MW01469225

OTTILIE DIVINE'S WAR

Thank you for choosing to read OTTILIE DIVINE'S WAR.

We wish you many happy reading hours.

Receive the first book FREE from the popular series,

99 Nightingale Lane

by joining Nightingale Lane Publishing

info@andreahicks-writer.com

CHAPTERS

PROLOGUE

End of July 1939

The young woman surveyed the impressive 18th Century buildings as she walked at a slow, meandering pace down Baker Street in London. She was looking for a particular house.

Dressed in a plain brown fitted dress, with hat and shoes to match, and a small bag over her right arm, she scrutinised the front doors of every house in the parade. Stopping in the middle of the pavement she sighed and looked up at the windows on the first and second floors of the buildings. Retrieving a slip of paper from her handbag she frowned and stepped back a little, searching the numbers on the doors.

'It must be here,' she said to herself. 'This is where she said it was.' She bit her lip and looked at the small note she had written to herself.

'221B Baker Street.' She turned and looked the other way down the street. 'Well, this is Baker Street.' She squinted at the note. 'I just can't find 221B.' She turned in a circle where she stood. 'Bet I've passed it.' It was then she saw the red and white striped awning of a café. She picked up her case and headed towards it.

'*They'll* know where 221B is,' she said under her breath, trying to convince herself she was more confident than she actually felt, 'and I could do with a cup of tea too.' She retraced her steps to the café and pushed open the door to a little bell ringing above her head.

The sound of the clinking of cups on saucers, the stirring of spoons in tea, and the chatter of happy voices met her as she went inside. The café owner, a portly man with a thin moustache and wearing a sparkling white apron, smiled at her as she went to the counter.

'Yes, love?' he asked her, his eyebrows raised. 'What can I get you?'

'A pot of tea for one, please,' she said returning his smile, 'and a direction to 221B Baker Street.'

He laughed as he poured hot water into a tiny teapot, placing it on a tray with a cup, saucer, and teaspoon.'

'You're there, ducks,' he said. 'Well, sort of.'

She blinked at him. 'Sort of?'

'This is 221 Baker Street. 221B is next door...Mrs 'Udson's place. I expect you've rented the top room. I know all about it. There ain't much that goes on along Baker Street what I don't know.'

A sense of relief went through her. 'That's right...a Mrs Hudson. I've rented the top floor from her.'

'We get people coming in 'ere all the time looking for 221B.' He nodded to the outside. 'You passed it when you came in here. It's a narrow black front door which looks like nothing at all. You'll see different when you get inside.'

She nodded and passed him the three pence-halfpenny he asked for. 'Thank you,' she said, smiling. 'I can't wait to see my room.'

'Mrs 'Udson's all right, she is. A bit forgetful at times, but a regular trooper. She likes our cream buns.' He winked at her and she nodded. He picked up one of the buns from the glass cabinet with a pair of tongs and placed it carefully into a paper bag. 'There you are ducks. She'll be your friend for life after giving 'er that.'

She passed him fivepence and nodded, finding a table by the window where the café owner brought her tea.

'You're not from around here are yer?'

'No…no, I'm not. I'm leaving home, although my family aren't far away.'

'Where'd you come from then?'

'Duke Street.'

'Oh?' The café owner looked surprised. 'Duke Street? You're right, it's not too far away. You sound like you come from somewhere posher than that.' She took a sip of tea and simply smiled at him. 'Any'ow,' he said. 'My name is Harold. I hope you'll come in here sometimes.'

'Oh, I definitely will…and I'm Ottilie,' she said, holding out her hand to him. 'Ottilie Divine.'

Chapter 1

The front door was where Harold said it would be, right next to the café, squashed between the café and the house next door. It had 221B in brass fittings high up on the door, but they were rather faded and needed a good polish. She thought about Duke Street and how Cecily insisted the numbers on the door and the brass letterbox should be polished at least once a week. She looked for a door knocker but there wasn't one, so she rapped on it with her gloved knuckles and stepped back. She waited for a few moments, then knocked again. A rather frail voice came from the other side.

'Just coming. Won't be a moment.'

Ottilie felt her heart thump in her chest. She was nervous, an emotion she wasn't used to. Her mother, Camille, and Richard, her stepfather, had always instilled confidence in her. The rolling stomach and fluttering heart was unfamiliar to her. This moment was important to her…her first time living alone. She so desperately wanted it to be…all right.

'Don't rush,' she called. 'I've got an appointment…with Mrs Hudson.'

There was a shuffle on the other side, the sound of keys being pushed into locks, and then the drawing back of bolts top and bottom. Finally the door opened with a judder revealing an older lady, short in stature, wearing a colourful wraparound pinafore. Her hair was quite white and her face was lined with life, but it was her eyes that startled Ottilie. They were the most beautiful blue. The sparkle in them was astonishing, and Ottilie could not help but smile.

'Hello,' she said brightly. 'I'm Ottilie Divine.'

The elderly lady frowned. 'Are you? Ottilie Divine you say?'

'That's right. I'm here to see Mrs Hudson.'

'I'm Mrs Hudson. I don't know anyone of that name.' Ottilie bit her lip, remembering what Harold had said about Mrs Hudson being a bit forgetful.

She suddenly sensed someone standing behind her and turned to find a young man on the bottom step who was clearly waiting to get inside. Ottilie smiled at him but he didn't return it.

'Hello, Mr Holmes,' said Mrs Hudson, peering behind Ottilie. 'You're back early.' She stepped back to allow him to go inside.

'I'm guessing this is your new tenant, Mrs Hudson,' he said, glancing at Ottilie then back at Mrs Hudson. He nodded at Ottilie, then ran up the stairs in the hall two at a time.

'Oh, so you're the new tenant?' cried Mrs Hudson. 'Why didn't you say so?'

Ottilie stepped over the threshold, relieved it had been sorted out at last. She was grateful to Mr Holmes that he'd reminded Mrs Hudson who she was but thought him rather rude. He hadn't smiled at her or welcomed her. It seemed he couldn't wait to get away.

'That's Mr Holmes,' said Mrs Hudson, almost reverently, as she shut the door. 'He's been here for a few months. He's studying. It's why he has all those books under his arm. Come into my sitting room. There are some house rules here, not that Mr Holmes pays much attention to them, but you're a young lady so I'm expecting you to follow them to the letter.'

Ottilie followed her into an old-fashioned downstairs sitting room and sat in a brown moquette fireside chair Mrs Hudson offered her. She removed her hat and took off her gloves, thankful to be inside at last. Mrs Hudson sat in the chair opposite. Ottilie held out the cream cake she had bought from the café to Mrs Hudson whose eyes lit up.

'A cream cake?'

'Yes.'

'From Harold's café next door?' Ottilie nodded. 'How lovely. Thank you, Miss Divine. Harold knows they're my favourite. Now, dear, your room is the one at the top of the house. I don't usually have tenants on the top floor but needs must. It was my storage room, but Harold, Mr Holmes and Dr Watson cleared it out for me. They're very good.'

'Dr Watson?' Ottilie asked, becoming confused.

'He's Mr Holmes's friend. He's just come back from overseas.' Mrs Hudson stared off into the distance. 'Oh yes,' she said, coming back from wherever she went. 'Then I got Ralph the decorator to give the rooms a lick of paint so it's nice and fresh up there. There's a bed in the bedroom, a dining room table and four chairs, and a settee, but if you want to bring your own furniture in you must let me know so I can move out what's up there already. Mr Holmes has the largest apartment...he likes to do experiments and whatnot in his kitchen.' She frowned. 'Not sure he's ever done any cooking in there. I can't say I approve and sometimes I have to go up there and give it a bit of a clean...and him a bit of a telling off.' She smiled indulgently and gazed at Ottilie. 'He's a man you see. Men don't have the first idea about running a household, but of course I expect you to run your own rooms. I'm sure you're used to it.' Ottilie lowered her eyes to her lap. She'd never cleaned a room in her life. Her mother hired a daily.

'Please make sure your rooms are kept clean and tidy. Don't cook anything too...well...pungent in the kitchen. Mr Holmes won't like it, and don't make too much noise. Mr Holmes's rooms are directly under yours and he will hear everything. And of course, no men. You can have friends in, females only, and I like the front door to be locked by eleven. If you're coming in late one evening you must let me know first and I'll leave it open for you, but only until twelve. Then the locks go on.'

Ottilie stared at Mrs Hudson, then remembered to nod. 'I think I've got all that.'

Her heart sank. Living in Baker Street was going to be more confining than living at home with Camille and Richard. She took in a breath and told herself to buck up.

'And the rent, Mrs Hudson? I'm guessing you'd like something in advance?'

'Yes, dear, but I think you should see the rooms first, don't you?' she said. 'They might not be to your taste. Mr Holmes is my only other tenant and he rarely comes down here. Sometimes I don't even know he's in…or out.' Ottilie left her hat and gloves in the sitting room and followed Mrs Hudson up the stairs, a slow ascent bearing in mind Mrs Hudson's age.

When they had climbed the three flights of stairs and reached the top floor, Mrs Hudson took a large keyring from her apron pocket and selected one of the keys, pushing it into the lock of a rather shabby door. She opened it with a flourish and invited Ottilie to go inside.

Ottilie stepped into a room which smelt of paint and Windowlene. There were two huge windows on the far wall which sparkled as the sunlight hit them. At one end of the room was a brick fireplace, and at the other end an arched entrance to the kitchen. Ottilie went into the kitchen and saw it was rather old-fashioned, lined with cupboards like the ones her mother had just removed from the kitchen at Duke Street, but clean and fully equipped with a small oven. It was big enough to house a table and four chairs in the centre. There was a window on the left hand side which had some frothy lace curtains dressing it. Ottilie grimaced then smiled when she saw them.

She ran her hand across the counter top, opened the cupboard doors to check for cleanliness, and inspected the oven, then made her way over to the windows in the living room where she looked out onto Baker Street. She could see the comings and goings of people in the street, some laden with shopping bags from the shops in Oxford Street and Regent Street; children in school uniform who had finished for the day, and men rushing to get to work. The ambience was one of busyness…a pressing need to get to wherever they were going, their thoughts simply on their destination. They didn't know she was there, watching them all as they went about their day, and she guessed they cared little. No one looked up. No one saw her.

She opened one of the windows and leant out, smiling. The afternoon sun was balmy and pleasant and warmed the skin on Ottilie's forearms as she leant on the window frame. She closed her eyes momentarily and soaked it all in…the noise of chatter from passers-by, the cars, and buses as they drove down the street, and the familiar atmosphere of a street that never slept. It reminded her of Duke Street.

A warm, cozy feeling rose from her toes to her chest, and she knew. She opened her eyes and turned to Mrs Hudson who had been watching her from the door. The wide smile still on Ottilie's face told her everything.

'I'll take it,' said Ottilie.

Chapter 2

The next day Ottilie and Richard arrived in Baker Street in a van which had been packed with Ottilie's furniture and the bits and pieces she'd wanted from her bedroom. Camille had suggested she join them, but Ottilie asked her not to, suggesting she was her first visitor once she'd settled in her new home at 221B Baker Street and everything was in its place.

This was a rite of passage for Ottilie, and she didn't want Mrs Hudson or her fellow tenant Mr Holmes to think she was a mummy's girl who couldn't do anything for herself. Richard had promised not to tell anyone who he was. He had laughed at the time when she'd requested his anonymity, but when he realised how important it was to Ottilie had agreed readily.

On the way from Duke Street to Baker Street, Ottilie and Richard had sung, "My Old Man Said Follow The Van" at the tops of their voices, Richard thumping the steering wheel at "And Don't Dilly Dally On The Way."

Ottilie was in good humour. She was quite sure she had never been so excited and nervous about anything in her life. She knew it was time for her to leave home, but striking out on one's own was always going to be fraught with apprehension. She was nearly twenty-eight and she knew her life had been too comfortable. There had been no pressure on her to leave home, not even to find a job, but she had done so, as a junior reporter at The Daily Express.

Her mother had been utterly supportive…female reporters were not widely recognised, and had encouraged Ottilie to make her way in what was a man's world. Her own life had shown she championed all women who wanted to step out of the moulds or restrictions men had made for them. She was an accomplished and modern woman. Because of that support Ottilie had been determined. She had always loved writing and had managed to convince the editor her skills were equal to any other reporter he employed.

'Do you think we'll go to war, Richard?' Camille asked her stepfather as they drove to Baker Street.

Richard had shrugged. 'Chamberlain had been so sure we would not go to war. The Munich Agreement was signed by him, Adolph Hitler, Mussolini, and Edouard Daladier. It was only last year, but there have been negative whisperings although no one wants to believe them. You must have read the papers, Ottilie. And what about your own editor at The Express. He must have his own thoughts about it.'

'He does.'

He glanced at her. 'And what are they?'

'He says the agreement isn't worth the paper it's written on.'

Richard widened his eyes. 'Well…there you are. I'm pretty sure it's what most of us think. We just don't want to consider it. The last war was horrendous. We lost so many young men…families broken, people living in poverty.' He shook his head. 'No one would want to return to a time like that.'

'Germany has already broken the agreement,' said Ottilie. 'In March this year they invaded the rest of Czechoslovakia. And now we've promised to support Poland in case of an invasion. The agreement has already been broken.'

'What we don't want is for Germany and the Soviet Union to get together.' Richard took in a deep breath. 'That would be extremely dangerous for Europe.'

'Thank goodness Simon is only fifteen. I couldn't bear it if my little brother were caught up in a war.'

Richard glanced at her. 'He's fifteen *now*, Ottilie. If there is a war and it lasts for some time he could well become the age of conscription.'

Ottilie bit her lip and closed her eyes momentarily. She adored her young brother and would do anything to protect him. 'We'd have to hide him.'

Richard pulled a grin. 'I have an idea it would be against the law, Ottilie.' He shook his head. 'I wouldn't want him to go any more than you, but he's a mature young man. He may consider it his duty to defend his country.'

'Oh, Richard!' Ottilie put a gentle hand on his arm.

'I know, I know, but we must hope and pray it doesn't come to that.'

Chapter 3

A knock on the door startled Ottilie. She was sitting at the kitchen table putting the finishing touches to an article for The Express on what would be expected of women should the country go to war with Germany. It was to counteract an article in the Daily Mail written by a reporter called Algernon North which strongly mooted the idea that a woman's place should be where it had always been…in the home and tending to men's needs. It was a misogynistic piece which had completely brushed over women's contribution in the 1914 – 1918 war.

Her research had been meticulous, even going so far as interviewing the women who had been employed to do work men could not do because they had been fighting in France, like planting food in the fields to bolster the war effort and feed those at home and working in munitions factories. Women had taken over the work gladly and had proved themselves to be the backbone of the country whilst continuing to look after their children and elderly relatives.

Ottilie frowned and tutted at the interruption but placed her spectacles on the kitchen table next to her old typewriter, a present from Camille and Richard for Christmas in 1925. She opened the door to the flat. In the frame stood Mrs Hudson, this time without the ubiquitous wraparound pinafore and head scarf. Instead, she wore a navy linen dress with a marcasite brooch at the neck. Her snowy white hair was swept up into a chignon, a tiny navy hat perched upon her curls.

'Mrs Hudson,' cried Ottilie. 'Oh, you look very nice. Are you going somewhere?'

Mrs Hudson nodded. 'I'm meeting my friend. We see each other once a month. She's a widow like me. It's good to go out sometimes, isn't it. Blows the cobwebs away.'

'I couldn't agree more,' replied Ottilie. She frowned. 'I'm not late with the rent am I?'

'No, Miss Divine, nothing like that.'

Ottilie glanced back to her article, still in the typewriter, wanting to get back to it as quickly as she could, but knew it would be impolite not to invite Mrs Hudson in, although she couldn't help wondering why she was getting a visit. She opened the door wider.

'Please, come in, Mrs Hudson.'

Mrs Hudson stepped over the threshold and looked around the flat.

'Oh, my, Miss Divine. You have been working hard. It looks lovely in here, so very feminine, such a contrast to Mr Holmes's rooms.'

'Would you like to see the bedroom? Mother suggested I brought my own bed and everything that goes with it. She thought it would make me feel more at home. I must say just having it here has been such a comfort.'

'I'd love to see it,' replied Mrs Hudson, clapping her hands together. 'I'm so pleased I chose the right person to share my home. It's such a worry you know. After all, we must all live together in harmony.'

Ottilie nodded and opened the bedroom door. Her huge bed from Duke Street was in the middle of the room opposite the window. The bedding, decorated with roses and hyacinths in shades of pink and cream with touches of pale green, gave the room a bright and cheerful ambiance. The bed was covered with cushions, and there was a pile of books next to the bed on a wooden bedside cabinet. There was a matching wardrobe and dressing table on the opposite wall. Mrs Hudson gave a little smile when she noticed a teddy bear tucked amongst the cushions.

'An old friend, Miss Divine?'

Ottilie went over to the bed. 'Mr Pickle. He's been with me for years. I can't remember a time without him.' She laughed. 'As you can see his fur is a bit bald and his nose is wonky, but it's because of all the cuddles I've given him. I couldn't have left home without him.' She hugged the teddy bear to her and placed him back on the bed. 'He's my lucky mascot.'

'Perhaps not today, dear,' said Mrs Hudson regretfully.

Ottilie frowned. 'Is there something wrong?' They went back into the living room and Ottilie shut the bedroom door behind her.

Mrs Hudson crossed her arms under her bosom and sighed. 'I've had a complaint.'

'A complaint!,' cried Ottilie. 'Who from?'

'Mr Holmes.'

Ottilie drew in a breath. 'What about?'

'Your music. He said one night last week you had a friend over and he could hear the music you were playing on the gramophone through the ceiling. He said there was a lot of thumping…like you were dancing. He said it sounded like a herd of elephants. He wasn't best pleased.'

Ottilie narrowed her eyes. 'Does Mr Holmes think I should live like a nun?'

Mrs Hudson shrugged. 'I don't know, dear. I must say I didn't hear it. I like to listen to the wireless of an evening, but I suppose it's because he's underneath you, so to speak.'

Ottilie could feel the heat of anger rising from her chest into her throat.

Her fellow tenant had done nothing to make her feel welcome, barely acknowledging her as they passed in the hall on occasion.

'What would you like me to do, Mrs Hudson.' Something occurred to her. 'It must have been last Saturday night. Rose, and sometimes some of my other friends, only come here on a Saturday because they work in the week. We were just letting our hair down a little.'

Mrs Hudson looked uncomfortable. 'Well, dear, to keep things nice, I wondered if you could apologise to him, you know, for the loud music, and the thumping. Were you dancing, dear?'

Ottilie nodded. 'Yes, Mrs Hudson. My friend Rose and I were dancing to show tunes. We felt the need to cheer ourselves up after the news we got last week. It seems Germany and the Soviet Union have cuddled up together.'

'I don't know, dear. I can't say I take much notice. The news is always so depressing. It makes me wonder why there's no good news reported. I listen to the music and the plays they put on. "In Town Tonight" is a favourite. I must say I don't want to hear what the other countries are doing, and who's at war with one another and who isn't.'

Ottilie nodded, understanding Mrs Hudson was an elderly lady who didn't want to be bothered with political machinations.

'I understand, Mrs Hudson. And I take it you would rather there not be a war between your tenants.'

'Exactly, dear. I knew you'd see the sense in it. Will you go and see Mr Holmes?'

'I'll do it for *you*, Mrs Hudson, but I think he's being rather a prig. I have to put up with the strange chemical smells coming from his kitchen. One can only wonder what on earth he does down there.'

Mrs Hudson nodded. 'Yes…he's a strange young man. Means no harm, and always pays his rent on time, but I think it would be for the best if you had a quiet word with him. You never know, you might become friends.'

Ottilie looked at her sceptically, then reluctantly nodded. 'Perhaps,' she answered, fearing she and her fellow tenant would never become friends.

Chapter 4

The days had begun to get shorter. Ottilie could feel it in her bones, the sensation autumn was waning, and winter was hiding, ready to pounce on them with its lower temperatures and warnings of inclement weather.

That afternoon, the Daily Express's editor Jonah Walsh had gone into the newsroom where the reporters sat whilst writing their articles or reports, his thumbs pushed into the pockets of his waistcoat, his expression glum. At his unusual appearance in the newsroom the typewriters had stopped their incessant clicking, conversations had ground to a halt, and quiet descended on the newsroom. He instructed some of the reporters with a raised hand to quieten the last few who hadn't noticed his arrival. He didn't attempt to sugar-coat the news.

'Germany has invaded Poland,' he said, his voice edged with a dark timbre, his expression the grimmest Ottilie had ever seen which was saying something. Jonah Walsh was not an easy man to please at the best of times and made his feelings felt, no matter how difficult. 'I think you all know what this means. We will be at war within days, maybe hours. I want everyone to work on the invasion of Poland and what it will mean to us.' He turned and glanced at his secretary. 'Marie here has a list of headings I want you to work towards. You can fight amongst yourselves about who does what. Miss Divine, your article will stand. It's more important now than ever the country realises what the war will mean to all members of society, including its women. I want it in tomorrow morning's issue, along with the other columns.

'Newspapers will be important now. It will be our responsibility to bring everyone in the country the latest news on what's happening here and in Europe. Holidays are cancelled, but there'll be plenty of overtime for those who want it. Good luck, girls and boys.' With that he turned and went back into his office, slamming the door behind him.

It was 1st September 1939 and the country had been informed Germany had invaded Poland. It had been less than a year since Neville Chamberlain had arrived back in England after declaring *'peace in our time'*. The promise Adolph Hitler had made had been readily broken and Britain was holding its breath, awaiting the announcement by Neville Chamberlain that the country was at war. The newsroom didn't return to its usual level of noise and chatter. It seemed everyone was absorbing what Jonah Walsh had told them and wanted to explore their own thoughts.

Ottilie knew she would never forget the surge of fear that went through her when she heard about Germany's invasion of Poland. She'd clenched her teeth and tried to quell the anxiety which had overtaken her. War! It was unthinkable, yet here it was. They would be a country at war.

Her thoughts went to Camille and Richard…and Simon, her younger brother. Tears gathered at her eyelashes and she brushed them away before she went across the newsroom to Marie to discover which article she should write. She didn't want the others to think she was crying, "the others" being men and some of them as hard as nails. She would never hear the last of it.

As she got to Marie's desk she was approached by John Clemence, Chief Reporter at The Daily Express.

'You don't need to get involved with this, Ottilie,' he said. 'That article you wrote about women in the 1914 – 1918 war was excellent. It'll appear in a special pullout we're doing for the centre of the newspaper tomorrow.'

'But these articles Mr Walsh wants us to write…'

He shook his head. 'You've done your bit for today. You work harder than anyone else here. Go home and put your feet up. Have a nice cup of tea.'

'Are you sure, John.'

He nodded. 'You can start again tomorrow. Mr Walsh has got a couple of things he wants to run by you. Looking ahead there will be plenty of subjects we can write about, and you look pale. Shocked you, hasn't it?'

'I think we all knew it could happen. I'm not sure any of us quite believed it when we were told we wouldn't be at war…as much as we wanted to think it wouldn't happen. I feel so sad…and afraid I must confess.'

'Anyone who isn't afraid is an idiot. I've got two boys who are in the right age group for conscription.' He drew in a breath. 'They'll be off to war no doubt.'

'I'm sorry, John.'

'Don't be. They'll want to do their duty.'

Ottilie decided to walk home after two buses had passed her by at the bus stop because they were full. She had felt exasperated when the first one went by, then philosophical and downhearted at the second.

'Well, I'm not waiting for a third,' she said grumpily to herself.

A woman in a headscarf tied under her chin and wearing a tweed coat that had seen better days who was also waiting at the stop, tutted.

'It's always the same at this time, ducks. I might as well stay at work for another hour and earn another hour's pay.'

'I'm beginning to think the same.'

'Not to worry. We'll be drivin' them buses when all the men 'ave gorn off to war. It's what we did in the last one. We'll never be short of buses then, 'cos there won't be no men to use 'em.' Ottilie nodded and swallowed hard. She bade the woman goodbye and began to walk to Baker Street, glad she was wearing her sensible shoes.

She didn't mind walking usually, except what she really wanted was her home and a hug. She decided to make a detour to Duke Street. The news they'd been given that Germany had invaded Poland had shaken her to her core and she craved the safety and warmth of her mother's home. When she got to Oxford Street, a sense of excitement went through her which made her frown. Did she really miss her old home so much, or was it because of what they had all learnt that day?

She still had her key to the house in Duke Street so she opened the door and called into the hall.

'Hello! It's me…Ottilie.'

She heard the rustle of a newspaper as it was placed on the ottoman. Camille came into the hall and engulfed Ottilie in a huge hug.

'You've heard the news, darling?'

'Yes, Mama. Mr Walsh told us. I can hardly believe it.'

'It's certainly a shock. Come into the sitting room and we'll have some tea. Knolly's made a fruit cake and I think we should make the most of it. There's bound to be rationing when we go to war, and I certainly don't think cake will be on the menu.'

Camille put Ottilie's coat on the stand in the hall and led her into the sitting room.

'Now, sit there and I'll ask Cecily to bring us a tray. They'll all want to see you.'

'It's only been five weeks, Mama. I stayed away far longer when I was at boarding school.'

'I know, darling,' she said, her face breaking into a smile. 'But we miss you,' she whispered. Ottilie nodded. She missed them too.

'Oh, Miss Ottilie,' cried Cecily as she brought the tray into the sitting room. 'It's so good to see you. I've missed you so much.'

'And I you, Cecily,' Ottilie said, rising to give Cecily a hug. 'It's strange living alone, but I'm gradually getting used to it.'

Cecily frowned. 'But won't you come back 'ere now that we'll probably be goin' to war. We all thought you would. I know we've got ter wait for Mr Chamberlain to tell us, but surely it will happen?'

Ottilie glanced at Camille who looked away. 'I don't think I'll change my plans, Cecily. Reporting on the news is more important than ever now. I've made the beginnings of a new life. Most women of my age have married and had families of their own. I must try to be self-sufficient.'

Cecily nodded, looking disappointed. 'It's what Madam said.'

Ottilie smiled, glancing at her mother again. 'I'm surprised.'

Camille poured them both tea and offered Ottilie cake which she readily accepted.

'I thought Knolly was going to retire, Mama. Has she said any more about it.'

'Well, there's the thing. She and Aaron were going to retire to the coast. They had already bought a little house there for them to retire to, but now...' she shook her head and sipped her tea, '...now I don't know. I'm not sure the coast will be the safest place to be.'

'Would you rather they stayed here?'

'Yes, I would. Knolly is sixty-five, Ottilie.'

Ottilie gasped. 'Is she really? I've never thought of her being such an age.'

'Aaron is two years older. They should have retired before now, but they were both reluctant to leave. It seems it was just as well. I couldn't bear for them to be frightened on their own. It's not as though they know anyone yet in the community where their house is. They haven't spent long enough there to make friends.'

'I hope they stay here, Mama. At least then we won't have to worry about them.'

'I agree.'

Ottilie took a bite of the cake Knolly had made which melted in her mouth. 'And what about Phillips?'

'Phillips is doing very well. He lives with his sister in the market town of Ampthill. I gave him a good lump sum for his retirement, and he has been enjoying life to the full. I'm so very happy for him. His sister has three children and any number of grandchildren. I should think he's loving every moment.'

'He deserves it. He was loyal to us wasn't he.'

'Oh, yes. I'll never forget the day he said he wanted to join me at Birdcage Mews. He became such a good friend to me. I don't know what I would have done without him. He's so quiet and steady. Exactly what I needed at the time.'

'Is Richard at Scotland Yard?'

Camille nodded. 'He's looking into the disappearance of a diplomat. The man had been in Germany trying to save the declaration of peace, but when all seemed lost he came back to London. All seemed well. He spent time with his wife's mother, father, and siblings, even went on holiday with them to Dorset.' Camille put her cup back on the saucer with a clink and looked quizzical. 'But then he disappeared,' she snapped her fingers making Ottilie jump, 'just like that. No one has seen him or heard from him for two weeks or more. His parents are beside themselves and now they've asked Scotland Yard to look for him.'

'Gosh,' said Ottilie, frowning. 'It sounds suspicious, doesn't it?'

'It does. And bearing in mind the news we've just had it seems to be getting more questionable by the day.' She picked up her cup. 'Richard is extremely concerned.'

'Mm,' Ottilie replied thoughtfully. 'I'm not sure I fancy the man's chances.'

'It's what Richard said, but you know Richard. He won't give up until the last moment. He says the diplomat could be held somewhere by people who think he knows more than he does…looking for information about how Britain would defend itself in a war.'

At that moment, Knolly joined them in the sitting room. She held out her arms to Ottilie and Ottilie sunk into them. Knolly had a permanent perfume of confectioners' sugar and vanilla which had always made Ottilie feel safe.

'It's lovely to see you, Miss Ottilie,' said Knolly. 'Are you here to stay?'

Ottilie grinned. 'No, Knolly. I'll be going back to Baker Street shortly.'

Knolly made a small smile but looked crestfallen. 'I just thought after the news we've had, and what's to come…'

Ottilie put a hand on Knolly's arm. 'I know, Knolly. But I need to look after myself, don't I? How many children did you have before you were my age.'

'Two.' She smiled at the memory.

Ottilie shrugged. 'I've only myself to take care of.'

Knolly nodded. 'Yes, you young modern women. Of course you want to make your way in the world. It's understandable.' She patted Ottilie's shoulder affectionately. 'You'll be all right, my dear.'

Chapter 5

Ottilie made her way up the stairs at 221B, suddenly feeling tired. The visit with Camille had been lovely, and seeing Cecily and Knolly had lifted her spirits. Knolly had sent her on her way with a bag of biscuits and cakes, clearly concerned Ottilie wasn't eating properly. Ottilie had glanced into the bag, thanking Knolly profusely, but thinking if she actually ate all of them she'd put on so much weight she'd have trouble getting up the stairs to her flat.

Duke Street was on the way to Baker Street, and if she decided to walk home she could always make a detour to see them all. She vowed to visit at least once a fortnight…and there was always the telephone, which Mrs Hudson had agreed to install in the hall, but not before making everyone promise they would pay for their own calls.

When she got to the first landing she glanced over at her fellow tenant's rooms and sighed, rolling her eyes. Ottilie had not seen Mr Holmes since Mrs Hudson had informed her of the complaint, and she thought it would be a good idea to get the asked for apology over and done with, otherwise it would have been even more embarrassing if they bumped into one another in the hall.

She gingerly rapped on the door, wondering if he would actually answer it. He seemed to live a solitary life with few visitors. She had seen only one man in the hall other than Holmes himself. He had smiled at her and said, "Good morning," seemingly a much friendlier prospect.

She waited for a few moments and was about to turn away when the door was opened by the man she supposed was Holmes's friend, although she couldn't recall his name.

When he saw Ottilie on the other side of the threshold the corners of his mouth turned up into a smile.

'Hello,' he said. 'Can I help?'

'I wondered if Mr Holmes was available?'

He frowned then retrieved his smile again when he realised who she was. 'Would you like to come in?' *Not really,* thought Ottilie. 'Oh, er, thank you.'

She stepped over the threshold and waited, clutching her handbag and her bag of cakes in front of her, feeling rather like a schoolgirl about to be reprimanded by the head teacher. The flat had a small lobby which Ottilie thought would have been very handy to have. Her flat did not have one, but instead opened onto her living room. 'Sherlock won't be long,' he said. 'Do sit.'

'Oh, no...er, I'm not stopping. I just needed to...

'Well, well, well,' said a voice to her left. 'It's one of the herd.'

'Holmes...' said his friend, admonishing him, clearly embarrassed.

'I think Miss Divine knows what I'm alluding to.'

'I'm here to apologise, Mr Holmes. I'm sorry if we disturbed you.'

He stared up at the ceiling. 'You did.'

Sherlock Holmes was dressed in a long brown dressing gown over a shirt, trousers, and waistcoat. Ottilie wondered why, then she saw his nose was bright red and she surmised he had a cold. He summarily sneezed and she took a step back. His friend was smartly dressed in a suit, shirt, and tie, and looked as though he had visited straight from his place of work.

The living room was dark, the windows dressed with heavy burgundy velvet curtains, partially pulled across the window, blotting out what little light there was. It was early evening and some of the streetlights were already lit, but the glow could hardly be seen.

The furniture was dark brown. In one corner there was an armoire loaded with books. The fireplace was brick and either side were more bookshelves. The coffee table was littered with paper. Ottilie glanced into the kitchen and her eyes widened. On the kitchen table were bottles of different sizes, some holding fluids of different colours, tubes, funnels, Bunsen burners and every piece of laboratory paraphernalia one could imagine if one were running a chemical experiment. She glanced back at Mr Holmes's friend and raised her eyebrows.

'It was a Saturday evening, Mr Holmes,' she said, trying not to get cross. 'I work to earn my living. It's the one evening in the week when I can relax and listen to music, and have friends round to the flat for a bite to eat. You told Mrs Hudson we sounded like a herd of elephants.' She frowned. 'There was only my friend Rose and I. Rose could no way be described as elephantine.'

Sherlock Holmes rose from his chair by the fireplace and leant with one elbow up against the mantelpiece, a pipe in his hand, a handkerchief in the other.

'Then perhaps you should consider, if you wish to dance, which of course I don't understand at all, going to a dance hall of which I believe there are a number in this part of our gracious city. No one would mind you dancing there.'

'I pay the same rent as you do, Mr Holmes and therefore believe it is my own territory and gives me leave to do whatever I wish in it. Your experiments often issue unpleasant smells, but in the principle of less said soonest mended, I choose not to say anything.'

Sherlock Holmes pushed himself away from the mantelpiece and sat back down in the large wingchair. He puffed away on his pipe without looking at Ottilie. In fact, she had realised, he had not once looked at her at all.

'My experiments are of an important nature, Miss Divine. Success could change the course of criminal investigations forever. I do believe they have more significance than your requirement to dance.' He turned to his friend. 'Watson, I do believe it's time for Miss Divine to leave.' He turned to face the fireplace without looking at her. 'I accept your apology, Miss Divine. I trust there will be no further cause for me to complain to Mrs Hudson.'

Ottilie narrowed her eyes and clenched her teeth for fear of becoming unladylike in her reply. The man was downright rude. He was not much older than she but had instantly taken the high ground. His friend, Watson, had made for the door and opened it for her, ushering her into the lobby.

'I'm sorry, Miss Divine,' he said sotto voce. 'Sherlock can be…rather brittle at times.'

'Brittle! He was rude.'

Watson nodded. 'He's that too. I can only apologise on his behalf. He's not well, and he doesn't take kindly to illness.'

'So, I'm not allowed to play music apparently. Nor use my flat, for which I pay the same rent as him, the way I wish to, because another human being's activities in the vicinity disturbs *him*.'

Watson smiled. 'You have a way with words, Miss Divine.'

'I should hope so. I'm a news reporter. Perhaps you could give some news to Mr Holmes. I will do my best not to disturb him but will continue doing what I wish in my own flat. Perhaps he should get some ear plugs if music offends him so much.'

Watson nodded. 'I'll pass the message on.'

'Please do,' said Ottilie as she made her way up to the second landing, her anger making her breath come in short gasps.

Inside the flat she flung her handbag onto the settee.

'Who the hell does he think he is?' she cried. 'Telling me what to do in my own flat.'

She took off her hat and threw it next to the handbag, then went into the kitchen and put the cakes on the table, not knowing whether to laugh or cry. The last thing she had wanted was to make an enemy of her fellow tenant, but it seemed she and Sherlock Holmes would not be friends.

'Sherlock, indeed,' she said to herself. 'Whoever heard of such a ridiculous name.'

She took one of the cream slices Knolly had given her and bit into it, the cream bulging from the sides of the pastry. She licked her lips, scooping the cream from the side of the slice with a finger.

'No, Mr Sherlock Holmes. I don't care how much everyone reveres you,' she said, her mouth full of cake. 'You won't win this time.'

'So, are you saying we're not allowed to play any music?' asked Rose the following evening, which as luck would have it was a Saturday. Rose had taken to visiting Ottilie on a Saturday evening and staying the night. She had told Ottilie it was her little nod to freedom away from the parents before taking up a job as an interpreter.

'Or dance?' cried Ottilie's friend, Nancy, who was a secretary at The Daily

Express. 'What are we meant to do then?'

'He sounds a real misery guts,' said Rose. 'Perhaps I should invite my mother here. She'd put him right.'

Ottilie threw back her head and laughed. 'Oh, my goodness, Elsie could start a war in an empty room. It might not be a good idea. In truth, I don't want to start an argument with, "he who lives downstairs",' she pulled a face, 'but as I said to him, this is my flat and I should be able to do what I like in it bearing in mind we both pay the same amount of rent, although I must say his flat is ghastly, so dreary and brown. Matches him perfectly. And it's only one evening a week for goodness sake. Let's make those cocktails we promised ourselves, then we'll put on some music and hope he doesn't notice.'

'What if he does?' asked Nancy.

'We'll cross that bridge when we come to it.'

They spent the next half hour mixing up cocktails and giggling over, "he who lives downstairs."

'You might end up marrying him, Ottilie,' said Rose.

Ottilie screamed. 'Not on your Nelly,' she cried. 'Only if I were unconscious.'

They all laughed, then went into the living room where Ottilie put on a "swing" recording of Ambrose on the gramophone. The girls put their glasses down and began to dance without their shoes.

'At least we're trying,' said Nancy. 'We're not wearing shoes. Surely, we won't make that much noise.'

'He said Rose and I sounded like a herd of elephants.' They burst into more laughter and pretended to be elephants, swinging their arms around like elephants' trunks.

Ten minutes later there was a knock on the door. Ottilie turned down the music and went to answer it. It was Holmes's friend. He stood at the door with his hands in his pockets and a wry smile on his face.

'I think you know why I'm here, Miss Divine.'

Ottilie shook her head. 'This is all so silly. It's one night a week.' She looked at him askance. 'I'm sorry, I've forgotten your name. Is it Mr Wilkins?'

'My name is John. My father is *Mr* Watson. I'm a doctor, a junior one, so it…it would be Dr Watson.'

'Well, *Dr* Watson, I truly think we're doing no harm. Just because he doesn't like music doesn't mean to say I can't play it in my own flat.'

'I agree.'

Ottilie widened her eyes. 'You do?'

'Yes, but I don't live here, well, not all the time. Holmes is a particular kind of fellow. It's one of the reasons it took Mrs Hudson so long to find someone for your flat. Apart from his rather sulphureous experiments, Sherlock causes no fuss. He pays his rent on the dot and Mrs Hudson appreciates it.' He looked into the flat and nodded to Rose and Nancy who were staring at him wide-eyed. 'Perhaps…perhaps you could turn it down a jot, or play a different kind of music, and perhaps not such boisterous dancing.'

'Why has he sent you? Is this not something he should do himself?'

'Sherlock isn't a people person, Miss Divine. He finds interaction with others somewhat difficult.'

'No surprise there.' She sighed. 'All right…*Dr* Watson. I give in. We'll play some quiet music. God forbid we upset the famous Mr Sherlock Holmes.'

John Watson laughed. 'He *will* be famous one day, Miss Divine. He is a clever chap, as well as a most infuriating one. Thank you for your understanding.'

Ottilie shut the door and leant against it.

'Well, girls. It looks like we must spend the evening gossiping instead of dancing.'

'I have some gossip,' said Nancy. 'But you must promise not to tell a soul.'

They grabbed their cocktails and sunk into the settee, pulling up their feet underneath them. 'What, Nancy?' asked Rose. 'Is it something you heard in Fleet Street?'

'Yes, but it's strictly on the QT.'

'Of course,' said Ottilie. 'Anything you tell us will not go any further than these four walls.'

'What about him downstairs? He might be listening.'

Ottilie went across to the gramophone and replaced the Ambrose recording with *Moonlight Serenade*.

'There. If he can hear us talking over this, he must have ears like an elephant.' They giggled and settled down to hear Nancy's news.

'Delia Wentworth.'

Ottilie frowned. 'What about her?'

'Her husband's missing.'

'Missing?' asked Rose. 'What do you mean…missing?'

'He's a diplomat at the Foreign Office. He had been in Germany trying to smooth things over in the wake of Chamberlain's visit and supposed agreement. He told Delia he didn't believe a word of the agreement. That he was sure Neville Chamberlain had believed it all much too easily…because he wanted to believe it. He said Adolph Hitler is a tricky character, rather a frightening prospect.'

'But you said he's missing,' said Rose. 'Delia Wentworth's husband.'

Nancy nodded, her eyes sparkling as she got deeper into her story. 'Well, yes. He came back from Germany, Delia said a little depressed, she thought. They went on holiday with his family to Dorset. Took their three children to play on the beach for two weeks. He returned to work, but then one evening he didn't return. She contacted his office, then the police. There's absolutely no sign of him.'

Ottilie bit her lip. She suddenly realised this was the person Camille had told her about, the case which was keeping Richard so busy at Scotland Yard.

'How do you know this, Nancy? Do you know Delia?'

'I've never met her, but one of our reporters went to interview her. It's not in the papers yet. The police have asked all the newspapers not to print the story until they have more to go on, but I know Jonah Walsh. He'll want to be the first to break the news. I reckon Delia Wentworth and the police have got two days at the most before it hits the stands. The Express will want to be at the forefront.'

'Did you type up the story?' asked Ottilie.

'It's how I know so much about it. The reporter who interviewed Mrs Wentworth went off sick with the flu, so I was asked to type it up. It's with Jonah Walsh now. I bet he's itching to publish.' She frowned at Ottilie. 'But don't you know Delia, Ottilie?'

Ottilie nodded. 'She was a pupil at our boarding school in Hampshire. St Agatha's.' She glanced at Rose. 'Do you remember her, Rose?'

Rose shook her head. 'Was she in your year?'

'Yes. She left under a bit of a cloud. Fell in love with Charles Wentworth when she was seventeen and absconded from school. There was quite the scandal. Her parents were beside themselves and the school was admonished for allowing her to leave.' Ottilie shook her head. 'Honestly,

I don't know what they expected the school to do about it. We weren't living under an armed guard. She simply slid down a drainpipe, ran across the gymnasium roof and he was waiting for her the other side.' She smiled. 'We all thought it was rather romantic.'

Rose grinned. 'I do remember her. She was very pretty wasn't she? Blonde hair and blue eyes. Looked like one of those dolls in Selfridges' window.'

Ottilie nodded. 'We were all rather envious of her at the time.'

'And now she has three children,' said Nancy. 'I'm not sure I envy her that.'

'Nor me,' said Rose. 'I'm not sure I want children.' She glanced at Ottilie. 'What about you, Ottilie?'

Ottilie shrugged. 'Maybe. One day.' She grinned at them and took a sip of her cocktail. 'But not if they grow up to be anything like "he who must be obeyed," Mr Sherlock flipping Holmes.'

They threw their heads back and laughed, and Ottilie hoped Sherlock Holmes could hear them.

Chapter 6

3rd September 1939

Rose stayed overnight. She and Ottilie had said goodnight to Nancy who had taken a cab from Baker Street at eleven-thirty the previous evening, just before Mrs Hudson locked the doors, and waved her off, all a little worse for wear.

'Oh, my head,' cried Ottilie, covering her eyes with her forearm. 'Someone's in there with a hammer.'

'I must have his workmate then,' said Rose. 'Gosh, did we drink so much last night?'

'It certainly feels like it. I'm a little worried to open the curtains. I don't think I could stand the light.'

'I've got some aspirin in my bag,' said Rose. 'You stay here and I'll get them and some water.'

Rose got out of bed and slipped on Ottilie's dressing gown. 'Oh, God,' she said, lurching a little. 'I hope I'm not going to be sick. I'm like my mother. She hates being sick too.'

'This is his fault,' said Ottilie when Rose returned with a glass of water and the packet of aspirin.

'Whose fault?' asked Rose, sitting on the bed and tipping two aspirins into Ottilie's hand. Ottilie pointed to the floor and Rose laughed, but grimaced, wishing she hadn't. 'Why is it his fault?'

'He stopped us from dancing. You and I both know the more we dance the less we drink, and even when we do drink it doesn't give one such a headache.' She sighed and lay back on the pillow, wincing at the pain across her eyes. 'I hope I haven't made a mistake moving here.'

'You haven't.'

Ottilie managed to smile. 'Why do you say that?'

'Because it's a beautiful flat. It reminds me of Duke Street…the hustle and bustle, the sounds from the market. When the sun shines through the windows in the living room it lifts my spirits. I think you've made the best choice…and as for him downstairs, I have no doubt you'll talk him round.'

Ottilie snorted a laugh. 'You think so?'

'I know so.'

A knock at the front door startled them. Ottilie looked exasperated.

'Oh, no, surely it's not him again,' cried Ottilie. 'Or his friend. We haven't made any noise this morning.' She threw her legs over the side of the bed and stretched. 'S'pose I'd better answer it.' Rose held out Ottilie's dressing gown. Ottilie slipped it on and tightened it around her waist, making sure the top was pulled across her neck. *If I appear too undone he'll probably accuse me of being a woman of the night*, she thought. *No lie in for him, I shouldn't wonder. He was probably up with the lark…annoying man.*

It wasn't Sherlock Holmes who stood in the doorframe when Ottilie opened the door, or his friend, Dr Watson. It was Mrs Hudson.

'Mrs Hudson,' said Ottilie, quietly. 'Good morning.' Mrs Hudson didn't answer and Ottilie frowned. 'Is everything all right?'

'I wondered if you and your friend would like to come down to my sitting room, Miss Divine. There's to be a broadcast on the radio. Neville Chamberlain. I feel quite sure it's not good news.' Her voice shook. 'I didn't want to be on my own. Would you mind?'

'No, no, of course not. How long have we got?'

'About ten minutes. It's due at a quarter past eleven.'

'We'll be there. We'll get dressed and be down right away.'

It took Ottilie and Rose five minutes to throw on their clothes from the previous evening, retrieving them from the floor where they'd left them. They splashed their faces with water hoping it would dispel the fogginess of the previous evening's imbibing and popped Parma violets into their mouths.

'What do you think it's about, Ottilie?' Rose asked her as they went down the stairs to Mrs Hudson's sitting room. 'The broadcast, I mean.'

'I don't think it's good news, Rose.' She shrugged. 'I could be wrong of course, but when Germany invaded Poland, I think the denouement was written. I think perhaps we *wished* Neville Chamberlain had agreed peace rather than believed it.'

A pot of freshly brewed tea, and plates of toast welcomed them when they went into Mrs Hudson's sitting room. She'd pulled one of her fireside chairs over to the huge radio which sat on a sideboard and was sitting pensively, her shoulders hunched, waiting for the broadcast to begin.

'Pour yourselves tea, girls,' she said in a whisper. 'And have some toast. I should imagine you need something in your tummies after last night.' Ottilie glanced at Rose and pulled a face. Were they really so noisy? 'It won't be long now.' She glanced at the clock on the mantelpiece looking worried. 'It's nearly a quarter past eleven.'

Both girls nodded, not wanting to fracture the quiet in the room. Ottilie poured the tea and Rose helped herself to toast. They waited.

The wireless crackled into life and Neville Chamberlain's voice filled the room.

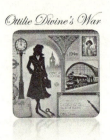

'I am speaking to you from the Cabinet Room at 10 Downing Street. This morning the British Ambassador in Berlin handed the German government a final note stating that unless we heard from them by 11 o'clock that they were prepared at once to withdraw their troops from Poland, a state of war would exist between us. I have to tell you now that no such undertaking has been received, and that consequently this country is at war with Germany.

You can imagine what a bitter blow it is to me that all my long struggle to win peace has failed. Yet I cannot believe that there was anything more or anything different that I could have done and that would have been more successful.

Up to the very last, it would have been quite possible to have arranged a peaceful and honourable settlement between Germany and Poland, but Hitler would not have it. He had evidently made up his mind to attack Poland whatever happened, and although he now says he put forward reasonable proposals which were rejected by the Poles, that is not a true statement. The proposals were never shown to the Poles, nor to us, and though they were announced in a German broadcast on Thursday night, Hitler did not wait to hear comments on them but ordered his troops to cross the Polish frontier. His action shows convincingly that there is no chance of expecting that this man will ever give up his practice of using force to gain his will.

He can only be stopped by force. And we and France are today, in fulfilment of our obligations, going to the aid of Poland, who is so bravely resisting this wicked and unprovoked attack on her people.

We have a clear conscience. We have done all that any country could do to establish peace. But the situation in which no word given by Germany's ruler could be trusted and no people or country could feel themselves safe has become intolerable. And now that we have resolved to finish it, I know that you will all play your part with calmness and courage.

'At such a moment as this, the assurances of support which we have received from the Empire are a source of profound encouragement to us. It is the evil things that we shall be fighting against…brute force, bad faith, injustice, oppression, and persecution…and against them I am certain that the right will prevail.'

'And that was a broadcast by the Right Honourable Neville Chamberlain,' said the announcer, who sounded no different from how he had sounded before the broadcast. And yet for those three women sitting quietly in Mrs Hudson's sitting room at 221B Baker Street, life was indeed about to change irrevocably.

They sat without speaking for a few moments until Mrs Hudson lifted her head and looked at Ottilie and Rose with tears in her eyes.

'The poor man. He did his best, didn't he? I mean, it sounds like it's the German man who has broken the agreement, not dear Mr. Chamberlain.'

Both Rose and Ottilie sat quietly looking into the fireplace. The few words Neville Chamberlain had uttered from the wireless had stunned them into silence, had chilled them to the bone. They couldn't bear to look at one another, they were so utterly shocked.

Ottilie had known for a while there had always been a prospect Britain would eventually go to war with Germany, but it had been something one could put at the back of one's mind. Yes, it had been a possibility; they had been carrying gas mask boxes around with them since 1938, but being involved in a war had simply been a notion. It hadn't been confirmed, so they had carried on with life in the usual way. Now it had been settled. They were a country at war. Their lives would never be the same again.

Ottilie rose from her chair and went across to Mrs Hudson, squatting on her haunches in front of her.

'Are you all right, Mrs Hudson? Is there someone we can get in touch with for you? Or you can come up to my flat if you'd like. I hadn't planned to do much today but I might venture out. I want to see for myself how the public have been affected by the announcement.'

Mrs Hudson patted her hand. 'I'll be all right, my dear…once I get over the shock. I'm an old woman with no family. The only way it will affect me is if they bring the fighting over here, and of course when the rationing begins, which it surely will. It's what happened last time. Life was so hard then.' She shook her head and gazed into the distance. 'I can hardly believe we're at war again. It doesn't seem so long ago since the end of the last one, but then time goes much quicker the older you get. Twenty years isn't such a long time though, is it? Not in the scheme of things. Those of us who were in the last war will remember it as clear as daylight. And all those young men who went to fight on the front…some of them not yet twenty. I expect it will happen again.' She closed her eyes.

'I confess I don't remember much about it,' said Ottilie. 'I was so young I don't think it registered too much. I remember Mama and Papa being very sad about all the young men being lost. I suppose we were the lucky ones.' Ottilie looked contrite. 'Is it what happened to Mr Hudson? Was he taken in the war?'

'No, dear. There isn't a Mr Hudson. Never has been.'

Ottilie heard Rose gasp, and she widened her eyes. 'No Mr Hudson?

But…you're *Mrs* Hudson.'

'Actually, I'm Miss Hudson, but when I realised there wouldn't be a suitor for me I decided the safest thing to do was to put a ring on my wedding finger, and tell everyone I was a Mrs.

'I'd bought this house you see, with an inheritance from my parents. I was an only child. We lived a quiet, somewhat solitary life, and I was never a beauty.' She smiled at Ottilie, then at Rose. 'Not like you two. There were never any gentleman callers, no one I wanted to marry to tell the truth. So I decided to live my life the way I always had, solitary, with my wireless and my books…and my tenants of course. Having you young people here is a blessing.'

'Can I make you a fresh pot of tea, Mrs Hudson?' asked Rose, getting up from her chair.

'No, thank you, my dear.' She levered herself out of her chair. 'I'll do it. And I have some washing to do.' She nodded, more to herself than to Ottilie and Rose. 'I'm simply going to carry on as I always have. I'm not going to let the Germans throw me off course. There's work to be done. I got through the last war alone. I can get through this one.'

Ottilie stood and reached for Mrs Hudson's hands.

'You're not alone, Mrs Hudson, and I won't have you thinking you are. You know where I am, and I'll drop in every now and then.' She grinned. 'I'll bring one of Harold's cream cakes.'

Mrs Hudson patted her cheek. 'You're a good girl. I knew you were as soon as I laid eyes on you.' She inhaled deeply. 'We'll be all right, my dear. We'll be all right.'

Chapter 7

Ottilie and Rose said their goodbye's outside 221B Baker Street, hugging, with tears welling at their eyelashes, both devastated by the awful news.

'You'll be all right, Ottilie?' Rose asked her, holding her hand. 'You could go back to Duke Street, couldn't you, or even come to us at Grosvenor Mansions. I just can't bear the thought of you being alone.'

'I'm not alone, Rose, please don't worry. I have a feeling I'm going to be even busier now we're at war. The public will want to know what's going on and it will be the newspapers they turn to. And I'm not sure I want to leave Mrs Hudson. I don't know her well, but she's such a sweet old thing. And now she's had a telephone installed I can ring both you and home. I'll be fine, honestly.'

'And what about our Saturday nights.'

Ottilie found some laughter for her. 'Rose, not even the Germans will call a halt to our Saturday nights.' She looked behind Rose and nodded. 'There's your car by the look of it. Your Mama and Lord Fortesque-Wallsey are making sure you're safe.'

Rose nodded. 'Gosh, they do worry so.' She glanced at Ottilie, and they laughed. 'It's obviously where I get it from. Take care, sweet girl. I'll be here on Saturday evening, on the dot.'

She walked towards her car and lifted her hand in a wave which Ottilie returned. She watched the car as it drove down Baker Street and turn into Oxford Street, experiencing a strange sense of abandonment as she watched it disappear around the corner.

The streets of London were quiet. It was Sunday, yes, but it was much quieter than usual. Ottilie often liked to wander the streets on a Sunday, particularly in the summer. It was the time for promenading, the young women of the city in the new fashions, some on the arm of young men in double breasted suits with padded shoulders and fitted waists teamed with high waisted unfitted trousers. Savile Row was the street men would patronise, but only if they could afford it. A suit by Gieves and Hawkes would set one back a pretty penny, so it wasn't for everyone, but there were lots of copies in the shops.

Girls would wear tea dresses with sweetheart necklines and puffed sleeves, often in floral or polka dot fabric. Many were designed by Norman Hartnell, but those who were not in a designers league would go to Marks and Spencer or Selfridges and find similar designs at an affordable cost.

Ottilie liked to dress down when she was observing people in the streets. Her usual working look was a blouse with either a Peter Pan collar or a pussycat bow, tied at the neck, often covered with a little jacket. A plain skirt, either in black, navy, or brown suited either the times when she was out for interviews or sitting in the press room typing her articles.

She wanted to appear as a woman of work. It was important to her that her colleagues see her as such, as she was the only woman in the press room. She had always felt a tea dress did not give the right impression.

As she walked to the corner of Baker Street Ottilie could feel tears welling under her lashes. The people of London were staying in the safety of their own homes. She could only imagine the feelings of families who were in utter shock, frightened for their lives and those of their children. She couldn't help shaking her head. Not only was London overlaid with a sense of fear, but also a feeling a sentence had been passed on them.

She found herself walking down Oxford Street, where the shops were closed, towards Oxford Circus. The Tottenham Court Road wasn't far, so she continued until she got to Drury Lane.

'I might as well pop into the office,' she said under her breath. 'Surely someone will be in.' Her pace picked up speed. She had a destination and somehow she knew she would feel more comfortable when she saw her desk and typewriter.

The front doors to the art deco building were open but there was no one in the lobby. She made her way to the first floor where the press room was situated. It was empty, quieter than she'd ever known it, eerily so.

She walked down the lines of typewriters to the office. Inside, with his head on his desk, was Jonah Walsh. As she reached the door he lifted his head, then straightened up.

'Miss Divine,' he said.

She stared at him. 'Mr Walsh? Have you been here all night?'

'Indeed. And so have your colleagues. We've got a memorable front page on the presses. It'll be out by lunch time. I've no doubt you know what it's about.'

Her mouth opened in surprise. Why hadn't he called her in? 'Why didn't you call me in, Mr Walsh? I would have happily worked through the night.' She bit her lip feeling upset, myriad thoughts going through her mind. *Did he think she wasn't a good enough writer? Did her colleagues not want her in the press room at such an important moment in the country's history? And how did they know what would occur that morning?'*

He took a pipe from the top pocket of his shirt which was crumpled and had ink patches on the rolled-up sleeves, and banged it on the desk, allowing ash to fall on the carpet.

'Sit down, Miss Divine.' Ottilie took the seat in front of Walsh's desk. 'I suppose you're thinking we didn't want you here?' Ottilie didn't answer. She couldn't quite bring herself to. 'Well, you can forget all that. I got the nod last night an announcement was to be made.' He tapped the side of his nose before filling his pipe with tobacco and lighting it with a lighter. 'Sometimes it's not what you know but who you know, Miss Divine. We're way ahead of our rivals. The Mail will be incandescent we've beaten them to the punch.' He took a long pull on his pipe and blew smoke into the room. 'But never mind about that.' He sat forward in his chair, his eyes narrowing.

'Are you up for a special job, Miss Divine?'

'Is it to do with the war?'

'In a manner of speaking.'

'What is it?'

'We've had a report of a disappearance of someone in the diplomatic service, a Mr Charles Wentworth.' Ottilie nodded. 'You know about it?'

'I know one of our reporters interviewed his wife, Delia. Charles has been missing about, what, two…three weeks now?'

'I'd like you to interview her again.' Ottilie blanched. 'Not to your taste, Miss Divine?'

'I'm just thinking it could be rather embarrassing, Mr Walsh. I know her. She went to my boarding school in Hampshire, St Agatha's. I remember it like it was yesterday when she left the school in the middle of the night to elope with Charles Wentworth. She was only seventeen. It caused the most almighty trouble I can tell you,' she smiled to herself, 'although we girls thought it was rather romantic.'

Jonah Walsh tutted and pulled a face. 'It's my belief young women find everything romantic, Miss Divine, but what is not romantic is the diplomat Charles Wentworth disappeared shortly after he returned from Germany. He was on the peace mission with Neville Chamberlain, he, and others, and was there when the historical document was signed.

'Of course, Chamberlain came back to this country with a contract signed by both him and Adolph Hitler which Chamberlain at least thought was genuine. I'm not sure the rest of us did but there we are. It has proved to have been not so. Charles Wentworth stayed in Germany to dot the i's and cross the t's, but he was apparently resisted at every turn, which he duly reported to the Foreign Office.'

'You think he knew there would be a war between Britain and Germany?'

'Without a doubt. He had apparently made a number of calls to the Foreign Office from the British embassy in Germany expressing his fears. Unfortunately, he wasn't listened to. The contract which had been flourished to us all by Chamberlain on his return to London was metaphorically waved at him as proof of Hitler's intentions.'

'So, he was shouted down?'

'Indeed.'

Ottilie frowned. 'He returned to London though, didn't he?'

'He went on holiday to Dorset with his family and returned to work two weeks later. One evening he did not return to his home. In the beginning, his wife thought he was working late, but when he hadn't returned by eleven that evening, she telephoned the police.'

'There hasn't been anything reported in the newspapers has there?'

'No, but the deadline is looming. Scotland Yard asked us to hold off reporting Wentworth's disappearance until they knew more. I spoke with Chief Inspector Richard Owen yesterday. They have until tomorrow evening and after that time they have agreed we can go to press on the story.' He raised his eyebrows. 'I understand Chief Inspector Owen is a relative of yours.'

Ottilie nodded. 'He's my stepfather.' The penny dropped. 'Is it why you've asked me to cover the story, Mr Walsh? Because of my stepfather? You think he will give me information no one else is privy to?'

'No…it isn't the reason why I've asked you to cover the story, Miss Divine.'

Walsh rose from his chair, still puffing on his pipe and went to the window. Ottilie couldn't help noticing how shabby his clothes were, perhaps not shabby, but certainly uncared for. She wondered about his home life. He certainly spent an inordinate amount of time in his office, and she'd noticed Marie, his secretary, often brought homemade cakes in for him. He stared out of the window onto Fleet Street, seemingly deep in thought.

'You must stop thinking you are less of a reporter than your colleagues, Miss Divine.' He turned to face her. 'I can assure you *they* don't think so. Your article on the necessity for women to pick up the pieces when the men went to war was timely and an excellent rebuttal to that rag, The Mail. You proved with in-depth research and salient facts that women are the backbone of this country, particularly when men go to war.' He nodded. 'And they will be needed yet again in the coming days. I've also decided to repeat the article in tomorrow's paper, just to remind everyone what will be expected of them, and there isn't a chance the women of this country will let the side down.'

Ottilie's demeanour suddenly brightened. It was rare for an article to be repeated. 'I thought you were friends with the editor of The Mail?'

'I am, but I still think it's a rag.' He grinned at her and she returned it. 'Are you willing to investigate the story, Miss Divine, or should I get one of the others onto it? I think you would find it an interesting undertaking. Charles Wentworth was present when the agreement between Chamberlain and Hitler was signed. It's very likely he would have spoken to his wife on his return about what happened in Germany. Most husbands tell their wives things they probably shouldn't, simply to take the weight off their shoulders for a while.

'The fact you know her is a plus, but it's not why I've asked you to interview her. You're good at it and I think you'll get more out of her than Nobby Clark did who's like a bull in a china shop at the best of times. He has a skill for rubbing people up the wrong way and I understand the interview didn't go too well. I'm hoping you'll pat her down again. You could suggest you meet at Browns for tea, or somewhere like it to make your chat informal…less of an interview, more of a catch up. I'm sure she's used to such places.' He looked at her from underneath his rather bushy eyebrows. 'I *know* you are.'

Ottilie thought about it. Charles Wentworth had been right at the centre of negotiations between Chamberlain and Hitler. If he told Delia about what happened it would make a marvellous story. She nodded. 'Yes, Mr Walsh, I'll take it on. How do I contact her.'

He sat at his desk and reached into his drawer, retrieving a slip of paper. He passed it to Ottilie.

'There's her telephone number. Ring her and try to arrange for a meeting immediately, tomorrow if you can. We need to get onto it. There's no need for you to come to the office tomorrow unless she won't agree to see you.' He smiled at Ottilie. 'I have every faith you'll talk her round.'

Ottilie nodded. 'She must be so worried about Charles. And she has three young children too. Poor Delia. What an awful position to find oneself in.' She swallowed hard as something occurred to her and she glanced up at Jonah Walsh. 'Do you think he's dead, Mr Walsh? Charles Wentworth, I mean.'

Walsh leant back in his chair, pulled another puff on his pipe then rested it in the filthy ashtray on his desk. He sighed and folded his arms over his stomach where Ottilie could see there was a button missing and his vest was showing through the gap.

'I've been thinking about the possibility. And so must you. Ask yourself questions, Miss Divine, those you wish to know the answers to. Why is Charles Wentworth missing? Has he absconded or was he taken? And if he was taken, why? Why would someone not want him to do the job he was given? And what exactly was the job? Was he spying?'

Ottilie gasped. 'Surely not. He was well-thought of wasn't he...someone to be trusted.' She looked shocked. 'I can't even imagine him being a spy.'

'They're the mistakes most people make, Miss Divine, and they're the mistakes reporters can't afford to make. I know he's part of the aristocracy and doesn't use his title, but he's privy to a lot of classified information. It's not beyond the imagination to wonder if he has thrown in his lot with the other side.' He shrugged. 'But of course he may not have done so. He might have been threatened and has gone into hiding. Perhaps Mrs Wentworth knows where he is but has had to report him missing to make things look...authentic. Or he may have been taken so he cannot tell the Foreign Office what he knows. He might have heard something that was not for his ears.'

He released a breath and sat forward, his eyes darkening.

'And in answer to your question, Miss Divine.' He nodded. 'It would serve you well to remember this. These people don't mess around. They are beyond ruthless. And, yes, I think he could well be dead.'

Chapter 8

Ottilie paced the living room in the flat, wringing her hands. She had been unable to sleep the previous night following her meeting with Jonah Walsh.

There had been so much to take in…the announcement the country was at war, and the faith and trust Walsh had put in her to interview Delia Wentworth; a girl who had been at Ottilie's boarding school but who had not been someone she had become close to. Ottilie had told Jonah Walsh she wasn't one of Delia's chosen circle of friends, but he had simply shrugged.

Ottilie was out of Delia's league, Ottilie had always thought. Delia was beautiful, popular, and paid absolutely no heed to the sporty, more academic types…like Ottilie. Delia had cast a long shadow over the girls Ottilie had called friends. She had always made them feel rather inferior. She and Ottilie had rarely spoken, and she certainly hadn't confided to Ottilie her plan to abscond from St. Agatha's to run away with Charles Wentworth. It had been a scandal that had never been forgotten at the school, one which had caused equal amounts of shock and admiration from the girls.

'Just be professional,' Ottilie said to herself as she sat on the edge of her settee. 'Delia probably won't even recognise you. We've all changed so much, and she'll have a lot more on her plate than thinking about Ottilie

Divine and the fact you were at school together.'

She took in a breath and went to her handbag to retrieve the coins she needed to make the dreaded phone call to Delia Wentworth. Then something occurred to her.

'It doesn't matter if she doesn't recognise me. I'll have to tell her my name.' She bit her lip. 'Damn. Oh, well. I've said I'll do it so I better had.'

She clutched the coins in her hand and made her way down the two flights of stairs to the hall. As she neared the bottom she heard voices, one of them Mrs Hudson's, the other she was quite sure belonged to Sherlock Holmes. *Oh, no,* she thought. *It's the insufferable man.* She tried to slow her steps, then realised if she didn't get to the hall before they'd finished speaking, she and Holmes would have to pass each other on the stairs. *No thank you,* she thought, and quickened her pace.

Sherlock Holmes and Mrs Hudson finished their conversation just as Ottilie stepped off the bottom tread. She tried her hardest not to look at him, but he stopped her as she made her way to the hall telephone.

'Miss Divine,' he said in the commanding voice Ottilie disliked because it made her feel like she was about to be reprimanded again.

'Yes, Mr Holmes,' Ottilie replied, averting her eyes.

He shifted his weight from one hip to the other. 'Two things. Number one, thank you for lowering the sound from your gramophone when Dr Watson paid you a visit at the weekend. I was conducting a particularly difficult experiment on Saturday evening which needed my utmost concentration.' Ottilie drew in a breath but said nothing. 'And number two. I understand you are a reporter for The Daily Express?'

She lifted her head and looked him full in the face. Her position at the Express was something of which she was proud. There was no need for her to be modest.

'Indeed.'

'I would imagine you will be kept extremely busy now war has been declared.' It was a statement more than a question. She simply nodded, wishing he'd get on with it…whatever it was. She couldn't imagine he'd stopped to speak with her out of any pleasurable expectation. 'I would like to offer my services.'

Ottilie blinked rapidly. 'Your services?'

'Indeed.'

'In what way?'

'I have certain contacts, Miss Divine, in the police department and in parliament. I have put my brain to good use for Inspector Lestrade at Scotland Yard. He and I have worked on a number of cases to which my invaluable help led him to arrest the villain involved. I also know men who are Members of Parliament, particularly in our fair city. I am currently on a hiatus with regard to cases.' He made a small bow. 'I am at your service if needs be.'

'I'm a reporter, Mr Holmes…not a secret agent. And I have my own contact at Scotland Yard.'

'I understand, Miss Divine, however, you are clutching money for a telephone call rather tightly in your hand which has made your knuckles whiten and seem to be in a state of high fever. You are about to make a telephone call to someone you would rather not speak to, but you have promised, in your capacity as a reporter for the esteemed Mr Jonah Walsh, you will do your duty.'

Ottilie looked surprised. 'You know Mr Walsh?'

'Indeed. He and I have crossed paths on many occasions. The man is in a state of flux I believe, since his wife died some six months ago.'

Holmes stared at Ottilie, and her mouth dropped open. How was it her fellow tenant knew about the death of Mr Walsh's wife when she, and she was quite certain, her colleagues did not.

'I...I... Well of course. It would have changed everything for him, poor man.'

'Am I correct in thinking you did not know, Miss Divine?'

'You must excuse me, Mr Holmes. The telephone call I must make is rather urgent. Good day to you.'

'And to you, Miss Divine.'

Ottilie lifted the telephone receiver, then watched Sherlock Holmes as he sprung up the first flight of stairs, two at a time. He was tall and wiry, but clearly strong. She shook her head, thinking she had never met anyone quite like Sherlock Holmes. And as for requiring his services...she giggled to herself as she dialled the number for Delia Wentworth, thinking she could not imagine anything worse.

The telephone rang four or five times and Ottilie waited wishing they would answer and put her out of her misery.

'Bayswater 1425. The Wentworth residence.'

'Good morning,' replied Ottilie. I wondered if I might speak with Mrs Wentworth.'

'Who shall I say is calling?'

Ottilie took a breath before replying, then decided to pull a little rank, hoping it would enable her to speak to Delia without any barriers placed in her path. 'Lady Ottilie Divine.'

'Yes, madam. Please hold on.'

'Ottilie? Ottilie Divine?'

'Hello, Delia.'

'I can hardly believe it. After all these years.'

'I'm surprised you remember me.

'Of course I remember you. What are you doing these days?'

Ottilie took a pause. *There it is.* 'I work for the Daily Express. I'm a reporter.'

'I see. I spoke to one of your chaps recently about Charles. I'm sorry to say he made me feel sicker at heart than I was already feeling. I wasn't expecting a bedside manner, but…shall we say…a little empathy wouldn't have gone amiss.'

'My editor, Mr Walsh is aware of what happened during your interview, Delia, which is why he suggested I call you. I wondered if we could meet for tea today…perhaps at Browns, my treat. You need as much help as you can get to find Charles, and newspapers often get the word out when someone is missing.'

'Do you think anyone will care?' Ottilie heard Delia's voice change. She sounded pessimistic as though she had given up and the end of the story was inevitable.

'Of course they care, Delia. Why wouldn't people care?'

'Because war has been declared. Our country is at war and it's inescapable people will be killed. Why would anyone be concerned about one man they have no knowledge of when they're worrying about their own?'

'It depends on the circumstances, doesn't it? Charles had a very important job in the Foreign Office, had recently been in Germany and has now disappeared. There's a reason it's happened, and we may be able to get to the bottom of it.' There was a pause. Ottilie could hear Delia crying. She felt awful, hoping she hadn't knocked down Delia's defences. 'I'm sorry, Delia, for upsetting you. It wasn't my intention.'

'It's not you, Ottilie. One feels so helpless.'

'Will you meet with me, Delia?'

'Yes, but not in public. I haven't been outside the house for nearly three weeks. The children and I have built a fortress around us. I don't think I could bear it if I realised I was being talked about. You know what people are like, Ottilie. It doesn't concern them that they're breaking someone's heart.'

'Should I come to you?'

'Yes, do, Ottilie. It will be so good to see you again and to reminisce about our days at St. Agatha's.' Another pause. Ottilie could hear Delia's breathing down the receiver. 'Will you write a story about Charles?'

'With your permission I will draft an article which will ask for our reader's help in finding him. It will be truthful and unemotional, and there will be no mention of your children, save to say you have three between you, and you, as Charles's wife, are of course extremely distressed at his disappearance.'

'Can you come this afternoon, about two?'

'I'll be there.'

Delia gave Ottilie her address which she wrote on a notepad which had been placed on the hall table beside the telephone for the very purpose. She tore off the relevant piece and put it in her pocket. She closed her eyes momentarily and thought about Delia, wondering how she would fare if it came to pass Charles was never found, or he was discovered to have been killed. Delia was always strong-willed and determined, but Ottilie was quite sure motherhood changed a person. Sighing, Ottilie decided to pay Mrs Hudson a visit as she had promised her when war had been declared.

'How are you, Mrs Hudson?' Ottilie asked her when the older woman had answered her door.

'Oh, I'm all right, Miss Divine. I'm bearing up now the shock has worn off. We're all feeling the same, aren't we? All shocked, all worried for the future. Have you got time for a cup of tea?'

'A very quick one. I'm meeting someone this afternoon.'

Mrs Hudson smiled at her. 'A young man?'

Ottilie laughed. 'Nothing like that. I've to interview a woman whose husband has disappeared. He works for the Foreign Office and was with Neville Chamberlain when the treaty was signed in Germany. He came back to England to be with his family, but he hasn't been seen for more than three weeks.'

Mrs Hudson poured two cups of tea from a pot that seemed to be forever full. She passed a cup to Ottilie.

'Oh, dear. What do you think has happened to him?'

Ottilie sighed. 'I wish I knew, Mrs Hudson, and I'm sure his wife would like to know too.' She took a sip of tea. 'I know Delia Wentworth. She went to my school.'

Mrs Hudson sat in her usual chair, her eyes widening. 'What a coincidence, Miss Divine. And what school was that?'

'St. Agatha's in Hampshire.'

'A boarding school?' Ottilie nodded and Mrs Hudson looked thoughtful. 'Did you like it, dear? I've heard some rum things about boarding schools.'

'I loved it. I felt privileged to go there and was incredibly happy in every year. Unfortunately, Delia Wentworth wasn't. She absconded one night and ran off with Charles, but obviously it worked for them. They're still together.' Ottilie blinked. 'Well, they would be if he hadn't disappeared.'

Mrs Hudson leant forward in her chair and said in a voice which spoke of an intrigue. 'You don't think he's dead do you, dear?'

Ottilie shrugged. 'I don't know, Mrs Hudson. Truly I don't know.'

Chapter 9

Ottilie got a cab to Bayswater from Baker Street. She could have walked to Bayswater, it would have taken a little over half an hour from Baker Street, but her stomach still fluttered with nerves and she felt if she got to her destination without fuss she wouldn't have time to think about her interview with Delia Wentworth.

In truth she would have preferred if they could have met somewhere public. Browns would have been perfect. The background of a busy tearoom was the perfect foil for any pauses in conversation. There was always something else to talk about, the beautifully cut sandwiches perhaps, or the selection of delectable cakes. Even the other diners. When one went to Browns there was always someone there one could gossip about. It was why her mother and her friend Elsie, now Lady Fortesque-Wallsey, frequented it so often. They were definitely ladies who lunched, but sadly Ottilie was quite sure their harmless fun would come to a close now war had been declared.

She looked out of the window of the cab. They were a country at war, but so far nothing appeared to have changed, apart from people on the streets carrying their gas mask cases over their shoulders. They were supplied with them in 1938, but some people said it wasn't worth it…just another encumbrance.

She looked down at hers on the seat beside her. It was a hideous thing, and she dreaded having to put it on her face, but it had been explained to her it could save her life. If she were to use an Anderson shelter should there be an air raid, or depending where she was at the time, the underground platforms where they were told to escape to, there was the danger of escaping gases should the area be bombed, which would kill her just as efficiently as any explosion.

The cab stopped outside a house in Kensington Gardens Square.

'Thank you, driver,' she said smiling. 'What's the damage?'

'Two shillings please.' She decanted the money into the driver's hand and stepped out of the cab, glancing up at the building in front of her.

Kensington Gardens Square was an enviable area to live. Ottilie had always wondered why her mother hadn't chosen a house like the one she was about to visit, but knew her mother had been happy at Duke Street and hadn't wanted to leave the house she called home. It was where Ottilie had made some wonderful memories and she couldn't help but be a little homesick when she thought of it, and Cecily, Knolly, Aaron and Phillips who had become her family.

She stepped back on the pavement a little, admiring the stucco exterior and the large floor to ceiling windows. It was an attractive house. The windows were dressed in frothy white curtains, not to Ottilie's taste, but they suited the style of the house. There was a balcony over the top of the porticoed front door which was filled with planters holding a beautiful array of red and gold autumnal flowers. It seemed life continued at Kensington Gardens Square, regardless of a husband and father going missing.

She went up the three steps at the front of the house and lifted the knocker which resounded loudly against the shiny, black-painted front door. After a few moments, a maid answered and invited Ottilie into the hall which was decorated in a palatial style, with wooden panelling and floral wallpaper above the dado rail. It was a feminine décor which Ottilie was sure Delia Wentworth would have chosen.

'Ottilie,' cried Delia as she joined Ottilie in the hall from a door to what appeared to be a front sitting room. To Ottilie's surprise Delia embraced her and slipped an arm through hers, showing her into the sitting room where there was a suite of comfortable-looking furniture in front of a large and elegant fireplace. 'I'm happy to see you, my dear.'

A maid was placing a large tea tray with a teapot, cups and saucers, and a selection of sandwiches and cakes worthy of any afternoon tea at Browns on an ottoman between two of the chairs.

'Do sit down, Ottilie,' Delia said, offering Ottilie one of the comfy chairs. Delia sat opposite her and lifted the tea pot, used to serving herself it would seem.

Ottilie watched Delia as she set out the cups and saucers and poured the tea. She was beautifully dressed in an expensive-looking tea dress, no doubt by Norman Hartnell. It gave her a delicate, girlish look which suited her, and which Ottilie was quite sure she, Ottilie, could never quite pull off.

The blonde hair was still there, although Ottilie felt quite sure it wasn't quite what nature had given her. Her face was devoid of cosmetics apart from bright red lipstick which looked somehow incongruous. Ottilie wondered if it was Delia's attempt at normality. Children would always notice if Mama was not at her best. Delia obviously wasn't. Her hand shook as she poured the tea and Ottilie's heart went out to her.

'A silly question I know, Delia, but how are you bearing up?'

Delia passed a cup of tea to Ottilie and sat back in her chair whilst clutching her own. 'I feel as though I'm in a dream…no, a nightmare.' She took a sip of tea. Ottilie was surprised she didn't seem to notice how hot it was. Delia shook her head. 'The thing is, because of his work, Charles is often away, usually abroad somewhere, so the children haven't asked me where he is.' Her eyes suddenly filled with tears, and she quickly put her cup back on the tray and took a handkerchief from her pocket. 'I'm sorry. I keep bursting into tears and it's so unlike me.' She wiped her eyes and blew her nose as Ottilie leant forward and placed a comforting hand on Delia's knee.

'Delia…you're being too hard on yourself. You must be incredibly worried about Charles. He's your husband. Why wouldn't you be?'

'I have to stay strong for the children.'

'But they are seemingly unaware their father is missing, and if I were in your shoes I would maintain their unawareness until you know what's happened.'

Delia nodded and retrieved her tea from the tray. She sat back in her chair and stared off into the distance.

'It's funny isn't it, the habits one gets into without actually realising it. I keep expecting him to come through the front door, a smile on his face, the children so happy to see him. They adore their father. He's very good. So very good. A good man.'

Ottilie tried a little smile. 'You made the right decision then, when you left St. Agatha's?'

Delia couldn't help but smile at the memory. 'I never doubted it for a moment. But then…when you're only seventeen you think you're invincible.'

'You *were* rather. You did it, didn't you?'

Delia looked reasonably consoled. 'I suppose so,' she said with a sigh.

'And what about Charles? How did he seem when he came back from

Germany? It was a momentous occasion, wasn't it? In 1938, I mean, when the Munich Agreement was signed.'

'A complete waste of time you mean.'

Ottilie nodded. 'I suppose one could say that, but they did their best, at least it's what my landlady thinks.'

'You don't live at home anymore?'

'I moved out recently. Found myself a rather lovely flat in Baker Street.'

'No beau?'

'No, and nothing on the horizon either.'

'Does it worry you?'

Ottilie laughed despite the melancholy atmosphere in the room. 'Not in the slightest.'

'I envy you in a way.'

'Really?'

'Don't get me wrong. Charles and I are happy, and we adore the children, but sometimes...sometimes I think it would be rather wonderful to consider myself before everyone else, just for once. When one is a mother one must see to everyone's needs before one's own. I began married life very young. I didn't really get the chance to see what I could do in the outside world.'

'The outside world can be a cruel place, Delia,' said Ottilie. She paused before asking her next question. 'Did Charles confide in you about what happened in Germany when he was with Chamberlain?'

Delia looked concerned. 'I like to think you've come here as a friend, Ottilie, but you're also a reporter. How much of what I say will go into an article?'

'Very little, and certainly nothing personal, and nothing that could rock the fine balance the country is poised on at the moment. I research my articles to the last nth; I make sure they're truthful, but if we're going to find Charles, we need to ask our readers for help. For example, a recent photograph would be very helpful. Someone must have seen him leave his office. They may think they saw nothing at all, but a photograph may well jog someone's memory. I know about these things because my stepfather is working on Charles's case.'

Delia's eyes widened. 'Is your stepfather Chief Inspector Owen? He came here when I reported Charles missing.'

'He is. Of course, he's not allowed to discuss the case with me; he's always scrupulous about it, but between us we could come up with something. Clearly if I were to be contacted by someone who saw Charles the day he disappeared I would inform Richard. If it points him in the right direction, it's worth it, isn't it?'

Delia suddenly looked more relaxed. 'At last, I feel something is being done. Let me find the photograph for you.'

Delia almost ran out of the sitting room and Ottilie heard her go upstairs, presumably to the bedroom. She looked around the room. There were photographs everywhere, mostly of the children, three blonde-haired mites who didn't know their beloved Papa was missing. A sob welled in Ottilie's throat, but she forced it down. She was doing her job and to do it to the best of her ability it wouldn't help if she became too emotionally involved.

A few minutes later Delia returned with a photograph in a silver frame. She sat in the chair opposite Ottilie and began to remove the photograph from the frame. Once she'd done so, she passed it to Ottilie.

'It's the most recent I have. I can hardly bear to part with it, but I know you'll take care of it.'

'I promise I will,' replied Ottilie. She held the photograph in front of her, then looked up at Delia, smiling. 'He's still handsome, Delia.'

Delia nodded. 'He's the love of my life. I don't know what I'll do if...' she cleared her throat and took in a breath. 'Is there anything you want to know, Ottilie? Anything I can tell you that would help find him? I just want to help. I want to do something practical, not sit here like a dying duck in a thunderstorm.'

'You can help by being scrupulous about your memories, even if it's the tiniest thing you think is irrelevant. It might be irrelevant to you, but it could be important.' Delia nodded firmly. 'What did he tell you when he came back from Germany?'

Delia sat forward, placing her hands between her knees. 'He was melancholy which surprised me. We welcomed him home like we usually do, with much excitement from the children and a glass of brandy from me. I was excited too because it seemed he and his colleagues had achieved a wonderful thing. I believed there would be no war between Britain and Germany. Charles had telephoned from the embassy in Germany to tell me Chamberlain and Hitler had signed the Munich Agreement last year. I was ecstatic, but Charles not so much. He was rather dour about the whole thing to be honest.'

'Did you ask him why?'

'Not when he telephoned, no. I simply thought he was tired. I know the whole trip had been rather exhausting for him.'

'And when he got home?'

Delia shrugged. 'Again, he was in a low mood. He said things had gone as planned but he wasn't convinced.'

'What was it that hadn't convinced him?'

'He said he was wary of Adolph Hitler.' Delia sighed again. 'You see, Charles had heard so many things about him...not particularly good things...and although Neville Chamberlain was obviously keen to get an agreement from him, Charles didn't trust him. He said Hitler seemed to have little interest in what was happening. He signed the agreement, then was heard making flippant remarks about Chamberlain and his entourage, in German of course, but Charles is fluent.'

Ottilie frowned. 'Charles must have wondered about it.'

'When Charles went back to Germany this last time, he heard rumours Hitler was scathing about Chamberlain and dismissive of the claim, "peace for our time." Apparently, he saw Chamberlain agreeing to a contract as feebleness and poured scorn on him and other leaders in the Western world. It seemed to Charles that Adolph Hitler had no intention of complying with the agreement.'

'Why did Charles go to Germany recently.'

'To keep things on course. There had been rumblings from the British Embassy in Berlin that the agreement wasn't stable. Charles is a good negotiator, but when he came back, he said, "Enjoy your holiday. It might be the last one we have for a while." And of course he was right, wasn't he?'

'You believe he was melancholy because he felt the agreement wouldn't stand?' Delia nodded. There was a question Ottilie wanted to ask Delia but was nervous of doing so. 'Did Charles make friends in Germany?'

Delia drained her teacup and placed it on the tray, sitting back in her chair. 'You're asking me whether I think Charles is capable of having an affair, aren't you?'

Ottilie looked contrite. 'It's just a question, Delia, and one I think worth asking. I know it's painful for you to think of Charles in such a way, particularly as you're so very worried about him, but we must explore every avenue.'

Delia nodded. 'The answer to your question is this. Charles and I have discussed the possibility of one of us finding someone else, but we agreed if it were ever to happen, we wouldn't let it come as a shock. We would tell the other one quietly and without drama because of the children. I can happily and firmly say no such conversation has ever taken place.' Ottilie nodded. Delia's statement was good enough for her.

'But his colleagues? He must have formed friendships while he was in Germany.'

'Of course.'

'And did they return to London with Charles?'

'All of them. The writing was on the wall. Some of them had families in Berlin. They had to return and bring their families and their households with them.'

Ottilie nodded again. 'Who was Charles closest to would you say?'

'Some of the Berlin lot came here for dinner once. I would say he was closest to William Shaw. They seemed to get on particularly well, and his wife, Tabby, short for Tabitha, is a pleasant person and very interested in the children. They seemed so very relaxed with them at dinner.

'The children liked them too which I always think is a good sign. The Shaws are like us; have been together for years and have three children between them. The only difference is they were stationed in Germany. William was an assistant to the Ambassador.' She thought a little more. 'Benedict Smyth was another colleague. He was also in Germany with his family.' She sighed. 'And then there were German colleagues too but I don't know their names. He was friendly with all of them until…well, until the agreement was broken.'

'Do you have William Shaw's address?'

'Yes,' said Delia, going to a bureau in the corner of the room. 'It's here somewhere.' She began to look through some papers in the bureau, then pulled out an address book. 'I think it might be in here.' She ran her finger down the page. 'Yes, here it is. I'll write it down for you. And his telephone number too.' She took a note of the address and tore a sheet out of a notebook. 'Here you are,' she said passing it to Ottilie.

'Has he been in touch with you?'

'Chief Inspector Owen paid him a visit I understand. William Shaw telephoned me when he discovered Charles was missing, utterly distraught.'

'Did Charles do or say anything unusual before he disappeared?' Delia shook her head. 'What about letters from an unfamiliar source, or perhaps phone calls?'

'Nothing like that as far as I know. I suppose if there was a problem Charles could have hidden it from me. He didn't like me to worry about anything.' She nodded. 'You know, Ottilie, the more I think about it the more I think he would hide something like that from me. He would never want to put something untoward on my shoulders.'

'Did Charles ever feel threatened?'

Delia took her time to answer. 'In Berlin he said he never felt safe. I remember him saying he was glad he wasn't posted to Berlin permanently because it would have meant moving us there and he would never have been able to rest. He wasn't…comfortable there, particularly on his recent trip. He seemed so very relieved to be home. Part of me wondered if he thought he would be stuck in Berlin, apart from us, held perhaps. I did wonder about it, but he seemed exhausted, so I didn't broach the subject.' She shook her head. 'I wish I had now. It might have told us so much more.'

'What about journals or diaries? Did Charles keep anything like it?'

Delia nodded. 'It was always in his briefcase, Ottilie. The one he took with him everywhere. It was with him when he left the last morning I saw him,' she said sadly.

'Could it be at his office?'

'Possibly, although I would have thought the police would have searched Charles's office, surely one of the first places they would have looked.'

Ottilie nodded, remembering what Camille had told her about the police sometimes missing evidence.

'I understand, although it's definitely worth following up?' She continued to write notes for herself in her notebook. She looked up and smiled at Delia. 'One last question, Delia. I promise it's the last one.' Delia nodded. She looked tired and Ottilie decided it was probably time for her to leave. 'Did Charles mention any rivalries within his department, perhaps between colleagues? And if there was did any of the rivalry concern him?'

'Charles was being groomed for greater things, we knew,' said Delia, looking proud and rather wistful. 'He had become a Charges d'Affaires, heading missions when perhaps the ambassador wasn't available, or the minister was absent. It had been mentioned Charles was in the running for Permanent Under-Secretary of State for Foreign Affairs, which meant he would have been the highest-ranking civil servant in the Foreign Office and would have acted as senior advisor to the Foreign Secretary. It would also mean he would oversee the administration of the Foreign Office and the Diplomatic Service. There would have been a lot of travelling involved…not just to Germany, which of course won't happen now because of the war.'

'You said he was in the running. Do you know who else could have been in the same position?'

'No, and Charles didn't know either. It could have been any of his colleagues, even those who were stationed abroad.' She pulled a despondent face at Ottilie. 'It's a plum job, Ottilie, one many of his colleagues would have wanted. I know Charles would have excelled at it. He felt wretched about what happened with Germany, but he was excited about being considered for such a position. Just being considered is a feather in one's cap…and my money was on Charles. I know I'm biased but he was excellent at his job. His colleagues told me themselves…he was the best person for the position.'

'And now he's out of the way,' Ottilie said under her breath.

Delia gasped. 'Ottilie, you can't think one of Charles's colleagues would have harmed him?'

Ottilie shrugged. 'We can't rule anything out, Delia. We must consider all possibilities.'

'When will the article be in The Daily Express?'

'The day after tomorrow. The police have asked the press not to divulge the story until then. It gives the police time to make enquiries, but I think our best chance of finding Charles is by asking the readers.' She leant towards Delia and grasped her hand. 'He didn't disappear into thin air, Delia. Something has happened to him and someone could know something, no matter how small. My stepfather is the best person you could wish for on the case.' She leant back and grinned. 'And now you have me. I will do everything I can to help.'

Tears welled in Delia's eyes. 'I've felt so alone, Ottilie. I've been utterly helpless not knowing which way to turn, but now I have you.' She made a watery smile. 'I feel so much better now.' She gave a small chuckle. 'You're rather like a police officer yourself.'

Ottilie laughed too. 'Investigative reporters aren't so much different I suppose, and we're not so confined as the police who must follow the letter of the law. Obviously, if I discover something I'll pass the information on to Chief Inspector Owen. Don't give up hope, Delia. If anyone can discover what happened to Charles, it's Chief Inspector Owen. He'll leave no stone unturned.'

Chapter 10

Ottilie stepped down to the pavement in Kensington Gardens Square after saying her goodbyes to Delia Wentworth. She hitched her gas mask over her shoulder along with her bag and looked around the square. There were few people on the streets, and she understood why. They were frightened, scared something might happen while they were away from their homes which would have been out of their control. The spectre of warfare had been on their shoulders for some time. Gas masks had begun to be issued the year before, but hardly anyone thought to carry them. They weren't at war then. There had seemed to be no need. The gas mask became just a bulky inconvenience to haul with them wherever they went. But now? Now it was different. They were at war, and everyone had to carry a gas mask, even children who were given Micky Mouse gas masks, so they weren't so intimidating.

Opposite the house were communal gardens where the leaves of the trees had begun to take on their late summer hue of green into pale orange. She imagined it would be beautiful in the depths of autumn when the reds and golds had come into play.

'I doubt Delia will notice,' she said under her breath, then noticed some men installing an air raid shelter in the gardens. Ottilie shook her head. Already her beloved London was changing. The face of the city was altering, and she wondered if it would ever look the same again.

She had eschewed the idea of finding a taxicab to take her back to Baker Street, choosing to walk instead. It was a pleasant afternoon, and she wondered how many opportunities she would get to walk these pleasant streets when the war was in full swing.

As she walked, she thought hard about the answers Delia had given to her questions regarding Charles's disappearance. From what Ottilie could gather Charles left his work in his office. He chose not to take it into his home and rarely discussed things with Delia for fear of worrying her. Ottilie was interested in Charles's colleagues though. She thought it was odd no one had visited Delia when they discovered Charles was missing. *Why would they not do so*, she wondered?

Delia said she felt alone, almost isolated from her husband's colleagues at a time when Ottilie would have thought they would have gone to her aid. She had mentioned a dinner party she and Charles had hosted and named some of the people who had been there, but only William Shaw had contacted Delia, Charles's closest work colleague, but not Tabby, or Tabitha, his wife, even though Delia said she was a pleasant person.

Ottilie frowned. Didn't women gather together at times like these? Ottilie thought about her colleagues in the press room. If something happened to one of them, would she not have made herself known to his wife, perhaps with a bunch of flowers to commiserate and to show she cared. Ottilie decided it's exactly what she would have done, even though she had only met her colleague's wives at Christmas parties.

She made a mental note to explore the hierarchy at the Foreign Office, and specifically William Shaw, and decided to get some background on him before she rang him. *Best to be prepared*, she thought.

Instead of turning left to make her way to Baker Street, she turned right and walked down Kensington Gardens Square until she got to Porchester

Gardens. The streets became busier the further she walked, and she turned into Inverness Terrace, walking the length of it until she got to Bayswater Road which edged Hyde Park.

Even the park had lost its sense of fun. Usually there were children playing in the park, a release from school in the afternoon, allowing them to shed the confines put on them during the day. They were often accompanied by harassed-looking mothers or nannies who would follow them slowly whilst pushing the youngest child in a pram. There were few children there…in fact the park was almost empty.

Ottilie sighed, sadness welling in her chest. She knew this was the sign of things to come. *It'll only get worse*, she thought. *The park will probably be full of Anderson shelters and the only time people will want to visit the park is when there's a raid on.* She shivered, praying things wouldn't be too bad, but her head told her she could be praying in vain.

The fear of the unknown was growing in London. She observed it in the eyes of those people who were going home from work and who passed her on the street. Where there might have been a cheery good afternoon from a passerby pleased to have finished work for the day, there was a hollow-eyed look instead. Ottilie bit her lip. What would the air raids be like? Would Germany go for London, or would they confine the raids to the coast where the ships and submarines were waiting? Would the war last for months, or could it be years as in the last war. It was unthinkable. All of it.

Ottilie found herself on the corner of Oxford Street and Duke Street. She hadn't realised she had walked so far, but her feet had guided her home. She didn't want Camille to think she wasn't coping on her own in Baker Street, but war had been declared. She wanted to hug her mother, and Cecily and Knolly. And she hoped there might be some news from

Richard regarding Charles Wentworth. She wanted to tell Richard she was the reporter who had been given the job of investigating the case.

She pushed her key into the front door and opened it.

'It's me,' she cried. Cecily ran into the hall from the kitchen vestibule where she had been folding some linen. She ran towards Ottilie, her arms outstretched.

'Miss Ottilie! We've been so worried.'

Ottilie frowned. 'Why, Cecily?' she asked, returning Cecily's hug.

'You didn't contact Madam when war was declared. I think she would have liked to have 'eard from you.'

Ottilie looked chastened. 'Am I in trouble?'

'No, darling, you're not in trouble,' said Camille, coming into the hall with Knolly. 'I have to keep reminding myself you are a fully-grown woman and quite capable of running your own life.' She shrugged. 'I suppose it's all come as a bit of a shock. One doesn't stop being a parent because one's child has grown and left the nest.'

Ottilie rushed to embrace Camille. 'Oh, Mama, I'm so sorry. It was thoughtless of me. The Express is so busy at the moment, and I've been given a special assignment.' She looked past Camille. 'Hello, Knolly. Are you and Aaron all right?'

'We're both as right as ninepence, but we feel like we've been rushed at and missed over this announcement what was made yesterday. I can 'ardly believe it, Miss Ottilie. We're at war. Again! And it's not much more than twenty years since the last one. I don't think I've got the energy for it, I really don't. Wish they'd all just shut up and go away.'

'Don't we all, Knolly,' said Camille. 'Is there any tea left in the pot. I'm sure Ottilie could do with one.'

'Actually, Mama, I'm awash with tea. I've just been to interview Delia

Wentworth over the disappearance of her husband Charles.'

They went into the kitchen where Knolly was putting the finishing touches to dinner. Sitting around the pine table that had been in the kitchen for more than two decades, they listened as Ottilie relayed her story about her assignment.

'So she were at school with you, Miss Ottilie?' asked Knolly as she basted a leg of lamb which looked and smelt utterly delicious.

'Yes, until she escaped.' Ottilie chuckled but then thought of Delia and how she must be feeling as another day without Charles was drawing to a close.

'And what do they think has happened to him?'

'There are no clues yet, Knolly. I hoped Richard would be here. I know he's working on the case.

'He is,' said Camille, 'but he's almost living at Scotland Yard at the moment. I'll be glad when he retires.'

Ottilie glanced at Camille, her eyes raised. 'You want him to retire?'

'He could retire now, but he says he'll stay until they make him go.'

'And you're not happy about it?'

Camille inclined her head to one side. 'I'd like to do some more traveling, Ottilie. We need to do it while we're both still healthy enough to enjoy it.' She shrugged. 'But of course I won't push him to retire if he doesn't want to.'

'Could you ask him to ring me at Mrs Hudson's please, Mama?' She fished in her bag for a piece of notepaper and wrote the number down, passing it along the table to Camille. 'I'd like to talk to him about Charles Wentworth. I know there are things he won't be allowed to tell me, but I would appreciate a chat with him.'

'I'll ask him, Ottilie, but you know what a stickler to the rules he is…and he wouldn't want you to write about anything he tells you.'

'I'll be relaying just the facts, Mama, nothing more. I've made a promise to Delia Wentworth anyway.'

'And you're determined to stay in Baker Street, even though war has been declared?'

'For the time being at least. Perhaps you, Cecily and Knolly could come for a visit. You'll see how homely it is, and how sweet Mrs Hudson is. It's begun to feel like home, my safe place. So, now I have two…here and Baker Street.'

Camille leant across the table and grasped Ottilie's hand.

'Just promise me if things get so very bad, you'll come back here. Just promise me, Ottilie. I'm not trying to live your life for you. I simply want you to be safe.'

Ottilie smiled and squeezed Camille's hand. 'I know, Mama…and I promise I'll come back if things take off.'

Ottilie made the short walk via Edwards Mews to Portman Street, then on to Baker Street. Preparations for war had been made the year before, but there had been a widespread expectation peace would ensue through diplomatic efforts. Those hopes and prayers had been dashed and as Ottilie surveyed the streets as she walked, it became even more real.

Already the cinemas, theatres and schools had been closed to reduce casualties during air raids which she knew would surely come. Sandbags were being piled around public buildings…places Ottilie knew well and used regularly; the Baker Street Underground Station in Marylebone Rd had sandbags placed around the entrance and she was sure many more inside. Communal shelters continued to be built in public spaces and basements of the larger buildings in the area.

She saw people behind their windows fixing blackout curtains to the curtain rails to ensure enemy bombers weren't aware of the cities and important buildings below them. Streetlights had also been extinguished. Ottilie had noticed when she had looked out of her window the previous evening…the rather comforting lights of Baker Street no longer illuminated the shops and pavements.

When she reached 221B Baker Street she released a breath of relief. The not knowing was worse than seeing her beloved London change before her eyes. She put her key in the lock and stepped over the threshold. Tears pricked her eyelids, and she brushed them away. She didn't want Mrs Hudson to see how upset she was feeling, and certainly not her fellow tenant who she was sure would have no sympathy whatsoever for "the silly woman upstairs".

As she passed Mrs Hudson's door it opened. Mrs Hudson stood on the threshold.

'I saw you pass my sitting room window, dear,' she said. 'Someone called you on the telephone…a man. He asked you to ring him.'

'Thank you, Mrs Hudson. I expect it was my stepfather. How are you?' Ottilie smiled, hoping her eyes weren't red.

'I'm all right. Seems to have gone a bit quiet, doesn't it. Since yesterday I think we've all been on pins expecting bombs to fall out of the sky and land on top of us, but I haven't heard anything.'

'Nor me,' replied Ottilie, 'but London is changing, Mrs Hudson. There are sandbags everywhere.'

'I suppose we should get some.'

'I've no doubt we'll be given some in due course. Baker Street looks so different without the glow from those lovely old lamps that line the street. It makes me feel rather sad.'

'Everyone's holding their breath, Miss Divine, that's what it is. I always say it's worse when we're waiting for something to happen than when it actually does. Don't know what we're going to have to deal with do we? And did you know they've started evacuating the kiddies to the country. The schools are closed of course, and the younger ones have been sent to stay with people they don't even know. How can a mother part with her little children?'

Ottilie closed her eyes momentarily and shook her head. 'I don't know, Mrs Hudson. It must be the very worst thing to part with one's children. This war could go on for months. They might never see them again. They must feel quite wretched.'

'Well, you go up, dear. I hope you don't mind me saying but you look a little peaky. I hope you're eating regularly.'

Ottilie chuckled. 'I am, Mrs Hudson, don't worry, but I *am* tired. It's been a trying day, but at least I'm not waving my children off to who knows where.'

'Very true, my dear.'

When Ottilie was finally in her flat she noticed a leaflet had been slipped under her door. She bent and picked it up as she dropped her bag and her gas mask on the settee.

'Protect Your Home from Air Raids,' she said to herself as she slipped off her coat. The leaflet went on to describe how one could best protect their surroundings and themselves from an air raid. It acknowledged the imminent danger which made Ottilie shiver, then went on to provide instructions on how to protect windows by taping the glass in a crisscross or diamond pattern, to use heavy blackout curtains and how to use sandbags to reinforce doors.

There was more information about where their nearest air raid shelter was, the use of gas masks and how to build an Anderson shelter. Ottilie sank down on the settee next to her gas mask, rested her head on her knees, and wept. The world was changing, even the small world Ottilie occupied, and she suddenly felt vulnerable.

When Camille had suggested she return home to Duke Street, Ottilie had been so tempted by the offer she had nearly agreed. She had watched the comforting and cozy rapport between her mother, Cecily, and Knolly, realising they still had each other.

The three women had known each other for decades, all living under the same roof for many years. They knew what made each other tick and she was sure they would rally each other when times became almost unbearable during the war as they surely would. Ottilie had researched the previous war extensively when she had interviewed women for her article and they had told her of the scarcity, the fear, the worry the war would continue for ever.

They told her about the losses of their loved ones, wondering how they could put a nourishing meal on the table when there was barely anything in the shops. One woman wept when she told Ottilie about rationing and how a shopkeeper had given her an extra egg because she had been a regular in better times, only to drop both eggs on the pavement when she'd left the shop.

"I believed those broken eggs resembled my life" she'd told Ottilie. "Broken, smashed to pieces and with no way of putting it all back again the way it was before." Ottilie had cried with her then, but they'd wiped their eyes and had a strong cup of tea afterwards, laughing at the difficulties of life the way women did.

Ottilie lifted her head and stared into the darkness. It had started to rain outside, and the wind was blowing the deluge towards the window, hitting the glass with force. She stood and went across the room to peer out.

There was nothing to see. It was dark and with no lighting the street looked gloomy and ominous, nothing like the street she had seen the first day she'd arrived when it was bustling with people going about their lives. It had all seemed so exciting then. She had been so full of hope and so proud she was at last in control of her own life. She frowned. Was she in control now?

So much had changed in a few short weeks. The country was at war, yet there was no noise, no imminent threat, no sign of danger.

She wondered if it was the calm before the storm.

Chapter 11

The following day Ottilie arrived in the press room early. She was anxious to get as much of her article written as she could before Jonah Walsh arrived. There was no one in the office so early in the morning, and she was glad of it. It meant she could type the article with no interruptions which there always seemed to be when the press room was full of reporters and their effulgent egos, which tediously led them to believe whatever they wrote was quite brilliant.

Her article regarding women in war had gone down well; the newspaper had all but sold out, and she was looking forward to submitting her article on Charles and Delia Wentworth. Again, she had slanted it to women's point of view, using a feminine touch and not allowing any bias or sensationalism to skew its meaning. At the end of the piece, she had typed a call to action, asking readers for help, repeating that Charles Wentworth had been an important member of the Foreign Office and could have information help make the war a short one.

"If you saw anything unusual on the day Mr Wentworth disappeared" she typed, "or recognise the man in the photograph, please contact The Daily Express or Detective Inspector Richard Owen at Scotland Yard." She typed two telephone numbers, then said a silent prayer over the article, hoping it was enough to jog someone's memory. Satisfied with what she had written, she whipped it out of her typewriter and placed it on Jonah

Walsh's desk for him to see on his arrival.

Gradually, the press office began to fill with reporters, and a lot of noise. Typewriters began to click and clack, balls of paper were thrown from one end of the room to the other because the other reporters thought it was a good game, and guffaws of laughter came from those who had nothing better to do, or so it seemed. Until Jonah Walsh arrived, when everyone bent their heads to their notes, and gave the impression of being industrious.

Ottilie was in the process of writing questions she could ask Charles Wentworth's colleagues, if and when she was given permission to question them. She had known she would need an entrée, and it was the subject she had spoken to Richard about the previous evening when she'd returned his call.

'Can you get me in, Richard?' she'd asked him. 'I need to be in the thick of it. Speaking to Delia Wentworth was one thing, but to be honest she didn't know much about Charles's day to day activities. I need information from the horse's mouth. I'm quite sure they're not going to allow a female reporter from the Daily Express to simply walk in and ask them questions.'

'You're right, they won't. They're not keen on reporters at Westminster. I think you're going to have a difficult job there, Ottilie.'

'But surely they want to discover what's happened to Charles Wentworth...particularly the Foreign Office.'

'I've already spoken to them of course. You need to speak with Lawrence Tebbit. He is the current under-secretary.'

'You've spoken to him already?'

'I have. I'm afraid he's not very forthcoming. He's like everyone at the Palace of Westminster. Buttoned up. They don't like outsiders delving into business.' Ottilie heard him sigh. 'I can write a letter of introduction for you. I'll send it to your office tomorrow by courier. More than that I'm afraid I cannot do.'

'Thank you, Richard. I'm very grateful.' She hesitated to ask him, but she couldn't help herself. 'Have you discovered anything?' she asked in a small voice.

'Ottilie…you know I can't say.'

'I know. I just wondered.'

'We're looking at every angle to find this man. He's important to the Foreign Office and therefore to the country. I *can* tell you it is thought he may have discovered something he shouldn't have, and he's been taken off the streets to protect someone. It's all I'm prepared to say…in fact, I've said too much. Just be careful, Ottilie. Men like Charles Wentworth don't go missing every day. There's a reason someone wants to keep him quiet, and that someone will be extremely dangerous indeed.'

'Miss Divine!'

Jonah Walsh called Ottilie into his office, startling her as she concentrated on her questions for the ministers, if she was ever allowed to ask them. She left her desk and went into his office.

'Shut the door, Miss Divine…and sit.'

Jonah Walsh was holding her article in his hands, his glasses pushed up to his forehead. His shirt looked cleaner than the one he wore on Sunday, and it had all its buttons. For a reason she couldn't fathom it made her happy. She relaxed while she waited for him to tell her what he thought of her article.

'We can go to print about Charles Wentworth now, Miss Divine. The police know an article will appear in this evening's edition. I've read your article, and it hits the spot.' Ottilie's heart soared. 'I'm glad to see it isn't an emotional account but simply states the facts. The call to action says what it needs to say. Well done.'

Ottilie smiled. *Another step forward,* she thought. *Now for the next one.*

'I need to speak to Charles Wentworth's colleagues, Mr Walsh. My stepfather has kindly written a letter of introduction. It should arrive this morning.'

Walsh searched his untidy desk, then held up another piece of paper. 'It arrived ten minutes ago.'

'Do you think it will get me in? Richard says…I mean, Chief Inspector Owen says those at Westminster aren't too keen on reporters asking questions.'

'They're not, but I've made a phone call. As I think I've said before, Miss Divine, it's not *what* you know, it's *who* you know. You have an appointment to speak with Lawrence Tebbit this morning at eleven. Take your letter of introduction with you. I can't guarantee it will go smoothly but it's a start. They need to get to know you. Any subsequent article you write after the interview will be closely studied by those at Westminster. Don't pull any punches and don't try to catch him out. He'll turf you out of Westminster in the blink of an eye and you'll never get back in again.'

Ottilie nodded. 'I understand.'

'And you're a woman, Miss Divine.' He held his hand up before she could protest. 'I know, I know, it shouldn't make a difference, but a female reporter is a rarity as I know you're aware. Those at Westminster would much prefer one of your male counterparts to speak with them, an occasion where they can go into the bar, get drunk and smoke cigars, with the reporter hoping the interviewee will drop something into the conversation that will interest them. Sometimes that approach works, but on this occasion, I feel it's too important for the country to treat Wentworth's disappearance in such a cavalier way.'

Walsh shuffled the papers on his desk which Ottilie knew was his way of dismissing her.

'Here's the letter from Chief Inspector Owen, Miss Divine.' Ottilie stood and took the paper from him. 'I won't wish you luck because I know you'll do a good job. I'd like you back here after the interview so we can discuss what you've learnt…if anything. They can be a cagey lot at Westminster.'

Chapter 12

10th September 1939

Ottilie sat in an outer office on a hard chair. Her handbag was on her lap and her ubiquitous gas mask was on the chair next to her.

There were three women in the office, all with typewriters in front of them. Two of the women were middle-aged, the other young and fidgety. She wore her bleached blonde hair in a roll at the nape of her neck and her lips were painted bright red.

Her fingernails were long and polished in a similar colour. They made an irritating clicking sound on the keys of her typewriter and were obviously not conducive to accuracy in her typewriting. She constantly made mistakes then swore under her breath while she used an eraser to rub out the offending errors. Both the middle-aged women would frown each time she uttered a curse, then glance at each other with an expression of frustration.

'Evelyn, really. Must you use such awful language?'

Evelyn turned to stare at the older woman whose desk was nearest the office door on which there was a brass nameplate which said, "Lawrence Tebbit".

'I don't know how you can hear what I say. I never say it loudly, and you're always typing so how do you know what I've said? I'm not harming anyone.' The older woman sighed.

A telephone rang on one of the desks and it was answered by the woman sitting closest to the door. Ottilie assumed she was Lawrence Tebbit's secretary.

'You may go in now, Miss Divine. Mr Tebbit has a small window in his schedule for you.'

Ottilie nodded and stood, placing both her bag and her gas mask over her shoulder. 'Thank you.' She was quite sure the phrase, "a small window in his schedule" meant he didn't want to speak to her, but felt obliged because of the letter of introduction, and because of Jonah Walsh's contact.

She opened the door to the office gingerly. She was nervous and butterflies fluttered in her stomach. This interview was the most important...and most difficult...she had ever undertaken, but then she straightened her back and pushed the butterflies away. She was a reporter, and she was trying to do a job. That at least deserved some respect.

Lawrence Tebbit's office was typical of a place of work occupied by a man of some stature. It was decorated in a rather dour fashion, brown everywhere, the wood panelling providing no relief whatsoever to what was clearly a male dominated environment. Above Lawrence Tebbit's head was a cloud of cigar smoke which gave the appearance of a halo. Ottilie wondered if he deserved such an aura.

Lawrence Tebbit sat behind a huge desk which was orderly and well-polished. He glanced up as she entered the room, pointing to the chair in front of the desk without asking her to sit down. Ottilie took in a breath. He had not welcomed her, nor made any attempt to make eye-contact with her. She smiled to herself. *He's not going to make this easy*, she thought as she sat in the proffered chair.

As he continued to write on the papers in front of him Ottilie took in his appearance. He was portly, a kind epithet, his face ruddy with large jowls which shook as he wrote. His hair was thinning but what had remained had been slicked back with Brylcream, making the separate strands look greasy. His eyes seemed to disappear into hooded eyelids occasionally narrowing as he read. Ottilie decided he was a bureaucrat through and through and getting information from him would be like trying to get blood from a stone.

'Miss Divine,' Lawrence Tebbit said without glancing up. 'I've spoken to Chief Inspector Owen regarding Charles Wentworth's disappearance. I'm not sure I can add anything more salient.' He picked up the sheaf of paper and bounced the ends on the desk to straighten them then put them into a tray on the right side of the desk.

'Now, Miss Divine,' he said, leaning his elbows on the desk and steepling his fingers together. 'As I've explained I had a long interview with Chief Inspector Owen who puzzlingly has seen fit to write a letter of introduction for you.' He shrugged and leant back arrogantly in his chair. 'I'm not sure there's much more I can say. Charles was diligent, an important member of the team, relatively popular, but I know nothing about his personal life. I don't ask members of my team what they do on their days off.'

Ottilie knew she was in for a fight but if Lawrence Tebbit thought she would crumble under his tone or his treatment of her he was much mistaken.

'Mr Tebbit, newspapers are the voice of the people. They can also help in investigations such as finding missing persons by asking the readership for information. The Daily Express has often helped Scotland Yard in this way because we can get the message out simply by placing an article or a call to action on the front page. I would imagine it is something you, as Charles Wentworth's superior, would want to utilise?' Ottilie's voice was the proverbial iron hand in a velvet glove. She made sure to hold Tebbit's gaze while she was speaking.

Tebbit's eyes narrowed and he took a breath. 'What is it you think I can tell you, Miss Divine? This is a professional environment. If you're looking for sleaze on Charles Wentworth I'm afraid you won't get it from me. I know what you reporters are like. You'll no doubt sell the article to the highest bidder, particularly if there's something unsavoury to be reported.'

'I work for The Daily Express, Mr Tebbit, and very proud to do so. We do not report sleaze as you put it. We report the truth, and since we're now a country at war, I would have thought you of all people would have been concerned about what Charles Wentworth knows. Who knows what's happening to him if it's true he has been abducted, which seems rather likely don't you think?'

Tebbit took a paperclip from his desk and began to unconsciously play with it, twisting it in and out of his fingers. He said nothing. Ottilie leant forward to face him, almost nose to nose. She knew he was trying to intimidate her, but she didn't care one jot.

'Would you and your seniors not like an explanation for his disappearance?'

She watched Tebbit harden his jaw. 'Of course.'

'So help me help you, Mr Tebbit. Were there any...anomalies you noticed in his work or schedule over the last few weeks?'

Tebbit threw the paperclip onto the desk. 'I'm sure you're aware I cannot comment on matters concerning either the Foreign Office or the War Office, Miss Divine. Those matters are classified and must remain so.

Seeing you this morning is a consideration to Chief Inspector Owen who I understand is a member of your family.'

Ottilie arched an eyebrow. 'So, are you telling me the ministry is not interested in Charles Wentworth's disappearance?'

Tebbit looked cross. 'Of course I'm not, but you must understand the department is in a difficult position.'

Ottilie bit her lip before playing a trump card she had invented on her way to Westminster.

'But what about the rumours, Mr Tebbit?' Tebbit flinched. *Got you*, thought Ottilie before Tebbit replaced his look of what could only be described as fear and replaced it swiftly with anger.

'I don't know to what you're referring.'

'I'm referring to rumours which could taint the reputation of not only the department, but those who work within it.'

Tebbit shifted in his chair. 'Miss Divine, I think your time is up. Scotland Yard is cognisant of the facts surrounding Charles Wentworth's disappearance. I have told them everything I know which is very little. Charles ran his own appointments.' He stood and stared down at her. 'I think you should leave.'

Ottilie returned his stare for a few long moments, watching as his trembling hand reached for the telephone receiver, presumably to ask his secretary to escort Ottilie out of the office. *You're hiding something*, thought Ottilie, *and if I'm not mistaken, you're frightened.*

'Then I'll leave you to it, Mr Tebbit. If I think of anything else I've no doubt you will want to help me with my investigation?' She allowed her voice to rise on the last word, almost like a threat. 'And I assure you I will not give up,' she continued, her voice quietly polite. 'I *will* uncover the truth into Charles Wentworth's disappearance no matter what it takes. I have made a promise to his wife, Delia Wentworth who is a close friend, and I never break a promise.' She turned to walk away, her heels tapping confidently on the parquet flooring.

She opened Tebbit's door and stepped into the outer office. The secretary, whose desk was nearest to the office looked up as Ottilie passed her desk. The secretary rolled a new document into her typewriter. Ottilie heard her take a breath. She stared at Ottilie and then averted her gaze, glancing towards Tebbit's office door.

Ottilie smiled to herself, her lips twitching when a thought occurred to her. Tebbit's secretary was in the know. Of course she was. Secretaries knew everything. They were often the best sources of up-to-date information.

Ottilie knew exactly what her next move would be.

Chapter 13

Ottilie stepped out into the sunlight, breathing in the fresh, crisp September air and feeling positive. Her interview with Tebbit had yielded less than she would have liked, but she was sure if she could meet with his secretary, she would discover something which would lead her to the next step. She smiled to herself. She had learnt this from Camille and Cecily. Baby steps they had always said led them to success when they had carried out their own investigations. Camille Divine and Cecily Nugent had attracted a certain amount of notoriety as amateur detectives. "Tangled threads," Camille would say when she and Cecily had a meeting of minds. "It's the tangled threads we must unpick. We must find the ends of the threads and pull them apart. It is when we'll find our adversary." It had stuck with Ottilie. It was a phrase that had been recited so often she could hardly not remember it.

Ottilie straightened her hat and pulled her gloves tighter on to her hands. The secretary had certainly interested her. All secretaries were likely more capable of doing the work of the man they served. They were the guardians of secrets, more precise in the carrying out of their duties than a man ever could be.

She took a breath. Ottilie hoped Tebbit's secretary had a loose tongue, as long as she knew how to tempt the secretary into parting with the information she held. And Ottilie was quite sure this particular secretary knew about Charles Wentworth.

Simply confronting her would likely make her take to her heels never to be seen again. No, Ottilie knew her next move must be handled with delicacy. She glanced at her watch. She had spent an hour at the offices in Westminster, mostly taken up waiting for Tebbit to deign to see her. It was just about lunch time. Did Tebbit's secretary leave the office and take herself for a walk, perhaps stopping for a quiet lunch at one of the many cafés and small restaurants in the area?

Ottilie decided to wait at the entrance, praying the woman had a daily lunch habit. She positioned herself to the side of the entrance so she could see all who were going in to and leaving the parliamentary offices. If Tebbit's secretary left the building she would tail her, discreetly, quietly, blending into the many passersby who were likely office workers looking for something to eat.

Fifteen minutes passed. Ottilie didn't mind. She was prepared to wait until the evening if it meant getting to the truth, but to her delight she saw it wasn't necessary.

Tebbit's secretary emerged from the parliamentary offices dressed in a calf-length twill coat in navy-blue with a hat and shoes to match. She looked smart; businesslike and heading for somewhere in particular Ottilie surmised.

The woman walked swiftly and with purpose. Ottilie left her position by the parliamentary offices and followed at a distance, keeping her quarry in sight while she wove through the melee of people walking towards her.

She followed Tebbit's secretary down a narrow side street. The shops and cafés were rather quaint, much to Ottilie's delight. This was the historical part of London Ottilie loved, but while she would have loved to stop and browse her eyes remained on the woman's back.

She drew in a breath as she observed her quarry entering a small tearoom. It was pleasant enough and as Tebbit had offered Ottilie nothing in the way of information or refreshment she thought it was the perfect time for a cup of tea. She took a seat near the front of the café so she would notice if the woman left, but Ottilie observed her as she order a pot of Lapsang Souchong and a plate of cheese sandwiches.

After ordering her own tea and sandwich she stood quietly, and picking up her tray made her way to the back of the café where the secretary was about to tuck in. As she got to the table she smiled her most charming smile. The woman looked up and frowned.

'Would you mind if I shared your table?' She didn't wait for a reply, simply sat down on one of the Bentwood chairs and placed her tray on the table.

The secretary stared across the table at Ottilie, frowning. 'Why would you want to join me? We don't know each other.'

Ottilie began to take her teapot, cup and saucer and sandwiches from the tray and lay them out onto the table.

'We don't know each other yet, but I think we have a mutual interest.' The secretary blinked. 'Charles Wentworth?' The secretary's lips formed a straight line, and she frowned. She poured herself a cup of tea, took a sip then put her cup down with a chink. 'I can't help thinking you know Charles quite well, and you're as concerned about him as I am, and certainly his wife and children. I am a close friend of Delia Wentworth. She is beside herself with worry. I felt sure you would want to help.' The secretary didn't answer. Ottilie leant forward to solidify her request. 'I'm good at keeping confidences and protecting my sources… but I would like to hear what you know regarding Charles's disappearance. And I am sure you know more than your boss was willing to impart this morning.'

The secretary sighed. Around them the café was business as usual; the odd release of laughter, women chatting because they knew time would be short now they were at war, and their opportunity to get together may well be taken away from them. It was a more joyful atmosphere than Ottilie had expected. Her spirits lifted.

'I'll lose my job, Miss Divine. If Mr Tebbit discovers I've been speaking with you he will not hesitate to sack me. He is a difficult man at the best of times, and he would not be impressed if he thought I was speaking to someone from the press. I can ill afford to lose my job. I'm the only earner in our home. I take care of my elderly mother and if I was dismissed it would be a disaster. We would have nothing to live on. It will be difficult enough now war has been declared. I have to leave her on her own all day, you see. She gets very upset when I'm not there, but having nothing to live on would be worse.'

'You won't lose your job, Miss…?'

'Cheam. Deirdre Cheam.'

'Miss Cheam, I will protect you, I promise. Lawrence Tebbit is hiding information about Charles Wentworth's disappearance. He was obstructive this morning, and from what I've heard from Scotland Yard he was equally so with them. This is your opportunity to help us find Charles or at least discover the people who have taken him off the street.'

'You have contacts within Scotland Yard?'

'I do, Miss Cheam. Close contacts.'

Deirdre Cheam picked up her sandwich from the plate. She observed it for a moment as though she was confronting an enemy, then bit into it. She was deep in thought and chewed silently as Ottilie sipped her tea, watching her. Finally, Miss Cheam lent forward and lowered her voice.

'Do you have any idea what sort of man Lawrence Tebbit is?' she shook her head. 'I really don't think you do. He clawed his way to the position he is in now, knocking his competitors for the post aside like chess pieces.' She took another bite of her sandwich. 'He has absolutely no compassion, and there have been some strange rumours circulating the parliamentary offices about him. I would leave if I could, but as I've explained it is imperative I keep my job, particularly now. He has already told the other secretaries and I there will no doubt be overtime, which means more money.' She shook her head again. 'He is not a man anyone with an ounce of sense would cross.' A sip of tea. 'I would like to help you, Miss Divine, really I would.' She gazed off into the distance. 'Charles is such a lovely man, a breath of fresh air compared to Tebbit. And so generous. Why, at Christmas he bought all us secretaries a present, and offered to meet us in the bar for a festive drink.' She lowered her eyes. 'Obviously, I couldn't go because of Mother, but it was so kind of him to offer.'

'Don't you think it is entirely the reason why you should help me find him. Your boss is covering up for something. I know from experience…time is of the essence. The longer Charles is missing, the greater the chance we won't find him alive.'

'Please don't say such a thing, Miss Divine. Surely it won't come to that?'

'It will if we don't do something. Lawrence Tebbit isn't about to. As far as I can make out, he wants to wash his hands of the whole affair, and he'll expect you and your colleagues to keep silent. It's why he wouldn't tell me anything this morning.' Deirdre nodded and Ottilie thought she was almost there. *Come on, Deirdre,* she thought. *You're all I've got.* 'Trust me, Miss Cheam…when Scotland Yard get involved in cases it's serious. The department only commits to the most significant offences.'

Miss Cheam settled back in her seat. She stared at Ottilie and narrowed her eyes.

'I don't want anything to happen to Charles, Miss Divine, but there are things going on in the department you couldn't possibly know.' She took a handkerchief from her bag and blew her nose loudly. 'What do you want me to do? How can I help? I'm just a secretary, that's all.'

'By listening to everything said in the office…and I mean everything, no matter how trivial you think it might be. It could be a lead. In other words, I need information. If a document passes your desk you don't recognise, make a mental note. If you're called into his office, try to scan what he has on his desk. It might be a memorandum mentioning Charles, Berlin, or Germany. If Tebbit receives visitors you haven't seen before try to remember their names. If Tebbit suddenly cancels a meeting or organises another, log it in your memory. But most of all, don't write anything down.'

Ottilie opened her bag and retrieved a small card which she passed to Deirdre.

'This is the telephone number you can reach me on during the day.' She turned the card over and pointed to the back. 'And this is the number of the house where I live. I might not answer it, but whoever does will be happy to take a message from you. Leave a number and I'll telephone you.'

Deirdre nodded and put the card into a zippered compartment in her bag. She clicked the clasp of her bag closed, then leant forward and gently grasped Ottilie's wrist, lowering her voice to a whisper, hesitating before she spoke.

'There was something last week actually.'

Ottilie caught the waitress's eye and asked for two more cups of tea. She leant towards Deirdre. 'What was it?'

'A man…someone I had never seen before. He was incredibly smartly dressed, definitely Savile Row, and he carried a cane that looked as though it was topped with gold.' She frowned and shook her head. 'Mr Tebbit certainly thinks of himself as being a cut above the other gentleman in the department because of his position, but he was not in the same league as this man.'

The waitress cleared their table and placed two fresh cups of tea in front of them. 'What happened?' asked Ottilie.

'He didn't have an appointment, but he expected to be allowed to see Mr Tebbit. Mr Tebbit never sees anyone without an appointment. The man had a cultured voice, but there was the trace of an accent there, possibly Irish, Celtic anyway.' She sniffed and wiped her nose again. 'Of course I could be mistaken. I'm not good with accents. Tebbit showed him into his office immediately. The man was there for over an hour. They spoke in hushed tones for the most part, but occasionally I heard raised voices, mostly the other man. When he left, he didn't say goodbye to the secretaries. Most people do out of politeness.

'Mr Tebbit called me into his office. He was sweating and had loosened his tie and collar. I asked him if he was all right and he asked me to fetch him a brandy from the console, which I did. He knocked it back in one gulp. I couldn't believe it. I didn't even know he drank alcohol.'

'Was there any paperwork to back up the meeting? I would have thought most meetings would engender a small amount at least.'

'I asked him if he had anything for me to type and he said no, then changed his mind. He quickly dictated a letter which I duly typed. Then I got a phone call from him asking me to bring the letter into his office. I took the letter to him, and he tore it up in front of me. He said he had changed his mind because the meeting had come to nothing so there was no need to worry anyone else about it. He also asked me to forget about it and not to mention it to anyone else.'

Ottilie felt excitement running through her veins. 'What was the letter about?' she asked, her eyes sparkling.

'It was about a consignment, but the letter didn't say what the consignment was. If I remember correctly, there was some kind of delay, that the return package would need to be in place on the date given, and they would ensure it would be in good condition.' Miss Cheam frowned. 'To be honest I couldn't make head nor tail of it, but it sounded important.'

Ottilie nodded. Something had upset Tebbit; the unknown visitor seemed to have some kind of power over him. Why else would he be so flustered when Deirdre Cheam went into his office? She took a breath. Had she found the end of one of the threads? Was it significant in Charles Wentworth's disappearance? She reached out and grasped Deirdre Cheam's hand.

'Thank you, Deirdre. I hope you don't mind my using your Christian name.' Miss Cheam shook her head. 'You've been a great help. I think what you've told me could point us in the right direction. It's the first step admittedly but…it is a step. We had absolutely nothing to go on before.' She released Deirdre's hand and smiled. 'Don't worry about any of this. Remain calm, do your job. Just carry on as you always have, but if you see or hear anything else you think is unusual, don't hesitate to contact me on either of those numbers.'

Deirdre nodded. 'You promise Mr Tebbit won't get to hear about this, Miss Divine. I can't stress enough what would happen to me if I was discovered passing information to you.'

'No one else needs to know about our connection, Deirdre. We won't meet again…there's really no need. I won't contact you. I'll wait for you to contact me. Whatever happens I'll protect you. Respectable reporters always protect their sources. If you ever need my help don't hesitate to get in touch.' Deirdre blinked at Ottilie. 'And don't forget, we're trying to save a man's life…a decent man, a family man. I know it means something to you.'

Deirdre Cheam left the café first. Ottilie remained at the table for ten minutes before she left, her mind full of possibilities. Charles Wentworth's disappearance was suspicious. What Ottilie couldn't understand was why Lawrence Tebbit was seemingly not taking it seriously. Was it because he knew what had happened to Charles? Was Tebbit in the know about the consignment, seemingly delayed, but with an expectation of a return on the consignment? And what exactly did the consignment consist of?

Ottilie took a breath and walked briskly to the taxicab stand. She couldn't wait to get back to the press room and document her ideas. It had begun. She knew in her gut she was on the right path. She was determined to continue her investigation until she discovered what had happened to Charles Wentworth. Nothing would stand in her way.

As Ottilie got into a cab she didn't notice Deirdre Cheam standing on the corner of the street, hidden by the shadows of the buildings opposite the café, watching as the cab was driven away, the corners of her mouth turned up into a smile of satisfaction.

Chapter 14

Ottilie shivered as she went downstairs to the hall at 221B Baker Street. The weather had suddenly turned to a biting chill she felt in her bones, and she was glad of her woollen coat and felt hat. Mrs Hudson did not provide heaters for the hall as she said it was an expense she could do without. It meant the tenants didn't linger there, apart from when they were speaking on the telephone. Ottilie made sure she at least wore gloves and a scarf.

She looked down at her new ankle length boots which had become *de rigeur*. She wasn't sure about them yet but was determined to persevere. They were warm and prevented her ankles getting cold when she was on one of her walkabouts.

The previous afternoon she had returned to the press room eager to enlighten Jonah Walsh on the events of the morning but discovered, to her disappointment, he had gone home early.

'Is Mr Walsh unwell?' she had asked Marie, his secretary.

'He had an appointment just after lunch and decided to go home when it was done.'

Ottilie lowered her voice, not wanting her colleagues to hear what she asked. 'Did Mr Walsh lose his wife?'

Marie nodded. 'At the beginning of the year.'

Ottilie frowned. 'Why didn't he tell us?'

'He's a private man, Ottilie. I know how much he misses his wife, but this press room has become his life.' She looked sad. 'I've been his secretary for five years and I've never known him to be so sad and withdrawn…but when it comes to the news,' she shrugged, 'he's like a dog with a rag. He wants to be the first in with a new story which is why he pushes all of you so much. Sometimes I think he's a bit harsh, but he says it'll make you all better reporters.'

Ottilie nodded and smiled her thanks to Marie. She had known not to expect soft treatment at the hands of her editor, but Mr Walsh was human, and she felt it was rather sad he felt he could not confide in his colleagues at such a distressing time.

She had spent the afternoon formulating an article which she hoped would be acceptable to him and to their readership. Nothing Deirdre Cheam had told her went into the article, she simply took another angle on Charles Wentworth's disappearance, almost repeating what she had written in her previous one yet emphasising the need for the readership to become involved and to look to their memories for a glimpse of the last sighting on Wentworth before he disappeared. The call to action was stronger than the previous one. Ottilie knew she must get the readership behind the investigation, but acknowledged they were likely taken up with thinking about what the war would do to their lives…and to their loved ones.

15th September 1939

'Good morning, Miss Divine.'

Ottilie halted her steps as she was about to exit the chilly hall onto the pavement of Baker Street and swivelled to meet the eyes of her fellow tenant, Mr Sherlock Holmes. He was dressed for the outside in an oversized full-length tweed coat with a black Astrakhan collar, a black Homburg hat, and black gloves. He was tall, yet wiry, with an extremely pale complexion, which for most would surely denote illness. His nose was long and rather sharp, along with his cheekbones which were in acute relief with grey hollows in his cheeks. For a man of his age, for Ottilie was sure he wasn't much older than she, he dressed in a rather conservative way. If she hadn't known better, she would have thought he was a more mature man.

'Mr Holmes.' She nodded to him and said a silent prayer that he did not begin a conversation with her. Her prayer was ignored.

'How did your meeting with Delia Wentworth fare?' he asked her. 'Did you discover anything to lead you to the whereabouts of her husband? I would be surprised if you did.'

Ottilie's eyes widened in astonishment. 'How…how did you know I was interviewing Delia Wentworth?'

He chuckled. 'An easy supposition.'

'In *what* way may I ask?'

'You wrote on the notebook by the telephone in the hall. I simply rubbed the tip of a pencil across the marks made in the note underneath it and the appearance of the wording revealed the address of your interviewee. The Wentworths have a house in Kensington Gardens Square in Bayswater, do they not?'

Ottilie wasn't quite sure what to say. Without a doubt he had invaded her privacy, but more than that, she wondered why he had done so?

'Why would you do such a thing, Mr Holmes?' she asked him, a frown knotting her eyebrows. 'You have invaded my privacy and have made me watchful about what I do in the future. It was a private meeting; one you should not have known about or been privy to.'

Holmes chuckled and held up a hand in supplication. 'Now, now, dear lady, please do not be upset. As a consulting detective I am constantly searching for new ways to help my colleagues and clients in their investigations and the mysteries within their lives. Please do not be alarmed. Of course, I had no intention of using the information, but simply to entreaty you to be more careful in future. It is an old trick, but it is not known by everyone.'

Ottilie inhaled a wobbling breath. She realised the way he had spoken had almost made it a fault in her that he had discovered where she had been going, simply because she had written a note for her private use. She wasn't sure how to proceed and didn't want to appear to him to be a woman who would become hysterical when something unusual happened. Ottilie suppressed her anger and eyed him with narrowed eyes.

'What do you think you have achieved by telling me what you discovered, Mr Holmes? I am curious.'

'I am a consulting detective, Miss Divine. I read The Daily Express last evening. Your article was precise and to the point and you have asked for the help of your readership. I am part of its readership and so therefore would like to offer my help.' Ottilie blinked at him. 'And may I say you seem rather troubled. Perhaps your questioning of Lawrence Tebbit of whom I have some experience, did not go well?'

Ottilie used her inner calm to stop herself from making a retort she would regret later.

'I think your imagination has led you onto some shaky ground, Mr Holmes. When I asked our readership for help it was simply to jog their memories. Someone may have seen Charles Wentworth before he disappeared.'

Sherlock Holmes nodded and pursed his lips. 'Unless of course he was taken while sitting in his own office. Then, of course, no one would have seen him. And as for my imagination...your cheeks are flushed even though you have yet to go outside. My instincts lead me to surmise there is something you are looking forward to this morning...perhaps a chat with your editor over what you have already discovered.' Ottilie was stunned into silence. 'You seemed businesslike as you were about to open the front door onto the chilly street, perhaps even a spring in your step which had not been revealed until now. My guess is you have found an "in" regarding your investigation which has given you confidence.'

Ottilie's breath caught up in her throat. The man was insufferable.

'Will you also be performing magic tricks for the children at Christmas, Mr Holmes? Those who are left in London may need a diversion between the dropping of bombs onto their homes.'

His lips curled into a laconic smile that did not reach his eyes. 'You are sceptical, Miss Divine. You think me a charlatan, a magician. A trickster perhaps?'

'What is it that makes you think I need your help if everything you have surmised is true? Surely my confidence will tell you I have my finger on the pulse of the investigation. And then of course there is the police force at Scotland Yard who is investigating Charles Wentworth's disappearance as we speak.'

'Your stepfather, Chief Inspector Owen I presume.'

'You know him?'

'Our paths have crossed,' he replied as he pulled on his gloves. 'In fact, we worked together on a case quite recently...a murder.'

'And you solved it for him,' said Ottilie, her voice laced with more than a little sarcasm.

'It is what I do.'

'And why do you do it? I was under the impression from Mrs Hudson you use the laboratories at St Bartholomew's Hospital for some of your experiments. I'm sure it would lead anyone to believe you are studying for a career in medicine.'

'Not so, Miss Divine. I have been given permission to use the laboratories, and it was particularly advantageous at the time and with some providence because it was where I met my good friend Dr John Watson.'

'Yes,' said Ottilie, pulling her gloves up to her wrists and rolling her eyes. 'He seems a reasonable man.'

'And he is, particularly when we are on one of our investigations.'

Ottilie looked astonished. 'He helps you?'

'But of course. The hive mind, Miss Divine. It can only do good, surely. Which is why I feel you should accept my offer of help.'

Ottilie shook her head, tiring of the conversation.

'Why are you so interested in Charles Wentworth's disappearance, Mr Holmes? Scotland Yard is carrying out an extensive investigation and I have been assigned to the story by my editor Jonah Walsh, who has connections with Scotland Yard and parliament. Do you feel you know better than either of them?'

Holmes straightened his back and looked her in the eye. 'I am a man who dislikes unsolved mysteries, Miss Divine, particularly when I know beyond a shadow of a doubt, I could be an advantageous addition to both your, and Scotland Yard's, investigations.'

Ottilie turned towards the front door and opened the latch. She allowed the door to swing open slightly before turning to Sherlock Holmes, her face expressionless.

'I will consider your proposal, Mr Holmes. It is as much as I can offer. I do not believe it is solely my decision to make. There are others who will need to be aware of your involvement. I hope it satisfies you.'

Holmes made a small bow in her direction. The laconic expression which turned the corners of his mouth in an upward direction in what could have been loosely described as a smile reappeared on his face.

'I will await your authorisation, Miss Divine,' he answered, his eyelids half-closed as though her agreement to his involvement had never been in any doubt.

Ottilie ran down the two steps at the front of 221B and walked swiftly down Baker Street. Her breath left her in short gasps and her heart thumped so loudly she could feel it pulsing in her ears.

'Unbearable man,' she said under her breath. 'There is one acquiescence I will make and only with myself. I will never…ever…ask Mr Sherlock Holmes for help!'

Chapter 15

17th September 1939

After sitting in Jonah Walsh's office for an hour and telling him everything she had learnt, Ottilie presented him with the article she had prepared. She had been mindful not to include any information Deirdre Cheam had given her but skewed the article with a rather sceptical slant as to exactly what the Foreign Office were doing to retrieve Charles Wentworth from his abduction, which, as she wrote in not so many words, was precisely nothing.

Returning home the previous evening, she had given herself time to think about her interview with Lawrence Tebbit, his reluctance to speak with her about Charles Wentworth, and what Deirdre Cheam had told her. She began to make notes in her journal.

Ottilie had purchased a blue leather-bound notebook from W H Smith on her way home from work, one of her favourite shops. She loved the polished wooden counters and glass topped cases. She also treated herself to a new fountain pen to match her journal, the one she used often leaked, and a new bottle of Quink ink. She had been sorely tempted to purchase a good deal more, the sumptuous letter paper with matching envelopes almost seduced her, but she entreated herself to keep her mind on the job and left the shop happily with her packages under her arm.

As she sat on the settee with her feet curled up underneath her she thought about Tebbit and his attitude towards Charles Wentworth. Looking back on his words Ottilie decided it wasn't the fact she was a reporter, and a woman, that had provoked Lawrence Tebbit into rudeness, but rather, he simply did not want to speak about Charles.

In her mind, before she had arrived at the parliamentary offices, Ottilie had mused Tebbit would have welcomed the Daily Express's involvement because it would have meant Charles Wentworth's disappearance would have been common knowledge. The public would know about it. Richard often said knowledge was power. So, Ottilie asked herself, why did Lawrence Tebbit not want to speak about him? She made a note in her journal to get interviews with Charles's friends, reminding herself to telephone William Shaw, apparently one of Charles's closest colleagues, and, if and when Deirdre Cheam contacted her again, to ask her about the hierarchy within the office, who Charles spoke to the most, and also if she had ever noted any antipathy towards Charles, and from whom.

Satisfied with her thoughts and her notetaking she had settled into her bedcovers which smelt comfortingly of home, thinking over the day's events. She had made progress. There was a long way to go she knew, but she relished the challenge. She had a contact right in the heart of parliament, a secretary who could quietly observe the comings and goings of everyone in the Foreign Office without raising suspicion. It had been a good day.

Jonah Walsh perused the article Ottilie gave him, nodding as he read.

'This all looks good, Miss Divine.' He glanced up at her. 'I like your angle on it. I take it from this the interview with Lawrence Tebbit didn't go well. I particularly like the phrase "seemingly vague".' He made a knowing smile.

'He was less than forthcoming, Mr Walsh. I must admit I was surprised. I thought he and Charles's colleagues would have wanted to help discover what happened to him, but it seems not.'

Walsh leant forward on the desk. 'He was obstructive?'

Ottilie shrugged. 'You could say that. He refused to discuss it. He mentioned he'd already spoken to Scotland Yard, but from what I heard from Chief Inspector Owen he wasn't much more forthcoming with *him*.'

'Are you suspicious?' Ottilie told him about Deirdre Cheam and her discussion with her. 'So, you followed her?'

'Yes.'

Walsh nodded. 'And you've asked her to keep you posted?'

'I gave her the number here and the one at the flat. Did I do the right thing?'

Walsh smiled. 'If you're going to become someone I can rely on, Miss Divine, you need contacts. Without them you'll get nowhere, but a word of caution. You must be careful there is no opportunity for anyone outside of what you're trying to achieve to discover her involvement. Part of it is for her safety, part of it is for your own. Nothing must be written down, and telephone calls aren't always secure, particularly if she makes calls from a parliamentary office. We don't know what is happening at the moment. Allegiances could be somewhat foggy. You must be careful.'

'I understand, Mr Walsh.'

He nodded, satisfied he had counselled her. 'What's next?'

'A telephone call to a man called William Shaw, one of Charles Wentworth's colleagues, in fact his closest colleague according to Delia Wentworth.'

Walsh nodded. 'Go to it, Miss Divine.'

Ottilie stood to leave.

'Before I go, Mr Walsh, do you mind if I ask you something?'

'Ask away.'

'Have you ever come across a man called Sherlock Holmes?'

Jonah Walsh leant back in his chair and folded his hands over his not inconsiderable stomach. 'I have…in fact I have met him.' He frowned. 'Why do you ask?'

'He lives in the flat below me in Baker Street.'

Walsh sat forward and grinned. 'And what do you make of him?'

Ottilie took a breath. 'I don't know to be perfectly honest. He tells me he's a consulting detective and he's helped Scotland Yard with some of their investigations.' She grimaced. 'I can't help thinking he's rather a fantasist.'

'I can see why you would think so. He isn't backwards in coming forwards about his achievements.' Walsh nodded. 'He's an unusual fellow I grant you, but I wouldn't dismiss him if I were you. I understand he's nothing short of a genius. He has an advocate at Scotland Yard. Inspector Lestrade. They're not exactly friends; from what I've seen and heard. It would not be easy to become friends with Sherlock Holmes. He is not an easy man, but he and Lestrade have an association which I think benefits them both.'

'Actually, he does have a friend. A Dr Watson.'

'Ah, yes, Dr Watson. They're like two ends of a piece of string. One wonders what the attraction is.'

'I rather think Dr Watson is more than willing to put up with Holmes's behaviour; he is certainly a most bigoted man. In fact, from the way Dr Watson speaks about him, he almost reveres him.'

Walsh frowned. 'Why the interest, Miss Divine?'

Ottilie sighed. 'He wants to assist me in my investigation into Charles Wentworth's disappearance.'

'Does he now?'

'He's most insistent. He makes comments about what he thinks I'm about to do or already done because of his observations of my behaviour. The other day he said I was about to make a telephone call I didn't want to make because I was reluctantly headed for the telephone in the hall and my face was rather flushed. He'd noted I was clutching the cost of the telephone call so tightly in my hand it had sent my knuckles white. I was quite astonished.'

'Was he correct, Miss Divine?'

'Correct?'

'In his observations?'

Ottilie rolled her eyes. 'Well…yes.'

Walsh nodded, then turned to gaze out of his office window, a dismissal of sorts, Ottilie thought.

'I'll leave it entirely up to you, Miss Divine,' he glanced in her direction, 'but I warn you. Don't forget we are at the beginning of a war. Sherlock Holmes has enemies.'

Ottilie returned to her desk, mindful of Jonah Walsh's warning regarding Sherlock Holmes, not that she had any intention of asking him for help. She didn't like the man. He was arrogant and full of himself. She'd been furious he had discovered the location of her interview with Delia Wentworth. She felt he was invading her privacy. Should she speak to Mrs Hudson about him, or should she deal with him directly? Speaking to Mrs Hudson was the coward's way out, she knew. No, she would speak to him candidly and tell him she did not appreciate his involvement in business that did not concern him.

She sat at her desk and eyed the telephone she shared with three other reporters. She should telephone William Shaw. Another call she would have preferred not to make, but it sounded as though he knew Charles Wentworth better than anyone else who worked with him. He might know something.

She picked up the receiver.

'I wondered when you would get round to me,' said William Shaw, quite light-heartedly. 'I telephoned Delia only this morning and she said she had passed on my telephone number. You're a reporter for the Daily Express I understand.'

'Yes, Mr Shaw. Delia Wentworth and I went to the same school, St. Agnes's in Hampshire.'

'Absconded, didn't she?'

Ottilie chuckled. 'A very different time.'

'Indeed.'

The was a pause and Ottilie wondered if he would say anything else. He didn't, so she took the plunge.

'Mr Shaw, what do you think has happened to Charles?' She decided not to use Charles's surname because she felt it would make it more personal, as though they were simply discussing a mutual friend. She heard William Shaw clear his throat before speaking. When he did speak his tone was consoling and polite, expressing regret and disquiet.

'I wish I could tell you, Miss Divine. It is completely out of character for Charles to have disappeared of his own accord. He is not a secretive man,' he corrected his statement by saying, 'at least not to my knowledge and experience of him. We have worked together for many years. I can only say how sorry I am this ordeal has been inflicted on his family.'

Ottilie couldn't help feeling William Shaw was choosing his words carefully, weighing and examining everyone before allowing them to leave his lips.

'What was he working on before he disappeared, Mr Shaw?'

She heard Shaw draw in a breath. 'He was of course with Chamberlain last year when the Munich Agreement was signed and then returned to Germany recently when there were rumblings of dissent, but I assume it is something you knew about. I'm sure Delia would have told you.'

'Was he distracted in any way? Perhaps not his usual self? Did you feel there had been a change in his mood?'

'Same as ever from what I could see. Charles isn't a man who wore his heart on his sleeve. He is a pretty closed book, but I would describe him as supportive, a strong shoulder if one was needed. Quietly confident. It's why he was being considered for Tebbit's job.'

'And what *about* Lawrence Tebbit? I have interviewed him and he was tight-lipped about Charles. You say Charles was in line for his position. Was Mr Tebbit being moved aside?'

'Not in so many words. He was being sent to Italy to oversee things there. Their political platform is unstable. We're hoping he can pat it down.'

Somehow Ottilie doubted it, but she was interested in Shaw's use of the word "we." "We", meaning he was somehow part of whatever Charles had been involved in.

'Do you think Lawrence Tebbit resented Charles being considered for his position? Tebbit seemed very comfortable in his parliamentary office.'

'I certainly did not detect any dissent from him. I'm sure if he was unhappy about the move he would have voiced his concern.' Another pause. 'You must understand, Miss Divine, it is a prestigious position Lawrence Tebbit has been given.'

'Does Italy not support Germany? They signed the Axis Agreement in May with Germany under Mussolini. Italy has an alliance with the country formalising their political and military coalition. It might well become a very unpleasant place to be.'

Shaw went quiet, then, 'You've done your homework, Miss Divine.'

'It's my job, Mr Shaw…and without trying to be impolite you have told me very little.'

'There's not much I can say, Miss Divine, partly because I don't know and I wouldn't want to lead your investigation astray, and partly because it's complicated. We have been cautioned by the Foreign Office. Walls have ears, and careless talk costs lives. That kind of thing. All I can say is there were some whispers some time ago…about Charles. It was never confirmed but you know how these things escalate.'

'What things?'

'Charles may have gone "off-piste" so to speak. There were rumours he had been speaking with people outside his sphere and position.'

'In Germany?'

'That's right.'

'Do you think he was?'

'Whatever Charles was doing he would have the greater good in his sights. He's a good person. I've always thought so and he has never given me reason to doubt it.'

'But others did.'

Another pause. 'I'm afraid so.'

'One more question, Mr Shaw. Could his disappearance be in any way connected to espionage?'

'Miss Divine. I'm fairly sure you don't expect me to answer that question.'

'Why, Mr Shaw? Are you telling me you had not thought of it yourself?'

'These are dangerous times. Extremely dangerous. You would do well to understand…even in this country there are sympathisers with Hitler and what Germany is attempting to achieve. You are a young woman just beginning her life in many respects. It would be a great shame if such a young life was brought to a close prematurely.'

Ottilie frowned. Was William Shaw giving her a warning…or making a threat?

'Thank you for your time, Mr Shaw.'

'Anything to help find Charles,' he answered.

Ottilie lowered the receiver onto the cradle. 'But you haven't helped,' she said under her breath. 'You're obfuscating and blurring the truth.'

Ottilie sat at her desk and thought about the conversation she'd just had with William Shaw. She had always considered herself a good judge of character. Camille had taught her to go with her gut, not her heart or her head. *What is my gut telling me,* she thought. She took a breath and allowed her body to point her in the right direction. *My gut tells me William Shaw knows more than he's willing to tell. I trust him about as far as I can spit.*

Chapter 16

20th September 1939

Ottilie found herself pacing her sitting room yet again. The evening had closed in early, and she had drawn the heavy velvet curtains across the huge windows in the flat to block out any light. She and the rest of the country had waited with bated breath for Germany to begin its bombing campaigns, but the skies had been silent.

There had been a double page spread included in The Express about the British Expeditionary Force leaving the country for France, but it had been reported they had seen little action. There had been mutterings of a "Phoney War" which had begun to gather pace.

It was like a cat fight, Ottilie decided. Who would strike first? Which country was the cat which would take the leap forward. Blackouts were still imposed across the country. Gas masks were *de rigeur*, and the air-raid shelters stood waiting for the first occupants to take up temporary residence.

Britain was preparing for a long conflict; rationing of butter, sugar, and ham had already begun. These items were imported and the importation of goods to Britain had been more or less ceased.

Ottilie sat heavily on her settee and picked up a fashion magazine. *The*

New Look was on the horizon apparently, but Ottilie's gaze swept over the pictures of models with their stunning hourglass figures sporting the latest suits and dresses without really taking much notice. She was frustrated because she knew what the next step should be in her investigation, and she was aware it would not be an easy one to achieve.

Her investigation into Charles Wentworth's disappearance had reached a standstill and it was sticking in her throat. There were questions to be answered, searches to be made. She was itching to take the investigation forward, but she had been stonewalled at every turn.

Her questions had met an immoveable wall and she searched the conversations she had had with Delia, Tebbit, and Shaw, looking for clues she may have missed. She understood Wentworth had disappeared at a most difficult time…they were at war after all, though the streets were still quiet and there seemed to be no sign of imminent danger. Approaching the bureaucracy and protocols at Westminster felt like wading through treacle. There was always something to stop her.

The following morning, she decided to call on Richard. She braved the low temperature of the hall at 221B, donning a pair of fingerless gloves and a scarf. September's temperatures had plummeted and the old house with its one-hundred-year-old bricks did not retain the heat.

'Richard, I'm sorry to call you at work.'

'Is everything all right?'

'Yes, everything's fine. I wondered…could I come and see you?'

'At Scotland Yard?'

'Well, yes.'

'You know I can't discuss a case with you.'

'Yes…yes, I understand.'

She heard the rustle of his jacket as he looked at his watch. 'You've got about an hour. I've got an interview with the Foreign Secretary at eleven. If you can get here within the hour we can talk.'

'I'm on my way,' cried Ottilie.

She ran up the stairs two at a time and grabbed her coat, shrugging it on as she ran back down the stairs, putting her bag and gas mask over her shoulder. On Baker Street she got a cab and within half an hour she was pushing through the doors into the foyer at Scotland Yard. The young constable at the desk stood to attention making Ottilie's lips twitch into a smile.

'Yes, miss?'

'I'm Ottilie Divine. I have an appointment with Rich...I mean, Chief Inspector Owen.'

Richard appeared out of the corridor behind the desk and beckoned her in. 'Through here, Ottilie. Constable, lift the flap will you, so Lady Ottilie can come through.' The young constable's eye's widened and he quickly lifted the top half of the desk so Ottilie could join Richard.

'You are mean, Richard,' Ottilie said, giggling as they went into an office.

'He's a bit green that one. Wet behind the ears, but he'll be all right. I was like it once.'

Ottilie giggled again. 'Now, *that* I wish I'd seen. The very young, very green Constable Richard Owen.'

'There are photographs,' he said, 'but I've hidden them. And no, you'll never find them.' He sat in one of the chairs and offered one to Ottilie. 'Now, what is it you want to see me about.'

Ottilie dumped her gas mask on the floor and unwound her scarf from around her neck.

'First of all, can I come with you to interview the Foreign Secretary?'

'No.'

She sighed. 'Oh, well. You can't blame a girl for trying.'

'What is it you really want?'

Ottilie leant forward and arranged her features into a beseeching expression. 'I need to get into Charles Wentworth's office.'

Richard inhaled a breath, smiling, his astonishment obvious. 'And what makes you think I can get you in there?'

'Because you're Chief Inspector Richard Owen. And you're my Papa, well, almost…and it's one of the perks.'

Richard nodded. 'So, I'm a perk am I?'

'Amongst other things.' She frowned. 'The thing is, Richard, without searching his office I can't get any further. I've questioned his wife, his superior whose position Charles is in the running for, and his colleague. I've nowhere else to go. It's so frustrating.'

'What did you find out?'

Ottilie sat back in her chair and pulled a grin, folding her arms in front of her. 'Quid pro quo, Chief Inspector.'

Richard pursed his lips and eyed her with amusement. 'Lady Ottilie, if you know anything about Wentworth's disappearance, anything at all, you must divulge it to the police. I would say you're obliged, darling.'

'William Shaw said there had been rumours and whispers about Charles. Shaw said he'd gone "off-piste" and had been talking to people outside of his sphere and position. I think it's how he put it.'

Richard nodded. 'It's very interesting. Did Shaw say what it was Wentworth had been doing.'

Ottilie shook her head. 'He wouldn't say. He said walls have ears and he couldn't say much more.'

'Perhaps the Foreign Secretary will be more forthcoming.'

'I so wish I could accompany you. I would learn so much.'

'But you need to be resourceful, Ottilie if you're to continue a reporting career. Find your own sources and contacts, and ways into those places which would block you. Then look after them. You never know when you're going to need them again.'

'It's what Mr Walsh says,' Ottilie said, looking glum.

'And he's right. However.' Ottilie straightened and crossed her fingers. 'As I should leave in the next few minutes, I've asked Inspector Lestrade to speak with you. He might be able to equip you with some ideas about how you can get access to Wentworth's office. Lestrade isn't working on the case, so it isn't a conflict of interest.'

'You can't help me, can you?'

Richard bent and kissed her on the forehead. 'I would love to help you, darling,' he said quietly, 'but you know I cannot. Wait here and I'll send Inspector Lestrade in to see you. He's not the brightest man we have on the force, but he might have a way in for you.'

Ottilie nodded. 'Thank you, Richard. It was good to see you.'

Richard grinned. 'And you, Ottilie.'

'Lady Ottilie.' Inspector Lestrade entered the room and gave a small bow. 'I'm pleased to make your acquaintance.'

'Inspector Lestrade. I'm hoping you will be able to help me. Chief Inspector Owen said you may have some ideas on how I can arrange a visit to Charles Wentworth's office.'

'Indeed.' Lestrade took the seat on the other side of the desk. 'Why do you wish to explore his office?'

'I'm a reporter for the Daily Express and also a personal friend of the family.'

'I can think of only one person who seems to have an entrée into Westminster. It is the consulting private detective Sherlock Holmes. He seems to have garnered trust and the patronage of not only Scotland Yard, but Westminster also. He has entrée to places we as policemen are not admitted.'

'You are an advocate of his, I understand, Inspector Lestrade?'

'Only in as much as he has been…useful…to me, Lady Ottilie.'

Ottilie felt her breath catch in her throat and her jaw tightened at the mention of Holmes's name. It's Miss Divine…or just Ottilie. I don't use Lady.' Lestrade bowed his head in acquiescence.

Ottilie sat back in her chair and folded her hands in her lap. It seemed she had no other choice. It was clear to her she needed to explore Charles Wentworth's office. What was also clear to her was she could not do it without Sherlock Holmes's assistance.

Asking for help was not how she had wanted to begin her career as a reporter on special assignments. Holmes's reputation and obvious arrogance probably meant he would take all the credit, should any be given, if they were successful in acquiring an "in" to Westminster. *Damn the man*, she thought. She closed her eyes and released a breath of frustration. There was clearly no other option.

She rose from her seat and wound her scarf around her neck and pulled on her gloves, then retrieved her gas mask from the floor.

'Thank you, Inspector Lestrade. I've noted your advice.'

'My pleasure, Miss Divine.'

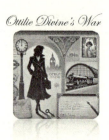

By the time the afternoon had drawn in and she'd had a rather scant evening meal of eggs on toast she realised she would have to capitulate. *He'll think I'm eating humble pie,* she thought as she forked her toast and egg into her mouth, realising she was ravenous because she'd missed lunch. *And he'll no doubt crow about it.*

Ottilie delayed the moment of surrender. She tidied the flat even though it was perfectly tidy, washed the few dishes she had used and looked about her for other things to do, of which there were none.

She applied a red lipstick before leaving the flat to descend the flight of stairs to Sherlock Holmes's apartment and spritzed her favourite perfume on her wrists.

'For confidence,' she said to her reflection in the mirror. 'And to show him I'm not going to beg.'

She took the stairs down to Holmes's flat slowly, breathing steadily as her mother Camille had shown her if ever she felt nervous. Standing outside his front door she lifted her hand.

'The point of no return,' she muttered and knocked on the door. It was opened by Dr Watson who was all smiles. *Why can't Sherlock Holmes be like Dr Watson,* she thought?

'Miss Divine. What a pleasure it is to see you. What can I do for you?'

'I wondered,' Ottilie cleared her throat, 'I wondered if Mr Holmes was available.'

'I believe he is. Do come in.'

Ottilie took in a wobbling breath and stepped across the threshold. 'Thank you.'

As usual the room was gloomy, not helped by the blackout curtains against the windows. The wall sconces were switched on but they did little to remedy the sombreness of the room.

Sherlock Holmes was sitting in a huge, rather lumpy wingchair smoking a pipe. He barely looked up when Ottilie entered the sitting room.

'Miss Divine,' he said in an overloud voice. 'I wondered when we would see you next.' He turned his head to face her, his complexion still pale, his cheeks seemingly hollower than before. Underneath his eyes were dark shadows and she wondered if he was ill. 'Is there something I…we…can do for you?'

'Would you like to sit down, Miss Divine?' enquired Dr Watson. He indicated a seat opposite the fireplace.

'Thank you, yes,' replied Ottilie. She took the seat and arranged her hands in her lap. Holmes took another puff of his pipe then proceeded to bang it against the fireplace where the contents fell into the hearth.

Holmes sat back in his chair and steepled his fingers in front of him. He leant his head back and closed heavy-lidded eyes.

'Well, Miss Divine. To what do I owe the honour of your visit?'

Ottilie gritted her teeth and proceeded. 'I understand you have contacts at Westminster, Mr Holmes.'

'I have contacts everywhere.' He bowed his head once. 'Westminster is one of those places, indeed.'

Ottilie decided to get to the point. Anything to cut short the conversation. 'As you know I'm investigating Charles Wentworth's disappearance for my newspaper. I require access to his office. I have spoken to my editor, and he informed me it is impossible to achieve unless one is with Scotland Yard.'

Holmes turned to look at her, his eyes bright like shards of glass.

'Bureaucracy is the devil, isn't it?' Ottilie heard Dr Watson sigh. 'Particularly if one does not have the connections to overcome it.' He turned away from her. 'Am I to be included in the investigation…along with my partner, Dr John Watson of course?'

Ottilie didn't want to say yes. He'd got her over a barrel, and he knew it. As did she.

'I would appreciate your help, Mr Holmes.'

'I take it your confirmation of needing help is a "yes" wrapped in tissue paper with a fine bow?' He blinked slowly at her.

'Yes,' she said quietly, lowering her chin.

'I'm not sure I heard you, Miss Divine.' He turned his attention to Dr Watson. 'Dr Watson?' he asked, his voice louder now. 'Did you hear Miss Divine utter in the affirmative?'

Watson looked embarrassed. 'Holmes, really.'

'Yes,' cried Ottilie.

Holmes rose from his chair and went across to the window where he pulled the curtain back ever so slightly.

'It is urgent I take it?'

'There have been rumours in Westminster, and whispers between his colleagues. It seems Charles could have been speaking with people outside of the Foreign Office regarding Germany and the war, and his closeness to them has influenced a belief it could have contributed to the reason for his disappearance.'

'Where did this information come from?'

'William Shaw, apparently Charles's closest colleague.'

'And does he believe the rumours?'

'He prevaricated somewhat.'

'He believes them.' Holmes allowed the curtain to drop and he returned to his chair by the fire which had reduced to a smoulder.

'It seems to me you have exhausted your contacts, Miss Divine, although I am surprised you did not use your title, or your mother's past position in society, to help you. Or your stepfather, Chief Inspector Richard Owen.'

Ottilie was miffed at his suggestion. 'I prefer not to involve my family in my work, Mr Holmes.'

'Really? Your arrival at Scotland Yard this morning was simply a social visit was it?'

Ottilie glanced at Dr Watson who slowly shook his head, as frustrated with Holmes as she was. It suddenly dawned on her and she sighed.

'Inspector Lestrade has spoken to you.'

'He rather felt you had nowhere else to go, Miss Divine,' said Holmes, 'other than to request the assistance of Sherlock Holmes.' Ottilie said nothing. Holmes glanced at his watch and nodded, more to himself than to Ottilie or Dr Watson. 'We will go to Westminster in three days' time,' he said with exactness. 'In the intervening days I will send a telegram to my contact requesting admittance. I will meet you in the hall at ten thirty, the morning of the twenty-fourth, whence we shall depart for the parliamentary offices. Wear stout walking shoes, Miss Divine. No heels or fripperies.'

'I'm short of fripperies, Mr Holmes,' replied Ottilie, her expression impassive. 'I think I can manage shoes which will see me through the morning.'

'I'm glad to hear it.'

'Will you require my presence, Holmes?' Dr Watson asked.

'Not on this occasion, my dear friend. We should be as unobtrusive as possible, and I rather think two investigators and a reporter may well over-egg the pudding. Should our explorations lead us to other prospects, I will of course welcome your support.' He turned to Ottilie. 'I'm sure Miss Divine agrees with me.'

Ottilie nodded and turned to Dr Watson with a smile. 'Of course, Dr Watson. I look forward to working with you.'

The smile dropped from her face when she turned her glance on to Sherlock Holmes. He had described her as a reporter, not as an investigative reporter. *Infuriating man*, she thought.

'Are you quite sure we'll be given admittance, Mr Holmes?' she asked him.

He looked surprised. 'Do you doubt it?'

'I'm not sure it's a matter of doubt, rather, why would they allow you to roam the corridors of Westminster, but not allow anyone else access? You are simply a member of the public, are you not?'

Dr Watson pressed his lips together to prevent a chuckle. He was beginning to like Miss Divine. He felt sure Holmes would not always get his own way when dealing with her. *It'll do him a power of good, he thought. There's nothing like a strong, confident woman to put a man like Sherlock in his place.*

Chapter 17

24th September 1939

Ottilie lifted her face to look up to the spires of the gothic architecture of Westminster, her hand on the top of her hat to prevent it from falling from her head. One couldn't help but be impressed, and her mind went to the history of the building and what had gone before in centuries past.

Holmes eschewed the front entrance, making for a side entrance instead, where a member of the police force was in attendance. He inexplicably waved them through with barely a look, leaving Ottilie perplexed.

'Do not attempt to wander off alone, Miss Divine,' Holmes said to her in a low voice. 'You will need my presence as protection.'

'Are you suggesting I can't look after myself, Mr Holmes?'

'I'm suggesting if you are discovered weaving through the corridors of Westminster alone you'll likely be arrested, particularly at a time of war.' Ottilie had no answer.

The Palace of Westminster was rather like a village. It seemed to be a conglomeration of buildings linked by corridors and alleyways. The passageways were convoluted, rather like a maze. The air in the corridors smelt of cigar smoke tainted with stale brandy. Each corridor was part of a complex arrangement, a clever assembly to deter those whose intentions were not trustworthy.

Ottilie considered one would need to know Westminster very well indeed to navigate the building with any success. Getting lost would be too easy. She decided to stay with Sherlock Holmes. She watched him as he walked briskly towards his intended destination, although he had not informed her of his plans. She practically had to run to keep up with him, and certainly she felt sure he had forgotten she was there. At last, he stopped.

'This is Wentworth's office,' he said, sotto voce.

The room was nothing like Lawrence Tebbit's which had had the atmosphere of a gentleman's club. This room was modest, austere perhaps. There were bookshelves on each wall, and in the centre of the room an oak desk which seemed incongruous when compared to the rest of the décor.

'I will begin my search left to right, Miss Divine. Please do not get in my way. Also we must try to leave no sign of our visit. I'm sure Scotland Yard has been over this room and its contents with a fine-tooth comb, but their fine-tooth comb is inordinately inferior to my own.'

He began to examine every part of the room, the shelves, the books on the shelves, the paintings of which there were few, the window and its curtains, the desk and its contents, and each drawer in the desk in turn. He bent towards the object of his examination, nose to entity, scanning everything with scrupulous precision.

'Ah, now,' he murmured. He turned and held up a piece of singed paper. In his hand he held a letter he had retrieved from inside the fireplace. It had been partially burnt, and was smeared with ash, but clearly the paper had not taken hold in the flames because it had billowed up to a shelf within the chimney; in the heat from the fire, Ottilie supposed.

'It's a letter…actually more of a note to Charles Wentworth.' He glanced at Ottilie. 'It refers to a Greta Dietz. I understand she is a German cultural attaché.'

'A woman?'

'Indeed.'

Ottilie narrowed her eyes. 'What is the job of a cultural attaché?'

'A diplomat, Miss Divine. Someone who promotes cultural relationships with the host country, in this case, Britain, and the country from where she hails. Germany. I think the modern description is international relations. Her remit would be vast I would imagine.'

'Is the note recent? Is it dated?'

'Indeed. The 8th of August.'

'He must have read it when he returned from his holiday with his family.' Ottilie frowned. 'But surely, he must have known what was on the horizon. All contact with a nation from which we're under threat would have stopped. Would it not be frowned upon, surely seen as collaborating, even though war had yet to be declared?'

Holmes nodded. 'One would expect so, bearing in mind Greta Dietz is now considered an enemy of Britain.' He sniffed. 'And yes. I'm sure if his superiors knew Charles Wentworth was still in contact with a German national, they would take a very dim view of it, particularly with the position he holds in government. Of course it is easy to read something untoward into it. Wentworth may have discovered some information; heard something he should not have heard. Perhaps he wished to question her.'

'Or they met in Germany and they're having an affair. Does it say anything else.'

A time…three thirty, and a place, Trafalgar Square.'

'He was to meet her there, do you think?'

'I imagine it was most likely.'

He placed the letter in the pocket of his coat and pulled out the slim drawer in the desk which sat over the occupants' knees. He glanced up at her with a knowing smile which was hardly a smile at all. Rather a grimace.

'What do we have here?' he said, shaking his head. 'The police are notorious for missing this drawer, much to my amusement.'

He pulled the drawer out of the desk and turned it upside down. He glanced up at her again and raised his eyebrows.

'A telegram if I'm not mistaken. Now, who could this be from?' He pulled the telegram from the underside of the drawer where it had been stuck with tape. 'Someone, presumably Charles Wentworth, wanted to hide this from prying eyes. One must wonder why.'

'What does it say?'

Holmes perused the telegram. 'If only I could read code.'

Ottilie widened her eyes. 'Do you mean you can't?'

He glanced up at her and narrowed his eyes. 'I assume your question was an attempt at humour, Miss Divine?' She simply shrugged but then frowned and turned her head towards the corridor outside the room.

''Footsteps, Mr Holmes. Perhaps we should leave now.'

Holmes pushed the telegram into his pocket. 'I do believe our time here is up.' He went to the door, passing Ottilie on the way, his fingers to his lips. 'Don't say anything,' he whispered, just follow.'

He slipped out of Wentworth's office with Ottilie following. There were voices at the far end of the corridor, and they were getting closer. Ottilie could feel her pulse hammering in her ears. She glanced at Holmes. His expression did not change. As usual it showed he was resolute and determined.

Within seconds, Holmes had turned into another corridor. He led her through the maze, turning here and there each time, he heard a voice.

Ottilie wondered why he was so eager to get away if he had clearance to be in Westminster.

Eventually they reached the corridor which led to the side entrance they had used to enter the building. Ottilie sighed with relief.

'Thank goodness,' she breathed. 'I thought we would never get out of the labyrinth.'

'It helps when one knows the layout of a building,' said Holmes. 'I made a study of an internal map of the parliamentary offices last evening.'

'Nothing less than efficiency, Mr Holmes,' Ottilie replied, unable to keep the admiration out of her voice. 'But you appeared to be as desperate to remain undiscovered as I was.'

He led her out of the side door, nodded his thanks to the same policeman standing guard, and walked down the street towards the main entrance.

'One should not advertise one's desire for information, Miss Divine. It is my advice to you if you wish to be a successful investigative journalist. Much of what I do is undercover. If we had been found in Wentworth's office, whatever has happened to him would have been instantly evaporated by those who know more than they're admitting. I have always been made welcome at Westminster; I have carried out covert private investigations for some of the ministers, but generally, no one knows what I do there.'

'The telegram, Mr Holmes?' Ottilie held out her hand. 'And the note.'

'I advise you to leave them with me, Miss Divine,' he said, pushing them further into his pocket. 'I wish to carry out some chemical analysis on both. If I find anything of interest, I will inform you and return them to you. Perhaps you could relay our investigation to Chief Inspector Owen.'

Ottilie lowered her hand, knowing she had lost both the telegram and the note to Sherlock Holmes, but curiously trusting he would do the right thing.

'I should thank you for today,' she said, her lips turning up at the corners.

'Careful, Miss Divine. I observed the glimmer of a smile in your expression. You may unwittingly give the impression you appreciate my skills, however grudgingly, and I'm sure you would prefer to keep me at arm's length. Most people do.'

He turned and walked away from her. Ottilie watched him as he strode down the street towards Westminster Bridge, a dark, tall, thin man who looked neither left nor right at the oncoming host of people as though he were the only person on the bridge. She took in a breath and hailed a cab to take her back to Fleet Street, wondering if she would ever understand her fellow tenant.

In the cab she had time to think. She settled back and gazed out of the window, not really seeing the streets as the cab passed through them. What was it about Sherlock Holmes? He was unlike anyone she had ever met. On the surface he was prickly, arrogant, and cantankerous. His attitude was indeed objectionable, a man full of his own self-importance. A person whose passion was investigating mysteries which involved members of the human race, yet was impervious, some might say despising of the feelings of others. One could even say he was downright rude.

So why did she feel sorry for him?

Chapter 18

When Ottilie arrived at the press room at the Daily Express offices she was surprised to see it was virtually empty. She looked down between the desks to the small office where Jonah Walsh's office was, situated in one corner of the press room and made her way towards it. When she got to Maria's desk, she stopped, frowning. Maria's eyes were red as though she had been crying.

'Maria?'

Maria quickly shook her head as she rolled paper into her typewriter. 'I'm all right, Ottilie. I'm just being silly.'

'Has something happened?'

Maria stopped what she was doing and looked up at Ottilie. 'Everything's changing, isn't it? It's only just hit me really. Took a while to sink in.' She shook her head again. 'It's just...I think my Frank is going to volunteer. He keeps going on about how it's his duty, and...well, part of me agrees with him, but Ottilie, what if something happens to him? What would I do?'

Ottilie drew up a chair and leant her elbows on Maria's desk.

'I can't answer your question, Maria. I've lost one person in my life so far, and that was my father. I can still remember, to this day, how I felt when I discovered what had happened to him. My mother and father had become estranged. He lived at Kenilworth House, my mother in Duke Street with her family of staff whom she adores to this day, and me when I was home from school. They weren't together, and knowing they didn't love each other anymore was difficult enough for me to accept, but when my father died…it was like the world had ended.'

Maria gazed at Ottilie. Ottilie reached out her hand which Maria gently took.

'All I can say is this. If something happens to Frank, it won't be the same as what happened to my father. My father was killed in an accident. Frank wants to go to war, to be part of the defense of Britain. It would be a shock of course,' she shook her head sadly, 'there will be many women feeling the same I should imagine. Frightened of the future and what it may bring. But Frank has chosen his path. He seems an intelligent person and I'm sure he knows what dangers await him. If I were you, I would make the most of your time with Frank before he leaves.

'He won't be alone. I'm sure there will be other men with him who feel the same way. There will be medical staff too, doctors and nurses sent to look after them. Before he goes to the front, you and he should enjoy your time together. Have some days out, go to the theatre or cinema before they're all shut down. There are still some open.

'I know how much you love him, and he knows too.' She squeezed Maria's hand. 'And we in the press room will always be here for you should you need us.'

Maria reached into her sleeve for her handkerchief. She wiped her eyes and blew her nose.

'Thank you, Ottilie. I think I needed to get my head on straight. I'm frightened of this war. To be honest I feel the anticipation is worse than things happening we can do something about. I thought it would begin as soon as the announcement was made.' She smiled, 'Maybe they'll call it off.'

'I hope so. It's what I'm praying for.' Ottilie stood, then noticed Jonah Walsh was beckoning her into his office. 'Will you be all right, Maria?'

Maria nodded and managed a smile. 'Don't worry, Ottilie. I'll be all right.'

Jonah Walsh's office smelt musty. There was a used plate with a knife and fork on the filing cabinet in the corner, and a bag of washing next to it. Ottilie frowned. Was her editor living in his office?

'What happened this morning?' he asked her.

'I went to Westminster…with Sherlock Holmes.' She turned to look out of the glass partition into the press room. 'Where are the other reporters? I expected them to be here.'

'They're out on other stories,' Walsh replied, waving away her enquiry. 'I'm more interested in today's events.' His eyes had widened in surprise, and he took off his spectacles to look at her. 'Now, there's a turn-up. You accepted his offer then?' He indicated the chair her side of the desk, and she sat down with a smile.

'Not exactly.'

'What do you mean?'

'It's the last thing I wanted to do, but I couldn't get into Westminster without him. Inspector Lestrade said as much.'

'And what was the outcome?'

'We got into Wentworth's office where Holmes found a note from a

Greta Dietz, a German cultural attaché, and a telegram stuck underneath a drawer the police had overlooked.'

'Do you have them?'

'No.'

Walsh frowned. 'Why not?'

'Sherlock Holmes took them to do a chemical analysis on them.'

Walsh sat back in his chair and sighed. 'I don't suppose there's much we can do about it now.'

'Should I have fought him for them?'

Walsh chuckled. 'I would have preferred to have used our own contacts but what's done is done. Will he keep you informed?'

Ottilie nodded. 'The telegram was in code.'

'Interesting. Do you think Sherlock Holmes will crack it?'

'He's not a man likely to give up until he does.'

'What do you make of him?'

Ottilie gazed out of the window and sighed. 'I don't know, Mr Walsh. He's a unique character, full of confidence in his own abilities, and not too modest to let one know about them. Yet...'

'Yet?'

She returned her gaze to Jonah Walsh. 'There's something almost...boyish about him. He's like a character from The Boy's Own magazine. His interest in the sciences, his passion for solving mysteries takes him on adventures which most of us wouldn't think of. He's a grown man of course, possibly not far from my own age, yet he has no personable traits which would attract others to him.'

'Apart from Dr Watson. Have you met him?'

'I have. He is a much different prospect than Sherlock Holmes. One wonders what would happen to him if he did not have Dr Watson to stand by him. It seems he has no other friends.'

'Perhaps he doesn't need friends. His work is enough for him.'

'Perhaps.'

'I called you in because I wanted to give you these.'

He passed a cardboard folder to her. It was crammed with hand-written letters.

'What are they? Who are they from?'

'You wrote a call to action in your article, Miss Divine. Hence…' He indicated the folder.

'These are the replies from the public?'

'Indeed.' He nodded towards the folder. 'There are letters there from every walk of life.' He raised his eyebrows. 'From people who fancy themselves as private detectives to conspiracy fantasists, from budding Miss Marples to people who want us to believe they're spies and have Charles Wentworth tied up somewhere. Good luck with it, Miss Divine, you're going to need it, but…there might be something within the pile of letters to interest you.'

She stood with the folder clutched to her chest, wondering what she had let herself in for.

'Er, thank you. I think.'

Walsh chuckled. 'By the way. Well done on what you said to Maria.'

Ottilie blushed. 'Oh. You heard.'

'I hear everything, Miss Divine. I keep my ear to the ground, particularly when it involves a member of my staff. I'd forgotten about Lord Divine's accident. I know it's been some years but I'm sure it was devastating at the time, particularly for a young girl. Maria's been out of sorts for days. You handled it very well.'

Ottilie nodded, her eyes going to the gravy smeared plate on top of the filing cabinet. Walsh caught her look.

'Maria has kindly brought in a few dinners for me,' he glanced at the bag of washing, 'and does some washing.'

'Could I make a suggestion, Mr Walsh?' He nodded once. 'A housekeeper. When our men go off to war women will have to work. They'll need money to provide for their families. It would help you…and the person you take on. You can't be expected to put the hours in here you do and run a house.'

Walsh shrugged. 'I wouldn't know where to start.'

'Would you like me to ask Cecily. She's been with my mother for years. Perhaps she'll know someone who's looking for work.'

He nodded. 'If it's not asking too much.'

'I'll ring her this evening.'

'Thank you, Miss Divine.'

'You're welcome, Mr Walsh.'

That evening, Ottilie sat at the table in her kitchen, the folder of letters in front of her. She flipped open the front cover and blinked, realising she would have to read each and every one of them in case there was information in any of them which could help find Charles Wentworth.

She had phoned Richard to tell him about her visit to Wentworth's office with Sherlock Holmes, and to inform him of what they'd found. She wanted to make it official because she still wasn't sure of Holmes, and she knew if he didn't pass on the note and the telegram to her, Richard would want to know why. He had made it perfectly clear any information they discovered must be passed on to Scotland Yard.

'So, my men missed it, did they?' Richard had sighed.

'Well, the note was up the chimney, probably swept up with the heat. It was only partially burnt so the message was legible. It mentioned a Greta Dietz who is apparently a German cultural attaché. Charles was requested to meet her on the 8th of August at three thirty in the afternoon at Trafalgar Square.'

She could almost hear the cogs and wheels in Richard's brain ticking over. 'Interesting,' he said.

'Is it?'

'No one saw him at Westminster after that time, so I'm thinking he kept the appointment.'

'But why? She's a German national. Surely, she's off limits. And why would she still be here?'

'Certainly, she's off limits, but there could be more to it.'

Ottilie took a breath, thinking of Delia Wentworth and her three children. 'You mean an affair?'

'It's possible.'

'Not Charles.'

'Why not Charles? He's a man like any other and perfectly capable of being led astray…or leading someone astray.'

'I suppose it depends on who's doing the leading.'

'Indeed.'

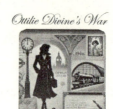

Ottilie leafed through the first few letters. Some were so bizarre it was laughable.

Dear Miss Divine,

I read in the Express your friend Charles Wentworth is missing. Please come to my house at eight o'clock on Saturday evening and I'll conduct a séance. I am a professional seer and we'll find him in a tick.

Madam Tallulah

Ottilie giggled and laid it on the "Oddity" pile. The next was just as outlandish.

Dear Ottilie Divine,

Chamberlain's servant vanished without a trace,

Secrets and lies took his place.

Whispers hover where truth once stood,

A whiff of treason, not understood.

I am available for readings and soirees.

Yours poetically,

Leopold James.

Ottilie raised her eyebrows and sighed. 'At least the poetry scanned,' she said, placing it on the Oddity pile. 'Sort of.'

She opened the next one. There was no salutation, and it wasn't signed. She glanced at the envelope. No postmark. The words were written on the flimsiest of paper and to the point.

The wolf is already in the shadows and has allies. They're closer than you think.

Disorder spreads fast. Many are being bled for the secrets they hold. The Ministry waits for power. Keeping silent will keep you alive. Who is the hunter and who is the hunted? Watch your back.

Ottilie shuddered. The words were rather too near the truth to be an amusing anecdote. Was it a prank sent to frighten her or was it real? A warning perhaps? She bit her lip. How was she to know? A new pile was established.

Her thoughts went to Charles Wentworth's office and what she and Holmes had found there. Then Richard mooting Charles had likely met with Greta Dietz. Who was this woman? Ottilie thought a visit to Sherlock Holmes was required. She closed the folder intending to go through the other letters the following day.

'I need to know about the note and the telegram,' she thought, suddenly itching to discover if Holmes had found anything. 'I need to know what they will tell us.'

'A timely visit,' Holmes said as she stepped across the threshold of his flat and entered his sitting room.

'I hope I'm not disturbing you, Mr Holmes. I've been going through some letters sent to the Express in answer to my call to action for information.'

Holmes went across to a side table where a bottle of brandy and two glasses sat on a tray. 'May I offer you brandy, Miss Divine. Forgive me for saying, but you look as though you might need one.'

She nodded and sat on the edge of the settee. 'Yes, please. Brandy would be very welcome.'

He passed a glass to her, then settled in his usual wingchair.

'Have you had a shock, Miss Divine?'

'Not a shock exactly. Some of the letters are quite ridiculous.'

'In what way?' He took a long drink from his glass.

'Offering seances and some with poetry. An offer from a Leopold James to read his own poetry at soirees and what have you.' She took a sip and welcomed the warmth and spicy tang.

'Are there any which we would find interesting?'

She nodded. 'One. It said there is a wolf in the shadows, and it has allies. The Ministry awaits power. And I should watch my back.'

'A wolf in the shadows. It very much sounds as though there is an infiltrator in the midst of Westminster.'

'But where?'

'I would suggest the Foreign Office, and perhaps now we are at war, The War Office.'

'You don't think it means Charles, do you? He's a diplomat, a man who was present when Chamberlain tried to divert war.'

'He could have been involved in counterintelligence.'

He rose from his seat and went to his desk which was by far the untidiest desk Ottilie had ever seen. She wondered how he could ever find anything amongst the detritus. He retrieved two pieces of paper from the top and handed them to Ottilie.

'These are the transcripts from the note and telegram we found in Wentworth's office. I carried out some chemical analysis on them. They proved to be rather interesting.'

'In what way?'

'Please read the transcript, Miss Divine,' Holmes replied impatiently.

'The note had more written on it than just a suggestion for a meeting?'

'Indeed. I carried out a surface residue test using a weak iodine vapour solution on the note's surface. This particular chemical analysis will detect hidden writing or traces of invisible ink.'

He sniffed in a rather pompous fashion. Ottilie thought he was rather enjoying himself because he was the centre of attention which she had learnt he expected and enjoyed. She looked up at him, her lips curving into a smile. Then she continued to read.

"We demand your decision is made by this evening. There are rewards waiting. Greta Dietz will lead you. Follow her instructions." And the telegram?'

'Read on, Miss Divine. The telegram was coded in the Cipher System…used by many. A little careless of them, I think. The code they used is a variant of that cipher, the Totem Cipher. I decoded the message by rearranging the letters and using a certain amount of mathematics in which I excel. Scientists use mathematics for all manner of experiments.'

"The emissary departs in two weeks. You will accompany him or face the consequences. K.F." Oh, good Lord. They're serious, aren't they?'

'I believe so. I have thought about the wording. "The emissary" could mean a negotiator, an agent, or even a ship or train. Either way, I would imagine they or it will be carrying critical intelligence or someone of importance if it is a mode of transport.'

'And who do think K.F. is?'

'Klaus Fogel…a dreadful man. He kills without compunction. I sincerely hope Charles Wentworth has not crossed him. If he has, he's very likely already dead.'

Ottilie gasped. 'Could Charles be a double agent working for both sides?'

Sherlock Holmes turned his head slowly and observed her with hooded eyes, his pale face seeming to materialise out of the gloom.

'What are your thoughts, Miss Divine?'

'My brain and heart tell me he is not.'

'What does your instinct tell you?'

Ottilie pulled a face. 'It's possible.'

'Anything is possible, Miss Divine. We simply need to get to the truth.'

'How do we do that?'

'By being as scrupulous and as astute as those we pursue. No clue is too small, no information is wasted.' He nodded. 'Do you understand?'

Ottilie's stomach rolled. They had discovered damning evidence Charles Wentworth could be giving Britain's enemy information to help them win the war. The investigation had become more complex than she had imagined. And she was part of it.

'It will be a dangerous undertaking, will it not, Mr Holmes?'

'We are discussing dangerous people who wish to overcome our war effort, Miss Divine. I'm wondering whether you have the strength of mind to see it through.'

Ottilie stiffened and narrowed her eyes. 'Please stop wondering, Mr Holmes. I brought this to you, not the other way around.'

'Yet you were unaware of the complexities of this particular investigation, were you not?'

He took his pipe out of his pocket and began to fill it with tobacco. When he had finished and had lit it with a spill from the fire he glanced at her.

'We are deliberating on espionage, Miss Divine. A dirty word in some quarters. A possible traitor who is an acquaintance of yours, and an enemy who would kill a fellow human being for saying one wrong word.' He nodded and began to puff on his pipe. 'It's all or nothing. No half measures.'

'And there will be none,' she answered, her voice as strong as she could make it.

He nodded and drew another puff on his pipe. 'I'm glad to hear it.'

Chapter 19

A dense fog had fallen over London. It swirled up from The Thames and was carried into the streets and around the buildings like ethereal ribbons by a breeze drifting from the river into the city.

London was well known for fogs which often plagued its streets and accompanied the development of London from the very beginning of its history. Peasoupers were famous. The fog swirling around Ottilie as she stood outside 221B Baker Street as she was about to open the front door was thankfully not a peasouper, but she watched the inhabitants of central London as they hurried by, some with scarves clutched to their faces, some coughing into their hands, children and adults alike.

Fog was an unwelcome certainty for those who lived in London. The Thames River was a friend to those who worked on her but became a foe when unsavoury conditions aligned. There was nothing one could do but accept it and protect oneself from the disease many thought was borne into their homes via the unstoppable onslaught of a miasma which carried illness.

Ottilie had spent the day reading the remaining letters in the press room which had been sent to The Daily Express in reply to her article. Most were from cranks who simply wished to be part of the investigation, Ottilie surmised, merely to give them some importance. Others she deemed as "possibles" but on a second reading were letters in the same vein as those placed on the "Oddity" pile but with improved grammar and more imagination.

She tutted and shook her head. The threads of the investigation appeared to be growing longer and more tangled the further immersed she became. She thought about what Sherlock Holmes had said to her the previous evening. He had almost suggested she wasn't up to the assignment Jonah Walsh had given her. She wondered if her editor had any idea how long the tentacles surrounding Charles Wentworth's disappearance were.

'I'm being elbowed out of my own investigation,' she said under her breath, 'by none other than Sherlock "blooming" Holmes.' The thought of Holmes receiving plaudits for the investigation she had begun angered her, but she took a breath and shrugged. 'Perhaps I'm being too previous. Unfortunately, I don't think I can do it without him…and I'm not sure I want to.'

She shrugged out of her damp things, vapour clinging to her hair and eyelashes and moistening her face.

Her coat she hung in the kitchen hoping the warmth from the oven would dry it. Her shoes she stuffed with newspaper and left by the fireplace. Lighting the fire in the sitting room with some kindling and a dwindling supply of coal she crouched in front of it, warming her hands, her face glowing orange from the flames. She closed her eyes, enjoying the warmth and the relative safety of her flat until a knock on the front door startled her.

She got up and went to the door, opening it a tad until she saw who her visitors were. Sherlock Holmes and Dr John Watson were standing outside on the landing. Sherlock Holmes invited himself in without waiting for an invitation. Ottilie mulled over how she simply accepted his behaviour now, unthinkable, a few weeks ago.

He strode into the middle of the living room, his black coat flaring as he walked.

'I've brought Dr Watson with me this evening, Miss Divine. I have always found his opinion on investigations pithy and well thought out. Of course, his observations are usually somewhat different from my own, but no matter. It is good practice to look at a problem from different angles. I have found his perspective to be surprisingly edifying.'

Ottilie blinked at him. 'Did we arrange to meet this evening, Mr Holmes? If we did, I must apologise because I had forgotten it.' Ottilie made a slight grin. There had been no arrangement.

'If it's inconvenient, Miss Divine, then we should apologise,' said Watson, 'and we'll leave immediately.'

'Oh, no, Dr Watson…please sit down. May I offer you some refreshment…tea perhaps or a cup of coffee?'

'Tea would be very acceptable, Miss Divine,' he said as he sat on the settee. 'And thank you. I don't drink coffee in the evenings. Keeps me awake you see.'

'I do see, and agree entirely,' Ottilie said as she went into the kitchen. 'I'm the same. Coffee is for the mornings.' She glanced into the room. 'Mr Holmes. Can I tempt you to have a cup of tea?'

'No, no thank you, dear lady.' Holmes had yet to sit. 'I prefer to concentrate on the matter in hand. Taking tea draws a rather informal veil over proceedings, and I want to be clear-headed.'

Ottilie glanced at Watson who returned her glance with humour. 'I understand,' she replied as she took a tray into the living room with a teapot, two cups and saucers, and a plate of biscuits. She set the tray down onto the coffee table and proceeded to pour two cups of tea, one of which she handed to John Watson. 'A biscuit, Dr Watson?' she asked him, offering the plate. Watson proceeded to take one, then reconsidered and took two. Sherlock Holmes tutted.

'John, we have not long eaten dinner.'

'But no dessert trolley, Holmes. I like something sweet with which to finish.'

Sherlock Holmes shrugged and sat on the other single chair, Ottilie noticed. The one situated in front of the fire. 'Very well. If your arteries harden you will only have yourself to blame.'

Watson rolled his eyes slightly. 'We're at war, Holmes. My arteries are not the first thing on my mind of late.'

Ottilie quietly observed John Watson from underneath her eyelashes as she sipped her tea. She was comforted by his warm and amiable personality. His looks were in stark opposition to those of his friend's. His hair was a sandy blond, his eyes a rather intriguing hazel, and he dressed in softer colours, tweeds, and pristine white shirts with a wine-coloured tie. Yes, he was an entirely different prospect altogether from his friend Sherlock Holmes.

They settled to an amiable quietness. Dr Watson sipped often at his teacup and enjoyed the biscuits with unapologetic gusto. Holmes, however, was restless. He persisted in jumping up from his chair, either to pace the room, or to go to the window and move the curtain aside with one finger so he could look out onto the street. Ottilie questioned whether he could actually see anything. The street was as dark as pitch with the familiar streetlights now extinguished.

When Watson finally placed his cup, saucer and plate onto the tray, Holmes finally settled in the chair.

'Watson, I have told you the events of yesterday, and our previous foray into Charles Wentworth's office. Can you use your military experience to offer some insight?'

'Indeed, Holmes.' Watson leant forward and rested his elbows on his knees. 'Diplomatic disappearances are rare. Most diplomats are surrounded by others because they are not only political, but they are also social too. They are the ones who ease the way for the main men such as the Home Secretary or even the Prime Minister to visit other countries or have meetings with the Prime Ministers or Presidents of those countries.' He glanced at both of them. 'But you should consider whether Wentworth's disappearance is masking something else, a political move the country wants to hide.'

'Which country?' asked Ottilie.

Watson leant back in his chair. 'Why, ours, Miss Divine.'

Ottilie frowned. 'But why would our own country want to hide something from its people?'

'There are many…many events happening behind the scenes at present. We are at war, yet not one bomb has been dropped on either country. People are calling it the Fake War, are they not?' He shook his head. 'If only it were. Preparations are being made. Men…and women, are being sent into France and Germany undercover. There are probably German nationals inveigling their way into Britain in retaliation as we speak. War games. Like chess, war is all about the moves our men of war make. One wrong move and it all comes tumbling down.' He glanced at her with soft eyes and pulled a small smile. 'What is your plan?'

Ottilie glanced at Sherlock Holmes. 'There isn't one at present,' she said with candour. 'There have been findings, of course, the note and telegram hidden in the office which I'm sure Mr Holmes has shown you.' Watson nodded. 'An odd message which arrived in a batch of letters sent to the Express press office.' She looked downbeat. 'I'm not sure we've made much progress.' She waited for Sherlock Holmes to contradict her, but he didn't.

'What do you know about Charles Wentworth, Miss Divine?'

'Not too much. He's married to a fellow pupil at my old school. They have a family...and I understand he is well-thought of and being considered for promotion as assistant to the Home Secretary.'

Watson's eyes widened. 'Really? That is interesting.'

Ottilie was loathe to speak about Charles in a derogatory manner, but she knew she could not avoid it.

'There have been whispers and rumours amongst his colleagues Charles has been rather too friendly with his opposite numbers in the German government. That he has been discussing what was then only the possibility of war. His closest colleague said he was involved with people above his position.'

Holmes suddenly spoke. 'I don't like to rely on whispers, Watson, but I will admit, sometimes they can lead one to the truth. I was thinking of your military contacts. Are you still in touch with them?'

'From time to time.' He thought for a moment. 'There is to be a soiree for the men from my unit on Friday. I had chosen not to go,' he nodded to himself, 'I wanted to put it all behind me, but I've changed my mind. I was on the front for just a year before the war ended. I was only eighteen years of age. I suppose I was one of the lucky ones,' he said gloomily. 'I made a lot of friends, some who sadly didn't come home.' He slapped his knee. 'Yes, it would be good to see the others again.' He glanced at Ottilie. 'I will be discreet, of it there is no question.'

Ottilie nodded. She had to confess to feeling a little sickness in her stomach. When she accepted the assignment from Jonah Walsh, nothing could have prepared her for the complex investigation she was embroiled in.

Watson glanced at Sherlock Holmes who returned his glance. He leant forward and spoke quietly.

'What you are undertaking is risky, Miss Divine. Make no mistake it will become dangerous. Holmes and I have been involved in a number of investigations where I did not think I would see the next day.' He smiled. 'But as you see we survived them.' His smile fell from his face. 'Someone has gone to great effort to hide their activities. They will not want to be discovered.'

'I'm ready, Dr Watson. I must finish this. This investigation may well define my career as an investigative journalist and my future. There has not been a moment since this began when I would have given up.'

Watson grinned. 'I think we have another Holmes amongst us. What say you, Holmes?'

Holmes expression remained deadpan. 'There is only one Sherlock Holmes, my friend. You see him in front of you. There can be no imitations.'

Watson guffawed with laughter. 'Of course not, Sherlock. I would never suggest it.' He raised his eyebrows to Ottilie, and she began to laugh.

Holmes and Watson left Ottilie's flat an hour later. Holmes had exited the flat in the same way he had entered it, with hardly a word. Watson, on the other hand, had shaken Ottilie's hand and did his best to reassure her.

'We will do our best, Miss Divine, whatever the outcome. Hopefully, I'll have more to tell you come Saturday. Holmes and I will support you in your investigation.'

Ottilie smiled warmly at him. 'I'm not sure it is strictly mine anymore, Dr Watson,' she whispered.

He squeezed her hand. 'It is just his way. He cares…but not in the same way as you or I perhaps.'

Ottilie closed the door and leant against it. The plan was in place. She had London's most intriguing mind, and a doctor who had served in the 1914-1918 war on her side. It was an odd partnership she had to confess, but she knew they were as determined as she to discover why Charles Wentworth had disappeared.

Were there wider ramifications? Could Charles Wentworth, a mild-mannered family man be involved in dubious activities that could damage Great Britain's chances of winning the war? And did Delia Wentworth know more about her husband's activities than she was admitting to?

Another visit is in order, she thought. *And I won't be nearly so trusting as before. Delia will need to answer some difficult questions, and I will not allow her to hide behind her children when answering those questions.*

Something told Ottilie the threads of her special assignment were gradually being untangled and beginning to jostle for position. Suddenly, she felt a surge of confidence that she, Holmes, and Watson would discover and lay bare the intrigues opening up in front of them.

'This isn't only about Charles Wentworth,' she said to herself. 'There is more under the surface of bureaucracy the Foreign Office has brandished like a shield, particularly from Lawrence Tebbit. And who was the man who visited him in his office and caused him such distress? I aim to find out. Lawrence Tebbit, I'm coming for you. Nothing will stop me now.

Chapter 20

Sherlock Holmes strode into Kensington Gardens Square as though he had more right than anyone to be there. Ottilie, whose legs were not as long, struggled to keep up with him and was rapidly running out of breath.

'Mr Holmes. Please,' she implored him as she stopped for a moment, leaning forward to placate a stitch forming in her side. 'You walk so fast I can barely keep up with you.'

'Do you not feel an urgency, Miss Divine? Time is of the essence don't you agree?'

'Yes, but I'm not an automaton.' She hung onto a gate, an entrance to one of the houses and took a breath. Holmes waited without turning his back.

The fog had not lifted. The houses around them appeared as though in a mist making everywhere look ghostly. Ottilie had not wanted to venture into Bayswater in what she sensed was going to be a lasting haze which everyone knew harboured diseases, particularly those of the respiratory system.

When Ottilie had suggested returning to the Wentworth house to Sherlock Holmes, he had reacted with enthusiasm, encouraging her to make an appointment for that day. She had agreed and had telephoned Delia, not without some trepidation as she had promised her she would not be bothered again. And certainly, Ottilie had not prepared herself for Sherlock Holmes's insistence he accompany her. Holmes had been unconcerned.

'My dear,' he had said to Ottilie, which Ottilie hated. It made her feel she had been called into the headmistress's office at St Agatha's. 'The Wentworth house is the beginning of it all. It would be remiss of us not to explore a situation I'm quite certain awaits us there. Wentworth has a hiding place in his home…information he would not want to take into the office. If I were a betting man, which I am not, I would say it is certain. The fact the note and telegram were sent to Charles Wentworth's office tells me he had a previous arrangement with Greta Deitz not to send communiques to his home address. One does not need a brain such as mine to come to such a conclusion. A search of the house is paramount.'

Ottilie had blown out a breath of irritation, but knowing he was likely correct, made the telephone call.'

'But, Ottilie,' said Delia. 'I thought your interview was complete. I read the article in the Express. It was well-written and as you promised did not allude to my emotional state.'

'I won't be alone, Delia. I wonder…have you ever come across the name "Sherlock Holmes"?'

'Charles mentioned him once. He's a detective I gather.'

'He is…and he has shown great interest in Charles's disappearance.' There was a pause and Ottilie was worried Delia would refuse. If she did so there would be nothing she could do. 'He has a brilliant mind, Delia. If anyone discovers what has happened to Charles it will be Sherlock Holmes.'

'Very well. Be here at eleven o'clock. I've taken on tutors for the children, so they don't fall behind in their school work. He is due here at one in the afternoon.'

Regardless of Ottilie's inability to keep up with her companion, they arrived at the Wentworth house promptly and were shown into the room where Ottilie had spoken to Delia previously. Delia joined them after a few moments, followed by a maid with a tray of tea things.

'I always have tea at this time,' explained Delia. 'Please, sit down. Perhaps you would join me.' Ottilie introduced Holmes to Delia who seemed a little perplexed at his presence.

'Mr Holmes, I'm surprised you are so interested in our case,' said Delia as she poured tea into two cups. Holmes had refused the offer of tea as usual. 'It is important Charles is returned to us, but surely our situation is a domestic matter?'

Holmes nodded and Ottilie surreptitiously bit her lip, wondering what Holmes would say. Since her acquaintance with him she had learnt he was not always diplomatic.

'I understand completely, madam, but we cannot be sure your husband's disappearance is purely domestic.'

His statement stilled Delia's hand, and she lifted her head, frowning. 'Whatever do you mean…not a domestic matter?'

Ottilie fidgeted in her seat, her breath held in her chest. *Please don't mention espionage*, she silently implored him.

'Your husband's disappearance has raised a number of issues, not least the codes of safety put in place for diplomats in the Foreign Office, particularly those who visited Germany before war was declared.' Ottilie breathed a sigh of relief. 'We do not want to intrude on your privacy, but it would be particularly useful to us if Miss Divine and I could examine your husband's office.'

Delia placed her teacup back on the saucer with a resounding chink. 'But he rarely works here, Mr Holmes. Our home is for family, not for work. We have always promised each other it would be so.'

Holmes bowed his head. 'I understand, Mrs Wentworth, but if there is anything in his domain which would make it possible to save your husband and return him to you, surely you would want to explore the possibility?'

Ottilie gazed at Sherlock Holmes with not a little admiration. He had made a proposition to Delia Wentworth she could hardly refuse. How clever he was. It appeared he could be subtle, but only when it would serve his purpose.

'I...I suppose it would be all right. Charles has always been very particular about who enters his office. The maids are not allowed to go in there, not even to clean.' She looked pensive. 'Please don't change anything. When he returns, I know he will notice if his papers and belongings have been disturbed.'

Sherlock Holmes and Ottilie glanced at one another. Delia Wentworth seemed to be under the illusion Charles Wentworth would simply walk back into their home as though nothing had happened. Neither wished to distress her further by disabusing her of the idea.

'Mrs Wentworth,' began Holmes. 'Did your husband leave behind any documents before he disappeared? He must have brought papers home with him occasionally.'

Delia reached for her cup and saucer from the tray and to Ottilie's concern began to blink rapidly, frowning as she searched for an answer. 'Er, yes, I suppose he did, but he would never have shown them to me. I'm aware much of the information he was given was of a sensitive nature.'

'Did you ever consider your husband may well have been involved in politically sensitive work that could have been dangerous or of a risky nature?'

'Charles's work as a diplomat was more of an administrative post. He dotted the i's and crossed the t's. His signature was often required on Home Office regulations. He had a position of responsibility. His work was more of a consultative nature.'

'Did your husband ever mention an unfamiliar visitor to the parliamentary offices, Mrs Wentworth? Please think very carefully. It is most important you answer candidly.'

Delia Wentworth looked cross. 'I'm always truthful, Mr Holmes.'

'I'm sure you are, dear lady, but one's memory can occasionally let one down. Please cast your mind back.'

Delia glanced around the room as she thought, then her expression changed, her face clearing as a memory returned to her. She suddenly nodded.

'He mentioned a man he didn't like the look of. It was rare for Charles to find fault with anyone, but he was most particular about this person. The man wasn't directly involved with Charles. Charles was in Lawrence Tebbit's office, the Under-Secretary for a briefing, when a man entered the office without being announced. Miss Cheam, the secretary was remonstrating with him because he didn't have an appointment. Apparently, he said, "Tebbit. A word."

'Apparently Mr Tebbit looked most embarrassed and asked the man to wait outside the office, but he refused. Charles was astonished at his rudeness. His briefing with Lawrence Tebbit ended and he left them together. He asked Miss Cheam who the visitor was, but she shook her head and shrugged. It was unusual for Charles to mention anything to me regarding what happened on a day-to-day basis at Westminster, but I think this occasion stayed with him.'

'Did he describe the visitor?'

'He said the man was impeccably dressed, Savile Row certainly, tall, and thin, with a receding hairline. Charles said he was scholarly in appearance. His voice was laced with an accent...Irish he thought, but he wasn't certain.'

Ottilie heard Sherlock Holmes draw in a breath. His back suddenly straightened, and his jaw hardened as he stared out of the window.

'Mr Holmes?' she asked, concerned at his change of demeanour.

He lifted a hand to silence her. 'I'm perfectly all right, Miss Divine.'

'Are you sure?'

'Quite sure.' He allowed his gaze to fall on Delia Wentworth. 'I should like to examine your husband's study, Mrs Wentworth. I appreciate everything you have told us. You have been extremely helpful.'

Delia looked doubtful. She rose from her chair and made for the door. 'I'll show you the way.'

She led them up a flight of stairs to the first floor, and then along a corridor to her husband's study. She lifted her hand and pushed the handle down, but the door was locked.

'I'm sorry, Mr Holmes, Ottilie. It appears my husband locked his study door before he left for business on the day he disappeared. I don't possess a key I'm afraid.'

'No matter, dear lady,' said Holmes as he reached into his pocket and pulled out a bunch of lock picks. 'I take these wherever I go. One never knows when they will be useful.'

Delia looked astonished. 'You intend to break into my husband's locked study, Mr Holmes? Is it not a criminal act?'

'Not under circumstances such as these, Mrs Wentworth,' he replied as he dexterously moved the lockpick about in the lock until he heard a click. 'Ah,' he said. 'There we are.'

Before he opened the door, he turned to Delia Wentworth with a soft smile which dumbfounded Ottilie. She hadn't known he was capable of such an expression.

'Thank you, Mrs Wentworth. Miss Divine and I can manage from now on. We will call if needs be.' Delia Wentworth looked uncertain. She nervously wrung her hands in front of her but then nodded and walked away. Holmes waited until he heard her descend the stairs and enter the hall before opening the study door. The study had been ransacked.

'Oh, my goodness,' cried Ottilie. 'I wasn't expecting such a mess.' She looked around the room, a formerly pleasant space with a beautiful oak desk and matching captain's chair, now laying on its side; the walls lined with bookshelves. Some of the books had been removed from the shelves and thrown onto the floor, the spines and covers ripped and the inside pages separated and spread across the rug.

A crystal inkwell and a selection of pens and papers, which looked like domestic invoices, had been swept off the desk. A tilly lamp had fallen from a cabinet, the glass shade smashed to pieces.' Ottilie shook her head.

'Do you think Delia knows about this?'

'I would say not, Miss Divine.'

Ottilie stepped forward but Holmes put a hand on her arm. 'Not yet, my dear. We must observe before we step into the disorder. It would appear someone has gained entry to this room. The "someone" was clearly looking for something, and they were in a flurry of haste. We must not muddy the evidence. Mrs Wentworth should be informed about what has happened here, as should Chief Inspector Owen. He will want his own people, forensics no doubt, to examine the room.'

Ottilie gazed at him in disappointment, then turned again to the room. 'But where does it leave *us?*'

'It leaves us where we should be, Miss Divine. Since our arrival I have been making note of indicators in the room informing us of Mr Wentworth's regular habits.'

Ottilie frowned. 'Oh!' she exclaimed, wondering what he could mean.

'The untouched bookshelf,' he said. 'Our malefactor was clearly disturbed during a rather hurried search. He or she did not have time to search the bookcases on the lefthand side.' He pointed to the bookcase. 'Do you see, Miss Divine?' Ottilie nodded. 'And do you see the volume in the middle of the third shelf. Its spine is rather well-used, let us say.'

'Yes, yes, I see it.'

Holmes made his way around the edge of the room so as not to disturb evidence and made for the row of shelves.

'As you can see by the condition of this particular volume it has been removed from the shelf repeatedly. The shelf is also somewhat scuffed. A favourite of the occupant one might say.'

Holmes gently pulled the book from the shelf. As the book was removed an almost imperceptible clink could be heard.

'What was that?' cried Ottilie.

Sherlock Holmes slid his arm into the aperture left by the removal of the book and retrieved a metal box. Replacing the book on the shelf he deposited the box under his coat.

'I think our work here is done, Miss Divine,' he said, his expression as poker-faced as before. 'We will peruse this item on our return to Baker Street.'

After informing Mrs Wentworth as to the condition of her husband's study and advising her to contact Chief Inspector Owen, Ottilie, and Sherlock Holmes left Kensington Garden Square and hailed a taxicab to take them to Baker Street. Just before they reached their destination Ottilie turned to him.

'Do you ever get excited about anything, Mr Holmes?'

He slowly turned to her; his face expressionless. 'I'm afraid I don't recognise your question, Miss Divine.'

'Do you ever have feelings of enthusiasm, or happiness, or an abundance of energy, something to make you feel glad to be alive?'

He turned his face away from her before he spoke, as though concentrating on the view out of the windscreen. 'Absolutely not. Those feelings you have described are erroneous, Miss Divine, and can usually be attributed to a hormonal imbalance.'

Ottilie blinked, taken aback. 'I see. Thank you for enlightening me.'

He bent his head to get out of the cab.

'It is of no consequence. Merely a scientific fact. Everything can be attributed to science, Miss Divine. I would urge you to remember it.'

Chapter 21

The fog still swirled around the redundant lampposts in Baker Street like ghostly ribbons. The time for lunch had come and gone and Ottilie's stomach rumbled. She was desperate to eat something, and she wondered why Sherlock Holmes had not mentioned a desire for food.

'I would like to telephone my stepfather, Mr Holmes. I want to be absolutely sure Delia telephoned him.'

'I would suggest if she has not there is information she's holding back.'

'I agree…and I have promised him I will pass on any information we discover. I believe it is our duty.'

'Indeed. I will take the box into my rooms. Perhaps you will join me there to discover the contents.' Ottilie nodded, deciding not to tell him she couldn't wait to find out what was inside. He clearly did not have an enthusiastic bone in his body.

Fortunately, Richard was in his office when Ottilie telephoned Scotland Yard. She asked him whether he knew about Charles Wentworth's study, and he confirmed Delia Wentworth had telephoned him.

'I wonder when it happened?' Ottilie asked him. 'It's a complete mess, books, and glass all over the floor. One would have expected Delia to have heard something.'

'Not if she wasn't at home at the time.'

Ottilie frowned. 'What?'

'Perhaps you could call me this evening, Ottilie. Your mother and I want to have a night in together. It has been a while. This case, and others, has prevented me from getting home at a reasonable time.'

'Are you sure. I don't want to disturb you both.'

'I'm quite sure.'

When Ottilie returned the receiver to the cradle she realised she hadn't told Richard about Sherlock Holmes's discovery of the metal box. *I'll tell him when I call this evening,* she thought. *And it will give Mr Holmes and I time to peruse whatever's inside.*

Before joining Holmes in his rooms, Ottilie ran up the stairs to her flat and rummaged in the cupboard for a packet of biscuits she had hidden there for a rainy day.

'I'm starving,' she said under her breath. 'And I'm counting today as a rainy day.'

She returned to the first floor hoping Holmes had thought to put the kettle on for tea but she didn't hold out much hope.

'There you are, Miss Divine,' said Holmes. 'I wondered what had happened to you.' She offered him a biscuit from the packet. 'No thank you. I don't eat biscuits. If Dr Watson had been here, I'm quite sure he would have accepted your offer of such an unhealthy comestible.'

Holmes had placed the box on the kitchen table. He invited Ottilie into the kitchen where they both sat staring at it, Ottilie munching on her biscuit.

'When are we going to open it?' she asked impatiently. 'You realise I will have to tell Richard about it. I can't keep anything from him. He would never forgive me.'

'Understood,' said Holmes, nodding, 'but I want to make sure it isn't a booby trap.'

'Oh, gosh,' she cried. 'I hadn't thought of that.'

'We must be aware of every possibility. I have examined the box and I'm sure it is safe to open.'

'It looks a bit like my old wooden pencil case I had at St. Agatha's, except it's made of metal of course. I would imagine the bit at the top slides back.'

Holmes picked up the box, pressing his fingers against the metal and sliding back the top. Inside was a bundle of papers, rolled into a cylinder shape and fastened with an elastic band. He removed the elastic band and laid out the papers on the table. Ottilie reached forward and took a sheet of paper from the top. Holmes retrieved the one underneath. They read their respective sheets, Ottilie's complexion gradually turning as pale as her companion's.

'This letter is addressed to Charles outlining an operation the government want him to carry out within Westminster.' She glanced up at Sherlock and he met her eyes with a frown. 'He's looking for a mole, Mr Holmes, he's not spying for Germany.' She picked up more of the papers. 'These papers aren't about espionage; they're about national security. He's working for...' she gasped. 'The signature!'

'Neville Chamberlain's I should imagine,' said Holmes.

'It has been signed by him.'

'Which is possibly why we have been stonewalled at every turn. Anyone in Westminster could be the mole, Miss Divine, and the powers that be would certainly not want to inadvertently warn the offender.'

'What do you think has happened to Charles?'

'His assignment has been uncovered by the wrong people, those with power who have dictated Wentworth's abduction.'

'Have you seen this?' She pushed one of the papers towards Holmes.

He nodded. 'Das Eisenhand. The Iron Hand. The insignia is impressive, is it not?'

Ottilie shuddered. 'It looks cruel,' she said in a whisper. 'Just the look of it makes me feel vulnerable.'

They continued to search through the papers until Holmes came upon one to interest him.

'If I am not mistaken, and I rarely am, this watermark is more than just an emblem. We are looking at a similar device of espionage to one on the note in the fireplace in Charles Wentworth's parliamentary office.'

He lit a candle and held the paper over the flame, not close enough to burn, but near enough to reveal the message.

Westminster Bridge. Seventh arch beneath. A package awaits. Confirm the package.

Ottilie could feel her heart thumping in her chest. She hoped Holmes couldn't hear it. He would never understand. 'Westminster Bridge. Right next to the Houses of Parliament. It's just too convenient.'

Holmes nodded. 'And it is where we should go.'

'To find the package?' Holmes gave a nod.

'When?'

'Tonight, my dear. Under the cover of darkness…and fog. Never have I been so tolerant of the miasma-carrying vapours exuding from the River Thames. We must assume they hold no danger for us.'

Ottilie grimaced. 'A poor night to venture out, Mr Holmes.'

He stared at her with hooded eyes. 'I am capable of venturing out alone, Miss Divine.'

'Not on your Nelly,' replied Ottilie. Sherlock Holmes looked at her in surprise which made Ottilie chuckle. 'A favourite saying of Knolly, my mother's cook. She has some wonderful sayings.'

He didn't look impressed. 'How entertaining.'

'What time will we leave?' Ottilie asked him.

'Seven on the dot. And dress appropriately, Miss Divine.'

'I know, I know, no fripperies.' She looked up at him and thought she saw a slight curling of a smile on his lips.

'You are a courageous woman, Miss Divine. I must admit my early experiences of you told me something quite different. I felt your music was of an unpleasant variety and played far too loud for a tenant sharing a house with other people, no doubt accompanied by copious amounts of alcohol. Perhaps you drink too much…a dangerous habit for an investigative reporter.'

'I'm not a lush, Mr Holmes,' Ottilie said, frowning at his audacity. 'You pay me a compliment on the one hand and with the other you sweep it away.'

'A compliment?' He frowned. 'I deal with facts, Miss Divine. My reputation goes before me. Facts solve crimes, not compliments. I cannot stress it too much.'

'Are we having our first argument, Mr Holmes?' Ottilie asked him with a twinkle in her eye.

Holmes did not answer her, simply turned away and sat in his wingchair by the fireplace where he stuffed his pipe with tobacco and lit it with a spill from the fire. Ottilie grinned, then scooped up the papers and put them back in the box, intending to give them to Richard. What they would find at Westminster Bridge that evening was anyone's guess.

Back in her flat she was too tired to cook a meal, so she poured a glass of sherry and toasted Sherlock Holmes.

'To Sherlock Holmes…a man carved from a block of wood.'

She lowered her glass to her lap feeling suddenly mean spirited. The gravity of what was in front of them hit her. Between them they had discovered a political conspiracy, one which would lead them into danger. With Sherlock Holmes's unique and brilliant mind, they had found what Charles Wentworth's abductors had been looking for, a simple metal box with details of his assignment.

She trembled when she thought of Das Eisenhand, an organisation waiting in the shadows to pounce and bring the country to its knees. Was Charles Wentworth still alive? Had he been tortured for information? Was he using Greta Deitz' position as a cultural attaché to infiltrate a German spy ring? Had he trusted her? Were they having an affair? There were so many questions remaining unanswered. Perhaps what they found under the bridge at Westminster would answer some of them.

Sherlock Holmes had proved to be a steady influence and a man of strong ideas. He had complete confidence in his own abilities without whom she could not have discovered the dangerous mission Charles Wentworth had been assigned. Some would describe him as arrogant. She had done so herself she remembered with a smile.

Holmes was a unique human being, a tour de force with a remarkable knowledge of science and the minds of criminals. His deducing skills were second to none, yet as brilliant as he was, he did not possess the skill of interaction with other human beings. Not for him an empty compliment or the sugar-coating of a distasteful pill.

The more Ottilie thought about it the more she wondered why one felt the delivery of difficult news was better served covered in icing. She smiled to herself. Perhaps Sherlock Holmes had discovered the art of living fearlessly. He neither worried nor cared about other people. He was his own man. Ottilie raised her glass again and drank to him.

'To Sherlock Holmes. A man who does not care for fripperies and possesses the most unique and brilliant mind in the country.'

Chapter 22

Just before she and Sherlock Holmes were due to leave for Westminster Bridge, Ottilie rang Richard at Duke Street. She kept her voice on the downlow...the fewer people who knew what they were discussing the better, although she was convinced Holmes knew what she was doing from one moment to the next.

'What was it you couldn't say when you were at Scotland Yard, Richard? Was someone with you?'

'Our telephone operator is always with us,' said Richard with a chuckle. She listens in, always has, even though she has been asked not to on a number of occasions. It's always better to discuss things in private if you know the conversation isn't straightforward.'

'And is what you're going to tell me not straightforward?'

'I wasn't sure if you had asked Delia Wentworth if she'd had any visitors.'

Ottilie frowned. 'I asked her in the first interview I conducted with her where her answer was in the negative. We didn't ask her yesterday...we were so eager to get back to 221B and open the box we found in Wentworth's study.'

'And did you?'

'Yes but tell me your news first.'

'I asked Mrs Wentworth if she'd had any visitors. She said not as such and I asked her what she meant by it. She said she had an appointment and she needed someone to take care of the children while she was away. She didn't want to leave them with the staff because half were on their day off and the other half were busy.'

'So what did she do?'

'She telephoned a woman called Tabitha Shaw and asked her to spend some time with the children while she was away. She said they knew her quite well and because she didn't want to see anyone else, Mrs Wentworth felt she was the only person she could ask.'

'Why not a member of her own family?'

'They live miles away apparently. I asked the same question.'

'So, Tabitha Shaw was in the house with the children, the only person permitted to visit the Wentworth family since Charles's disappearance.'

'It would seem so.'

'And there wasn't a full staff which meant Mrs Shaw was at liberty to explore if she wanted to.'

'Exactly.'

'Are we barking up the wrong tree do you think?'

'I've always thought when one is investigating one needs to bark up every tree.'

'Thank you, Richard.'

'My pleasure. What's next on the agenda.'

'I'll tell you when it's done. I don't want Mama to be alarmed.'

She almost heard him frown. 'Be careful, Ottilie.'

'Always.'

Baker Street was shrouded in remnants of the fog and so dark Ottilie could barely see her hand in front of her. The pavements were sodden where the fog had touched the flagstones with vapour, but there was no comforting glow from the streetlamps. It was grimy underfoot, and an unpleasant smell accompanied the smog.

Holmes dug his hands into his coat pockets and strode along Baker Street with Ottilie doing her best to keep up with him.

'Could we not get a cab?' asked Ottilie, already puffing from exertion.

'Absolutely not,' Holmes answered. 'The driver would be a witness to our activities.'

'How long will it take us to walk to Westminster Bridge?'

'About an hour…less if we can keep up a good pace.'

Ottilie nodded, not wanting to use her breath to answer.

Every street was in darkness. There were few people venturing into the damp, foggy night, when every building was obscured by mist until they had almost come upon them. People were no doubt tucked up warm in front of their living room fires. Ottilie wished she were one of them.

They reached Westminster Bridge a little over an hour later. The Houses of Parliament loomed up in front of them as they made for the Thames. Everything was still, everything quiet apart from the dense, pitch-black water below them, slapping against the historic brickwork which joined the riverbank to its opposite.

Occasionally, a hazy moon peeped out from behind a cloud, casting chinks of light into the water as they stepped onto the bridge. A few vessels, tied up for the night, creaked and scraped against one another. A pungent smell rose from the water and Ottilie grimaced, wondering if they would need to enter the river to find what they had come for. She hoped not. The Thames was home to all kinds of detritus. She knew from listening to Richard, or eavesdropping as she had been at the time, Scotland Yard often found bodies in the murky depths. She shuddered at the thought of it. The pitch black would give every wrong doer an opportunity to get rid of something in the river they did not want to be discovered with.

She glanced up at the clock tower, affectionately known as Big Ben, and the Houses of Parliament looking for some comfort from their familiar sight, but there was none. There were no lights emanating from the diamond-patterned windows. The lights heralding the front entrance had been extinguished. London had all but disappeared.

'How will we see where we're going?' she whispered to Holmes as they looked over the bridge into the black water, debris floating on the surface.

He took a small flashlight from his pocket. 'This should suffice. Using light will be dangerous but we have little choice. We won't use it until we're under the bridge.'

'Which arch is it?'

'The seventh.'

'There are seven arches underneath Westminster Bridge.'

'I'm aware of it,' he said sniffily.

'So which end is it?'

'What do you mean?'

'Well, if there are seven arches and the instruction is to search the seventh arch, which end of the bridge must we search?'

She knew Sherlock Holmes was staring at her because she could just see the whites of his eyes. He cleared his throat, turned to look away from her, then turned back.

'We will have to check both ends.'

Ottilie sighed. 'I thought so.'

'It matters not, Miss Divine. Which end do you propose first.'

'Might as well begin here.'

He nodded. 'Come, we have nothing to lose and everything to gain.'

'Could Charles not have already picked up what was waiting for him?'

'I think not.'

'Why?'

'My instinct tells me he was "disappeared" before he had the opportunity.'

'Your instinct?'

'Indeed. Now, let's get on. I would like to get back to my hearth before too long.'

Ottilie followed Holmes to where the pavement and the bridge met. At the juncture there was a flight of stone steps leading down to the water's edge. They were covered in slime making them slippery underfoot.

'Be careful, Miss Divine,' Holmes said over his shoulder. 'I wouldn't like you to slip and fall into the river.'

She eyed his Homberg hat and broad but bony shoulders as they sunk further down the steps. If it had been anyone else in front of her, she would have rested her hand on his shoulder to steady herself, but she could not even imagine doing such a thing with Sherlock Holmes, so she placed her palm on the crumbling brick of the bridge, discovering firsthand what the slime felt like under her fingertips. She grimaced but gritted her teeth and hoped whatever they were looking for would be their side of the bridge.

She heard a squelchy splash as Holmes's boot reached the bottom of the stone steps. Her own footing had become precarious, and she said a silent prayer for strength of mind and a secure foothold. She suddenly thought of her father and directed her prayer to him. *Please don't let me slip, Papa. I think it would be the end of me.*

'I'm going to step underneath the nearest arch, Miss Divine. There is a small ledge I think, which we can stand on to explore the brickwork. Whatever has been left for Charles Wentworth will not be clear to the naked eye but will have been hidden. One can only assume it will be in the wall of the bridge. *That's if it's there at all,* Ottilie thought. She wondered what they would do if they didn't find anything.

She followed him gingerly onto the ledge. Facing the wall of the bridge she scuffled along the ledge wishing Holmes would switch on the torch.

'When are you going to switch on the torch?' she asked him in a whisper.

In answer to her question a pale light shone from Sherlock Holmes's hand, illuminating the crumbling, detritus laden walls on Westminster Bridge. The bricks were covered in bird droppings, green and black slime, and a brown foam smelling of sewage. Ottilie felt her stomach rise to her throat and she fought to keep it down.

'Oh, my goodness,' she said while covering her mouth with her hand. 'This is awful. How on earth will we find anything?'

'By looking, Miss Divine,' Holmes replied tartly. 'If there is something here I will find it. Ha, what have we here? Hold the torch please.'

He passed the torch to Ottilie, then leant forward and began removing some of the crumbling bricks from the bridge wall. Ottilie winced, hoping he wasn't planning to remove too many. She looked up to the top of the bridge and swallowed hard. What if the bridge came tumbling down on top of them.

'Do not upset yourself, Miss Divine. Westminster Bridge has stood here since the 18th Century and replenished in 1862. It has seen more history than either you or I could imagine and will be here long after we are gone.

And the ghost too, I've no doubt.'

'Ghost! What ghost?' Ottilie pulled her collar up around her neck and shivered.

'Thomas Page. He designed the new bridge in 1862 but died under mysterious circumstances in 1877.' Sherlock pulled a few more of the bricks out of the wall then reached into the gap he'd made and pulled out a long box. 'Apparently there were unofficial modifications made to the bridge when it was rebuilt, and Page knew about them. Many think it was the reason he was done away with.'

'And his ghost walks the bridge?'

'Indeed.'

Ottilie frowned. 'The aperture must go a long way back to have got the box inside.' She peered at it. 'I recognise it. It's a flute case. We had them at St Agnes's…or at least, those who played the flute in the orchestra did.'

Sherlock Holmes glanced up at her, his expression unreadable. 'And what was your instrument, pray tell?'

'I'm not musical I'm afraid. I can play the opening bars of *"Tea for Two"* on the piano, but that's about it.'

'Quite elementary, I should think.'

Ottilie looked indignant, then shrugged. 'What's in the case?'

'We should take it up to the bridge, Miss Divine, where we can open it in a little more comfort.'

Ottilie nodded, then turned and picked her way through the detritus and ordure on the ledge as she held onto the wall. The stench from the ordure was still in her nostrils when she scaled the broken steps leading up to the bridge, looking forward to a bath when she returned to the flat to wash away the smell which she was sure was on her skin and clothes.

Sherlock Holmes followed her, and when he reached the bridge set the flute case on the ledge which ran the length of the bridge. He unclipped the buckles and lifted the metal clasp on the case.

The case was water damaged and smelt strongly of filthy river water, but was still intact. Inside were some sheets of music, old, yellowing at the edges. There were notes written on the sheet music. Sherlock Holmes peered at them.

'Do you read music, Miss Divine?'

Ottilie shook her head. 'No, I'm afraid not.'

He sighed. 'I play the violin but I play through sound. I can recollect how to play a piece of music by listening to it.' He shook his head in frustration. 'I have never read music but I'm fairly sure Watson can, although he doesn't bother himself to play an instrument. I've never understood why.'

'We'll have to wait until he takes a look at it. There's something underneath the sheet music.' Ottilie carefully lifted the sheet from the case. 'Oh, it's a card case, and look at the engraving. It's Charles Wentworth's initials…C. W.' Ottilie lifted out the card case and flipped it open. Inside was a small piece of paper, folded in two. Ottilie handed it to Holmes.

'Time runs amok. Tick tock, tick tock. The answer lies beneath the clock.'

Beneath the card case were two train tickets to Zurich. They were dated for a week hence.

'I wonder who the train tickets are for?' asked Ottilie.

'Wentworth and with whomever he was going to Zurich. A double agent perhaps.'

Ottilie gasped. 'You think so?'

Holmes shrugged. 'We know he was looking to discover a mole inside Westminster. Let us not rule out the possibility it could be someone close to him. A friend perhaps. If it is he'll want them out of London as soon as maybe.'

'You mean Charles might want to save them?' Ottilie said, frowning, wondering why he would want to save a traitor to the country.

'Indeed.'

'But what's all this for? The cryptic clues? The train tickets…and what's this?' She reached into the bottom of the flute case, then held something up in her fingers. 'A coin. Why is there one coin in the bottom of the case?'

Holmes held out his hand and she dropped the coin into his palm. He took a small magnifying loupe from his pocket and examined the coin.

'It's a 1938 Reichsmark…' he pushed his nose further to the coin, 'and there is an engraving on the rim.' He pushed the loupe back into his pocket and placed the coin into the flute case.

'What does it say?' asked Ottilie.

'Nightingale.'

'Nightingale?' Ottilie frowned. 'I don't understand.'

Holmes was about to answer when a noise from underneath the bridge startled them. They both looked over the bridge to see a man in a dark overcoat walking along the shelf underneath the bridge. To Holmes and Ottilie's astonishment the man was singing, his low voice was laced with an Irish accent, and gruff to the point of throatiness, which suggested a heavy smoker.

Ottilie was about to call out, but Holmes held her arm and put a finger to his lips. 'Listen,' he mouthed. Ottilie nodded and listened intently.

When adversaries meet in Mayfair,

So I've heard,

A bird will sing in Mayfair,

So I've heard.

A bird resides within,

Where the night is smoky and dim,

The nightingale waits in Berkeley Square.'

The singing suddenly stopped, and Holmes and Ottilie leant further over the bridge to see a figure fleeing at the other end, his coat flying out behind him as he held his top hat to his head.

'He's gone,' sighed Ottilie. 'I wonder who it was?'

Sherlock Holmes looked decidedly uncomfortable. 'If I'm correct Miss Divine, it was a man who I know to be one of the most dastardly criminals who ever walked the streets of London. He knew he would not need to sing in a loud voice. There is a strange anomaly in the architecture of Westminster Bridge. It used to be called the Whispering Bridge because if a person whispered a message under the arches, anyone walking on the bridge above would hear what was being said.'

'So, a man familiar with the anomaly.'

'Indeed. There is little he does not know.'

'And it is someone you know?'

'I wish I did not know him, dear lady. When I heard about Tebbit's visitor and the way he inveigled himself into Tebbit's office I was convinced immediately his visitor was none other than Moriarty.'

'Moriarty?' Ottilie frowned. 'It isn't a name I've heard before, Mr Holmes.'

'He is known only in the smallest of circles, mostly criminals, and those where he thinks he will discover the most power for himself.'

'But *you* know him.'

Holmes's face darkened. 'He is my sworn enemy. It seems he knows I'm involved in this case.'

'Could he be the mole?'

'It is a distinct possibility, but I have no doubt he has recruited someone on the inside…a person who knows the condition and circumstances of the Foreign Office…and very likely the War Office.'

'He was singing about adversaries meeting in Mayfair. Could he have been suggesting it is what we would find if we went there…to Berkeley Square?'

'I assume it is exactly what he meant.'

'So…should we go there? Do you think he meant for us to go there?'

'I believe he did.'

'Will we go tonight?'

'I think not.'

Ottilie's eyes widened. 'But they, whoever it is, might be waiting for us.'

'Exactly, Miss Divine. I would say it is certain.'

'So…?'

'Have you not considered it could be a trap? Someone was keeping an eye on Westminster Bridge were they not? They knew we were here…rather a coincidence don't you think? And it would seem my old adversary Moriarty is playing his part. He likes nothing better than to be involved in wrongdoings. I'm sure he would very much like to bring the British government to its knees, and me along with it. I am certain now he is involved with Klaus Fogel, head of Das Eisenhand.'

Ottilie bit her lip, thinking she had a lot to learn, then looked up to the soulless windows of the Houses of Parliament where no lights shone from the diamond-shaped glass in the leaded light windows, and would not until the end of the war. The Houses of Parliament would be the perfect target for German bombers.

'Someone from up there,' she said in a whisper. 'Someone who's known in Westminster. A person who wouldn't raise eyebrows if they were working late in their office.'

'My thoughts exactly, Miss Divine. I do believe we are thinking alike at last.'

'Perhaps we should go inside. It might be Tebbit. It seems your Moriarty knows him. Am I right in thinking he is the man who pushed his way into Tebbit's office?'

Sherlock Holmes raised his dark eyebrows. 'Indeed, it could be, or his loyal right-hand man, Sebastian Moran who also hails from the Emerald Isle. And he is not *my* Moriarty, Miss Divine. Heaven forefends. Whoever it was who tipped off Moriarty, he…or she…will be long gone. They are a number of steps ahead of us I'm afraid, but our aim is to get into step with them and, in time, overtake them.' Ottilie nodded, knowing he was right. 'We will return to 221B and examine the objects in the flute case. I also wish to document everything we have heard, and found, and subsequently plan our next move.'

They hailed a cab for the journey back to Baker Street. Their presence at Westminster Bridge was already known so it seemed to Holmes quite pointless to hide the fact. Ottilie sat back into the seat with a sigh.

'It all seems rather a mess. It feels as though we have a jumble of clues and are no further forward.'

'On the contrary, Miss Divine,' Holmes answered with gusto. 'We have made great progress. We must also await Watson's contribution after attending the soiree held for his unit. Don't forget he has promised to make enquiries on your behalf about Charles Wentworth.

Sherlock Holmes sat back in his seat looking forward as he always did, looking neither left or right, or in her direction when he spoke.

'Watson is rather an easy-going fellow, phlegmatic in his outlook, and certainly not of a nervous disposition. It's because of these traits he is skilled in asking for information in such a way the person he is asking will think Watson isn't bothered whether his target divulges information or not. Watson will make them feel safe, that what he asks for has no importance.' He made what Ottilie thought was a small smile, a slight turn up to the corners of his mouth, a rare occurrence. 'Which is exactly why they will tell him what he wants to know.'

Chapter 23

Ottilie joined Holmes in his rooms on the first floor. She had begged for a few moments to freshen up after their ordeal under the arches at Westminster Bridge.

The stink of the arches had clung to her clothes, and she was glad to divest herself of them and change into something fresh. For reasons she could not fathom, the odour remained in her nostrils, even though she had washed her face twice and applied a skin tonic. She tutted and picked up a perfume dispenser which she sprayed onto her neck and wrists, and her clothes.

'It'll have to do,' she muttered as she opened the door to her flat to make her way to Holmes's rooms. 'Holmes probably smells worse.'

As he opened the door to his rooms, he looked at Ottilie askance and wrinkled his nose.

'Miss Divine. There seems to be a surfeit of perfume about your person.'

'Oh,' she said, reddening. 'Is it a bit strong? It's just the smell of the river, you see. I can't get it out of my nostrils, and I don't understand why.'

Holmes showed her into his sitting room and reached for his pipe on an occasional table by his wingchair.

'You do not smell of the river, Miss Divine. Your nostrils are playing tricks on you. The smell from the river was strong, I grant you, but your nostrils have nothing to do with it. Your brain is simply remembering the unpleasant smell, probably because it was an unusual aroma to you. Never fear. You will forget it in time.'

'Gosh, I hope so. It made me feel quite sick.'

Holmes lit his pipe and rubbed his hands together.

'So, to business. I have taken the liberty of writing a timeline of our investigations. You may wish to give a copy to your stepfather, and perhaps one to your editor, Mr Walsh. I'm sure he will be interested to see how you have been filling your time.' He passed her a sheet of paper on which was his flamboyant handwriting.

Wentworth's Office at Westminster

A note which I believe Wentworth tried to burn without success, referencing an upcoming meeting with Greta Deitz at Trafalgar Square. Did Wentworth make the meeting? A telegram from an unidentified sender, instructing Wentworth so: The emissary departs in two weeks. You will accompany him or face the consequences. K.F., undoubtedly Klaus Fogel. Desk rifled through, though methodical—either by Wentworth himself in haste or an intruder with specific intent.

Wentworth's Study (Home)

Study had been ransacked…books strewn, drawers emptied. The search was thorough but reckless, suggesting someone in a great hurry. Well-used books on a shelf which had not been searched yielded a small, ornate box. If Wentworth was taken, it was after he attempted to secure or retrieve something from this study. The house appeared untouched, suggesting either a well-maintained cover or deliberate concealment of recent activity. Desk contained documents on foreign trade agreements—official business or a façade? No immediate evidence of espionage. Paper discovered in box points to Charles Wentworth conducting an investigation into person or persons who are passing classified information regarding Britain to German nationals. A security breach.

Beneath Westminster Bridge

Narrow aperture in the bridge's stonework, concealed from casual view. Inside: a flute case, worn with age but recently handled. Case contained a false bottom, secured with a hidden latch. Contents to be examined further. The bridge's location suggests a prearranged drop point—but for whom? An unknow miscreant followed Miss Divine and me to the bridge. He sang a rewritten rendition of A Nightingale Sang in Berkeley Square. The verse, when dissected I am sure will lead us to more clues regarding Wentworth's disappearance and who he is investigating.

Preliminary Conclusions:

Wentworth was engaged in covert activity—an investigation into a suspected mole in Westminster, most likely the Foreign Office. The telegram and note indicate urgency; he was running out of time. The box and flute case were deliberately hidden—each likely containing pieces of the same puzzle. If Wentworth was compromised, the individual or individuals responsible are still at large—and aware of our movements.

Further analysis required.

Ottilie read the page twice then passed it back to Holmes, her eyebrows raised.

'You've made no mention of Mr Moriarty, Mr Holmes. Is there a reason?'

Holmes puffed on his pipe deep in thought. 'He is involved in this case, Miss Divine, of it there is no doubt, but his first thought will be to antagonise me and to put obstacles in my path to induce me to fail. He would like nothing better…unless he could kill me of course. I am a thorn in his side and he will endeavour to rid the world of me. If I'm correct he will have been paid handsomely by his German friends to infiltrate Westminster. It would seem Lawrence Tebbit is also involved with him.

For that I am sorry. Moriarty will chew him up and spit him out without a modicum of concern. The man is already dead I'm afraid. A matter of time only. When he becomes less useful, he will be eliminated. It is why I felt it best to keep my own counsel on this matter.'

Ottilie nodded, thinking it best to allow Sherlock Holmes to make his own decision. 'I see.' She glanced at him. 'Will my stepfather know about him?'

'Possibly. Inspector Lestrade most definitely.'

Ottilie nodded and inhaled a breath. 'Should we look at the case do you think?'

'Certainly,' answered Holmes. 'I have made a preliminary examination. The crossword is of course cryptic which will offer no problems to me whatsoever. As the nightingale is prominent on the coin and in the verse our friend sang to us this evening under Westminster Bridge, I looked in my extensive collection of books and documents. There is a nightclub called The Nightingale in Mayfair.' Ottilie gasped. 'I believe it is a club for those who can afford it, namely those of a certain society,' he looked tellingly at Ottilie, 'and perhaps those who are in well-paid positions at Westminster.'

'Are you planning for us to visit? We must, mustn't we?'

'I am, but I would prefer Watson to be with us. Safety in numbers of course, and he often provides a thoughtful take on whatever is happening around us. It does concern me they are going to a great deal of trouble to direct us towards The Nightingale Club in Mayfair, but…sometimes one must act on a hunch. At the very least we may discover who is involved.' He sniffed and took another puff of his pipe. 'Clearly Watson's method of logistical thinking is not as fine-tuned as my own, but,' he waved the pipe in the air, 'his conjectures are always welcome even if they are sometimes incorrect.' Ottilie wanted to giggle but stopped herself just in time. It would not have done to upset the genius who was Sherlock Holmes.

'I must call in to my office tomorrow, Mr Holmes. Mr Walsh will think something has happened to me.'

'Something *has* happened to you, Miss Divine. You are now working with the most celebrated consulting detective in the country. You will give Walsh my interpretation of the investigation, will you not?'

'Yes, of course. Thank you for taking the time to write such a comprehensive timeline. It will provide Mr Walsh with a perfect explanation of how far I have travelled in the investigation.'

'*We*, Miss Divine. A perfect explanation of how far… "*we*"… have travelled in the investigation.'

Ottilie nodded. 'Of course, Mr Holmes. It is exactly what I meant.'

Chapter 24

Walsh held Sherlock Holmes's interpretation in his hands. He glanced up at Ottilie and raised his eyebrows above his spectacles. She wondered if he was impressed by it or whether he would have been more impressed if she had written it herself.

'And your article, Miss Divine? It will be based on this…timeline?'

'My article?'

'You are an investigative reporter, Miss Divine, most particularly on the reporting. Is Sherlock Holmes leading you astray? He has his own methods of investigation which some may well think are downright dangerous.' He frowned. 'Do you think he is leading you into danger?'

Ottilie shook her head. 'As you can see, we have found clues to Charles Wentworth's whereabouts. We think he isn't spying for Germany…at least all the evidence points to it not being so, rather he is carrying out an investigation for Neville Chamberlain to discover the mole within the Foreign Office.'

'Is Sherlock Holmes convinced there is a mole?'

'I believe so. He also mentioned a man he called Moriarty. Have you heard of him?'

Walsh laid Holmes's interpretation on his desk and took off his spectacles. He lent back in his chair, his expression hard to fathom. He glanced out of the window then back at Ottilie.

'Now, there's a name I haven't heard in a while.'

Ottilie sat in the chair opposite Walsh's desk without being invited. 'So you *do* know of him?'

'Unfortunately, yes.'

'Sherlock Holmes thinks he is involved in Charles Wentworth's disappearance.'

'Does he now?' Walsh folded his arms over his chest. 'And why would he think it?'

'Deirdre Cheam who is Lawrence Tebbit's secretary said Tebbit's visitor, the one who pushed his way into Tebbit's office, was tall and impeccably dressed, and had an Irish accent. Charles Wentworth told Delia he was having a meeting with Tebbit when the same man came into the office without invitation and certainly without an appointment. He said the man had an Irish accent and was tall and wearing a Savile Row suit.' Ottilie shrugged. 'I suppose Charles would know. I should imagine he goes to Savile Row all the time.' She bit her lip. 'Well…did. And last night Sherlock Holmes said the man under Westminster Bridge was none other than Moriarty. He was singing in a gruff voice, but he had an Irish accent. Holmes was certain it was an accurate description of his nemesis, although he also mentioned a man called Sebastian Moran who seems to be a colleague of Moriarty.'

Walsh nodded. 'Lots of people have Irish accents, Miss Divine, particularly if they were born in Ireland. Holmes might be mistaken.' He shrugged. 'Could it just be Holmes is reading too much into it? He hears an Irish accent and immediately thinks it's Moriarty. And Holmes described him as his nemesis, did he? I can understand why. The man is a psychopath of the highest order, in fact psychopath does not describe him fully. He is highly intelligent, can be charming and manipulative, is criminal in his behaviour, and has no empathy for any human being.' He raised his eyebrows at Ottilie again. 'Apart from the criminal behaviour does the description sound like anyone we know?'

Ottilie sighed. 'You mean Sherlock Holmes, don't you?'

Walsh pressed his lips together and nodded. 'They are similar in many ways, Miss Divine. Apart from the criminal behaviour, Holmes and Moriarty could be one and the same person. Both respect each other's intelligence, yet both would like to see the other done away with.'

'How do you know so much about them, Mr Walsh?'

'Inspector Lestrade and I are good friends, Miss Divine. We occasionally meet socially. He likes a brandy, or five, which can sometimes embolden him to be loose-lipped.' He smiled. 'Perhaps it's unfair of me to encourage him, but I've written many an article because of a snippet of information he's let slip.'

'And he told you about Sherlock Holmes and Moriarty.'

Walsh made one nod. 'He said they were having their own personal war. Who knows who will win.'

'You were expecting an article from me, Mr Walsh. I hope you understand I cannot give too much away. It could be detrimental to the investigation.'

'Forget the article for now. You can write it up when you've found Charles Wentworth. It will be a coup for Express, certainly. What is your plan going forward? This,' he pointed at the sheet of paper in his desk, 'tells me what you and Holmes found, not how close you are to finding Wentworth.'

'Because we don't know. All of those things points to someone trying to divert Wentworth from his original course. My money is on Greta Deitz, the cultural attaché, who it seems he was friendly with both here and in Germany. What we do know is Wentworth was searching for the person who breached Westminster's security, that someone on the other side discovered he'd been recruited by Neville Chamberlain to find the mole who it seems has been passing information to our German friends, so not only do we have a mole but also someone passing on information about Charles. We have a couple of names…Greta Deitz who Charles was meant to meet at Trafalgar Square, and Das Eisenhand…the Iron Hand, a group of men and women who are implicated in Charles's disappearance. The note we found mentioning Das Eisenhand and revealing its insignia requested Charles to confirm the passage. We think Das Eisenhand wanted Charles Wentworth to confirm the passage of the mole. Charles was clearly playing a double hand. We think he was found out via this other person. We just don't know who it is but it's likely someone close to him.

'Holmes, Dr Watson and I will go to the Nightingale Club in Mayfair, possibly tomorrow evening. Holmes thinks the man under Westminster Bridge was directing us to go there, but of course it might be more to the singer's advantage than ours. Unfortunately, there is only one way to find out.'

'I would say it is certain, Miss Divine.' He leant forward and narrowed his eyes. 'Be careful, Miss Divine. I do not want the wrath of your stepfather on my head. I hope you're going to tell him of your next steps.'

'Of course. He has already told me it is my duty to inform him of what we are doing.'

'You think he'll object?'

'Very likely, but I rather hope he will offer to help.'

That evening Ottilie called Richard from the telephone in the hall at 221B Baker Street. She had already couriered Holmes's analysis to him at Scotland Yard during the afternoon and silently prayed he would be impressed.

'You've been busy,' he said. 'I suppose it's what comes of having Sherlock Holmes directing operations.'

'He certainly has an understanding of the criminal mind. He has mooted we are a few steps behind the opposition but is confident we will eventually catch them up and overtake them.'

'What do *you* think, Ottilie? I'm more interested in your opinion.'

Ottilie positively glowed. It was the first time Richard had asked her for her opinion on a case and it inspired a belief in herself.

'This is my first assignment, Richard. I'm not sure I know what to think. Just a few days ago we discovered Britain is at war with Germany, but I've had little time to think of it, or be concerned about what it means. Being with Sherlock Holmes is a little like being on a roller coaster, but one on which one doesn't know where one is going or where it will end.'

'I've heard Inspector Lestrade say something similar about him. I understand he is a force to be reckoned with.'

'Yes, I suppose he is.'

'Do you like him a little better?'

Ottilie thought about it. 'I'm not sure Sherlock Holmes inspires friendliness, Richard, in fact I would say he eschews it entirely. He doesn't need friends. He is self-contained and seemingly only trusts one person, his associate Dr John Watson, although he is quite disparaging about him, mainly I think because Dr Watson is the human face of the partnership. He is a kind man, has a softer side to him which is in complete contrast to Holmes.'

'Have you telephoned to inform me of your next intentions, Ottilie?'

'I thought I should, Richard, and Mr Walsh expressed a wish that I should let you know what is going to happen next.'

'And what *will* happen next?'

'Holmes, Watson, and I are to visit the Nightingale Club in Mayfair. Holmes is convinced we're being directed there.'

She could almost hear Richard frowning down the wires. 'But if they're directing you there it will be for their own advancement and will likely be detrimental to you and your associates.'

'I know.'

'It could be dangerous. I wish you would reconsider, Ottilie.'

'How can I, Richard? It's everything I've ever wanted. For so long I've been relegated to writing articles about flower shows, and the latest fashions, and what the best hostess offers her guests over Christmas. All I ever wanted was to be taken seriously as a reporter. An investigative reporter, one who wrote about something that mattered, something important which just might change people's lives. It's my chance to prove myself. I can't give up.'

She heard Richard sigh. Then after a pause. 'What do you need?'

'Plain clothes at the club. It may come to nothing, but…if it does, it would be good to know you're there.'

He took in a breath. 'I'll see what I can do. Tomorrow evening you say?'

'Yes. Sherlock wants Dr Watson with us. Should I tell him about the police?'

Richard chuckled. 'It might be best. He likes to be kept in the know. Making plans outside of his knowledge will not please him.'

'Will Inspector Lestrade be there?'

'I'm quite sure it's something he won't want to miss. You know, Holmes always lets Lestrade take credit for his successes whenever they have worked together.'

'I didn't know that. Why?'

'So Lestrade has no reason to object to Holmes being involved in any future investigations. Holmes is very astute. And of course, Lestrade is happy to take the accolades.'

Ottilie shook her head. 'I'm learning more and more about Sherlock Holmes.'

'He is an enigma, a man of mystery. I'm not sure anyone truly knows him, not even Dr Watson. No one can get close enough to him to learn who he actually is.'

'I trust him, Richard. And Dr Watson.'

'It's important, probably the most important thing of all. We can never work authentically and sincerely with someone if we don't trust them. Do you think he would protect you?'

'Yes, Richard. I rather think he would.'

'It's good enough for me...which is just as well because I have a proposition for you.'

'Oh?'

'I've arranged a meeting for you in the back of a shop in Bayswater with operatives who are part of British intelligence. It's discreet and will provide you with cover. We often use it for meeting our sources.'

Ottilie could not contain her surprise. 'But why, Richard? Does anyone else know about it? Could you not get into trouble?'

'Yes, very much so, but by some quirk of fate you have managed to elicit the skills of the most famous detective in the country, and I think we should use those skills to our best advantage.'

'I'm worried. If your superiors find out…'

'They won't.'

'Who are they, these men?'

'Ah, well…I don't know. They'll decide who to send.'

Ottilie nodded to herself. 'All right. Give me the details and I'll let Mr Holmes know.'

Richard chuckled. 'Mr Holmes? Not Sherlock?'

She laughed too. 'Absolutely not. Mr Holmes would never allow such informality. I would imagine his own mother calls him Mr Holmes.'

Ottilie, Holmes and Dr Watson who had joined them, sat in the back sitting room of a pet shop off Bayswater Road, waiting for the intelligence officers to arrive. The owner of the shop had simply nodded to them as they walked in, and Ottilie surmised he was on the government's payroll.

The shop smelt of wood shavings, hay, and an indeterminate odour which Ottilie assumed came from the animals…rabbits, guinea pigs, and rats.

'Who would want a rat for a pet,' she said sotto voce.

'Rats are extremely intelligent animals,' answered Holmes, 'certainly the most intelligent of the rodent family.'

'Please don't say that word.'

'Which word, Miss Divine?'

She flinched. 'Rodent.'

Sherlock Holmes frowned as Dr Watson chuckled. 'Why ever not? They are a species to be admired.'

Ottilie didn't have time to answer because two men entered the back sitting room of the shop. Ottilie wasn't sure what she had expected but they looked like two ordinary men off the street, one puffing a pipe, the other with a newspaper rolled up under his arm.

'Mr Holmes,' nodded one, then another nod to Dr Watson. 'And Miss Divine?'

Ottilie swallowed hard, her stomach churning with nervousness. 'That's right.'

The men each took one of the dining chairs and turned them to face Ottilie, Holmes, and Watson.

'It seems you have uncovered some intelligence as to the whereabouts of Charles Wentworth.'

Holmes took charge as Ottilie knew he would. 'We have. I have deduced Charles Wentworth is playing a double game, not because he's a spy, but because he is on a mission to discover someone at Westminster who is.'

Both men nodded, eying the three warily. One spoke up. 'He had been recruited to feed propaganda to the Germans through his contact, Greta Deitz, a cultural attaché who had been working with the British Foreign Office before war was declared. He knew how dangerous it was, but because of his position in the Foreign Office he was the perfect agent for the job. Because he was known to the German government some of their members were loose lipped around him, information which he passed on to us. The German contingency liked him.'

'Liked?' asked Ottilie with a frown.

'Unfortunately, there is someone within the Foreign Office who saw fit to blow his cover. Greta Deitz sent Wentworth a message asking him to meet her at Trafalgar Square. It was a set up. Deitz wasn't who she purported to be. She is part of a group calling themselves "Das Eisenhand" … "The Iron Hand".

'Wentworth's disappearance isn't an accident. Information was passed on about Wentworth to someone in the German government. What we don't know is why, who passed it on, and to which government operative the intelligence was passed on to.'

'Financial gain perhaps?' asked Sherlock Holmes. 'Money talks, does it not?'

'Possibly…or a personal vendetta against a successful man who had the ear of Neville Chamberlain. We understand his efforts were to be rewarded with a promotion many have surmised would be the Permanent Under-Secretary…but we have it on good authority it could be even higher up the ladder. There's always going to be someone who thinks they deserve it more. Getting him out of the way would solve the problem.'

'Could it be one of his close associates?' asked Ottilie.

'I assume you mean William Shaw,' said one of the men. Ottilie nodded. 'We're keeping a watch on him, and three others Wentworth works with, Lawrence Tebbit, Robert Halifax, and Victor Lerman. They are all high-ranking officials, Deputy Under-Secretaries of State, who are privy to intelligence. Lawrence Tebbit is Permanent Under Secretary but he's being moved sideways to a post in Italy. Not so "permanent" for him, much to his chagrin. They would know what the department is trying to achieve.'

'But would they know about Charles Wentworth?' asked Dr Watson. 'Surely his involvement would be classified information.'

'Indeed,' said the other man, 'but there are always leaks. We don't know how it happens, but it does. It's why we're employed by the government, to try and stop the leaks, or plug them up.'

'Do you have any advice for us?'

The first man spoke up. 'We understand you're going to the Nightingale Club in Mayfair this evening.' Holmes and Ottilie nodded, and the man turned his attention to Ottilie. 'Miss Divine, I'm sure you know of Ye Olde Cheshire Cheese in Fleet Street?'

'Of course. Everyone in the newspaper industry knows it.'

'What happens there?'

Ottilie shrugged wondering why he was asking. 'Reporters swap stories, pass on information…get drunk, and say too much quite often. Editors have dismissed reporters who have lost a lead report.'

'Which is exactly what happens at The Nightingale, except it's government officials and civil servants, not reporters. We have people placed there on permanent watch. You won't know who they are, they're trained to be unobtrusive, but we think it's where many of the leaks are established. We have been successful in the past. Men have been dismissed from Westminster because they were too open with what they knew, but the Wentworth case is one we can't get a handle on. Any information you can find we'll be grateful for, as will the Prime Minister.'

That evening, after returning to Fleet Street to pick up any messages left for her, Ottilie hailed a cab to take her to Baker Street. She often caught the underground train from the Temple Street Station which would take her to Baker Street for half the cost, but it was a convoluted journey which would take more time, and time was something she didn't have.

That evening's visit to the Nightingale Club loomed in front of her and she couldn't help smiling to herself. She thought about the previous three years working at The Express and the articles she had been asked to write by Jonah Walsh. They had all been what reporters called "soft articles", the baptism of a child born to someone important, the funeral of a local dignitary, a cake sale from which the proceeds were sent to areas of poverty, usually places like St Giles or Seven Dials. They may have been rebuilt but the people living there still had little to live on. Nothing had really changed.

That Walsh had offered her an investigative assignment told Ottilie one of two things. Either, he had accepted she was a good writer with an enquiring mind and had learnt how to write an enticing article, or…he hadn't realised how important Charles Wentworth was, and how significant it was he should be found before he was forced by his enemies to give away the country's secrets. She hoped it was the former, but she couldn't help but think it was probably the latter.

She sighed, deciding it didn't matter either way although obviously she would have preferred the former. She was fully entrenched in the case, and the fact Sherlock Holmes and his long-suffering companion Dr Watson was involved had added more power to her elbow.

She watched the people and buildings go by as the taxicab got nearer to Baker Street, not really seeing them in any detail as her mind was on The Nightingale Nightclub. The way it had been described by the men she and the others had met that morning from political intelligence had made it sound like a louche den of iniquity, and if it was anything at all like Ye Olde

Cheshire Cheese in Fleet Street it definitely was.

She frowned to herself, thinking she had been sheltered from such places. Her mother, Camille, had been insistent Ottilie try to find friends, and possibly romantic attachments, from within their own circle. It was precisely the reason why she had not found a soulmate; someone she had wanted to marry. Apart from Wil Askew.

She sat back in her seat and thought about Wil. He was Lord Nathanial Fortesque-Wallsey's nephew, as strikingly good-looking as his uncle, and as intelligent and interested in world affairs as Ottilie was.

They had immediately struck up a friendship, both realising they had similar interests and could enjoy each other's company for hours on end, the time together seeming to slip by in an instant. Camille and Nathanial's wife, Elsie, previously Elsie West, had been friends for many years and often sought out each other's company. Everyone had noticed of course, whenever Camille and Ottilie were due to visit, Wil had ensured he would "just drop by" on some pretext or other. There had been gently raised eyebrows, and glances between the friends each time Wil had turned up at Grosvenor Terrace, Elsie, and Nathanial's home.

Camille had asked Ottilie how she felt about Wil. Ottilie remembered she had nodded and said, 'He's rather nice, Mama.' Camille had been convinced Wil would ask Ottilie to marry him, although Richard had urged caution. At the time Ottilie had wondered why. Had she expected Wil to ask her to marry him?

As she thought of him as the streets of London went by she desperately wanted to say no, but it wasn't the truth. She had prepared herself for him to ask her, had wanted him to ask her. She had fallen for him, had dreamt of his velvet-brown eyes and dark hair curling seductively on his pristine white shirt. He was always so impeccably dressed she couldn't fault him in any way. In her mind she pictured their wedding, and their future home, so elegant, so of the moment. She took in a breath and released it slowly, trying not to allow the memory of her humiliation unravel her.

When Nathanial had suggested to his sister her son seemed interested in Ottilie Divine she had laughed and told him he was being ridiculous. Wil had been promised to Lady Daphne Porter, a daughter of one of her oldest friends. She had also said Ottilie's mother's fall from society would never allow Ottilie to make such an illustrious marriage. Wil had known about it for years and she couldn't understand why Ottilie had thought he was available.

It was an old-fashioned view Nathanial had found insupportable, Camille had simply married out of the aristocracy after her estranged husband, Lord Henry Divine, had been killed in a motoring accident, but never the less he informed his wife and implored her to break the news gently to Camille and Ottilie.

Ottilie had straightened her back and kept her eyes on the fireplace, her fingernails cutting into the palms of her hands with contained distress. She had been devastated Wil, the only man she had fallen for, could have treated her so shabbily. He had allowed her to think there was a future in their friendship which had become closer over the weeks and months. Had she misread his intentions? If she had then so had her mother, and Elsie, her mother's friend. She was certain they had assumed Wil would propose to her. Richard had been correct when he had urged caution.

The cab jarred to a halt a few doors away from 221B Baker Street.

'I can't park right outside, love,' the driver said to her over the front seat. 'There's a car already there, do yer see?'

'It's perfectly all right,' answered Ottilie, handing over the fare. 'It's only a few doors away.'

She got out of the cab and proceeded to fasten her coat when a shadowy figure slid out of an alcove on the other side of the street. As Ottilie walked unknowingly towards 221B, a shot rang out from the other side of the street, just missing her and splintering a doorframe on the other side of Johnny's café. Ottilie ran towards the car outside 221B and crouched down, her heart hammering against her chest. She swallowed and tried to steady her breathing. The shot was meant for her, she was sure of it. Someone was trying to kill her.

Another shot shattered the windows of the car parked in front of 221B, showering tiny shards of glass over Ottilie's head and shoulders. She screamed, lowering her head even further. Shrieks were heard from passersby who ran up the street to get away from the danger. When a third shot came from behind her and flew across the street, she turned on her haunches to see where it had come from.

'Stay down, Miss Divine,' said a familiar voice. 'I think I have winged him. Yes, there is blood on the pavement. He won't get far. I will telephone Lestrade to tell him of the incident, but first you must come inside.' Ottilie hesitated. She could see nothing but the legs and feet of those frightened people fleeing the shots, and the side of the car where she had taken cover. Sherlock Holmes walked towards her, leaving the doorway of 221B and reaching down for her arm. 'He is gone, Miss Divine,' he said quietly. 'He cannot hurt you now.'

Ottilie gradually straightened up and leant against the car.

'Who was it?' she asked, her voice shaking with shock. 'Is it because of our investigation do you think?'

'Without a doubt. Quickly now, come inside. Mrs Hudson will make you some tea and I will telephone Lestrade. We must let the police know we are being targeted. The quicker they get after the miscreant, the better the chance they have of catching him.'

Ottilie allowed herself to be led into Mrs Hudson's sitting room.

'Sit down, Miss Divine, please,' exclaimed Mrs Hudson who was trembling with fright.

Ottilie did as she was asked as Holmes went into the hall and picked up the telephone receiver. Her legs were shaking and she felt sick with shock. She placed her arms on her knees, then her head on her arms trying to regulate her breathing. She wished fervently she was in her own flat, away from the noise and ministrations of those who meant well.

'Oh, Mr Holmes, what have you led this poor girl into,' Mrs Hudson cried into the hall. 'She could have been killed. And on our beloved Baker Street too. I've never heard the like of it before. A gun being fired in Baker Street.' She thought for a bit, then turned to Ottilie. 'Except when Mr Holmes fired a gun at the wall in his room. Yes, yes, I remember it now. He said it was for an experiment, so I suppose it's different. He wasn't trying to kill anyone.'

She went into the kitchen and came back with a tray of tea things.

'Now, my dear. You have a cup of tea. It'll steady your nerves. I've made it nice and strong and put in lots of sugar…for the shock.'

Ottilie took the cup and saucer from her and sipped gingerly at the hot tea.

'Thank you, Mrs Hudson.'

'It's all right, my dear. Now, you mark my words. Don't you let that young man drag you into one of his investigations. I know he thinks he's always right, and I dare say some of the time he is, but he's made of flesh and blood just like you and me.' She nodded to herself. 'And he's a man, and they can get themselves into all kinds of trouble without even trying. It's very nice you're friends, but I should leave it at that if I were you. I'm sure your mother would agree with me. Don't forget, will you?'

Ottilie stared at Mrs Hudson, suddenly feeling very tired. 'I won't forget, Mrs Hudson.'

Mrs Hudson nodded, satisfied she had made her point. 'I'm glad to hear it.'

Chapter 25

A knock on her door startled Ottilie. She was still shaken from what had happened earlier, reeling from the thought that if the gunman had hit his target she would likely be no more.

As she had bathed and changed into an outfit she thought appropriate for a nightclub, one of her mother's spangly dresses, a castoff, dripping with bugle beads and revealing more than she was usually comfortable with, her thoughts had gone to Charles Wentworth and how her view of him had changed.

She had met him of course. He was part of the aristocracy and had moved in the same circles as Ottilie and Camille. When he and Delia had married, she had seen less of him, but his parents always attended the same soirees and balls. They had been disappointed Charles had encouraged a young girl to leave her school and run away with him, but as the years had gone by their angst at the situation had lessened, and in fact it had become rather a family anecdote, simply because Charles and Delia had done well, buying a beautiful home for them and their three children, and Charles rising high in the Foreign Office. All had been forgotten. All had been forgiven.

Charles was a mild, rather pallid looking man, pale blond hair, tall, lean, and Ottilie had always thought a little too quiet. She shrugged at her reflection in her dressing table mirror. One could not know the real person inside anyone. Her thoughts then went to Sherlock Holmes and she shook her head. The man was a conundrum indeed. She wondered if he'd ever been in love, but then giggled to herself. *We have to love ourselves first,* she thought, *before we can love someone else.* She didn't think Holmes loved himself, even though he was an expert at blowing his own trumpet.

She smiled at herself in her mirror then rose from her chair to answer the knock on the door. As expected, it was Sherlock Holmes and Dr Watson. Holmes strode into her flat without being invited.

'Miss Divine,' he stated in a loud voice. 'We were rather of the opinion you would not join us this evening after the shock you had this afternoon.'

Ottilie had anticipated this. 'I'm perfectly all right, Mr Holmes, as you see.'

He eyed her outfit and sniffed disapprovingly. 'Must your attire be quite so revealing?'

'This is the only dress I own I felt was appropriate, Mr Holmes, one given to me by my mother. As you know it's not my usual style of dress.'

Holmes sniffed again, an annoying habit Ottilie thought. 'I understand your mother was quite the girl in her day.'

Ottilie raised her eyebrows and opened her mouth to reject his statement but was prevented when Dr Watson interjected. 'I think what Holmes means…your mother was a unique, rather beautiful individual, her style of dress being of the day.'

Ottilie pursed her lips. 'It was.' She went to the settee where she had thrown her coat and gloves. 'And of course I'm joining you this evening.' She felt a twirl of anger in her chest as she pulled on her gloves. 'The search for Charles Wentworth is my investigation, Mr Holmes. Whilst I am grateful for your skills and input, and those of Dr Watson, I feel I should remind you of it.'

Holmes observed her under hooded eyes, then bowed his head slightly in acquiescence. 'Thank you, dear lady, for prompting me.'

Ottilie raised her head and looked at both of them. Watson's lips were twitching with a chuckle he did his best to conceal. She made a small smile.

'Right, gentleman. I'm ready. It's time to go. There's a cab waiting for us outside 221B. I took the liberty of hailing one half an hour ago and asked him to call for us to ensure we do not have a repeat of this afternoon's drama.' The doorbell downstairs rang. 'Ah, there he is.' She looked at her watch. 'And right on time.'

Her eyes went to Holmes who looked slightly wrong-footed. He stepped back and allowed her to exit the flat first followed by Dr Watson. Ottilie heard Holmes sniff again, and she grinned.

The cab pulled up outside The Nightingale Club. There were myriad lampposts lining the drive to the entrance, but not one was lit due to the blackout.

'It all looks rather droll,' said Ottilie, peering out of the cab window. 'Although I'm sure it isn't inside.' Watson paid the cab fare and they walked towards the entrance, a large porticoed building with a dark mahogany front door. Watson lifted the brass knocker, and they waited for the door to be answered.

A young maid stood in the frame. Behind her stood a tall, burly man who looked as wide as he was tall.

'Yes, madam? Gentleman? How may I help?'

'We would like entry,' said Holmes in an officious voice which Ottilie was sure would not ease their way inside. She gave him a quick look. 'If you please, my dear,' he continued.

'Are you regular guests?' the maid asked.

'We are not,' said Ottilie before Holmes could say anything. 'But we would love to be part of The Nightingale's clientele.' She took two shilling coins from her bag and gave one each to the maid and the burly doorman, smiling widely and hoping it was enough to gain entry. The maid curtseyed and the man stepped back.

'Thank you, madam. Welcome to The Nightingale Club.'

Ottilie nodded and smiled and stepped over the threshold into a rather dark foyer, wood panelled and lit by sconces which emitted yellow beams onto the brown carpet, followed by Holmes and Watson. They left their coats at the cloakroom where an attendant gave them each a number and told them to take care of it. The double doors to the club were closed, but at a knock from the doorman they were opened and Ottilie, Sherlock Holmes, and Dr Watson were permitted to enter.

Inside, the club was decorated as if in homage to the art deco style. The walls were mirrored as was the bar which was situated in the centre of the room so guests could order drinks from wherever they were in the club. At present the barkeep was expertly making cocktails for a group of guests who were entranced. When he poured the shaken drink into the beautiful glasses the guests cheered and passed tips across the bar to the barkeep who smiled and bowed his head. The grandeur was breathtaking.

'Gosh,' uttered Ottilie.

Above their heads were crystal chandeliers with lights reflecting off the marble floors and the mirrored walls. A jazz band positioned to one side of the room played Glenn Miller's "In The Mood", and glamorous couples danced to the music which seemed to fill every pore. A haze of cigarette and cigar smoke hung just under the chandeliers, and the scent of alcohol and expensive perfumes pervaded the air.

Around the room were booths styled in pink leather with a sparkling black trim. Each had a canopy under which guests sat in luxury, many who were in intense conversation. Ottilie eyed them with interest, thinking it would be a good idea to move as close to them as was possible without appearing to be eavesdropping.

'Should we find a seat?' asked Watson. 'We look a bit suspicious simply standing here.'

Ottilie nodded. 'Yes, Dr Watson. A good idea. We should look as unobtrusive as possible I think.' She turned to Holmes. 'Mr Holmes, perhaps you could go to the bar and get us some drinks.'

Holmes looked horrified. 'I think not, dear lady. I have never…Sherlock Holmes does not…'

'It's all right, Holmes,' interrupted Watson, placing a hand on his friend's arm. 'I will go. Perhaps you and Miss Divine could find a table.' Watson turned to Ottilie. 'Miss Divine, what is your pleasure?'

Ottilie looked around at the tables of the other guests. 'A glass of champagne, please.'

'Holmes?'

'A brandy of course. Anything else would be an insult.'

Watson rolled his eyes with a grin. 'Come now, Holmes. You enjoy a good wine as much as the next man.'

'On occasion, but not this evening. I need to retain my clarity of thought.' Watson nodded, glancing at Ottilie, and made for the mirrored, circular bar.

Ottilie and Holmes looked for an empty booth from where they could observe the other guests. Just as they were beginning to think they would not be successful, a couple left one of the booths and they quickly commandeered it.

'We're in luck,' breathed Ottilie, sliding into the middle of the seat. 'We can just about see everyone from here.'

Watson joined them with their drinks and quickly sat down. 'Well, Holmes. Have your eagle eyes spotted anyone interesting?'

'I have...and she's about to come to our table and introduce herself.'

Ottilie and Dr Watson both turned to see a tall, elegant, blonde woman dressed in black, walking towards them. She used a walking stick in her left hand, also black, with a beautiful pearl handle.

She was difficult to age, but Ottilie thought she was in her late thirties. Her clothes looked expensive, black lace sleeves, and a lace bodice lined with black satin. Her black satin skirt was cut to fit, tight and just below the knee, with a long kick pleat at the back. Around her neck were myriad strings of pearls, the real thing by the look of them, and not the fake ones sold in London's department stores. She was so slender her clothes sat immaculately on her. Ottilie decided she looked like a model in Vogue magazine, of which Ottilie was a fan.

'Sherlock Holmes,' the woman cried in an attractive French accent. 'I am very surprised to see you here after all this time. Why, I thought you had left the country. Why have you not visited me?'

Ottilie placed her elbows on the table and rested her chin on the heel of her hand. She smiled to herself. This *was* an interesting development. Sherlock Holmes had a woman friend.

Holmes stood and bowed. 'Madame Albertine. It is good to see you. I was not aware...' He indicated the nightclub.

'When my husband died, I decided to invest my widow's inheritance in a business venture. This club came up for sale, although I must say it was nothing like this when I purchased it. The renovations and style are all my own.' She smiled around the table at them. 'I'm rather proud of it.'

'Your husband passed, Albertine?' asked Holmes. 'I'm sorry for your loss. When did it happen, pray?'

'About two years ago.' She sighed. 'It was a blessing in the end, but as you know he was much older than I. I needed something to fill my time. Nightingales has filled the void so perfectly.' She smiled her dazzling smile again.

Sherlock Holmes looked flustered. 'Yes, yes of course. But you should have let me know so I could pay my respects.'

Albertine leant on her stick. 'Ah, Sherlock, you are always the busy man are you not? Always, how you say, the investigator, too busy for fripperies.' Ottilie bit her lip to stop a giggle. She had learnt quite early in their acquaintance Sherlock Holmes was not fond of fripperies. 'But here you are,' said Albertine, 'although I am surprised to see you here. I did not think a nightclub would be your chosen mode of entertainment.' She made a small frown.

'I am here with my colleagues,' he nodded towards Ottilie and Dr Watson. 'We have business to discuss.'

'Ah, yes, many a business agreement has been made here.' She made to leave them. 'I hope you enjoy your evening, my dears. Nightingales is *"le meilleur endroit pour les affaires"* mon ami.'

Ottilie's eyes widened. *The best place for business,* she thought. *I wonder what she meant by it?*

'An old friend, Holmes?' Watson asked him, his eyes sparkling with amusement. 'You have never mentioned a "Madame Albertine".'

Holmes straightened his back and sat upright, his hooded eyes watching the dancers.

'A long time ago, Watson.' He took a breath and swigged from his brandy glass. 'Simply an acquaintance from the past, Albertine Renault.'

'She would know everything that happens within these walls, would she not?' enquired Ottilie. 'Do you think she would be a good person to speak to with regard to her guests? She may be able to tell us something about them; point us in the right direction. It would provide us with a starting point and perhaps save a lot of work.'

Holmes stiffened. 'I think not.'

Watson frowned. 'Why, Holmes?'

Sherlock Holmes turned to his friend; his expression fixed. 'Because we would not want to alert her to the reason we're here, John. If she knows about our investigation into Wentworth's disappearance, she might alert others to our scrutiny of the people who come here. It would be of no benefit to us.'

Ottilie frowned. Was Holmes saying he didn't trust Albertine? 'You don't trust her, Mr Holmes?'

'It is a moot point, Miss Divine.' Holmes returned his eyes to the dancers. The conversation was at a close.

Chapter 26

'What...or who are we looking for, Mr Holmes, asked Ottilie. 'I'm not sure how we're going to spot anyone involved in Charles Wentworth's disappearance.'

'I rather think we must wait until we're approached. We were led here by...well, someone who is involved, not just with the disappearance but very likely underhand doings in Westminster.'

'You mean this Moriarty person you spoke of?'

'Indeed.'

Dr Watson frowned to himself, then turned to Sherlock Holmes. 'Were we not recently approached, Holmes...by your acquaintance?'

Holmes straightened. 'Albertine?'

'Indeed. She approached us directly then disappeared. Perhaps she wishes us to follow.'

Ottilie nodded. 'It was rather odd, Mr Holmes, she should approach immediately after our arrival. I can only assume she knew we were on our way by some means.' She glanced at Dr Watson. 'Perhaps she is involved.'

Sherlock Holmes drew in a breath, looking uneasy. 'Perhaps.' He surveyed the room. 'She is not in the club at present.'

'No, she went up those stairs,' replied Ottilie, indicating a staircase leading to the first floor.

Sherlock Holmes looked surprised, then impressed. 'You observed her?'

Ottilie shrugged. 'I was curious.'

'We should follow her,' said Watson. 'I have a feeling it's what she wanted.'

Holmes said nothing, simply stood, threw back the last of his brandy and proceeded to make his way towards the staircase. Watson did the same and followed Holmes, lifting his chin to Ottilie to go in front of him.

'Do you think she's involved?' Ottilie whispered to Watson.

'Without a doubt, Miss Divine, although whether Holmes wants to accept it remains to be seen. He seems strangely attached to her.'

'Why strangely?'

'I've never known him become attached to anyone, least of all a woman.'

She glanced at him as they got to the staircase. Holmes had already disappeared to the top of the flight. 'Except you, Dr Watson.' Watson made a small smile and nodded, telling her he accepted it as fact.

The staircase led to a shadowy upper floor which held private booths. The atmosphere was even more illicit than the one pervading the ground floor. In the booths were groups of men with their heads together, discussing subjects they didn't want anyone else to hear.

A door at the end of the room was intermittently opened and shut again, with men…and women going in and others coming out. Ottilie narrowed her eyes and said, 'I wonder what's going on in there?' under her breath.

'A gambling den I shouldn't wonder,' said Watson.

She turned to him. 'But isn't it illegal?'

'Bit of a grey area I understand. Places like this operate under the law, and let's be clear, many of the men here make the laws. It seems to worry them not at all.'

Ottilie shook her head in disgust. 'One rule for them, and one for everyone else.'

'Exactly.

'They're guarding it well. I've just noticed those two men who are standing either side of the door. There must be a reason.'

'Intriguing,' said Watson.

'Dangerous,' replied Ottilie, 'yet I have a feeling it's where we must go.'

'I think Holmes is already negotiating our entrance.'

Ottilie peered through the gloom to see Sherlock Holmes speaking to another burly man who had his arms folded in front of his chest. His body language shouted loud and clear, no entry, yet Holmes appeared to be opposing him in his own unique way.

'If anyone will convince him, Mr Holmes will.'

Watson chuckled. 'I won't argue the point.'

'Do you recognise anyone, Dr Watson?'

'Have you not spotted Mr Tebbit, the Permanent Under Secretary at present. He is part of the aristocracy, but he refuses to use his title.'

Ottilie stared at Watson open mouthed. 'How on earth did you discover it?'

'From the soiree I went to the other evening.'

'Did you find out why he refuses to use his title?'

'He doesn't believe in them. He thinks they're unnecessary. He has been extremely vociferous on the matter.'

'And the government placed him in such an elevated position?'

'Apparently it wasn't viewed as a problem, at least not one which affected the country, although I beg to differ. One would wonder why he would have such an aversion to a family title. He told his counterparts it was a personal decision and nothing to do with his feelings about his country.'

Ottilie shook her head. 'I don't believe it.'

Watson raised his eyebrows and took a breath. 'Neither do I.'

'Where is he?'

'Third booth down, deep in conversation with a large, dark-haired gentleman.'

'I wonder who he is?'

'I've no doubt Holmes will ask him. He'll introduce himself and remind Tebbit he knows who he is. Tebbit won't stand a chance.' Watson grinned.

'Tebbit is a repellent man. Only the good Lord knows how he's got as far as he has.'

'It's nothing to do with the good Lord, and everything to do with politics.'

They looked over to where Sherlock Holmes had been remonstrating with the man guarding the door. He wasn't there.

'Where is he?' asked Ottilie, looking about the room and suddenly spotting someone she knew very well in the gloom. 'Oh my God. What on earth…'

Watson frowned. 'What is it, Miss Divine.'

'Rose. Rose Fortesque-Wallsey, Nathanial Fortesque-Wallsey's stepdaughter.' Ottilie swallowed hard. 'What on earth is she doing here?'

'May I suggest you go to her, Miss Divine, and I will try to discover where Holmes has got to.'

Ottilie pushed her way past people standing in front of the bar, winding her way towards Rose. When she reached the booth, she put a hand on Rose's shoulder who startled, gasping before looking up at Ottilie.

'Ottilie? What are you doing here?'

'I might ask you the same thing, Rose.'

Rose stood and grasped Ottilie's hand, pulling her to the edge of the room. She was dressed in a short, satin dress, an unfamiliar style for Rose.

Ottilie drew a breath.

'Good God, Rose, where on earth did you get that dress?'

Rose pulled a face. 'I could say the same for you, darling. Isn't it one of your mother's? And why are *you* here of all places? Does Camille know you're here?'

'Absolutely not. And Elsie?'

Rose snorted. 'Don't be ridiculous.' She smiled at Ottilie. 'Nathanial told us you'd been working with the great detective Sherlock Holmes. Is it true?'

Ottilie nodded. 'He's here with Dr Watson.'

Rose smirked. 'I didn't think you liked the…what was it you called him, "the insufferable little man"?'

'He is a man it is difficult to like, Rose, and he *is* insufferable. But he is also the cleverest man I have ever met…a scientist and a consulting detective. Did I want him involved in my investigation into Charles Wentworth's disappearance? No, of course not, but I think it would have been rather stupid of me to turn down such a brain. He is a man of many talents, particularly in deduction, has never considered the word empathy, for him it does not exist, and he couldn't care less what the rest of the world thinks about him.'

'And Dr Watson?'

'Different.'

'Aye, aye, aye!'

Ottilie sighed, grinning. 'He's a nice man, that's all.'

'I trust you.'

'Do. Anyway, you didn't answer my question. Who are you working for?'

'I'm translating for Colonel Sebastion Moran. He works for a munitions company. He's not in the best of moods. He has an injury to his leg which has made him crabby.'

Ottilie squinted into the shadows of the booth. 'You might want to reconsider working for him, Rose. From what I've heard he's not one to be trifled with.' She looked over Rose's shoulder. 'I think he's waiting for you.'

'I expect he is. He's trying to broker a deal with the Italians. Moran only speaks English, and with a broad Irish accent. Even *he* is quite difficult to understand...and he's not very patient either.'

'What kind of deal?'

'I'm sorry, darling. I can't tell you.'

'Rose!'

Rose tossed her head and looked across to the booth. Moran waved her over and she nodded.

'I must go. What about Saturday night at your place?'

'Will you tell me then?'

'Only if you tell me what you're doing here with Sherlock Holmes and the delightful Dr Watson.'

'It's a date.'

Ottilie watched as Rose returned to the booth. She frowned as Moran remonstrated with Rose, hoping Rose was being well paid for having to translate for such a man. Rose simply shrugged and spoke to the other man in Italian. *I hope you know what you're doing, Rose,* she thought. *Something tells me those men are not quite what they seem.*

Dr Watson found Holmes just as the guard looked as though he was about to force Holmes's exit from The Nightingale Club.

'Holmes!'

'Watson, this man is determined we will not be given access to the room the other side of the door at the end of the room. I've offered him every inducement, including a payment which almost made my eyes water, but to no avail. He will not be swayed.'

'Is this because you want to speak with Madame Albertine?'

'I want to know what her involvement is. *She* came to *me*, Watson. Is she in danger? Could she be warning me of something? Until I speak to her, I will not know.'

'Forget it, Holmes. We have a more serious encounter to consider.'

'What could be more serious than discovering what she knows? I am sure she is connected to Wentworth's disappearance.'

'She may well be, but if you look over to where Miss Divine is,' he indicated with his chin, 'and then cast your eyes to the booth just in front of her, you might see someone you recognise.'

Holmes squinted into the gloom. 'Miss Divine's friend is it not?' He frowned. 'Why is she here?'

'Now look beyond her, Holmes. Who do you see?'

Holmes moved his vision along the back of the booth. 'Good God! It's Moran.'

'Indeed. What does it tell you?'

'Moriarty is either close by or is conducting events from another location. He usually sends his henchman when he does not wish to be exposed. Moran is a vicious fellow.' He frowned. 'I must ask why Miss Divine's friend is sitting with him. I am concerned regarding the connection.'

'I think it is an excellent idea, Holmes. I can only assume Miss Divine's friend isn't aware of whom she's sitting with.'

Watson allowed Holmes to lead the way as was his habit. Sherlock Holmes's coat flew out behind him as he strode up to Ottilie, his long legs giving him seconds over Dr Watson.

'Miss Divine!'

Ottilie turned and nodded. 'Mr Holmes. We wondered what had happened to you.'

'We need to get behind the door at the far end of the room but I'm being prevented.'

'So, there's something they wish to hide?'

He ignored her question. 'Your friend is it not?' he asked, indicating Rose with a lift of his chin. 'From the other evening.'

'Rose? She's working for Colonel Sebastian Moran.' Ottilie stared at Holmes. 'I believe you know him,' she said, sotto voce. 'He has told her he works for a supplier of munitions. Rose works for a company who sends translators to business negotiations. Moran asked her to translate while he negotiates a deal with the Italian gentleman.'

'He is no gentleman, Miss Divine. He is Luca Vitali, known as "Corvo del Ombre" ... Raven of the Shadows. He is a criminal devoted to Benito Mussolini. He speaks five languages including English which he speaks fluently. Your friend has been duped. If she is working for Moran, then she is in the grasp of Moriarty's right-hand man. He is ruthless. A word out of place will see her killed. We must interrupt them immediately.'

Ottilie frowned. 'Who is he, Mr Holmes? I don't understand. And if Vitali speaks English...then why does he need a translator?'

'Does she work for the government?'

'I have no idea.' Ottilie looked worried. 'I'm sure she would have told me...' she sighed, 'but perhaps not. Rose is loyal and serious about her work. She speaks any number of languages, a prodigious polyglot whose memory is like a sponge. As far as I know she works for the embassies in London, and various companies. She has never mentioned the government.'

As mendacious agents of their respective countries discussed deals, secrets, and their plans for wartime mayhem, a single gunshot cracked through the air, so loud the sound rose above the music.

Rose screamed as a bullet missed her by mere centimetres. The atmosphere was shattered as chaos reigned, erupting into confusion. There were screams, glasses smashing on the marbled floor as people knocked over their tables, eager to get away from the gun-wielding guest.

Ottilie grabbed Rose by the arm and pulled her out of the booth where she was sitting with Moran and Vitali, pulling her onto the floor. She pulled a table down in front of them, screaming at Sherlock Holmes and Dr Watson to get away. More bullets thudded into the top of the table, the only thing saving Ottilie and Rose from being killed.

Ottilie slid her hand into her clutch bag and pulled out a small pistol. 'Did you see in which direction the bullets came from, Rose?'

Rose, still cowering with fear, stared at Ottilie's pistol. 'It came from the opposite corner from where I was sitting, perhaps from the stairs.' She lay on the floor and peeked out from the side, quickly pulling her head back in again. 'There's one man.' She had the temerity to chuckle. 'He looks a bit portly to be wielding a shotgun, not military at all, and rather florid of complexion. It looks as though he came up to the first floor from the nightclub.'

Ottilie frowned. 'Is his hair thinning?' Rose nodded and Ottilie sighed. 'Tebbit. What on earth is he doing?'

'Who's Tebbit?'

'He works for the Foreign Office...Charles Wentworth's superior in fact.' She glanced at Rose. 'Was it you he was shooting at?'

'Perhaps.'

'Rose?'

'I don't think this is the time or the place, Ottilie.'

Another wave of bullets hit the table they were hiding behind, making them startle. Rose gasped and put a hand to her mouth.

'I'm going to try and wing him,' said Ottilie. 'I've never done this before so I don't know how successful I'll be, but I think I must try.'

Suddenly, a shot came from behind them and she heard a groan and the sound of a body slumping to the floor. Ottilie knelt up and turned to see Inspector Lestrade with a smoking gun in his hand. Ottilie breathed a sigh of relief, thankful her shooting skills, or lack of them wouldn't be put to the test.

She peered over the table to see the heads of other people gradually emerging from the floor, underneath tables where they'd hidden for safety, from behind the heavy curtains at the windows, and guests crawling out from behind the bar. Lestrade and his men had hidden themselves well. She had not spotted them. They had used their experience as undercover police to slide quite effortlessly between the other guests of the club.

On the floor, at the entrance to the stairwell, was Lawrence Tebbit. He was in pain and groaning. Lestrade had successfully brought him down, Tebbit's arm shattered by Lestrade's bullet and he was trying to stand. Lestrade's men ran towards him to prevent him from getting away.

'I don't think so, Mr Tebbit. You have some questions to answer,' said Lestrade.

'I have nothing to say,' said Tebbit, his voice garbled with pain. 'I need a hospital.'

'And you will be taken to one, but it will be under an armed guard.' Lestrade looked unsympathetic.

Albertine Renault slipped out of the door at the back of the room and made her way to where Holmes was standing as he observed Tebbit's arrest. Dr Watson had joined Lestrade to offer his help.

'Well, well, Sherlock,' she said, a look of mirth crossing her features but not quite reaching her eyes. 'It seems trouble follows you everywhere, even to my little club. Nothing changes, does it?'

Holmes turned to her, a slight frown between his pristine, dark eyebrows.

'Are you suggesting trouble was not already here, Albertine?' His hooded eyes observed her closely as the mirth disappeared from her face. 'You are as beautiful as you ever were, but you have yet to master the art of the poker face.'

'I run a nightclub, Sherlock. That is all. Why would you think anything different?'

'With an illicit gambling den behind the door from whence you came.'

Albertine breathed in deeply. 'I wasn't aware you played the tables or the cards, Sherlock. It was never one of your passions when I knew you.' She stared at him, her eyes narrowing.

'Of course not, Albertine. Gambling is the devil's work. I see no reason for it, but…it is not gambling I came here for, of which I'm sure you're aware.'

'I understand you were trying to get into the far room.'

'It is where I think I will find my quarry…and I think you are aware of it, although I imagine he has now left your premises.'

Albertine tapped her walking stick on the floor in frustration. 'Who can you mean, Sherlock?'

They were interrupted as Watson joined them.

'Tebbit has gone to hospital in an ambulance. I don't think it is just the bullet wound which ails him. He might not survive.'

Holmes shrugged and raised his eyebrows. 'A great shame. There is a reason for what he did here this evening. Knowing it will help our investigation,' he turned to Albertine, 'and so will knowing who my friend Madame Albertine was hiding in her gambling den.'

Albertine shook her head. 'It is all in your imagination, Sherlock. You always had such an imaginative streak. It is why you interested me.'

Ottilie and Rose had left their hiding place behind the table. They glanced around the room which was now almost empty.

'Where have the men gone you were working for?' Ottilie asked Rose.

Rose shrugged. 'Who knows. You and I both know they were not negotiating a deal.'

Ottilie stared at her. 'So, what were they doing?'

'Discussing Mussolini and his growing strength in Italy. Moran was looking for information he could use.'

'In what way?'

'I don't know.'

'Tebbit had been assigned to Italy. He was to head the British Embassy in Rome, a position he will now not hold for obvious reasons. Who was he trying to kill I wonder?' She widened her eyes at Rose. 'You were nearly his victim.'

Rose nodded, looking contrite. 'Can I come back to Baker Street with you, Ottilie? I'll tell you everything.'

Ottilie nodded. 'Will I be disappointed? You're my best friend. I can't imagine being disappointed by you.'

'I hope not, but I haven't been entirely truthful with you.'

The four of them left the nightclub. Ottilie had never been so pleased to leave somewhere. The club was a den of iniquity, and she had felt uncomfortable within its walls. Lestrade approached them on the path, a cigarette burning between his fingers.

'This could have ended extremely unpleasantly, Sherlock.' He shook his head in frustration. 'Why are you not keeping me informed of your actions? What is going on here? If it hadn't been for Miss Divine and Chief Inspector Owen, I would have known nothing about it.'

Sherlock's heavy-lidded eyes observed Lestrade. 'You know how I work, Lestrade. I'm not a child to be reporting my whereabouts. We are on an investigation which I know you're aware of. It was you who pointed Miss Divine in my direction.' He turned away and sniffed. 'All will become clear.'

Lestrade's mouth pulled an upside-down crescent showing his rancour. He turned to Dr Watson and glared at him. 'And it seems you are also involved in this "investigation", Dr Watson?' Watson made a single nod. 'Why do I feel I'm being kept in the dark?' Neither Holmes or Watson answered him. Lestrade tutted with impatience and followed the remaining plain clothes policemen down the path.

'It's unusual for you not to keep him in the picture, Holmes,' said Watson.

'I have my reasons, dear man.'

As the four of them walked down the path towards the street, Watson made a low chuckle.

'How quickly a gunshot can clear a building,' he said.

'Most of the men we saw here tonight work for various governments and foreign organisations looking to profit from the war between Britain and Germany, but they are inherently cowardly. One sign of trouble and they disappear into the woodwork.' As they walked to a cab waiting for them, a voice came from the shadows.

'Sherlock Holmes. As I live and breathe.'

They stopped and looked across to where the voice had come from, a group of trees at the side of the drive leading up to the nightclub entrance. The hiss of a match reached their ears, then the glow from the end of a cigarette lit the owner's face as he pulled on it. He stepped out of the shadows but kept his distance.

He was more than six feet tall, with a strong broad-shouldered build. His features, highlighted with every pull on his cigarette, were rugged and weathered. His hair was dark, his gaze stern and predatory. He wore an army greatcoat over a dark suit, a crisp white shirt, and red tie. In his right hand he held a cane. His sights were firmly set on Sherlock Holmes.

'Colonel Moran,' said Sherlock Holmes, his voice low and laced with abhorrence. He sniffed his displeasure. 'I should have known you would be involved in this debacle. I wonder where your General is?'

Moran gave a small chuckle as he squinted at Holmes through cigarette smoke.

'I have a message for you.'

'Is Moriarty too cowardly to deliver it himself?'

Moran threw back his head and laughed loudly. 'He has more important fish to fry.'

Holmes's face darkened. 'Well, give me the message, man. Get on with it. I too have important fish to fry.' Moran began to speak in a husky, Irish accent.

"The game we play is never truly over, not until one of us is no longer here to play. You are hunting kidnappers and secret agents while my focus is war with men whose sinews are ready for a fight...a conflict to change the world. Our world will never be the same again. Only the strong will survive.

Germany is rising, and with its rise there will be anarchy and madness, an open door for men such as we. Tell me, Sherlock Holmes, when there are no more kings and treachery is the name of the game, who of us will be the last piece on the board of opportunity?"'

As he spoke the last line, Colonel Moran disappeared into the trees leaving a cloud of cigarette smoke behind him. All that could be heard was the breathing of the four. No one dare break the silence...it seemed too intrusive to interrupt a monumentally significant moment.

Moran's message from Moriarty was clearly a challenge. He had, in essence, described himself and Holmes as chess pieces on a board, challenging Holmes to be the last piece remaining. Not only was it a challenge, but a threat to Holmes's life.

'Holmes?' Watson broke the silence, a frown between his eyebrows

Holmes held up a hand. 'No matter, Watson. Moriarty has thrown down the gauntlet. Nothing has changed.' He turned to observe Rose and Ottilie, clutching each other, the embrace of two frightened women who suddenly realised the situation they were involved in was even more serious than they had anticipated. 'And now ladies, you can see we are not simply up against those who kidnap and maim, but those antagonists who see the war in Europe as a game. Moriarty is one such man.'

The taxi driver sounded the horn and the four made towards it. Rose glanced up at Ottilie and Ottilie raised her eyebrows, her mouth a straight line. Sherlock Holmes had an enemy, one who was strong and confident and took great pleasure in taunting his opponent.

One who could facilitate his demise.

Chapter 27

Ottilie took Rose's coat and hung it on the stand next to hers. There had been little chatter in the taxicab after the shocking events of the evening. They were enveloped in their own thoughts and weren't inclined to make conversation.

'Tea?' asked Ottilie.

Rose sat on the settee and glanced up at Ottilie with sad eyes. 'You're angry with me.'

'Because I offered you tea?'

'Because I've kept something from you.'

Ottilie softened her expression, then sat next to Rose, taking one of her hands from her lap.

'Only because I was worried, darling. You were in that awful place all by yourself. I was astonished, Rose. You were the last person I expected to see there.'

'I know, and I'm sorry. I should have told you.'

'Is it something you can't talk about?'

Rose sighed. 'I will tell you, Ottilie, but please don't share the information. It could have terrible consequences, and not just for me.'

Ottilie blanched, taken aback by what Rose said. 'Oh!'

'Let's have that tea,' said Rose. 'I need something to steady my nerves after what happened tonight. No more alcohol. I'm sick of the sight and the smell of it.'

They went into the kitchen. Ottilie filled the kettle while Rose set the cups and saucers out on the table and got the teapot from the cupboard. Ottilie measured in two scoops of tea, then one for luck. They waited in silence for the kettle to boil. When the tea was made Ottilie piled everything onto a tray along with a packet of biscuits and they went back into the living room, sitting on the settee. Once they had their tea Ottilie spoke.

'Right, darling, I'm ready. Tell me all.'

Rose took a sip of tea, then a deep breath. 'I work for underground intelligence. It's a network set up by the war office to infiltrate the conversations between our enemies about Britain's war with Germany.' She glanced up at Ottilie and blinked.

'Gosh.'

'I have a handler, a Mr Groves, but I don't think it's his real name.'

Ottilie nodded, then bit her lip in consternation. 'Why were you at The Nightingale Club tonight?'

'Mr Groves sent me there. He said he wanted me to watch Sebastian Moran who had told the Foreign Office Luca Vitali was working for Benito Mussolini in Italy. Vitali is a double agent, a terrible man, a criminal. It was why Tebbit was being seconded there…to infiltrate the Italian network.

'Sebastian Moran is an ex-army officer with a network of his own. He had inveigled his way into the Foreign Office, we think with help from Tebbit. Mr Groves insisted I went along to keep an eye on both Moran and Vitali. Moran tried to argue the point but Groves would not be pushed. He told Moran he would be arrested if I wasn't included in the meeting. Groves told me Vitali could speak English, but we needed a reason for my presence at the meeting. Vitali didn't question it…was happy to pretend he didn't understand English and speak in Italian because it meant those people sitting around us would not know what was being discussed. Moran was none the wiser. I stashed everything Vitali said in my memory and was expected to relate it to Moran after the meeting, but of course it didn't happen.'

'Moran knows you're connected to me now, Rose. And to Sherlock Holmes.'

Rose nodded and frowned, then took another sip of tea. 'I suppose he does.'

'Will it cause problems?'

'I expect so.' She made a small smile.

'He'll look for you?' Rose nodded. 'Should you not go into hiding?'

Rose shook her head. 'I can explain it away. *You're* my friend, not Sherlock Holmes. Tonight is the first time I've been in his company for any length of time. I'll tell him we're friends and I don't know Sherlock Holmes, which is the truth. I'm to report to Mr Groves tomorrow. I've no doubt Moran will be there. He'll want to know what was said.'

'And what about Tebbit?'

'Tebbit was just a name to me. I had never met him, so I didn't know who he was. He had been under investigation for a while. He has some questionable contacts…like Moran.'

Ottilie frowned. 'So why was Moran allowed to continue?'

'Better the devil you know, Ottilie. Mr Groves knows he's up to know good even though Tebbit told him he was ex-army and wanted to be included in the fight for Britain's victory and to be included in British intelligence because of his career in the army…which I must say was impeccable.

'The thing is Groves knows different. He has allowed Moran a long tether because he is sure Moran will lead him to the others he's working with. Moran is also a double agent, or even a triple agent, working for Britain, Germany, and Italy. He is part of an outfit called " Das Eisenhand".'

Ottilie gasped. 'The Iron Hand. I know about it. We think they abducted Charles Wentworth.'

Rose nodded. 'It's what Groves thinks too. The question is which side will Moran come down on? Probably to the highest bidder. He is incorrigible and holds no loyalty to anyone apart from The General, the man Holmes mentioned this evening. He is currently the receptacle of a lot of information, particularly after this evening. Vitali told him a great deal about what is happening in Italy. I found it quite amusing. He was clearly under the impression I had no idea what he was talking about because of the numerous codewords he used.'

'But why did Tebbit do what he did tonight?'

Rose shrugged. 'Groves has been under the opinion Tebbit was being squeezed by someone, likely Moran, and seemingly another man who apparently forces his way into his office without invitation and without an appointment. Charles Wentworth was present once when it happened. We have intelligence in the department.'

'Who?'

Rose shook her head. 'I don't know.'

'Would you tell me if you did?'

'Yes, I would. It might help you find Charles Wentworth.'

They went quiet. 'I'm not sure if we'll ever discover what happened to him,' said Ottilie sadly.

'Don't give up, Ottilie. I think you, Sherlock Holmes, and Dr Watson are getting closer.'

Ottilie glanced at Rose. 'Do you?'

Rose nodded. 'It can take quite a while to unravel everything.'

'How do you know?'

Rose hitched her mouth into a sideways smile. 'I've been doing this for a time.'

'A time? How long a time?'

'Three...no, four years.'

Ottilie gasped. 'Four years! How did I not know?'

'I started with small assignments. There was already talk of war even then and the Foreign Office was recruiting. I was getting bored working for businessmen who couldn't be bothered to learn the language of the people they were doing business with.'

'But how did you hear about it?'

Rose sighed again and stared into the distance, arguing with herself about whether she should tell Ottilie. 'Nathanial.'

Ottilie's mouth dropped open. 'No!'

'He knew what was happening. Nathanial is an incredibly clever man. It's no wonder Mama is so proud of him. He drew me aside one day and told me about the recruitment drive for intelligence officers for the Foreign Office, knowing how wearied I was becoming with what I was doing. He explained everything to me. He said I would be an asset to my country because I not only speak most of the European languages but can pick others up "at the drop of a hat", as he put it.'

'Well, that's true.' Something occurred to Ottilie. 'Does Elsie know?' Rose shook her head and Ottilie pulled a face. 'Oh, dear.'

'Quite.'

'What will happen if she finds out?'

'All hell will be let loose, then Nathanial will calm her down like he always does.' She chuckled. 'They're like chalk and cheese, those two. Goodness knows how they ever got together.'

'But still madly in love.'

Rose nodded. 'Sickeningly so.'

'So…you know all about The Nightingale Club?'

'It's the place to go if you want clandestine information. This evening, I recognised men and women from the Foreign Office who were working there covertly. I've learnt so much, Ottilie. Much of the information is trafficked through unbiased embassies. Obviously, translation is easy for me, but I've also become familiar with codebreaking and deciphering intelligence hidden in cocktail menus, political pamphlets, and even bus tickets.'

'Bus tickets!'

'I know. It's mad, isn't it? But information can be passed on anything.'

'So what did Vitali say?'

'Mum's the word, right?'

'Of course, darling.' Ottilie tapped the side of her nose.

'He's working with Mussolini who has thrown in his lot with Hitler. He spoke in coded words which I'm sure Moran is unaware I know. He thinks I'm a translator and nothing more. He is a sneaky individual, used to ducking and diving, as is Vitali. Vitali and Moran are working together. Groves doesn't know it yet, but he will tomorrow morning.'

'There is a mole in Westminster, Rose, passing on information directly to a German national. It's what Charles Wentworth was investigating. He had been chosen by Neville Chamberlain to smoke them out. We think the German national is a woman named Greta Deitz who was a cultural attaché in London before war was announced, but we're not certain. We're fairly sure the mole isn't Moran, and not Tebbit. It's definitely someone who is a Westminster employee; someone who can come and go without questions being asked. Any ideas?'

'I hate to say this Ottilie, but it could be anyone. I'm guessing Charles Wentworth knew who it was and it's why he was abducted. Discovering the mole will reveal the tentacles of how the information is being passed on. Once a collaborator has been discovered it would mean closing down the whole system and starting again. Whoever's leading the agents within Westminster and beyond will do everything they can to prevent it from happening. It has likely taken a long time to build the connections between the conspirators. I would say almost certainly it is why Charles Wentworth has been abducted.'

'Do you think he's still alive, Rose?'

'There's always a chance he's still alive. Don't forget, Wentworth has information about Britain too. The defectors will think him a valuable commodity and will get as much as they can from him before killing him.'

'Torture?' Ottilie asked in a small voice. Rose closed her eyes momentarily and simply nodded.

Chapter 28

'There's a telephone call for you downstairs, Miss Divine.'

Mrs Hudson had puffed her way up the stairs to deliver the message to Ottilie.

'Oh, Mrs Hudson, come in and sit down in my living room for a minute. Those stairs are getting too much for you. I'm wondering about having a telephone connected in my rooms.'

'Oh, there's no need, my dear. It's good exercise for me, isn't it? I don't get out much.'

'I'll run down and take the call, Mrs Hudson. You come down when you're ready.'

'All right, dear. Thank you.'

Ottilie ran down the stairs two at a time, leaving Mrs Hudson to rest, wondering who it was who was calling her so early in the day.

'Ottilie Divine,' she said into the receiver.

'Ottilie, it's Delia. Delia Wentworth. I need to see you.'

'Delia! Are you all right?'

'Yes, I'm all right, but I've received something in the post you need to see. I can't make head nor tail of it, but it was addressed to me. The envelope has a strange sign on the flap which I don't recognise. Can you come?'

'Yes, of course. I'll be there in an hour.'

After ending the call, Ottilie telephoned Jonah Walsh who she knew would already be at his desk.'

'What's happening, Miss Divine? I hadn't heard from you, and I was becoming concerned.'

'I'm all right, Mr Walsh. I had planned to come into the office today to reprise you of everything that had happened since our last conversation, but I've just had a rather urgent telephone call from Delia Wentworth. She said she needs to see me. She's received something in the post she can't read. I said I'd go there this morning.'

'All right, Miss Divine…then come into the office, will you?'

'Of course, Mr Walsh.'

'I hope you're journalling everything with regards to your assignment, Miss Divine. I'd also like an article from you, a general overview of why there has been no progress in the war.'

'I'm writing everything down, Mr Walsh. I'll write the article you want when I come into the office.'

'Fair enough.'

Ottilie sat patiently in Delia Wentworth's drawing room as she waited for her to get the letter she had received. Delia explained she had been so frightened of it she had locked it away in her husband's study. Ottilie understood. Delia had been patiently awaiting her husband's return for weeks to no avail, and had seemed vulnerable and shaky when she had answered the door to Ottilie.

She told Ottilie she would not allow her maid to answer the door to callers in case whoever sent the letter had plans to visit the house. She needed to see the callers for herself before she allowed anyone into the house, citing she was frightened for her children who had still not returned to their schools. Ottilie wondered at the wisdom of keeping them home for so long but said nothing.

Delia returned to the drawing room with a forced smile on her face, followed by a maid carrying a tray of tea things.

'I'm sure it's nothing, Ottilie, but it needed to be seen by someone, and you were the person who came first to mind. I expect you'll show it to your friend?'

Ottilie nodded as she took the envelope from Delia. 'If it's in code I've no doubt Sherlock Holmes will want to see it.' She opened the envelope where Delia had previously run a paper knife along it and pulled out a sheet of paper. Unfolding it she studied the contents. She scanned the page immediately recognising it for what it was….a coded message, written coldly like a business communique but was worded in such a way one could be quite clear of its intentions. Ottilie wasn't surprised Delia had been unnerved by it. It read…

Dear Mrs. Wentworth,

*You are no doubt experiencing the effects of your husband's disappearance. Unfortunately, our **business arrangement** has encountered some **unforeseen hindrances**. Those hindrances will certainly affect the timescale of your husband's planned return. May I suggest cutting all ties with those hindrances and allowing us to do what is important work which will benefit both the country and your husband.*

Please do not change the terms under which your husband was working. It will cause his conditions to become adverse to his well-being.

If you are unsure of the terms of this letter, may I suggest you refer to my previous correspondence where you will find an address to which you may reply. Certainly, if you wish to help your husband's cause and you have the means to do so we expect to hear from you.

As in all things utter discretion is paramount and certainly should not be disclosed to those hindrances who persist in threatening Charles Wentworth's life.

We hope to hear from you without delay.

A Well-wisher.

Ottilie glanced at Delia who had picked up the teapot to pour the tea, but whose hands were trembling to such a degree she had spilt the tea onto the tray.

'Delia, my dear. Please leave the tea. I will pour it when we have discussed the letter.'

'I'm not sure I want to discuss it,' said Delia, wringing her hands in front of her as she sat opposite Ottilie. 'I don't want anything to do with it. I know what it is, Ottilie. It's a threat, isn't it?'

'Did Charles receive anything like this before, Delia? The truth please. You won't help yourself, or Charles, by lying.'

'As I told you, Charles was discreet about his work, but well, there were one or two occasions when letters came through the door, he pushed into his briefcase without reading.'

'One…or two?'

'Three, actually. I never thought Charles would be afraid of anything, but he seemed to pale when they arrived. He took to making sure he was near the hall when the postman arrived so he could pick up the post himself. I don't think he wanted me to see the letters.'

Ottilie turned the envelope over and blanched at what she saw on the other side. It was the symbol for Das Eisenhand. She investigated the back of the envelope further. There was nothing on it but the emblem. She turned it over to look at the writing on the front. It was written in an attractive style, a cursive script with a slight lean to the right. Written by someone with a good education, she decided.

She examined the letter again. It was written to promote fear. The threat was clear. Tell us what you know…or else. Ottilie frowned. She turned the letter over in her hands a number of times, then took it to the window and held it to the light. She frowned again. There was a faint dent in the paper.

She recalled the day Sherlock Holmes had discovered she had visited Delia the first time. He had simply rubbed a lead pencil over the surface of the paper underneath the note she had made and had discovered Delia Wentworth's address. She reached into her bag for a pencil, then lightly rubbed it across the indentations. A series of numbers appeared.

'Oh, my goodness. They're coordinates. And there's a date and time. The 18th of November. Three o'clock.' She looked up at Delia with bright eyes. 'That's tomorrow.'

'Coordinates to where?'

Ottilie shook her head. 'I can't tell you, but I know someone who will. May I borrow your telephone?'

'Of course. It's in the hall.'

Ottilie dialled the number for the operator. When the operator answered Ottilie gave her the number for 221B Baker Street. To her delight Dr Watson answered.

'It's Ottilie.'

'Miss Divine, where are you? Holmes has at last cracked the code for the cryptic crossword you found under Westminster Bridge.'

'I'm glad to hear it, but Dr Watson I need you to find these coordinates. I'll explain everything later but it's important you and Mr Holmes do this now.'

'Right away, Miss Divine. Are you at the Express?'

'No, I'm at Delia Wentworth's. Mr Holmes has the number. Please work out the coordinates immediately. I'll wait for your call.'

She gave him the coordinates and replaced the receiver, sitting on the chair in the hall. She closed her eyes and leant back against the panelled wall. She was suddenly overwhelmed with tiredness. The previous weeks had been rather like sitting on a fairground ride which had no stop button. Her shock at discovering Rose was an intelligence officer had taken her breath away and she realised both she and Rose were keeping things about their work from their mothers. It couldn't be helped. If they discovered what they were involved in they would surely do their best to put a stop to it, even though she and Rose were fully grown women. She realised mothers never stopped worrying and nurturing. She could only wonder what it was like.

The telephone rang with a shrill bell, startling her out of her thoughts. She picked up the receiver, not without some excitement.

'Yes?'

'Mrs Wentworth. I understand you received my letter this morning.'

Ottilie froze. She tried to remain calm, swallowing hard before she answered. She had fully expected the call to be from John Watson. Taking a breath she pretended to be Delia Wentworth. 'Yes,' she answered. 'What do you mean by it?'

'We all must know where we stand. I have been informed one of the hindrances I mentioned is presently at your address.'

'My visitor is a friend.'

'More than a friend, Mrs Wentworth. She has been seen in the company of Sherlock Holmes who I understand is investigating your husband's disappearance.'

'Do you have him?'

'Who?'

'My husband.'

'We need something from you, Mrs Wentworth before we impart any information. Quid pro quo.'

'I'm afraid I don't know what you mean.' At that moment Delia joined Ottilie in the hall. Ottilie put a finger against her lips. 'What could I have you could possibly want? I don't know anything.'

'First of all, we suggest you stop passing information onto those who would hinder us. Second, your husband has a metal box in his possession. We would like it.'

'I know nothing about a box, or where Charles would have kept it if he had it.'

'Perhaps you should look in his study, Mrs Wentworth. I should hope you would leave it in better condition than the last time it was searched.'

'Will it save Charles?'

'It will help us find a more comfortable outcome for him.'

'Please don't hurt him.'

'I will be in contact, Mrs Wentworth. Good day.'

Ottilie replaced the receiver and closed her eyes. She opened them again to find Delia Wentworth watching her.

'Who was it?'

Ottilie put a finger to her lips again. 'You must leave this house, Delia,' she whispered.

Delia frowned. 'Why?'

'Because I believe you are in danger if you stay here. Is there anywhere you can go.'

Delia thought for a moment. 'I suppose I could go to the Shaws.'

'No,' cried Ottilie in a loud whisper. She shook her head. 'You can't go there.'

Delia frowned. 'Why ever not? They're our friends.' Ottilie raised her eyebrows and Delia blanched. 'You don't think so?'

'I'm afraid not. Obviously, I could be wrong, but if Holmes and I have read them correctly they might be exactly the people you should *not* go to.'

'My parents have a holiday home in Dorset.'

'Perfect. Go there and stay there until I contact you. You mustn't come home until we can be sure you are out of danger.'

'What about Charles? He might come home, and we won't be here.'

Ottilie blew out a breath. It was time for the truth. 'I don't think it's likely, Delia.'

Tears welled in Delia's eyes. 'You think he's dead, don't you?'

'Actually, I don't. I think he's being kept by someone who wants information from him.'

'When should we go?'

'Today. Pack a small valise and some things for the children. Don't take any risks. Get a cab to the station and go to Dorset by train.'

'How can I get hold of you?'

'You have both my numbers, Delia. Use them at any time.'

Delia nodded. 'All right.'

The telephone rang again and Ottilie answered it.

'Miss Divine. The line was engaged.'

'Don't worry, Dr Watson. I'm coming to you now.'

'Do you want this information before you leave.'

'All right.'

'It's Waterloo Station. The coordinates are for Waterloo Station.'

'Oh, my goodness,' cried Ottilie. 'Tick tock, tick tock. The answer lies beneath the clock.'

'I beg your pardon?'

'I'm on my way, Dr Watson. Tell Sherlock Holmes I'm on my way.'

Chapter 29

'Miss Divine. You must have flown here.'

Dr Watson opened the door to Sherlock Holmes's rooms, a frown crossing his face.

'I got a cab,' Ottilie said, rushing into the sitting room without being asked. 'And he was pretty fast. I used an Americanism… "step on it". And he did. I'll certainly remember it for next time.'

Sherlock Holmes rose from the desk which was covered in pieces of paper which had been cut into strips and then into squares. In the middle of it lay the crossword puzzle and the clues Ottilie and he found under Westminster Bridge.

'Was it a difficult one, Mr Holmes?' asked Ottilie, knowing he would never own up to something potentially defeating his intellect.

'Absolutely not, Miss Divine.' Ottilie glanced at Watson who hitched one corner of his mouth. 'I simply utilised my method for solving all cryptic crosswords. Of course, one must have a profound knowledge of words and how they can be used to divert. Once I'd set my mind to the solving of the crossword the technique prevailed.'

'I'm glad to hear it.'

'I understand Mrs Wentworth has received a contact. Who was it **from?'**

'Das Eisenhand. They sent her a letter.' She passed the letter to Holmes who read the text.

'And the coordinates?'

'I used your trick, Mr Holmes. I ran a lead pencil lightly over the paper and the coordinates and the date and time revealed themselves. Whatever is happening is set for three o'clock tomorrow afternoon at Waterloo Station.'

'How do you know it is from Das Eisenhand?'

'Their emblem is on the back of the envelope.' She passed the envelope to him. 'And if you remember, Mr Holmes, the message we found in the flute case. *"Time runs amok. Tick tock, tick tock. The answer lies beneath the clock."* Surely it is too much of a coincidence to be anywhere other than the clock at Waterloo Station for which we have found the coordinates and which I'm quite sure they did not mean us to find.'

'I agree,' said Holmes. Ottilie looked surprised. Holmes rarely agreed with anyone other than himself. 'We shall go there tomorrow afternoon at three of the clock.' He turned to Dr Watson. 'You will join us, Dr Watson?'

'I wouldn't miss it for the world, Holmes, although I must say one wonders what could possibly be found under a clock above a busy train station.'

'I was so excited when I used the trick Mr Holmes told me about…the pencil rubbed across the indentations. It's worked beautifully in this case.'

Sherlock Holmes sniffed. 'It is not a "trick", Miss Divine. It has been used for centuries as a way of passing on information, although obviously in some cases the writer of the original notes has not been aware of the indentations they leave in the page below. It is often used to discover the intentions of a person who is trying to hide information, rather than pass it on.'

Ottilie pursed her lips. 'I do beg your pardon.' Holmes made a small bow. 'What was the outcome of the crossword puzzle?'

'If you and Dr Watson will join me at my desk I will show you.'

He led them over to his desk and sat behind it.

'Here is the crossword puzzle, and here are the clues which were in the flute case along with it. The clues are thus. There are no numbers pertaining to the clues or the puzzle. One must construct a method with which to find the correct boxes for each word. It has taken some time I grant you, but once one finds the key it is relatively easy.' Ottilie picked up Holmes's notes and began to read.

Spy in the fog (3 letters) Answer: MIST ... (Double definition: "spy" as a verb meaning to see, and "fog")

Covers for the dead obscure secrets (7 letters) Answer: SHROUDS "Covers" refers to the definition of shrouds as something that conceals, and "for the dead" hints at burial shrouds. "Obscure secrets" also suggests hiding or covering something. (Double definition—both as burial coverings and as something that hides or conceals.)

Secretive by loyal (4 letters) Answer: TRUTH (Double meaning: faithful, concealed loyalty)

Organ at the centre of affection (5 letters) Answer: HEART (The heart is both a physical organ and metaphorically at the centre of love)

A quiet retreat in Paris (5 letters) Answer: ELOPE (Hidden word in "retreat in Paris": also means escape)

Key agent holds document (7 letters) Answer: DOSSIER (Key is DO, agent is

SIR, together hiding a document)

Code encrypted in scarlet message (6 letters) Answer: CIPHER ("encrypted code" and a possible, scarlet-themed twist hint)

Initials mark danger ahead (3 letters) Answer: SOS (common distress signal)

Hidden agent takes cover (5 letters) Answer: MOLES (Double meaning: "hidden agent" and burrowing creatures)

Operations concealed in layers (7 letters) Answer: MISSION ("Concealed" implies secrecy, layered task in espionage)

London district where Parliament meets in the west (10 letters) Answer: WESTMINSTER ("London district" gives the location. "Where Parliament meets in the west" confirms the location)

Loyal partners honestly support each other (10 letters) Answer: TRUE ALLIES ("loyal" suggests true. "Partners" hints at allies. "Honestly reinforces true")

Enemy spy taps into British intel (6 letters) Answer: ASSETS (Double meaning: "enemy spy" and valuable agents/information)

Escape with coded warning (5 letters) Answer: EVADE (Means "escape")

The traitor seen in cloak-and-dagger tale (6 letters) Answer: DOUBLE (Reference to a "double agent")

Solved the case but slightly broken (7 letters) Answer: CRACKED ("Solved the case" suggests cracking a mystery or code. "Slightly broken" hints at something being cracked or damaged).

Engagement that floods the field (8 letters) Answer: A WATERY BATTLE – ("Engagement" suggests a battle, and "floods the field" hints at water.)

Spot timepiece in sodden disguise. (13 letters) Answer: WATERLOO CLOCK – ("Spot means to notice or see. In sodden disguise hints at a clock in a place with water in the name. The famous clock at Waterloo Station.

Ottilie stared at Sherlock Holmes. 'I imagine you have already worked out what it means, Mr Holmes.'

'Yes, of course, but I'd like to see if you can "crack the code", Miss Divine.'

Ottilie took a pen from the Chinese brush pot on the desk and wrote the answers to the crossword clues on a notepad. They were jumbled, but within a few moments she had unjumbled them and revealed a message.

'Mist shrouds truth in the heart of Westminster. Mission to find mole. Elope to safety with dossier, cipher cracked. Evade double asset. A watery battle reveals the clock. True allies reveal danger… SOS.'

'Well done, Miss Divine,' cried Holmes. 'You did not find it too strenuous after all.' Ottilie rolled her eyes at Dr Watson who grinned. 'To be precise the message points a finger at someone who is the heart of Westminster. It alludes to the mission which was to discover the mole. There is a dossier. The cipher from the enemy has been cracked. There is a double agent who must be eluded. The said dossier is being held under the clock at Waterloo Station…the watery battle. Rather clever I must confess…worthy of one of my own cryptic crosswords.'

'You devise cryptic crosswords, Mr Holmes,' asked Ottilie, her eyes widening.

'I do, Miss Divine. It keeps my brain in fine form, and they take minutes to construct.' Ottilie shook her head and smiled.

'What happens now, Sherlock?' asked John Watson.

'We keep the appointment, my dear friend. It would seem there is a dossier to be relieved from he who currently holds it. The clues were left to send the enemy in the wrong direction, but we apprehended the flautist's case under Westminster Bridge before Moran and his cohorts could find it. I believe they were left there by Charles Wentworth before he was captured. I think he has been rather clever. A man after my own heart. I would be interested to meet him.' He turned to them. 'You see. Everything is as it should be.'

'As long as he's still alive,' said Ottilie, glumly.

'Oh, I think there is no doubt he is still alive, Miss Divine.'

'Why is there no doubt, Mr Holmes?'

Sherlock Holmes made for his wingchair by the fireplace, took up his pipe, and began to stuff it with tobacco. He lit a spill from the fire in the grate and touched it to the tobacco, puffing on the pipe until he was satisfied.

'There are some people in the world who are valuable to others, Miss Divine. Like myself, Charles Wentworth is one of them. He has a good brain, and his brain holds a good deal of information extremely valuable to our enemies. They will keep him indefinitely until they have exhausted all means of wringing the information from him.'

Ottilie winced. 'But surely it means they will torture him.'

'They may do, but if he is as determined as I think he is he will withstand it.'

Ottilie looked quickly at her watch.

'Oh, gosh. I'm supposed to be at the office at the Express. Mr Walsh is not going to be happy. He may want to torture *me*. I'm sorry, but I must fly.'

'I'll join you, Miss Divine,' said Watson. 'We'll get a cab from Baker Street.'

Ottilie frowned as they went down the stairs to the hall together.

'Do you have an appointment in Fleet Street, Dr Watson?'

'I thought I'd pop into Ye Olde Cheshire Cheese, buy a pint, find a discreet table...and listen.'

'I wish I could get away with doing it. Women are frowned upon in there. I was warned off when I started work at the Express.'

They found a cab quickly and settled into the back seat.

'Why did you want to be a reporter, Miss Divine? Most women from your society are happy to settle for a much more domesticated life.'

'I think it was because of what happened to my mother, Dr Watson. She was treated appallingly by her peers when my father asked her to leave Kenilworth House. She realised she had very few friends she could turn to. Those women who wanted to be in her circle when she was Lady Divine didn't want to know her when she was no longer mistress of Kenilworth House. She said it was a harsh lesson to learn at a time when she was at her lowest ebb.'

'I understand she did some rather successful investigating of her own.'

Ottilie chuckled. 'Indeed, she did. I was so very proud of her...and Cecily, her lady's maid. They weren't afraid of anything or anyone. She was determined not to be buckled by what society thought of her, or of the pigeonhole they tried to place her in.' Ottilie turned to him. 'It sowed a seed inside me, Dr Watson. From when she and my father parted she led

her own life on her terms.' She smiled at him. 'I intend to do the same.'

Chapter 30

Her article written and Mr Walsh patted down because of her late arrival, Ottilie left the Express and stepped into the darkness of another foggy evening. She thought about her conversation with Dr Watson and how gentle he had been when she talked about Camille.

He had heard of her of course; there weren't many people Ottilie spoke to who hadn't heard of her and her escapades as an amateur detective. She smiled to herself. She had always wanted to join her mother and Cecily, her loyal lady's maid, on their investigations, but Camille had always refused, even though Ottilie had been caught up in one or two by accident. She thought back to those times, then realised she was simply following in her mother's footsteps.

Looking into the shop windows reminded Ottilie Christmas was on the horizon. Windows had been beautifully decorated, a little early she thought, but knew it was to provide some cheer for the beleaguered inhabitants of London's streets who could think of nothing but war and when the first bombs would drop.

This is a strange war, Ottilie thought. There they all were with their boxes over their shoulders carrying their gas masks, something they could all do without at present, but too frightened to leave them at home for fear the day they left them behind would be the very day Hitler decided to drop his poisonous bombs. She sighed as she made her way to the underground.

The people around her seemed to be the same as they were before war was declared, but she knew in her heart they did not feel the same. They felt as she did…breath held almost for the duration…almost wishing for the war to start because the anticipation was so very awful.

Arriving in Baker Street she made her way to 221B, passing the café on the way to the front door. She backtracked and looked inside. There was Sherlock Holmes and Dr Watson speaking with Harold the café owner. She opened the door, the bell over it tinkling. They all looked up.

'Miss Divine,' said Dr Watson. 'We were just talking about you.'

'All good I hope,' she answered, her eyes going to Sherlock Holmes, whose facial expression gave nothing away.

'Of course, Miss Divine,' said Dr Watson, smiling affectionately. Ottilie returned his smile and sat at the table. 'Would you like tea?'

'Thank you, yes. And I'll take a cream cake for Mrs Hudson please, Harold.'

Harold smiled. 'I notice she's beginning to get quite stout, Miss Divine,' Harold said with a grin. 'I dare say it's due to all the cream cakes you take for her.'

Ottilie grinned. 'We all deserve a little treat sometimes, Harold. Anything to cheer us up in these dark days.' She turned to Sherlock Holmes. 'Don't you agree, Mr Holmes?'

He frowned. 'A treat, Miss Divine? You mean like a lapdog which craves treats from its master? 'No, I must say it has never been one of my habits to treat myself…or anyone else…with food. It is the path to destruction.'

Ottilie wanted to ask why but decided not to.

Back in Holmes's rooms, Ottilie thought he looked rather agitated. First he sat in his favourite chair, then went across to his desk, tut tutting as he went, then back to his chair by the fire where he knocked out his pipe. He picked up his violin as though to play it, examined it, and placed it back where he had found it. Dr Watson shook his head.

'Holmes, whatever is the matter, man? You're like a cat on a hot tin roof.'

'We must infiltrate Westminster,' said Holmes, a frown between his eyebrows. 'One of us must go there and be on the spot. This is the problem we have, don't you see? Events are happening away from our purview. Yes, we have tomorrow afternoon at Waterloo Station, but if we are thwarted there we must consider taking the next step.' He turned on his heel, enthusiastically into his subject now. 'In fact, it is something we should consider nonetheless.'

'And who will it be, Sherlock?' asked Watson. 'You and I are both well-known to the police who guard the house.'

Holmes turned to Ottilie. 'Then I venture to suggest it is Miss Divine who should inveigle her way into the House.'

'And how do I do that, Mr Holmes?'

'I will speak to one of my contacts there. You could pose as a secretary, or perhaps a cultural attaché. It will give you a chance to examine the department, filing cabinets, documentation, correspondence. Perhaps listen to conversations in the vicinity.'

'I think you're forgetting Deirdre Cheam knows who I am, Mr Holmes.

I have spoken to her, yes, and she gave me information, but I'm not totally sure of her loyalty. She could be involved.'

Holmes nodded. 'A chance we should take, however.'

'A chance *I* should take, you mean.'

'We will be in the vicinity, Miss Divine….I promise you. You will not technically be alone. I have yet to be turned away from the Houses of Parliament.' Ottilie blew out a breath and nodded. 'You accept?'

'Do I have a choice?'

'Everyone has a choice, Miss Divine,' said Dr Watson. 'If you feel you would rather not put yourself in any position you have the right to say so.' He glanced at Holmes, waiting for him to agree.

'Of course, Miss Divine,' said Holmes reluctantly, bowing his head once. 'It is your choice of course.'

'Perhaps we should wait and see what happens tomorrow afternoon,' answered Ottilie, praying they would get the information they needed so she would not need to go into Westminster.'

'A good idea,' said Dr Watson. 'We should not make plans too far in advance. Who knows what might happen.'

Chapter 31

The following morning seemed to drag as far as Ottilie was concerned. She had arrived at the Express office early, wanting Jonah Walsh to notice her there. The previous day he had reminded her of where her office was and she had reluctantly admitted she had spent many of her working hours away from it, but assured him it was all in a good cause. He had raised his eyebrows and pushed his glasses up to his forehead.

'Yet I have no evidence of it, Miss Divine. Perhaps I should take a look at your journal to see what you've been up to.' Ottilie had been happy to provide it. She had logged everything that had happened since she'd been given the special assignment. Walsh's eyes had widened at the situations she had found herself in.

'Are we any closer to discovering what happened to Charles Wentworth?' he asked her.

'I believe so, sir,' she said. 'I am assured by Sherlock Holmes we are just a few steps away from the perpetrator, but as you see from my journal this story is not just about Wentworth. There is a mole at Westminster,' she said sotto voce. 'And we think it has everything to do with Charles Wentworth's abduction…for he *has* been abducted. There is no doubt of it.'

'And you think it's this…mole?'

'We think the mole has been passing on information to a German national who was close to Charles before war was announced. It is likely information is still getting through.' Walsh nodded. 'And this afternoon I have an appointment at Waterloo Station.' She pointed to the journal. 'It is all there in my journal. We are quite sure whatever happens at Waterloo Station will be significant.' Walsh nodded again. 'Is it dangerous?'

Ottilie considered her answer. Should she play it down or should she be truthful about the dangers she was likely to confront.

'Yes, Mr Walsh.'

He narrowed his eyes. 'How dangerous are we talking, Miss Divine?'

'I think there could be guns involved. I've already been shot at. Someone took a potshot at me outside my flat in Baker Street. It's all there in my journal.'

Walsh bit his lip. 'I could prevent you from going…take you off the assignment. I'm not happy with how serious this has become. Your parents…if anything happened to you it is me they would blame.' He smiled at her. 'Perhaps you're too good at investigative reporting, Miss Divine.'

She returned his smile. 'I'll take it as a compliment…but I must see it to the end. We are close to a conclusion, Mr Walsh. We are definitely close.'

Ottilie, Sherlock Holmes, and Dr Watson stepped onto the main concourse of Waterloo Station. It was noisy with the chatter of many travellers, the steam engines releasing the vapour from the engines out onto the tracks which engulfed the men working on them.

Overhead, the roof loomed over them, the glass and iron suspended above their heads. In the centre was the clock. *The* clock, the famous clock which had been in Ottilie's thoughts since she had rubbed the pencil over the letter sent to Delia Wentworth and had found the coordination and the date and time of whatever the afternoon would produce.

Ottilie had become increasingly nervous about what could happen at the station, particularly after her discussion with Jonah Walsh. He had mentioned Camille and Richard, and her stomach had rolled at the thought of them grieving should anything untoward happen to her. It had brought her up sharp, reminded her of who she really was, a reporter with a newspaper who wanted to discover the truth.

Working alongside Sherlock Holmes had changed everything. She had found a different perspective, had begun to think like he did. Was it necessary for her to do so to become a successful investigative reporter? Was she tough enough to withstand what could come her way? She was in so deep, immersed within Holmes's world she wondered if she would ever come to the surface.

They made their way to the part of the station underneath the clock where passengers gathered before boarding their trains. It was too crowded for Ottilie to see if there was anyone waiting there. In front of her were men, women, and children, some waiting to board the trains to be evacuated to the countryside. The children had name tags tied around their necks and were holding small cases, with their favourite toys, Ottilie hoped. Her heart sank.

There were tears from the children and parents alike. How must it have felt to say goodbye to one's beloved child, to send them off into the hands of people they did not know, who might not have been suitable as parents for the children they had worked hard to raise. Ottilie swallowed back her tears. This was the price they were paying for a war they did not want. She could only pray they were going to safety. The children's safety was paramount.

As the crowd cleared, and she and the others got closer to where the clock hung over the station, she could see someone waiting. A woman. When she saw who it was, she gasped.

'Oh, no! Oh, no, but it can't be.'

'What is it, Miss Divine?' asked Dr Watson.

'Delia Wentworth.' She turned to Watson. 'She was supposed to go to Dorset...take the children with her. A secure place for her and the children. Why is she not there?'

Delia Wentworth stood underneath the clock. Her face was pale. She looked close to tears. Ottilie, Sherlock Holmes, and Dr Watson approached her guardedly. She held a battered briefcase in her hand and she looked about her, searching for someone. Ottilie was the first to speak.

'Delia?'

She saw Delia swallow, although a flash of relief flashed across her face. 'Oh, Ottilie. No...you must go...go away from here.'

'Delia, what are you doing here? I thought you were going to take the children to Dorset.'

'When you left someone came...a man. He would not leave. He said he and his friends were holding Charles and if I didn't do as they said I would never see him again.' She burst into tears. 'A woman came and took the children. They threatened me. Said the children would be sent away if I didn't cooperate.'

'What?'

'Delia nodded. 'I have to give this to someone...not you, Ottilie, and not your friends. The man is here, Ottilie. At the station. He's watching me to make sure I don't run. You need to get away. I don't know who he is. He never gave me a name.'

Holmes, who had been listening, suddenly grabbed Delia's arm.

'You must run, dear lady.'

'But the children,' cried Delia. 'I cannot leave the children with these people. Who knows what they will do to them.'

Holmes dipped his hand into his pocket and inclined his head towards Watson who did the same.

'Run, ladies. Run as far as you can. We are being watched.'

Ottilie looked across to where Holmes was looking. A large man wearing a long army great coat and a bowler hat stood in front of one of the trains, steam impairing their view of him. Ottilie grabbed Delia's arm and pulled her towards the exit. As they ran the man sprang at them.

As he tried to grasp Ottilie's arm he pulled a pistol from his coat and pointed it at them. Delia screamed and Ottilie ducked, still running towards the exit. She had the sleeve of Delia's coat in her hand, and she tightened her grip, determined not to release it.

The sound of gunshots ripped the air. The chatter subsided to be replaced by screams from the waiting women and children, the fathers dragging them away from the platforms.

As Ottilie and Delia ran, Ottilie was aware of someone close behind them. She wove through the people at the exit, dodging startled porters as she pushed by them, too out of breath to apologise. She could feel the man gaining on them. He had a gun, and she knew if they stopped or were held up by passengers he would shoot.

Delia was fast getting out of breath and Ottilie was terrified she would need to stop.

'Not long, Delia,' she puffed. 'We're nearly there.'

'I can't....' puffed Delia. 'Ottilie...I need to stop.'

'Not yet, we're nearly there. Please, Delia don't stop. He'll kill us.'

Delia burst into tears. 'I don't care.'

Ottilie pulled her even harder. 'Yes, you bloody well do.'

They ran on until they reached the main entrance where travellers were still coming into the station.

'We're here,' cried Ottilie. 'It's the Victory Arch. We're here.'

She pulled Delia out of the entrance, down some steps and onto York Road. A bus pulled in at the kerb just as they got to the pavement. Ottilie pushed past the people getting off the bus who tutted and made comments about "the rude young today" and "wait until they have to fight a bloody war". She pulled Delia up the stairs to the top deck where she pushed her into a seat. Ottilie dragged Delia to the floor so they could not be seen by the agent through the windows.

'Not long now, Delia,' she said between gasps. Delia couldn't reply. She was breathing heavily and retching into a handkerchief.

Ottilie peeked out of the window at the top of the bus. The agent in the long coat and bowler hat had pocketed his gun and was looking up and down the street. When he realised he had lost them he scowled, then turned on his heel and went back under the Victory Arch into Waterloo Station. Ottilie lay back on the seat, her eyes closed, her breathing finally slowing. Delia leant her head against Ottilie's arm.

'Is he gone?' The bus driver started the engine, and the bus began to move off down York Road, leaving Waterloo Station and their adversary behind.

'He went back into the station. I hope Holmes and Watson deal with him.'

'What happens if they don't.' Delia sat up in her seat and stared at Ottilie. 'I hope they kill him.'

Ottilie pressed her lips together. 'They might. Do you have the briefcase?' Delia held it up and Ottilie nodded. 'Well done, Delia. You were very brave.'

Delia made a slight chuckle. 'No, I wasn't. I was ready to give up. I would have if you hadn't been with me.'

'We'll go back to Baker Street. You can stay with me in my rooms until we find out what the next step is…and of course what those documents are in the briefcase.'

'Are they important?' asked Delia. 'They told me they would shoot me on the spot if I even tried to get a glimpse of them.'

'They were meant for someone else, Delia. And I think I know who. And in answer to your question…yes, they are extremely important.' She sighed, her lips hitching into a smile as she looked out of the window. 'I think this is where the tables turn.'

Holmes and Watson positioned themselves by the exit. They had to believe Ottilie and Delia would get away and the agent would return to the station, perhaps to meet up with one of his cohorts.

'Can we hold him?' asked Dr Watson. 'The station is running with police. If we could grab him, we could have him arrested, then call Lestrade.'

'My thoughts exactly, dear Watson. We are thinking alike today. An unusual occurrence I grant you. It all hinges on whether Miss Divine and

Mrs Wentworth were able to shake him off.'

They waited by the florist's kiosk, obscured by foliage, their eyes trained on the entrance to the main concourse. Patience was not Holmes's most obvious quality, and he persisted in tutting and sighing which made Watson shake his head with weariness at his friend, although he did it with a wry smile.

A whistle shrieked as a train was about to leave the station. Passengers had begun to drift back onto the concourse when they realised the danger was over and the police were present at the station.

Suddenly, Holmes darted out of his hiding place moving at astonishing speed and launched himself at a man who buckled under him. The man's bowler hat fell from his head and rolled into the crowd.

'Get off me, Sherlock Holmes,' the man shrieked. He threw out a fist in an attempt to connect with Holmes's face, but missed, catching his shoulder in the attempt. Dr Watson ran over to the two fighting men and grabbed the man's arm, pushing it up his back.

'It's all right, Holmes,' he said. 'I've got him.' He pushed his knee into the man's back which disabled him, making him shriek even louder in pain. Two policemen ran across to them, and when Sherlock Holmes told them who he was and the man they had pulled down was an enemy agent they pulled out a pair of handcuffs and put them on the man's wrist.

'What's your name, sir?' one of the constables asked him.

The man turned and sneered at him. 'You'll never know,' he said, showing his teeth.

'We'll see about that,' said the constable, who with his colleague, hauled him off.

'Inspector Lestrade will know soon enough,' said Holmes, 'as will Chief Inspector Owen. They have someone now, as well as Tebbit.'

'Who do you think will break first?' asked Watson.

'Tebbit. He's already broken, Watson. It was why he took a shotgun to the Nightingale Club. My guess is he didn't want to go to Italy because he knew he would be in the clutches of Vitali and Moran and made to do what they wanted.'

They began to walk towards the Victory Arch entrance.

'And who was it who pushed his way into Tebbit's office do you think, and why?'

'As soon as they discovered Tebbit was to be seconded to Italy, they made him a target. Mussolini and Hitler are singing from the same song sheet and aligned in their beliefs. Tebbit would have made the perfect go between…the mole here, and Tebbit in Italy, which means Das Eisenhand would have agents in both places. All they would need now is one in France when the war gets started.' He glanced at Watson, knowing he would be delivering a shock. 'And the man who forced his way into Tebbit's office was none other than Moriarty.'

Watson's mouth dropped open. 'You think he's involved?'

'Involved?' Sherlock Holmes chuckled. 'He is the instigator, my dear Watson. It is quite elementary. If the government is to be brought down, if Britain is to lose its sovereignty, it is Moriarty who will make sure it happens…at least…he will do whatever it takes to see he is on the right side, the side who will pay him the most money and push him to the highest status.'

'You think it's the Third Reich who will do it?'

'Of course. Hitler wants to rule the world, and it is likely Moriarty has already made many promises to him. Britain simply wants to retain its independence, control over its dominion. It's not enough for Moriarty. One little island does not suit his ambition. If Hitler is to rule the world

Moriarty will want to be right there with him.'

'Do you think the Third Reich know how devious Moriarty is?'

Sherlock Holmes pulled a slight hitch of the right side of his mouth which Watson determined could have been a smile.

'I doubt it…in fact I would strongly suggest they do not know the man and what he is capable of.' He sniffed and nodded. 'In fact, Watson, I'm counting on it.

Chapter 32

Ottilie took Delia to her flat in Baker Street. The bus they had leapt on to had been a blessing in disguise. It took them from Waterloo Station, across Westminster Bridge and onto St Pancras where they alighted and found a taxicab to take them to Baker Street. Once there they kicked off their shoes and fell onto the settee.

'I need a cup of tea,' said Ottilie. 'Why do we always turn to tea I wonder?'

'I have no idea,' answered Delia, 'but I couldn't think of anything better at the moment.'

Ottilie made tea. When it was made and each of them held a hot cup of everyone's favourite beverage in their hands, Ottilie walked to the window and peered out onto Baker Street.

'It's getting dark,' she sighed. 'I do hope Holmes and Watson are all right. I can't imagine them letting the man get the better of them, particularly Holmes. It would be something he wouldn't want to admit to.'

'Do you like him?' asked Delia.

Ottilie laughed. 'Hmm, not a question I can answer.' She turned to Delia, her head on one side. 'I'm not sure Holmes is someone one likes…more someone one admires for his intellect.' She shrugged. 'He would much prefer it anyway. He does rather insist his prowess as a consulting detective to be admired. I'm almost sure he would never admit to liking anyone so wouldn't expect to be liked in return.'

Delia frowned. 'But what about Dr Watson. They've always been friends have they not?'

Ottilie nodded. 'I believe so.'

'But he is his only friend.'

'They don't call each other friends,' replied Ottilie. 'They're colleagues.' She nodded. 'I must admit it's a strange relationship.'

'Dr Watson is an attractive man.'

'And very kind.'

'Kindness in a man is so important. It's why I adore Charles. He is kindness personified.' She put her face in her hands and wept. 'And now they have my children.' She looked up at Ottilie, her face streaming with tears. 'Will I ever see them again?'

Ottilie left her place by the window and sat next to Delia on the settee, a look of concern crossing her face.

'Yes, yes you will. We are getting closer…much closer. We were too many steps behind the infiltrators but the nearer we get to them the easier it will be to discover where the children have been taken.' She indicated the briefcase. 'What is in the briefcase is clearly of great importance and wasn't meant for us, but I think I know who should have met you under the clock.'

Delia nodded; her face still wet. Ottilie passed her a handkerchief which Delia took with thanks and wiped her face. 'Who?'

'There was a woman standing by the newsagent's stall, watching everything. It was when we were running through the exit that I spotted her. She was hard to miss; tall, wearing a jet-black coat cut to fit, and a Forest Green hat with a half-veil. I couldn't help noticing her because they are the colours of Das Eisenhand. She is clearly one of them and I wondered afterwards if she was Greta Deitz.'

'Greta Deitz? Who is she?'

'A German cultural attaché who Charles liaised with when he was in Germany, and who also travelled here, apparently to smooth the relationship between Britain and Germany.'

'Huh, well, she didn't do a very good job.'

'No, but I don't think she was meant to. Rather, I think she is playing a double game...pretending to be a friend to the British while at the same time stealing our secrets.'

Delia shook her head. 'What have we got ourselves into?'

'I must confess I've wondered about it a few times myself.'

A knock on the door startled them.

'Gosh, I hope it's them,' said Ottilie. She sprang up from the settee and pulled the front door open a little. 'Thank goodness,' she cried. 'We were wondering what had happened to you. Did he get away?'

Sherlock Holmes looked miffed. 'No, Miss Divine, of course not. We caught him, and he has been taken to Scotland Yard for questioning.'

'So, with him, and Lawrence Tebbit...they should discover some information, don't you think?'

'One would hope so. I'm sure your stepfather has his own well-cultivated techniques to get information out of suspects.' Ottilie nodded. 'So...dear ladies. The briefcase. It was of course not meant for us. I noticed a tall woman standing by the newsagent's kiosk. It was meant for her I'm sure of it. She did not flinch when shots were heard on the platform...a woman with a good deal of experience in that area, I shouldn't wonder.'

'I saw her too,' said Ottilie. 'It wouldn't surprise me if it was Greta Deitz.'

Sherlock Holmes bowed his head. 'My thoughts entirely.'

Dr Watson stepped around Sherlock Holmes and sat next to Delia

Wentworth.

'Mrs Wentworth. Are you holding up?'

'Only just, Dr Watson.' She closed her eyes and shook her head. 'I must get my family back. I would do anything.'

'Never fear, dear lady,' said Holmes in a loud voice. 'Watson and I are singular in our investigations. We never fail and we shall not on this occasion. Have faith in us, do. We will not let you down.'

'Would you like to lie down, Delia?' Ottilie asked her. 'The bedroom is just through there.' Delia nodded and rose from the settee. She glanced at Holmes with reddened eyes.

'Please find them, Mr Holmes. There will be nothing left for me otherwise.' Sherlock Holmes looked towards her with his heavy-lidded eyes and nodded sagely. Delia made a small nod and made for Ottilie's bedroom.

'The briefcase, Miss Divine,' said Holmes, pointing to the case which Delia had left on the settee.

Ottilie picked up the briefcase and took it over to the kitchen table where she opened it and pulled out the contents. She spread the papers, maps, and diagrams across the table and stepped back. Holmes and Watson stepped nearer the table and began to peruse the contents.

'Mm,' muttered Holmes. 'As I thought…in code.' He sniffed. 'No matter. We will eventually crack the code. It may take some time but I'm sure we will prevail.'

'Rose cracks codes in her work, Mr Holmes,' said Ottilie. She was careful how she worded her suggestion. 'I'm fully aware you are capable of working out which code has been used, but as you say, it may take some time. Do you think it would be a good idea to invite Rose here? She may be able to help us.' Ottilie glanced across to Watson who was wincing.

Sherlock Holmes lifted his chin, his eyes on the ceiling as though deep in thought. 'Rose?…Rose? Your friend, Miss Fortesque-Wallsey?'

'Yes, Mr Holmes.'

He nodded then brought his attention back to the papers. 'Contact her, do. It would be fortuitous for this consultative detective to have the solution to the code forthwith.'

Ottilie ran down the stairs to the telephone in the hall and rang Rose.

'Can you come, darling? We need your skills.'

Within the half hour Rose arrived, driven by Nathanial Fortesque-Wallsey who had suggested Rose for the secret services the government undertook. Ottilie opened the door on Rose's arrival at the flat with some relief. *Another woman. Thank goodness*, she thought.

'Come in, Miss Fortesque-Wallsey,' cried Sherlock Holmes. We have need of your talents this evening.'

Rose nodded and went across to the table. She fished in her bag for her spectacles, then after fastening them on her nose picked up one of the sheets of paper. And read aloud…

'Agent HAND8 aligns transference in fog. Evade central paths; danger at midnight. MISSION compromised by inhibitors. Safehouse over river. Any evening, any day do the walk. Move contraband. Don't dilly dally.'

'What do you make of it, Rose?' Ottilie asked her.

Rose pulled up a kitchen chair and sat at the table, her eyes fixed on the clue.

'Well, Agent HAND8 would seem to refer to an operative codename "HAND", although it says HAND8 which can only mean they call all their agents HAND with given numbers. Fog…or mist could very likely mean somewhere where the fog is always at its thickest which would be an embankment, a bridge, somewhere near the river, so I think we can assume the place they allude to is The Thames.'

She pushed her glasses up her nose and hunched her shoulders in concentration.

'Avoid central paths.' She looked up at the three of them standing around her. 'It would usually mean no direct approaches to the location. There could be surveillance, or ambush points.' She glanced at the sheet again. 'Mission compromised.' She chuckled. 'They are probably referring to the three of you who have been trying to thwart their mission to get classified secrets. Safehouse over river.' She shrugged. 'It depends where they're situated, but if as you say the mole is ensconced at Westminster, then over the river would mean south of the river, across one of the bridges.' She grinned. 'Ah, they've forgotten how embroiled and proud we Londoners are in our history. "Any evening any day. Do the walk.' She shook her head and chuckled. 'They're referring to the song, the Lambeth Walk. Mr Holmes, I do believe you must go to Lambeth.' She began to sing. *'Any time you're Lambeth Way, Any evening any day.'* Do you recall it? It was in the musical, "Me and My Girl" a couple of years ago. And northerly over 50 and westerly not quite 12 months, refers I would imagine, to the map coordinates. Perhaps you could look them up. And move contraband means move whatever, or whoever, they've got locked up there. They even use the term "don't dilly dally", another line from a song. I suppose it means get on with it.'

'Yes,' replied Dr Watson, nodding. 'I took a young lady to see Me and My Girl.'

Sherlock Holmes stared at him. 'A young lady, Watson? When did this occur?'

'When it first opened at the theatre. She's a friend of my sisters and she wanted to see it but didn't have a beau to take her.'

'So *you* did?'

'Why, yes.' Dr Watson looked perplexed. Ottilie decided to step in before the conversation between Holmes and Watson went any further.

'So what is the result, Rose?'

Rose began to scribble feverishly on a clean sheet of notepaper passed to her by Dr Watson. She sighed when she had finished and held it up in front of her.

'Here we are. Agent HAND8 organises handover in the mist…meaning somewhere near The River Thames. Avoid central paths, meaning the area could be overlooked by those surveying it. Mission compromised, referring to Sherlock Holmes, Dr Watson, and Ottilie. Safehouse over the river. Meaning it's likely to be south of the river, which is confirmed by any evening, any day, do the walk, which means Lambeth. And the coordinates are,' Ottilie handed her a map of London, '51.4950° N, 0.1232° W.

'There we are. All is clear. You must make your way to Lambeth Bridge. There are all kinds of storage buildings there, warehouses, and such like. I can only assume it is where they're hiding the so-called contraband.' She pulled a face. 'I would say haste is the order of the day.'

Chapter 33

'When should we go to Lambeth, Mr Holmes?' Ottilie asked. 'It would seem time is of the essence.'

'Indeed.' He nodded to himself. 'I would agree, Miss Divine.' He pulled himself up and took a breath. 'There is no time like the present. I am concerned I must confess. As the other side knows we have got the briefcase they will move the so-called contraband tonight. We must pre-empt their plan. If, as I suspect, the contraband is Charles Wentworth and his children, dilly dallying will not help us.' He turned to Ottilie. 'Miss Divine, you and Miss Fortesque-Wallsey need not accompany Watson and myself. The going will be difficult and dangerous, not the place for a lady.'

Ottilie narrowed her eyes and lifted her chin.

'Thank you for your concern, Mr Holmes, but I intend to see the investigation through to the end. Should, as you say, the contraband turns out to be Charles Wentworth and his children it is irrefutable the children will need a female presence. Apart from which I believe it is a decision to be made by myself and Rose...Miss Fortesque-Wallsey.

'I have been shot at more than once during this investigation, searched for clues under Westminster Bridge in the dead of night during blackout, and dealt with my editor Jonah Walsh, who is becoming increasingly cantankerous at my lack of presence at the Daily Express offices. I rather think I have earnt my place when the threads of this investigation are untangled, and your permission is something I am not seeking.'

The room went quiet. Dr Watson glanced across to Sherlock Holmes then to Ottilie and Rose. He knew Holmes had never been challenged in such a determined way in the past, particularly by a woman, and he wondered what the outcome would be.

Holmes drew in a breath then turned to Ottilie; his expression impassive.

'You are right, of course, Miss Divine. I was simply concerned for your safety. However, you seem determined to join Watson and myself on our foray to Lambeth, and your presence, and that of Miss Fortesque Wallsey, will be of great benefit, I'm sure.' He turned to Watson who nodded his approval, then turned again to Ottilie. 'Please be ready within the half hour. Sturdy boots and heavy coats will facilitate a more comfortable journey for you both.'

He picked up his coat, took his hat from the hat stand, and left the flat. Watson raised an eyebrow at Ottilie and grinned.

'You have a way with words, Miss Divine...and a determined countenance. Holmes rarely capitulates, but I truly think he was concerned for your safety. On more than one occasion he has suggested this particular enquiry is rather a baptism by fire for you, as you are a novice investigative reporter.'

Ottilie closed her eyes momentarily then slowly lowered herself onto the settee.

'It was a bit strong, wasn't it? The trouble is he has a way of bringing out the fighter in me. Why did he not explain it...said what you've just said.' She put her head in her hands. 'Perhaps we shouldn't come.'

'Ottilie,' cried Rose. 'Don't be silly. You have a point. This is your investigation. You were at the beginning of it. Of course you want to be there at the end. Who wouldn't?' Rose sat next to Ottilie and put an arm around her shoulders. 'It is only right you go, Ottilie. Your job is on the line. Mr Walsh wants the ending, doesn't he? He'll expect you to write the full story. How can you do it if you're not there?'

Ottilie took her hands from her face and leant against the back of the settee. 'Oh, God. Why does everything have to be so difficult?'

Watson chuckled. 'Holmes is already thinking about something else entirely, I can assure you, Miss Divine. His thoughts will no doubt be concentrated on what will happen this evening and what he can do to bring about a successful outcome. Don't upset yourself unduly.'

They took a cab from Baker Street to Lambeth. Unlike before war had been announced it was not an enjoyable journey. Everywhere was in darkness…no lights shone from the diamond-paned windows of the Houses of Parliament, there were no lights shining from the boats moored on the banks of the river. Shops had closed down their window displays even though it was close to the festive period. Usually, fairies, goblins, elves, Father Christmas would have been seen in all of London larger stores.

'You're lucky to 'ave got me, ladies and gents,' the driver called from his cab. 'I was just goin' orf. Don't get much business in the evenin's now, well not 'til the weekends any'ow when the toffs go dancin'. Will yer want ter come back again?'

They looked at each other. It was something they hadn't thought of.

'No, thank you, my good man,' said Sherlock. 'We'll hopefully have other methods of returning.' Ottilie and Rose looked at one another. They wondered what Holmes meant, but neither wanted to ask him.

They arrived at Lambeth Bridge, an undeniably recognisable structure even in the darkness, and left the cab. Dr Watson paid the fare as the others looked at the area and surveyed their surroundings. They had asked the driver to allow them out of the cab some way from the warehouses. If they were under surveillance the last thing they wanted was to be observed.

Ottilie and Rose gingerly walked across the cobbles underfoot, slick with damp and puddles of oil. River water from the Thames slapped against the wooden planks fixed against the bank to stop erosion. The smell was suffocating, oil, the pungent odour of wet wood, and the overwhelming detritus from the Thames. Ottilie shook her head at the unsavoury conditions, and Rose covered her mouth with a gloved hand and tried not to breathe too deeply.

A fog, dense and carrying with it the smells of the surroundings lingered like odorous ribbons around the buildings; pungent air from nearby factories, wet rope, and whatever cargo was stored on the boats moored in the sludge wafted around them. In centuries past it was thought all illnesses known to man were borne in the miasma coming from the river. Ottilie could understand why they would think so. The awful smell was completely overpowering.

Warehouses loomed ahead of them, so darkened by soot and pollution the names of the companies using them could not be seen. The buildings blended perfectly with the darkness surrounding them.

'We should find a hiding place,' said Holmes, sotto voce, 'and keep watch for any movement. When we are sure the coast is clear we will make our move and search the warehouses.'

'How will we gain entry?' asked Ottilie. 'They're bound to be locked.'

Holmes produced four sets of lock picks, handing a set to each of them. 'They will do the trick,' he said. 'One of those picks will afford you entry. If the warehouse is not locked do not enter but find us. It may mean there are others already here. It would be strange if a company left its warehouse unlocked. The darkness pervading our country at night is the perfect cover for burglars and footpads.'

They made their way to a loading bay where myriad crates and barrels had been left bereft of cargo, stacked high, and the perfect cover for them until they decided to make their move. There was no sound…only the constant slapping of the water against the wooden sleepers lining the banks. In front of them was a barge moored at the banks by long, smelly ropes and covered by a large tarpaulin. An unstable-looking walkway led to it from the cobbled bank. It was eerie. The quiet adding to the unnerving atmosphere. Ottilie shivered and grabbed Rose's arm.

'I know,' whispered Rose. 'Gosh, it's very spine-chilling.'

'Would you have come if you'd known,' Ottilie asked her, her eyes shining in the darkness.

Rose squeezed Ottilie's hand. 'Yes, of course,' she whispered.

They stayed hidden for an hour. Ottilie and Rose had given up on squatting…it was too hard on their knees, and were sitting on the filthy cobbles, the damp edging nearer and nearer to their skin through their clothes. They leant against one another for comfort and warmth and said nothing, waiting for Sherlock Holmes to give the sign they could move.

'We've waited long enough,' said Holmes, eventually, much to Ottilie and Rose's relief. 'We can move now. I feel quite certain there is no one currently observing the warehouses.' He nodded to them. 'Each take a warehouse…ladies, the nearest ones to us. If it is locked use your lockpicks…if not signal to us. We will join you. We may need to go forward in numbers.'

Rose blew out a breath. Numbers? There were four of them. She raised her eyebrows yet began to move forward, crouched down and ran gingerly towards the nearest warehouse. Ottilie followed her, making for the next warehouse along the bank.

The warehouses were brick built with large arched entrances with iron doors. When she reached the doors Ottilie looked to her left to see Rose trying her set of lockpicks in the padlock keeping the doors to her warehouse locked. Rose was frowning. Ottilie wondered why. She heard a dull scraping sound, then watched as Rose opened the door. Ottilie held her breath. She loved her friend and hoped she had not dragged her into danger.

She lifted the padlock away from the door to her warehouse and began to try the lockpicks. Eventually one clicked and she swiftly undid the padlock and pulled it out of the metal loop. She took a breath, wondering what she would find inside.

As expected, the air was musty and fetid; the smells of the river permeating the atmosphere. She took a tiny flashlight from her coat pocket and trained it on the back of the warehouse. The ceiling was incredibly high, the buildings were large and voluminous, with room for multiple stacks of crates and barrels.

The walls were covered in soot and Ottilie wondered if she should have worn her gasmask to protect herself from the miasma captured within the warehouse's walls. The ceiling was supported by huge wooden pillars, some wrapped in thick rope which dripped water coming in from gaps in the metal roof. Cargo hoists and rope pulleys hung from the huge wooden rafters.

There were hessian sacks with coal spilling onto the floor, some were tied at the top with rope. On the floor were lumps of coal, spillages of flour and wheat. There were metal barrels with strange labels, some with cryptic markings. Ottilie assumed they contained fuel or chemicals. This unpleasant, evil-smelling place was a criminal's dream.

The only sounds were the scraping of scurrying rats disappearing into the walls, and the plink-plink-plink of dripping water. There was no sign of any human presence. Ottilie was satisfied Charles Wentworth and his children were not being held in the warehouse.

Pushing the padlock together to secure the warehouse she glanced across to the left where the last she'd seen of Rose was as she'd opened the doors to the warehouse. She frowned. The doors were closed but there was no sign of her.

She looked to her other side and spotted Sherlock Holmes padlocking the warehouse he had searched. He looked across at her and she beckoned him. She heard him say "Watson" and Dr Watson appeared by his side. There were two more warehouses left to be searched but Ottilie had an uncomfortable feeling they had found their quarry. Holmes and Watson joined her at the door to the warehouse.

'Rose went in there,' she whispered, indicating the warehouse, 'but I haven't seen her since. She would have finished searching the warehouse about the same time as I finished searching mine, yet there's no sign of her.' Holmes nodded, then lifted his chin to survey the warehouse from under his heavy-lidded eyes. Watson put a finger to his lips. Holmes was strategizing and he must have no interruptions.

Unexpectedly, the door to the warehouse creaked open. Holmes, Ottilie, and Dr Watson moved quickly into the gap at the side. Holmes took in a deep breath then narrowed his eyes. He flattened himself against the wall of the warehouse then peeped around the corner. He swiftly pulled his head back and nodded.

'This is the place,' he whispered. 'There is a guard standing outside. Watson, Miss Divine, make your way around the back of the warehouse and secrete yourselves on the other side. We need a pincer movement to remove the guard so we can get inside.'

Both Ottilie and Dr Watson nodded and quietly moved behind the warehouse and made their way to the other side where they hid out of sight. Just as Holmes was about to give the signal for them to move the warehouse, the door opened again, and another man joined the first.

'Otto, what are you doing here?'

'I'm having a smoke. We've been waiting for those knuckleheads for hours. They will not come. They do not have the faintest clue we are here, nor the intelligence to work it out from the papers they stole. We are in no danger.'

'We can't be sure…and you should not be smoking here. There is oil and petrol in these barrels. They could go up in an instant.'

Otto sounded aggrieved. 'I'm not an idiot, Anselm. I know the dangers. I needed a smoke. Don't tell me what to do. The boss isn't here so I'm making the most of it. There will be no explosion. There is no danger of it.'

Anselm released an expletive and went back into the warehouse. Holmes peered around the corner of the warehouse and spotted Watson doing the same. He nodded to his friend. With striking agility Holmes ran towards Otto and felled him, kicking him in the back of the knees. Watson dived on top of Otto, pulled back his arm and delivered a punch which sent Otto unconscious, blood pouring from his nose.

'Well done, Watson,' said Holmes, puffing. 'It was the punch, I'm sure. You have strength in your arm, my dear friend.'

'I knew my army boxing training would come in handy one day,' breathed Dr Watson, standing upright and straightening his clothes. 'What will we do with him?'

'We must gag him then find some rope and tie him up. He must be hidden out of sight. There will be lengths of rope in one of the other warehouses.'

'I'll go,' said Watson. 'If he stirs punch him again.'

'I am convinced there is no danger of him stirring after such a punch,' said Holmes, paying Dr Watson a rare compliment, although I will use my own boxing training if he wakes, and it is necessary.'

In minutes, Watson had returned with a length of rope with which they tied Otto's hands and feet, and an oily rag they used to gag him should he regain consciousness.

'We should hide him the other side of the furthest warehouse,' said Holmes, 'as far as we can. We do not want him to be discovered.'

They lifted the guard, Holmes at his head, Watson at his feet, and deposited the inert body at the end of the line of warehouses. They returned to the first warehouse, Watson brushing off his clothes, Holmes leading the way.

'Where is Miss Divine?' asked Watson when they'd reached their destination.

'Still hiding I've no doubt,' said Holmes. 'She is safer there.' Watson nodded, thinking if Ottilie had heard him her wrath would know no bounds.

Ottilie crouched next to the warehouse. She had watched as Holmes and Watson had taken the guard down, surprised and admiring at the velocity of Dr Watson's punch which had rendered the guard unconscious. Not only was Watson a kind man, he also packed a punch. It had amazed her and was convinced the quiet, unassuming man had hidden depths.

She was just about to join them when they returned to the warehouse after depositing the guard at the other end of the warehouses when a hand slipped over her mouth.

'Don't make a sound,' whispered a voice.

Chapter 34

Ottilie trembled with fright. She had been caught, and they would use her as bait. Everything was ruined. Why hadn't she moved sooner? She slowly glanced up, terrified at who she would find holding her, into the eyes of…Rose.

She pushed Rose's hand away from her mouth.

'What are you doing, Rose?' whispered Ottilie.

'Sorry. I didn't want you to call out. I had to hide,' replied Rose. 'I was nearly caught trying to get inside. You saw the guard. He was just walking towards the warehouse door as I opened it a crack. Thank goodness I saw him or I'd be hog tied by now.'

Ottilie stifled a chuckle. 'I think we've found the place, don't you?'

Rose nodded. 'What happens now?'

'We'll go around the back of the warehouses and join Holmes and Dr Watson. We need to get inside. I have a feeling in my gut, it's where we'll find Charles Wentworth.'

'And his children?'

'Oh, Rose, I hope so. It doesn't bear thinking about. I'm afraid there are no guarantees the children are being held in the same place as Charles Wentworth.'

They took the path around the back of the warehouses, clinging onto the brickwork and each other. They found Sherlock Holmes and Watson still hiding down the side of the warehouse. Watson smiled at them as they approached them. Holmes simply nodded.

'Yes, yes, singular.'

As a group they waited for a decision to be made. Ottilie wanted to speak but she was in no doubt her voice would be drowned out by Sherlock Holmes who would have his own ideas on the matter.

'The stakes are high,' he whispered. 'The other guards may leave the warehouse because Otto did not return. They'll no doubt look for him, which means we must strike before they realise he isn't with them. A moment's hesitation could mean disaster. We must not be discovered before we have found Wentworth. I for one feel this is where he is being kept.'

'What should we do?' asked Ottilie.

Sherlock Holmes turned his attention to Ottilie, his eyes like polished flint shining in the dark. 'We move now, like shadows in the night. Watson, stay with Miss Fortesque-Wallsey. Miss Divine, you and I will infiltrate the warehouse. If we're captured, we have Dr Watson and Miss Fortesque-Wallsey as backup.'

They heard a noise from inside the warehouse, shouts, and footsteps running across the floor. Time was running out. Ottilie pulled her pistol from her pocket.

'I'm ready.'

Holmes and Ottilie used the towering stacks of crates outside the warehouse as cover.

'Will we wait for the guards to come out?' she whispered, 'or should we take them by surprise?'

Holmes put a finger to his lips. 'If we go too fast it will be ourselves who receive the surprise, Miss Divine,' he whispered. 'We must be circumspect in our movements.'

They watched as three guards left the warehouse through the front entrance. They were holding rifles and peering into the darkness.

'How are we to find Otto with no lighting?' asked one. 'It is pitch black out here. Where the hell is he?'

'Gone for a leak,' said another. 'He is always complaining about his bladder. The trouble with Otto is he's a complainer. I'd be glad to see the back of him. We should lock him out. We wouldn't have to listen to him.' The guards left the front of the warehouse. The large iron double doors were left open just a crack. Ottilie was sure she and Holmes could slip inside without being seen.

Holmes took a step forward but as he moved there was a dull click at his feet. He looked down, his sharp eyes examining the ground around him.

'A trap,' he said, sotto voce. 'Damn.' Another step and it would sound an alarm which would alert the guards to their presence.

'Can you disarm it, Holmes?' asked Dr Watson, a whisper behind them. Holmes bent down to examine the device. He scowled, realising if he took his foot off the wire the game would be up.

'Maybe we could distract them,' said Ottilie. 'They're searching for the other guard. It needs to be something which will take them away from the warehouse.'

'A fire,' said Rose in a loud whisper. 'A fire would do it. It's dangerous but what's the alternative?'

Ottilie took a breath. A fire would certainly grab the guard's attention, particularly if it was big enough. The guards would abandon their search, but it would give them time to slip into the warehouse.

'I'll do it,' whispered Ottilie. She ran across to a pile of crates and a couple of barrels which had been left the other side of the warehouse. When the guards saw it they would need to deal with the fire, particularly if it was big enough.

She hesitated when she saw the word "Flammable" on one of the barrels, then shrugged. They wanted a big fire. She was sure they were about to get one.

Holmes threw a box of matches to her which she deftly caught. She turned to see where the guards were and was relieved they were on the other side of the compound. She struck a match, the tiniest of flames lighting up her face. She opened the lid of the oil barrel, threw the lit match in, then ran to the warehouse entrance, followed by Holmes, Dr Watson, and Rose.

Behind them the barrel was emitting a hissing noise. Within seconds it had exploded into a huge fire, taking the crates with it. An alarm rang through the compound as Holmes took his foot from the tripwire but was almost lost in the sound of the explosions coming from the fire on the bank which had now spread along the cobbles and had set fire to some of the mooring ropes. Ottilie smiled as she ran towards the entrance. The fire had served its purpose, and it would take some time to get it under control.

When the four of them had entered the warehouse, Holmes and Watson pulled the door to and locked it from the inside. The guards had lit lanterns which emitted a yellow beam, not enough to show on the outside but enough for them to play draughts and dominoes which were on a table made from some crates and a piece of tarpaulin.

'And here you are, Mr Holmes. Of course, I knew you would come for him eventually. The others were convinced you and your comrades would not have the intelligence to work out the codes left by Das Eisenhand and by Charles Wentworth himself, but I knew better.' A deep voice laced with an Irish lilt met them as they entered the warehouse.

A tall, lean man emerged from behind the crates, startling them. He wore a cashmere coat and a bowler hat and looked like a gentleman. In his hand was a pistol which was pointed towards them.

Sherlock Holmes sniffed and raised his chin, staring at the man with flinty, hooded eyes.

'Moriarty!' he cried. 'I wondered when you would put in an appearance. You hate to be left out, do you not?'

'Yes, Sherlock Holmes,' the man said, smirking. 'Your nemesis, Moriarty...the one who decides whether you leave here alive or be taken out in a shroud.'

'What is all this to you, Moriarty? I thought the holding of one man was beneath you. I rather thought you were more interested in conquering the world.' Holmes lifted his chin in disapproval.

Moriarty threw back his head and laughed. 'I see you have still not acquired a sense of humour, Holmes. You are so dry, almost arid.'

He moved closer to them, peering at Ottilie and Rose through narrowed steely-grey eyes, making them shudder.

'And now you are working with the female of the species. How odd. This is something I thought I would never see. But of course, this little investigation of yours is not actually yours, is it?' He turned his gaze to Ottilie who tried to return it but felt herself trembling in the attempt. 'The lovely Miss Ottilie Divine is the instigator, am I right, Miss Divine?' Ottilie nodded.

'Now...let's get down to business. I'm getting bored, which I knew I would. You want Charles Wentworth, and I want the secrets he holds. It is important to my friends he does not leave my control until he has passed them to me. I must say he is a man with a strong constitution.

'He looks what he is, a member of the aristocracy, those insipid men who expect to be given the world on a plate, but surprisingly, no, his condition is somewhat different to those men I have taunted in the past.'

Sherlock Holmes snorted. 'You mean "tortured" of course.'

Moriarty was incensed at Holmes's interruption. 'There is much more to Charles Wentworth. We have tried everything to get him to talk,' he shook his head and tutted looking frustrated, 'but he will not. Unfortunately, we have had to try to persuade him.' He pursed his lips and shrugged. 'I don't think he enjoyed it.'

'Does he have any fingernails left?' Holmes asked Moriarty, his voice hard. 'Or perhaps it was his toenails this time? Or did you use a cattle prod, or a branding iron? They seem to be your favourite toys.'

Moriarty ignored him. 'As he had become useless to me I'm afraid he will be done away with…the Thames is favourable, particularly at this time of year, perhaps with bricks tied to his ankles…unless you have information you would like to unload, but first I would like Miss Divine to unbolt the door to the warehouse so my friends can join us.' He turned to Ottilie. 'Miss Divine?'

Ottilie narrowed her eyes and stared at him. 'No.' She lifted her chin in defiance. Rose bit her lip and glanced at Ottilie.

'No?' asked Moriarty. He hitched the corner of his mouth into a tight smile. 'You have spirit, Miss Divine, but I suggest if you ask your friends here, you will know it is ill-placed. 'Open the door!'

Ottilie lifted her chin even higher to show Moriarty she was not intimidated. 'No.'

Moriarty's face darkened. He raised his pistol and pointed it at Ottilie. 'Open. The. Door!' Ottilie shook her head.

A shot rang out from behind Ottilie, winging Moriarty and sending his pistol flying to behind one of the crates. Holmes and Watson ran forward to hold him as his knees buckled and he fell to the ground. Blood seeped from a wound in his arm. His eyes were closed and his expression changed from one of triumph to a man who was in desperate and debilitating pain.

Ottilie frowned, then turning to look behind her, gasped. Rose stared at Moriarty looking unrepentant, pistol in hand, vapour curling out from the barrel, her face a picture of determination.

'Rose,' cried Ottilie. Her mouth dropped open. 'I didn't know…'

'It's best to keep any suggestion of shooting skills hidden,' said Rose, 'otherwise he would have known I had a gun and was capable of hitting a target.'

Otilie smiled. 'You look as though butter won't melt.'

Rose chuckled. 'I know. And it works so well. He took absolutely no notice of me. I was insignificant to him…which is exactly what I intended.'

'Clever,' said Ottilie, admiringly. Rose grinned.

Sherlock Holmes and Dr Watson tied Moriarty at his hands and feet with the rope they found in the warehouse before turning to Rose.

'A singular skill, Miss Fortesque-Wallsey,' said Holmes. 'One which has saved the day.'

Dr Watson nodded. 'Well done, Miss Fortesque-Wallsey. A crack shot.'

'The government shooting instruction is second to none. I was reluctant at first, but then I rather fancied myself as Annie Oakley, so I decided to take part.' She inhaled. 'Thank goodness I did.'

'What about the guards outside?' asked Dr Watson. 'Once they've got the fire under control the doors won't hold them forever.'

'All the more reason why we need to act swiftly,' said Holmes as he ran towards the wooden stairs in the centre of the warehouse. 'We need to find Wentworth, and quick smartish. You search the ground floor; I'll examine up here. Make haste, make haste, we must not let them deter us.'

They searched the warehouse from top to bottom, in every crate, barrel, and box, knowing Charles Wentworth had to be somewhere. Sherlock Holmes asked Moriarty time and again of his whereabouts, reminding him there was nothing he could currently do to prevent them from finding him.

'You may as well tell us, Moriarty,' said Holmes. 'You are simply delaying your own suffering as well as his.'

'My suffering is nothing compared to what you will suffer when I'm free to continue what I've begun,' Moriarty replied. Blood pooled on the ground around him from the wound in his arm, but Dr Watson assured Holmes…Moriarty was in no danger. 'There is only one ending to this and it is your death, Sherlock Holmes. When the day comes, I will be triumphant. You will never find your objective.'

The guards outside used everything they could find in the compound and under Lambeth Bridge to infiltrate the warehouse, but the heavy doors, the padlock, and the bolts they themselves had fixed to prevent the warehouse from being assailed stood up to them, the perfect defense, constructed by the guards, but which had been used against them.

'Where is he?' asked Ottilie when they had completed the search of the warehouse, her breath coming in short gasps. 'We've looked everywhere. He must be here, yet there is no sign of him.' She frowned. 'Those guards and Moriarty were protecting their prize, yet it would appear on the face of it their prize isn't here.'

Rose stood away from the others. She had yet to find the confidence to speak as one of them, yet her mind would not stop working. She remembered hearing once, from somewhere she could not recall…when every thought has been considered and it has not solved the puzzle, the remaining thought, no matter how unlikely, is the obvious answer.

'The floor,' she said quietly. 'We haven't searched the floor.'

Holmes, Watson, and Ottilie stared at her. Ottilie nodded. 'It's the only place we haven't looked.'

Holmes immediately fell to his knees and began to peruse the floor on which they stood. For fifteen minutes he searched, his nose almost touching the detritus underfoot. Rose frowned at Ottilie, who grinned. Watson put a finger to his lips, then smiled.

'Ah ha,' said Holmes finally. He began to scrape some of the debris away, revealing four gaps in the shape of a square.

'A trapdoor,' breathed Rose. 'Is it a trapdoor, Mr Holmes?'

'Indeed, Miss Fortesque-Wallsey.' He stood and rubbed the dirt from his knees and hands. 'I'd wager this is where we will find Charles Wentworth.'

'Is there a padlock?' asked Watson.

'No, dear friend. It is secured by magnets.' He squatted in front of it, slipping a penknife underneath one of the sides. It didn't budge. He tried the other three sides until one lifted as though by a hidden hand. 'Clever,' he said, replacing his penknife in his pocket. 'The mechanism is quite ingenious.'

'What's there, Holmes? Is it a container of some sort?'

'No, Watson.' Holmes pulled the trapdoor up and pushed it back onto the floor. 'A flight of stone steps I think you'll find.'

Ottilie, Rose, and Dr Watson stepped near to the edge and peered down. Below them was a flight of stone steps which continued into a darkened space.

'How far does it go down?' asked Ottilie.

'We won't know until we throw caution to the wind and follow the steps down, Miss Divine. Are you prepared to step into the unknown?'

Ottilie shrugged. 'It's all I've been doing since this began, Mr Holmes.

Everything is unknown until one confronts it, don't you think?'

'Absolutely. I will lead, then you and Miss Fortesque-Wallsey, followed by Dr Watson.' He glanced at them. 'We will prevail,' he said. 'We have come this far.'

They remained silent while they followed Sherlock Holmes through the trapdoor.

'Leave it open, Dr Watson. I wouldn't like us to be imprisoned under the floor of the warehouse.'

Holmes went first, followed by Ottilie, Rose, then Dr Watson. The further down they travelled, the colder and mustier the air became. There were cobwebs hanging from the stone ceiling, and rats scuttling into their hiding places in the walls. Holmes had flicked on a flashlight, and the others followed suit, their shadows becoming squatter and shorter the further down the steps they went.

Their footsteps made a hollow echoing noise as though there were not just the four of them, but many more. It was mind-chillingly eerie; the thick dust as they followed the steps down almost choaking them. The constant drip of water was almost torture, and Ottilie wondered how any human being could survive in such a place so putrid with mildew and black mould.

'I've reached the bottom of the steps,' cried Holmes, stamping his feet on the wet stone, his every sound echoing around the walls. He peered into the gloom. 'There is a chamber here,' he said as he moved his flashlight over the walls. The others joined him, looking around the chamber with horror. Rose suddenly gasped in revulsion.

'Are they cells?'

'Indeed,' answered Holmes. 'They're rather like medieval prison cells. Those iron bars have no doubt been in situ for hundreds of years.'

Ottilie slowly pushed by Holmes and stepped towards one of the cells, her heart in her mouth. 'There's someone in there.'

In the last of these cells, hunched in the corner on a dirt floor, was a man. His clothes were rags, his face bloodied and bruised. He was emaciated, his eyes and cheekbones deep, dark hollows. Next to him was a metal plate with a hunk of hard bread and a bowl of water. There was an evil-smelling bucket in the other corner of the cell which was overflowing with ordure.

The man in the cell was Charles Wentworth.

Chapter 35

Ottilie was stilled with disbelief. Charles Wentworth's eyes were swollen with ill-treatment and the lack of food had turned a once lean but fit man into nothing more than a skeleton. She could hear his breathing, shallow breaths, rather like the tuberculosis sufferers back in the twenties when it was rife, then occasionally, a deep laboured breath depicted by a phlegmy rattling sound reverberating from his lungs.

She stepped closer to the cell and knelt down onto her haunches.

'Charles…' she whispered.

Charles Wentworth tried to open his eyes. He stared at her through narrow slits which showed bloodshot rims and broken blood vessels. With great difficulty he lifted his hand.

'Delia?' he said, his voice hoarse with lack of water.

'No, Charles. It's not Delia, I'm afraid. I'm Ottilie Divine.' His face gradually showed a flicker of recognition, a remembrance of the name. 'We're going to take you out of here, Charles.'

Holmes, Watson, and Rose joined her at the bars of the cell. Holmes and Watson examined the locks which were archaic and crude and attached to chains with huge rusting links. Holmes took his lock picks from his coat pocket and began to open the locks. Watson did the same.

'He's malnourished to the point of starvation, Holmes,' said Dr Watson, staring at the grim scene in front of him, 'and totally dehydrated, but if we can get him to safety quickly, he has a chance of survival. His injuries will heal in time. I'll check for broken bones.'

Once the padlocks were unlocked and the chains unravelled from the iron bars Watson pulled the cell door open and rushed to Charles Wentworth's side with Holmes following. Both squatted to speak with him.

'Are you able to stand, Mr Wentworth?' Watson asked him gently.

Wentworth tried to speak but began to cough, a rough phlegmy cough that made him wince in pain. 'Two days ago,' he said in a rasping voice. 'I could stand two days ago.' Tears ran down his leathery, emaciated cheeks. 'I've seen no one since then. I've had no reason to stand.' He leant a head against Dr Watson's shoulder. 'I have no reason to live.'

'You have every reason, sir,' said Sherlock Holmes. Your wife awaits you.' He stood and went out into the chamber where Ottilie and Rose were waiting, tears rolling down their cheeks with horror and sadness.'

'Wait here,' he said. 'We need help.'

Ottilie's eyes widened. 'But the guards?' she said. 'Mr Holmes, they will not mind how much damage they do to you. Listen to them, trying to get into the warehouse. They are angry, violently so.'

'Not as angry as they shall be soon.'

Holmes ran up the stone steps and emerged into the warehouse where Moriarty lay prone on the dirt floor.

'You've found him then?' said Moriarty with a sneer. 'I doubt the man has much life left in him, although the sight of a certain woman might stir his juices. It's the only thing I've discovered, his love for her.'

Holmes narrowed his eyes and gave Moriarty a flinty look, his jaw hard with repugnance. 'Regardless of how much life he has left in him, we will ensure he survives and thrives, sir. You need say no more.'

Holmes went to the warehouse entrance. The guards outside had made some progress in demolishing the doors. The had found a piece of metal in the compound which they were using as a battering ram. Holmes pulled a whistle from his coat pocket and blew it as hard as he could. Moments later there were shouts and expletives from the guards, the sound of punches being thrown and bodies hitting the cold, hard ground.

'We have them, Mr Holmes,' said a voice through the doors.

Sherlock Holmes unfastened the huge bolts the guards had installed, and opened the padlocks, allowing one of the huge doors to swing open. In the frame was Inspector Lestrade.

'We thought you weren't going to need us, Mr Holmes,' said Lestrade. 'We have been waiting for some time.'

'I had anticipated overcoming any sentries here would not be plain sailing, Inspector Lestrade, which is why I begged your presence. I am grateful to see you. We not only have a desirable prize in our possession, we have an injured man in the cells.'

'A desirable prize?' Holmes led him to where Moriarty was tied up. 'Good Lord. Is it who I think it is?' cried Lestrade.

'Indeed,' said Holmes, 'but please instruct some of your men to follow me into the chamber underground where Charles Wentworth has been held. They will need to carry him to one of your vehicles. He must be taken to hospital immediately. There is no time to wait for an ambulance to arrive. The man is almost dead and clings to life with but a thread.'

Lestrade instructed those officers who were not occupied by the guards to follow Holmes through the trapdoor and into the chamber. Once they had seen Charles Wentworth's condition, some of the officers returned to the warehouse and fashioned a makeshift stretcher from wooden planks and a piece of tarpaulin with which they carried Wentworth up the stone steps and into the chamber.

Moriarty's guards had been arrested along with Moriarty, who had been bundled into the back of a police vehicle amidst expletives, cries of police brutality, and the indignities being rained upon him to which Sherlock Holmes scoffed. He put his head into the vehicle and tutted.

'Now, now, Moriarty. Think yourself lucky Charles Wentworth did not die. At least you'll be charged only for abduction and mistreatment of your prisoner. It could have been murder.'

'Not so, Sherlock. I did not touch him. You…and they…cannot prove anything.'

'Tell it to the judge,' cried Holmes as he slammed the vehicle door.

The compound was duly searched by the police to ensure none of the guards escaped. A cavalcade of police vehicles left the compound apart from one, the driver of which Lestrade had instructed to wait so Sherlock Holmes and his friends could be returned to Baker Street.

Sherlock Holmes, Dr Watson, Ottilie and Rose stood on the embankment staring into the night sky. The warehouse compound was as it was when they had arrived, almost calm after the stormy moments which had passed, the sound of river water lapping the sides of the wooden sleepers as it moved to and fro in the wind. The burning remains of the barrel and crates Ottilie had set a match to still smouldered, little flashes of flame occasionally flickering amongst the ropes and detritus.

'What now?' asked Rose. She frowned. 'Finding Charles Wentworth has surely completed your mission but is there not unfinished business.'

'Indeed, there is, Miss Fortesque-Wallsey.' said Holmes. 'The Wentworth children.'

'We should have asked Moriarty,' said Ottilie. 'Damn, their mother will be beside herself.'

Holmes scoffed at the suggestion. 'And you think he would have told you what you wanted to know? He cares nothing for them. They were simply used as a pawn to ensure Delia Wentworth did as she was told. Of course, one would do anything to protect one's children. He may be an arch criminal, but he was fully aware of the fact.' Ottilie raised her eyebrows and glanced at Dr Watson. Holmes turned on his heel and spoke over his shoulder as he walked towards the river. 'However, I have thought about the problem in a logical manner and deduced they are not far away.'

The others turned and watched him as he left the cobbled bank and walked up a roped gangway which had escaped the hottest of the flames and made his way to a cargo barge. When he reached the barge, he grabbed the tarpaulin covering the cabin and pulled it aside. Ottilie and Rose ran to the barge and looked in through the windows. There, on the banquettes, were three children, tied at the hands and feet, and gagged.

'Well done, Holmes,' cried Watson.

'Elementary, Watson,' said Holmes looking rather satisfied with himself. 'Rather a rudimentary deduction. Moriarty and Das Eisenhand would have wanted the children close so they could use them as bait whenever they had need to. I could not understand why a tarpaulin would have been pulled over a barge with a cabin. I deduced it would most likely be to hide something.' His lips twitched with self-congratulation. 'And of course, I was correct.'

Ottilie and Rose stepped onto the barge and went inside the cabin where they proceeded to untie the children and remove the gags.

'My father?' asked a boy, who looked to be the eldest child. 'Is my father safe?'

'He's safe,' answered Rose. 'He has been taken to hospital where I think you may be going too…just to make sure. Dr Watson will have a quick look at you. He's very gentle and kind. You will be all right.'

'And my mother? Penelope has cried for her every hour. I wasn't able to console her.' He indicated the smallest child, a little girl aged not more than four-years-old whose eyes and nose were swollen and bright red from crying. Ottilie put an arm around her.

'Your mother is staying at my flat,' said Ottilie. 'I'm sorry, we don't know your names.'

'I'm Dom…Dominic,' said the boy. 'This is my brother, Stan, and of course, Penelope, the littlest.'

'We'll take you to her as soon as we can,' said Ottilie, helping the children off the banquettes and encouraging them to walk through the barge. 'Do your legs feel wobbly?'

'Yes, a bit…and we're ravenous. They didn't give us much to eat, and just water sometimes. Stan said he thought it came out of the river, but it looked all right.'

Ottilie and Rose grinned. 'Oh, I think you would have known if it had come out of the river,' said Rose. 'Let's get you to Dr Watson and he'll take a quick look at you.'

On the bank, Watson spoke to each child asking if they had any injuries or whether they hurt anywhere. All three said no…all they wanted was to see their parents.

'Should we take them to Baker Street?' asked Ottilie. 'They don't seem to have suffered any ill effects, not like… well, anyway, I'm sure they would like to see their mother.'

'Can we go home?' asked Penelope in a small voice. 'I just want to go home.'

'Very soon,' said Ottilie, hugging the little girl who still had the pink ribbons in her hair from before she was abducted, although they were filthy and hanging like rags. 'You'll be at home with your mother very soon.'

'Promise?' Penelope said in a lisping whisper. 'Pinky-Pinky, Bow Bell?' She held out her little finger.

Ottilie's heart melted, and tears sprang to her eyelashes. 'Pinky-Pinky, Bow Bell,' she answered in a whisper, and cupped her little finger around Penelope's.

Chapter 36

Ottilie woke late the following day. Her bed was warm and so very comfortable she didn't want to leave it. She heard the sound of crockery being taken out of the cupboard and laid on the table in the kitchen. Reluctantly, she swung her legs out of bed, stretched her arms above her head, and yawned.

She flung on her dressing gown and tied it tightly around her middle, pushing her feet into her slippers. She hoped Rose had made the tea and maybe cooked the small amount of bacon she'd flirted with the butcher for.

'Morning, Rose.'

'Ah, you're awake.'

Ottilie chuckled. 'Mm, only just. Gosh, I had such a good sleep.'

Rose giggled. 'I know. You were snoring.'

'No! Honestly! Oh, dear. I didn't know I snored.'

Rose put the teapot on the table and checked the bacon under the grill. 'You don't usually, but you were sleeping so deeply. We were both exhausted after what happened last night.'

Ottilie pulled out a chair and sat at the table. 'I can hardly believe what happened. It's like a dream.'

Rose snorted. 'Or a nightmare. Moriarty. I'd heard of him of course. I shouldn't think anyone who works for the government hasn't, but to actually meet him.' She shook her head. 'He doesn't like Sherlock Holmes, does he?'

'Oh, my goodness, no. In a strange way I think they have an admiration for each other, but there is huge animosity between them. In one of his cryptic messages to Mr Holmes he alluded to them being chess pieces in the game and asked which one of them would be knocked over at the end. I can't help thinking it's exactly the situation between them. They're both incredibly intelligent men, one with a darkly criminal mind, the other the exact opposite.'

Rose forked two pieces of bacon from the grill and placed them on a slice of bread before laying another slice on top. She cut the sandwich in half and put half on a plate for Ottilie; the other half on a plate for herself.

'Breakfast. You don't have much in.'

'I know,' said Ottilie through a mouthful of bacon sandwich. 'I haven't had time to go shopping and everywhere is so empty already. The bacon was flirted for, so enjoy it.'

Rose laughed, then took a big drink of tea. 'Oh, tea. There's nothing like it is there. So comforting.'

Ottilie smiled. 'You're a typical English Rose.'

'It's what Mama says.' It went quiet. 'She promised to tell me more about my father. I know some already.' She pulled a face. 'What a legacy.'

Ottilie looked up. 'Oh? Why now?'

Rose sighed. 'She thinks it's time I knew. I mean…I'm twenty-five. I'm not a little girl who can't take it on the chin.' She stared at Ottilie. 'Do you know about him?' Ottilie nodded. 'I thought you might. Camille would have told you.'

Ottilie nodded. 'Well, it's only right you should know. As you say, you're not a child. I had to learn things about my own father, not all good I hasten to add, but it's not right we think of them as saints, or picture them through rose-tinted glasses.' Ottilie shrugged. 'I don't like to feel as though the wool has been pulled over my eyes which is why Mama told me about him.'

'Did it upset you?'

Ottilie nodded again. 'A bit…but then,' she sighed, 'he was human, with human frailties. I don't think he treated Mama very well. It wasn't her fault, you know…Mama and Papa didn't have another child.'

'Of course not. She and Richard had Simon.'

'He's a dear. I never thought I would have a little brother.' Ottilie smiled at Rose. 'And you have one too. Leo.'

'He's well-named, that's for sure. He's the lionheart of the family. So tough. I do love it rather.'

'Perhaps we should have asked him to help our investigation.'

'Please don't say that. He would have taken over, and I know one Sherlock Holmes who wouldn't have liked it at all.' They both burst into laughter. 'What's on your agenda today?'

'Holmes wants me to infiltrate an office in the Palace of Westminster. He certainly likes to be in control, it's one thing I've learnt about him.' She drained her teacup. 'You've reminded me, I must telephone Mr Walsh and tell him what's happened. I should think he's ready to sack me. I've barely been to the office.'

'He won't after you tell him what happened last night. You have quite a story to write, don't you?'

'I do.' Ottilie nodded. 'But how much to reveal and how much to conceal?'

Chapter 37

'When will I have your story, Miss Divine?' Jonah Walsh asked her.

'I'll come in today, Mr Walsh. I slept in because of what happened last night. We'll be the first with the story.'

'And Charles Wentworth? How is he faring?'

'He was taken to hospital directly. As far as I know he has a good chance of recovery. He has a strong constitution which has saved the day, but he was extremely badly treated. They had beaten him, starved him, and kept him in the most horrendous conditions.'

'There was a pause before Walsh spoke again, his voice serious. 'You did a good thing, Miss Divine. I'm proud of you.'

'Thank you, Mr Walsh, but I wasn't alone. We were a team. We all had a part to play.'

'Is the investigation finished? Are you satisfied with the conclusion?'

'There is some unfinished business, Mr Walsh. I will write Charles Wentworth's story and have it on your desk by this afternoon, but there is another story, one important for the country.'

'Fair enough, Miss Divine. Look after yourself.'

''I will, Mr Walsh, to the best of my ability.'

'And will you want to return to writing about Births, Deaths, and

Marriages of the aristocracy? Or flower shows, or fashion?'

Ottilie chuckled. 'I'd rather not. I don't see myself as that reporter now. I want to be your investigative reporter, Mr Walsh.'

'I think you've earnt it, Miss Divine.'

When Ottilie's story hit the newsstands, the scandal was unstoppable. Charles Wentworth's treatment horrified the good citizens of Britain who could hardly believe one of their own had been subjected to such cruelty. He was hailed a hero for not divulging state secrets and his name fast became a household name…the story spreading like wildfire.

Two weeks later, Ottilie received a telephone call from Sherlock Holmes while she was at the Express offices.

'Miss Divine. Are you in a situation where you can speak freely?'

'Yes, Mr Holmes. The office is almost empty.'

'I take it you and I are of the same mind we need to prevent Charles Wentworth's mission from fading into obscurity?'

'I would rather it didn't. It would mean everything he has gone through, and our own work in finding and rescuing him would be for nothing.'

There was a pause from Holmes and Ottilie grinned to herself. 'Not quite, Miss Divine. We rescued Wentworth and his children. I rather think it was quite the coup.'

'You're right of course, but I couldn't help noticing in most of the newspapers you were hardly mentioned, Mr Holmes. Inspector Lestrade had the accolades heaped on him by a grateful public.'

'Indeed, Miss Divine. I prefer not to attach my name to investigations. I'm perfectly happy for Inspector Lestrade to take the kudos and admiration, which he is happy to do.'

'And you don't mind?'

'Not at all. We have worked in a similar way in the past.'

'So, what's next, Mr Holmes? I'm quite sure you didn't call me at work to discuss the weather.'

'Indeed, I did not. We still have work to do to draw the investigation to a close.'

'You mean the mole?'

'Exactly, Miss Divine. I have devised a plan and put the plan into operation.'

'Oh?'

'I've spoken to a contact at Westminster…'

Ottilie interrupted him. 'Your contact, Mr Holmes? I would like to know who your contact is. He, or she, seems to live in the shadows. I think you should tell me who this person is.'

'I understand your curiosity, Miss Divine. In usual circumstances I would not divulge the name of my contact, however, I see no harm on this occasion. My contact is my brother, Mycroft Holmes.'

'And what is his position?'

'I'd prefer not to say.'

'Mr Holmes. Let me be clear. You have devised a plan which apparently involves me without any hint of a suggestion as to what you're expecting me to do. I'm quite certain whatever it is you're planning; it will put me in a dangerous position. Therefore, I think it is imperative I know who your brother is, and what he does, bearing in mind he is at Westminster. I may need his help.'

She heard Holmes sigh. 'Very well, Miss Divine. You are most insistent. I should have expected it to be so. You are of an enquiring personality.' Ottilie nodded to herself. 'He is First Secretary to the Cabinet Office, Head of the Intelligence Coordination Committee. He is at the core of Britain's intelligence and defense machinery and reports only to the Prime Minister. He oversees MI5 and MI6, and Naval Intelligence. He is, in fact…Westminster…one could say.'

Ottilie was taken aback at his answer but managed to regain her composure.

'Gosh…I…didn't know you were so well connected, Mr Holmes.'

'I rather think he is the sibling who is "well-connected", Miss Divine.'

Ottilie swallowed a chuckle. 'Yes, of course. Perhaps you would like to divulge what you've planned for me.'

'You are to enter the lion's den, Miss Divine. You have a position at Westminster as a cultural attaché which will give you an entrée into all departments and all diplomatic circles. You have the perfect credentials, dear lady, refined manners, and a familiarity with members of the aristocracy which you will need if you are to encourage those involved to share confidences with you.'

Ottilie frowned, suddenly feeling nervous. 'But will the staff know I'm a fraud?'

'Absolutely not. It would be a pointless exercise.'

'But I know Miss Cheam. She is…or was…Lawrence Tebbit's secretary.'

'Then you may have to lie, Miss Divine. Perhaps say you grew tired of working for the newspaper and have always had an interest in politics, in fact, it is a relationship you could cultivate. She is secretary to the Under Secretary, after all.'

Ottilie took some time to mull over what Sherlock Holmes had suggested to her.

'I'll have to tell Mr Walsh, my editor.'

'I have spoken to Mr Walsh. He has accepted there is more work to do.'

Ottilie's mouth dropped open. 'You've contacted Jonah Walsh behind my back?'

'I wouldn't put it quite as such. He accepts the investigation will not be over until we discover the mole. It would be a coup for the Express. He has accepted your absence.'

'And if I don't wish to comply?'

Sherlock Holmes sniffed loudly down the receiver. 'I cannot imagine you would turn away a chance to get to the nucleus of Westminster, Miss Divine. It would be quite an accomplishment for a novice investigative reporter.'

Ottilie looked out of the window at the passing buildings as she was taken to Westminster in an unpretentious government vehicle.

She had dressed very carefully for her new role as a government cultural attaché, a tailored grey suit, black gloves, and a black hat. She had been given a cover story from Sherlock Holmes who had been advised of it by his brother, Mycroft.

According to her instructions she had been sent from a school in France where she learnt French and skills of diplomacy, to massage relations between Britain and France before travel was impossible. Ottilie could speak French, she had been taught at St Agnes's in Hampshire. She knew

Latin too, but doubted if she would need it. She sincerely hoped not. She was rather rusty.

When the car reached Westminster, the driver jumped out and opened the door for her. He was very easy on the eye, and his uniform was perfect, but Ottilie simply made a small smile, nodded once, and said thank you. She ran up the steps at the front of the Palace of Westminster and made for the large reception hall.

She had been instructed by Holmes as to the layout of the floors. Her office was on the second floor and her new superior was a Mr Jaspar Fairchild, the man she was to report to on arrival. When she entered her small office, there was a woman standing by the desk looking out of the window.

'Miss Divine?' she asked, turning when she heard Ottilie's heels on the polished wooden floor.

'Yes,' said Ottilie with a bright smile. 'I'm told I'm to report to Mr Fairchild.'

'I'm Miss Butterfield, Mr Fairchild's secretary. He's expecting you. If you'd like to hang up your jacket, and remove your hat and gloves, I'll take you in to him.' Ottilie nodded. 'You can put your gasmask in this cupboard. We all have places allotted for us so our gas masks aren't always obviously present. They can leave one rather depressed when they're on show all day.'

Ottilie nodded and smiled. 'I know what you mean.'

Miss Butterfield waited for Ottilie to compose herself then led her out of her office, along the corridor, and into another office.

'This is my office, Miss Divine. Should you need anything, please don't hesitate to ask. I know how difficult it is when joining a large staff...' she looked sad, 'particularly at the moment.' She pointed to a door on the other side of the office. 'Mr Fairchild's office.'

She went across to the door, knocked on it swiftly, then opened it and poked her head in.

'Miss Divine has arrived, Mr Fairchild. Shall I show her in?'

'Yes, yes,' Ottilie heard Fairchild say. 'Let's see what this is all about.' Ottilie's heart sank. She was afraid she would be asked questions she didn't know the answer to.

'Miss Divine,' said Fairchild, leaving his desk and holding out his hand. 'A pleasure to meet you.'

'And you, sir,' answered Ottilie.

'Please sit,' he said, inviting her to sit in the chair opposite his. His desk was incredibly tidy. There were a couple of photos on it, an inkwell, rather beautiful, and a folder which was in front of him. 'I'm surprised you've been sent here, Miss Divine. Culture is the last thing on our mind right now, but I'm reliably informed you speak fluent French and will be available to translate any papers we get from France. I had my doubts when the First Secretary of the Cabinet office informed me he had taken you on…but I suppose he has a point. We must at least keep up the appearance we know what we're doing.' He laughed heartily, and Ottilie smiled, hoping she had done the right thing by agreeing to Holmes's plan.

'I wondered what I would be working on?' Ottilie asked Fairchild, determined to look eager.

'I have a folder of some recent cultural reports and some conversations that were had during meetings with Lawrence Tebbit who I'm afraid no longer works for the department, and some attachés from France and Germany.' He frowned and blinked at her. 'Any German?'

'A little, yes. I went to Germany on a school exchange trip. I picked up some of the phrasing and what have you?'

'How long were you there?'

'Only two months.'

'Long enough to get a grip of it I should think. There are an equal number of each. I would like you to work on them for now.'

'Should I report to you, Mr Fairchild?'

'When you've completed them. Miss Butterfield would usually be available to you, but she is to go on a training course from tomorrow.' Ottilie frowned. Miss Butterfield had said she would be available if Ottilie needed her. 'Before you go home, I would like you to give the folder to Miss Cheam. Her office is one floor down. She was secretary to Mr Tebbit before he left us. There's a temporary officer in Tebbit's old office at the moment, Mr William Shaw, who will more than likely be taking Tebbit's position when all has been finalised.'

Ottilie's eyes widened when she heard Deirdre Cheam's name, and even wider when she heard William Shaw's. She nodded.

'Certainly, Mr Fairchild.'

'I think it'll be all. I understand you used to work for the Daily Express.'

'Yes, sir.'

'Then you should be exemplary at writing reports. I would like a full report on the folder by Friday evening.'

'Yes, sir.'

She turned to go but Fairchild halted her. 'I hear you are a personal friend of Delia Wentworth.'

'We were at the same school; St Agnes's in Hampshire.'

'You've read about her husband, Charles?'

'I should think everyone knows about Charles Wentworth by now. All the newspapers have been full of his abduction by a gang.'

'How well do you know him?'

Ottilie frowned, wondering why Fairchild wanted to know. 'Not very well. We met once or twice…we used to socialise in the same circle, but our paths didn't cross much.'

Fairchild nodded, his lips a straight line. 'Fair enough. Get on, then.' He flapped a hand at her. She was dismissed.

Ottilie returned to her office. As she went through Miss Butterfield's office, the neat and well-coiffured woman with the cat-framed glasses looked up and smiled. Ottilie realised how perfect Miss Butterfield was, rather like a model in a magazine. Her skin was dewy, her eyes, almond shaped and pure blue, her hair an aristocratic blonde swept up into the most immaculate chignon Ottilie had ever seen.

'Everything all right, Miss Divine?'

'Yes, yes, thank you, Miss Butterfield.

Miss Butterfield chuckled, her laugh a tinkle of bells. 'Miss Butterfield is my maiden aunt,' she said with a smile. 'You can call me June.'

Ottilie smiled. 'Thank you. And I'm Ottilie.'

'I know,' she said. 'Your mother is Camille Divine.'

Ottilie nodded. 'Was. She's Camille Owen now. She and my father, Lord Divine…well,' she looked down at her hands, 'he was killed in an accident.'

'I know. I'm so sorry.'

'It was a long time ago.' She smiled at June again, hoping she wasn't the mole she was seeking. 'I'd better get on,' Ottilie said, indicating the folder. June nodded.

Ottilie went back to her office, a private room and not much bigger than a cupboard. Some would have complained about it, but not Ottilie. She felt safer there, hidden away, and hopefully forgotten.

She went across to the window and looked out over the Thames. The river was a dull grey ribbon snaking past the Palace of Westminster and under Westminster Bridge. A fog was banking up on the horizon which obstructed her view.

She sat at her desk, but kept her door slightly open so she could hear conversations, and the coming and going of the other staff. Throughout the day she noticed people going into June's office, the mumble of conversation, even a moment of a raised voice from Jaspar Fairchild.

At lunchtime she made her way to the staff restaurant. She spotted Deirdre Cheam, and the other secretaries who sat outside Lawrence Tebbit's office, now occupied by William Shaw, which had surprised her. With them was the new young secretary who had uttered the expletives, and seemingly whose typing wasn't up to scratch. One of the other secretaries standing at the counter called over to her.

'Evelyn, what are you having?'

'An egg sandwich.'

'No eggs.'

Evelyn looked cross and uttered something under her breath which Ottilie was sure was a rude word. 'Toast then, if it's all they're capable of.'

The secretary nodded, then glanced at Deirdre Cheam who shook her head and momentarily rolled her eyes.

Ottilie made sure she sat far enough away from them so as not to be noticed, but close enough to hear what they were saying. The conversations were far from interesting and Ottilie got bored as she ate her cheese sandwich, a floppy and rather damp facsimile of the ones she made at home, until she heard Charles Wentworth's name mentioned. She sipped her tea and looked the other way, her ears on alert.

'Got himself in a right pickle, didn't he,' said one. 'Makes you think.'

'What about,' asked Deirdre as she bit into her toast.

'What he was doing.'

'Not what he was meant to be doing, I shouldn't think.'

'Which was what?'

'Stopping the war.'

'Didn't do much of a job, did he?' replied Evelyn. 'I reckon he was an agent for Germany. Probably giving them all our secrets.'

The other women stared at her. 'Evelyn, I really wish you would stop saying such things about our superiors,' said Deirdre Cheam, sotto voce. 'Mr Wentworth did a fine job until he was abducted. He was severely treated and tortured and has been called a hero for not divulging the country's classified information.' Miss Cheam turned back to her Brown Windsor soup. 'I really think you should keep your opinions to yourself.'

Evelyn shrugged. 'I'm allowed an opinion. It might not be the same as yours, but I'm entitled to say what I think.'

'Yes, but not everyone wants to hear it. And why would you think such a thing? You barely knew him.' Evelyn pulled a face then narrowed her eyes

Ottilie watched her closely. The girl couldn't have been more than twenty, and very likely the poorest paid of all the secretaries, yet she wore beautifully cut clothes, and around her neck was a string of pearls Ottilie was almost sure were real. The pearls were irregular in shape and not all the same shade of cream. So how could a junior secretary on the first rung of the payment ladder afford such a beauty.

That afternoon Ottilie continued to go through the folder, translating the mostly French language and the conversations between Lawrence Tebbit and the cultural attachés from France. She read nothing to pique her interest or sound any warning bells; the conversations were mostly those of hosts welcoming guests with snippets of personal information thrown in for good measure. There were enquiries about family and work, questions about what Lawrence Tebbit thought would happen and how they would mitigate difficult circumstances during a war that seemed more than likely to occur. Ottilie sighed. It was all rather boring, but she reminded herself she was at Westminster for a reason and the reason was to find the mole who was leaking information to Germany.

At five o'clock she closed the file, put on her coat, hat, and gloves and made for the stairs in the corridor. Jaspar Fairchild had instructed her to return the folder to Deirdre Cheam as June Butterfield would not be in her office. Her destination was Deirdre Cheam's office on the first floor.

As she reached the bottom of the stairs, Evelyn came out of the corridor leading to Deirdre's office.

'Is it the folder for Deirdre?' she said. 'I'll give it to her.' She held out her hand.

Ottilie smiled. 'Thank you, but no, I've been instructed to put it into Deirdre's hands.'

Evelyn's face darkened. 'I'm quite capable of giving it to her.'

Ottilie nodded. 'So am I,' she said brightly, and pushed past the girl. She heard Evelyn inhale with annoyance but continued to Deirdre's office. At the door she turned to find Evelyn still standing in the corridor staring after her. Ottilie lifted her chin and went into the office.

Deirdre was the only secretary left in the secretary's office. The others had left.

'Deirdre. We meet again,' said Ottilie cheerfully as she placed the folder on Deirdre's desk.

Deirdre looked up and gasped. 'Miss Divine! What on earth are you doing here?'

'I work here. I got rather fed up with chasing people for information they didn't want to give, so I switched careers. How are you?'

'I'm well, Miss Divine. I must say I'm surprised to see you here. Are you a secretary now?'

'A cultural attaché for France. I speak fluent French so I'm carrying out translations for Mr Fairchild. The conversations are all between Lawrence Tebbit and the French contingent.'

Deirdre nodded. 'Poor Lawrence.' Ottilie was surprised to hear Deirdre call Lawrence Tebbit by his first name. 'He was badly served.'

'You think so? Did he not try to kill some men at the Nightingale Club?'

Deirdre nodded. 'He was breaking down. So much was expected of him.' She shrugged. 'And then of course he lost his job and was being sent to Italy, a place he did not want to go.'

'Why?'

'Because it's becoming so dangerous over there and Lawrence knew it.

He was sure he was being got rid of so someone else could take his place.'

'Would it not have been Charles Wentworth?'

Deirdre bit her lip. 'You're still asking questions, Miss Divine.'

'Charles and his wife are friends, Deirdre. If anyone has been poorly served it's Charles. He was fortunate to survive his abduction.'

Deirdre nodded. 'Yes, yes of course, I understand. His wife must have been beside herself with worry.'

'Indeed.'

Suddenly, the door to the main office opened and a man stepped out. He was dressed in a pearl grey suit and wore a pristine white shirt and navy and red tie. He was fair-haired, slightly tanned, and he had a fair pencil-slim moustache. He was the picture of elegance.

'Miss Cheam. I'm leaving now. Have you anything more for me to sign?'

'Not today, Mr Shaw. Enjoy your evening.'

Shaw nodded without returning the compliment and made a slight glance towards Ottilie before taking a cashmere coat from the coat stand and leaving. Deirdre and Ottilie watched him as he walked down the corridor, putting on his coat.

'William Shaw?' asked Ottilie.

Deirdre nodded. 'He's Lawrence Tebbit's replacement.'

Ottilie changed the subject. 'Your colleague wanted to give you this, but I was told by Mr Fairchild to put it into your hands.'

Deirdre frowned. 'My colleague?'

'Evelyn, I think her name is.'

'Evelyn Green.' Deirdre pressed her lips together. 'That girl.' She shook her head. 'I wouldn't call her a colleague. I honestly don't know what she's doing here. She's a terrible typist, makes mistakes all the time, which I have to correct because there's no point in asking her to do the letters again.

She just makes more mistakes. And she doesn't follow instructions. She also has pert opinions which no one wants to hear.'

'What about?' Ottilie frowned, trying to look only mildly interested in what Deirdre was saying.

'Everything…particularly the war which she says is Britain's fault because we didn't try hard enough to avert it.' She sighed. 'I don't know what to do with her.'

'Why don't you have a quiet word with Mr Shaw. He won't appreciate mistakes in important letters.'

Deirdre chuckled. 'Because he was the one who suggested her for the job.'

Chapter 38

The evening had settled on Baker Street by the time Ottilie returned home. She knew Sherlock Holmes would be eager to see her for a debriefing, but all she wanted to do was kick off her shoes and get into the bath. Unfortunately, he and Dr Watson were waiting for her as she got to the first-floor landing.

'Miss Divine,' called out Sherlock from his rooms. Dr Watson was standing at the door, a wry grin on his face.

'Would you rather go to your rooms, Miss Divine. You've done a day's work. I should think bath and bed are calling you.'

Ottilie smiled and nodded. 'They are, Dr Watson, but so is Sherlock Holmes and I know if I do not tell him what happened today his call will get louder.'

Watson opened the door wider and showed her into Sherlock Holmes's rooms.

'Would you like some tea, Miss Divine?' asked Watson, 'Or perhaps something stronger?'

'Something stronger sounds tempting.' Watson invited her to sit and poured brandy into three glasses, handing one to Ottilie and to Holmes.

Sherlock Holmes was sitting in his favourite wingchair, sucking on a pipe which had no tobacco in the bowl. He looked up as she sat in the opposite chair and observed her under eyes she knew were examining her.

'So, Miss Divine,' he said, placing the pipe in the hearth. 'What have you to tell me?'

'My boss is Jaspar Fairchild. His secretary is June Butterfield who went on a course this afternoon. I report to Deirdre Cheam,' Holmes raised his eyebrows at the mention of Deirdre Cheam's name, 'in the evening. This evening, I returned the folder Mr Fairchild asked me to translate from French to English. There was nothing of any interest there, simply conversations Lawrence Tebbit had with a French contingent who visited the Palace of Westminster last year.'

'Nothing to pique your curiosity?' Ottilie shook her head. 'Anything else?'

'I returned the folder to Deirdre Cheam before I left for the evening. There is a young secretary who works in the same office. Her name is Evelyn Green. She's trouble. I heard her in the staff restaurant making disparaging remarks regarding Charles Wentworth's abduction. The other secretaries were scandalised but she would not shift her stance. Then, this evening, when I was making my way to Deirdre Cheam's office I met her in the corridor. She offered to take the folder to Deirdre for me, but I refused to which she seemed less than pleased. When I turned at the office door, she was standing in the corridor watching me.

'Deirdre and I talked about Charles Wentworth which led onto Evelyn Green's remarks and her belief we're at war with Germany because Britain was inept in some way, and it was Britain's fault because more could have been done to avert war. Deirdre despairs of her because she's a dreadful typist and makes lots of mistakes which the other secretaries are forced to correct. When I suggested she spoke to William Shaw who is now occupying Lawrence Tebbit's office, and his position, she laughed and said it was William Shaw who had suggested Evelyn Green for the job.'

Sherlock Holmes looked up to the ceiling and looked remarkably attentive. Ottilie glanced at Watson who hitched the side of his mouth into a half grin.

'Mm, now…quite a development, Miss Divine,' muttered Holmes.

'Is it?'

'Indeed.' He rose from his chair as quick as a flash and began to circle the room, his eyes still on the ceiling as his brain brought together the information Ottilie had given him.

'You say William Shaw is already ensconced in Lawrence Tebbit's office, no doubt carrying out the tasks of the Home Office's Under Secretary?'

'I saw him before he left the Palace of Westminster to go home.'

'And he suggested Evelyn Green for the position in the secretary's office?'

Ottilie took a sip of her brandy, relishing the warmth of the amber liquid as it went down her throat. 'Indeed. It was what Deirdre Cheam told me.'

Sherlock Holmes stood by the window, looking out as though there was no one else in the room. Ottilie glanced at John Watson who shrugged. 'So, we can deduce William Shaw and Evelyn Green are connected in some way.'

'I would imagine so.' Ottilie frowned, a little knot of curiosity appearing between her eyebrows. 'It doesn't mean they've done anything wrong though, does it? It could be a coincidence, or he wanted to help the daughter of a friend.'

'Not if she had been an exemplary typist who could type eighty-five words per minute without mistakes, no. But the reverse is true. She is not a trained typist, yet William Shaw recommended her for the position. If she is connected to him in some way, a familial connection let us say, she is not short of money.'

'I know she isn't.'

Holmes glanced at Ottilie, his eyes narrowing. 'You know? How, pray?'

'Her clothes. Extremely well-cut and if I'm not mistaken certainly not off the peg, but rather, designer made. She was also wearing a string of pearls around her neck. One could be forgiven for thinking they were fake. A young woman who needs to work can surely not afford such beautiful pearls. They were irregular and beautifully strung. In fact, they were not fake. They were real. I know the difference.'

'I am in no doubt you do, Miss Divine.'

He returned to his favourite chair in front of the fire and nodded to himself.

'We have suspects then.' He turned his head swiftly to look at Ottilie, startling her. 'And you must discover more about them, Miss Divine. I haven't forgotten William Shaw's wife visited Delia Wentworth just before Charles Wentworth's study was broken into and ransacked.'

'Tabitha Shaw…known to her friends as Tabby.'

'Another connection. Ah ha! The threads are beginning to unravel. How worried they must be at the probability Charles Wentworth and Lawrence Tebbit will spill the beans.'

'Is Lawrence Tebbit still in custody?'

'He has been sent to a hospital for the mentally infirm. He tried to escape the police when they took him to Scotland Yard. He was raving unfortunately. He told them he would now be Das Eisenhand's target because he had refused to give information to Luca Vitali who has a connection with Mussolini, and who has shown where his loyalties are. He is frightened because of Vitali's links to the Third Reich through Sebastian Moran who was one of the men who forced their way into his office when he did not comply. The other of course, was Professor Moriarty.'

'Professor?' asked Ottilie.

'Indeed. He is a professor of mathematics, a genius. It is a dilemma indeed to analyse where his life went wrong, and he took to crime. He comes from an excellent family, although I have often thought he sees crime as a mathematical equation. It interests him far more than doing good works. His intellect is phenomenal...at twenty-one he wrote a treatise upon Binomial Theorem which is referred to today.'

'I see. When one thinks of a criminal, one thinks of someone who was forced into crime by reduced circumstances. It seems Professor Moriarty chose his path.'

'Indeed...but he is incarcerated...at least for now.'

'Why do you say that, Mr Holmes?'

'Because Moriarty always finds a way of evading justice. I am expecting him to do so on this occasion. It's only a matter of time. He will find an anomaly in the law, or his cohorts will rescue him, usually by foul deeds and with weapons. He is beyond ingenious.'

After her bath and cuddling up on the settee with a blanket, Ottilie placed her journal on her knee and began to map out connections. The spider's web, between everyone she had come into contact with during the investigation; names, places, and the possibility they could be the mole they were seeking. She knew with each day passing the infiltrator had the opportunity to pass on secrets. It was paramount they find him...or her...

and bring them to justice.

She felt at the centre of it all was Das Eisenhand. The Iron Hand was clearly an extension of Moriarty's criminal mind, the empire he built when he realised war was looming. At his right hand…Sebastian Moran, the man who enforces Moriarty's wishes and who recruited Luca Vitali and very likely Greta Dietz, the cultural attaché Charles Wentworth had become close to when working in Germany and when she had visited Britain. There was no doubt in Ottilie's mind she was involved in his abduction.

Then there was Klaus Fogel who was overseeing Moriarty's reprehensible operations in Germany. Ottilie shook her head. *Where will it all end*, she thought?

She wrote everything on a page in her journal, then wrote the heading…WESTMINSTER. The first name she thought of was William Shaw followed by Tabitha Shaw. Tabitha Shaw had been a visitor when Charles Wentworth's study had been ransacked. Was it Tabitha Shaw who had used the opportunity Delia had given her to look for the metal box Sherlock Holmes had found? Deirdre Cheam came next, then Evelyn Green who had been given a position in the central office. This was where every document sent and received at the Palace of Westminster for the Foreign Office, and now the War office, passed through. Anyone working there would have the opportunity to read the documents, much of the information classified.

Ottilie omitted Lawrence Tebbit because of his current stay in hospital but then included him because it was likely he had information on Moriarty and Moran's plans, particularly for those in Italy where Tebbit had been due to be sent. Luca Vitali's links with Mussolini were well founded. It was Luca Vitali Tebbit had been trying to kill at the Nightingale Club, and presumably Moran too who had Tebbit in a vice.

The foreign assets were easy to document. Greta Deitz was an enigma. She had been at Waterloo Station when they had retrieved the briefcase from Delia Wentworth who had been waiting under the clock, seemingly to take the briefcase from Delia. As for Luca Vitali he was a different prospect. It was true his tentacles ran as far as Mussolini, but what else did he know? Who else did he know? And how far had those tentacles infiltrated the Palace of Westminster? Was he a member of Das Eisenhand or did he operate alone?

Ottilie considered June Butterfield and Jaspar Fairchild. June Butterfield had gone on a course which had been very sudden, Ottilie thought. June had not mentioned it when Ottilie had arrived at Westminster to take up her new position, but Jaspar Fairchild. He had also been very interested in her friendship with Delia and Charles and how close she was to them. Was she too close for comfort, she wondered?

A knock on the door interrupted her deliberations. At the edges of her consciousness, she thought she'd heard the telephone in the hall ring, but being two flights up she had dismissed it as likely to be for someone else, perhaps even Mrs Hudson.

She pushed the journal off her lap, got up from the settee and opened the door. Mrs Hudson stood in the frame, her hair in curlers and wearing a man's navy blue dressing gown with a silver tassel.

'There's a telephone call for you, my dear, a Delia Wentworth. I thought you'd want to speak to her.'

'Thank you, Mrs Hudson. I'll come right away.'

She left Mrs Hudson on the second-floor landing and ran down the stairs. 'Delia?' she said into the receiver. 'Is everything all right?'

'I just wanted to let you know Charles is coming home from hospital today.'

'Oh, Delia, that's wonderful news. How is he?'

'Very much better. Still bruised and a bit sore. He had three broken ribs where they'd kicked him and beaten him, and a dislocated shoulder, but the hospital was marvellous with him. Treated him rather as a hero which of course he lapped up.' She chuckled.

'And how are you, Delia?'

'Ottilie, I can't tell you how grateful I am. You and your friends…if it wasn't for you, I don't know what would have happened to Charles…and the children. Penelope has been asking after you, and Dominic says he wants to be like Sherlock Holmes.'

Ottilie laughed. 'I'm not sure the world is ready for another Sherlock Holmes. He is rather unique I must say.'

'Charles says he's a genius.'

Ottilie laughed. 'Well, if you meet him again, please tell him. He loves to be praised and told how wonderful he is.'

'Well, that's the thing. Charles and I thought it would be rather nice to have a small get-together…in two weeks…Friday evening if it suits. Some of his colleagues from Westminster will be there and we hoped you, Mr Holmes and Dr Watson would care to join us.'

'Oh, Delia, thank you. We'd love to come. What time should we arrive?'

'About seven thirty. We'll continue until about ten I should think unless Charles wishes to continue. Time flies when one's having fun.'

'Indeed, it does. Thank you so much, Delia. We'll be there.'

Ottilie ran up to the first-floor landing and rapped on Sherlock Holmes's door. It was opened as usual by Dr Watson.

'Miss Divine?' he said, looking at Ottilie quizzically. 'Is there an emergency?'

Ottilie suddenly realised she was wearing her dressing gown and slippers.

'Oh. What? No, no emergency. I just wanted to let you both know we have been invited to a get-together at the Wentworth's. Some of Charles's colleagues will be there. I thought it would be a good opportunity for us.'

'Indeed,' shouted Holmes from his chair by the fireside. 'Accept on our behalf, Miss Divine.' There was a pause. 'Singular. How very interesting.'

Chapter 39

Ottilie continued to work at the Palace of Westminster, but her mind was on the Friday of the Wentworth's get-together. Her days were rather boring…June Butterfield was attending a mysterious course which had seemingly hastily been arranged, and Jaspar Fairchild was someone who hardly came out of his office. She looked forward to five o'clock when she could take the folder down to Deirdre Cheam with the translations, not just because it was the end of another tedious day, but because she felt strongly the central office was where the infiltrator was discovering information.

She *had* realised Evelyn Green left before Ottilie arrived. Whether this was accidental or by design Ottilie couldn't fathom. What she did discover was that Deirdre Cheam had been invited to the Wentworth's gathering.

'I hear you're to join us on Friday, Miss Divine.'

'Join you? Are you invited to the Wentworth's?'

'I'm rather looking forward to it. It's not very often I get invitations to soirees.' Ottilie smiled at the old-fashioned word. 'I've arranged for my neighbour to sit with Mother for a few hours. It will be quite a relief to have some time for myself.'

'Perhaps we'll have an opportunity to let our hair down, Miss Cheam.'

Deirdre Cheam looked scandalized. 'Certainly not, Miss Divine. I firmly believe one's hair should remain very definitely up. Tasteful and elegant at all times, I think. It's what Mother taught me.'

Ottilie felt as though she had been dismissed, her thoughts going to the Saturday evenings she spent with Rose and her other friends in her flat in Baker Street, dancing crazily to show tunes, and drinking cocktails.

'I'm sure you're right, Miss Cheam,' replied Ottilie, a slight grin on her lips. 'I'm sure it will be very tasteful. Just as you say.'

The wardrobe doors were flung open. On the bed were a number of different dresses, considered and discarded with a sigh. Ottilie could not make up her mind what to wear. Was she there as an old school friend, or was she there as a professional, an investigative reporter who had helped to rescue Delia Wentworth's husband? Thankfully, the other guests, whoever they were, would not know she had been present at his rescue. She had telephoned Delia to suggest it might be wise if it was not made public, she had been involved and Delia had agreed it was wise the other guests should not know.

'We don't want to blow your cover,' Delia had said.

Ottilie laughed. 'Where did you get such a phrase from?'

'Don't tell Charles, but I'm reading one of Agatha Christie's books. It's about a lady detective called Miss Marple. Oh, Ottilie, it's so exciting.'

The three of them met in the hall of 221B. Sherlock Holmes was in his usual attire of black; suit, Homburg, and coat. Dr Watson wore shades of brown and claret. Neither looked happy about their intended destination.

'So serious, gentleman?' asked Ottilie with a small smile. 'I take it you're not looking forward to this evening.'

'Only in as much as we may learn something new, Miss Divine,' said Sherlock Holmes. 'It is dependent of course on the guests Delia Wentworth has invited. Am I too hopeful it could lead to an arrest?'

Ottilie looked sceptical. 'As you say, Mr Holmes. It depends on who the guests are. I think we could be in for a noteworthy evening.'

The cab dropped them outside the Wentworth house at precisely seven thirty. Ottilie was glad she had chosen one of her suits, a Digby Morton her mother had given her. It was fashionable, formfitting, feminine without being overdone. The fabric was a fine plaid wool in charcoal grey with a burgundy overcheck. The jacket was single breasted and cinched in to show Ottilie's beautifully slim waist. With a matching just below the knee-length skirt it precisely gave the look she wanted...professional but with a feminine twist.

The drawing room at the Wentworth's looked beautiful. Everything had been polished, the cut glass decanters sparkling in the light from the chandeliers. Delia had pulled out all the stops. In the corner of the room was a string quartet, and the drinks cabinet held every type of alcohol anyone could possibly desire.

There was not to be a dinner at the dining table but rather a buffet style offering which suited Ottilie perfectly. Sitting at a table meant the guests would be separated and therefore would not have the opportunity to speak with one another. Ottilie hoped the guests, after a few drinks, would separate into different groups and let their guard down. It meant she could wander around the room with a listening ear.

When she, Holmes, and Dr Watson were announced by the maid all chatter stopped. They were seemingly the last guests to arrive and Ottilie was surprised to see who had been invited.

She noticed Deirdre Cheam right away. She was standing near Charles Wentworth who looked entirely different from the man they had rescued from the warehouse. His face had filled out and lost the sallow look acquired during his captivity. He was leaning on a cane, yet his eyes were bright. Delia stood on the other side of him, looking happy and relaxed. When she saw Ottilie, Holmes, and Watson enter the room she came forward immediately and held out her hands to Ottilie.

'Ottilie,' she said gently, kissing her on both cheeks. 'I'm so glad you came.' She leant forward and whispered into Ottilie's ear. 'Charles is too. He wants to thank you.' She shook the hands of Holmes and Watson and offered them a drink which they accepted.

Ottilie sipped at her champagne whilst scanning the room. She wasn't surprised to see William Shaw and his wife Tabitha who professed friendship to the Wentworths. She was, however, rather shocked to see

Jaspar Fairchild and Evelyn Green. Ottilie frowned to herself. Why was Jaspar Fairchild present? And Evelyn Green? She must be closer to the Shaws than at first thought.

The evening went by without incident. Sherlock Holmes and Dr Watson had begun a lengthy conversation with Charles Wentworth. She noticed that Holmes stood with his back to the fireplace and was facing the centre of the room. Ottilie watched him for a moment. She knew he was not just listening to Wentworth; he was also surveying the other guests. Ottilie's concentration was interrupted by Deirdre Cheam who was nursing a glass of sherry which she had held since she'd arrived.

'Miss Divine. I'm so glad you're here.'

'You are?'

'Why, yes. We are both professional women, are we not?' She leant forward and whispered. 'You're the only person here I have anything in common with.'

Ottilie decided to agree with her. 'I know what you mean, Miss Cheam.'

'Oh, Deirdre, please. We are enjoying a social occasion after all.'

'Thank you. Of course. May I get you another drink, Deirdre?'

'No, no thank you. One sherry is all I'll allow to pass my lips of an evening. Mother wouldn't like it.'

'I understand. It wouldn't be right to upset your mother.'

'No, indeed.'

Ottilie averted her eyes to a corner of the room. Evelyn Green and William Shaw were also in conversation, their heads tilted towards each other, too close for politeness.

Across the room Tabitha Shaw released a loud laugh. She was standing with Delia Wentworth who looked a little nervous, Ottilie thought. She wondered what they had been discussing. The children perhaps. Delia certainly looked uncomfortable.

She turned back to Deirdre Cheam, but she had disappeared. The room seemed to reshuffle. Evelyn Green and William Shaw parted and joined the others in the centre of the room. Sherlock Holmes and Dr Watson shook Charles Wentworth's hand then made their way over to where Ottilie stood.

'Where is Jaspar Fairchild?' asked Holmes.

Ottilie shrugged. 'I have no idea.'

He looked about the room. 'And Tabitha Shaw?'

'She was talking with Delia a moment ago, but I see she is now being occupied by Evelyn Green.'

'Mm,' said Holmes. 'Charles Wentworth has explained Evelyn Green's presence here. She is Tabitha Shaw's sister.'

'Which is why William Shaw suggested her for the job in the central office.'

'It's one of the reasons,' said Dr Watson. 'We've watched the guests. The room is rather like a board game with the pieces moving around as though choreographed. There is something going on here.'

Ottilie placed her champagne glass on the drinks console.

'I'll go to the cloakroom. One must wonder why three of the guests have disappeared.'

'Be careful, Miss Divine,' said Dr Watson. 'We don't know what we're up against.'

'There's only one way to find out.'

Ottilie left the room and went down the corridor. Deirdre Cheam was just leaving one of the rooms. She smiled at Ottilie.

'Are you looking for the cloakroom, dear?' Deirdre asked her.

'I was, Deirdre.' She pointed to the room Deidre had just left. 'Is this it?'

'Yes…and beautifully appointed it is too. I wouldn't expect anything less from the Wentworths.'

Nor would I,' replied Ottilie, returning Deirdre's smile.

She went through the door Deirdre Cheam held open and sat on a perfectly upholstered chair by the mirror, waiting for Deirdre to go into the drawing room. After a few moments she stood and opened the cloakroom door, peering around it. Deirdre Cheam was no longer in sight.

Ottilie left the cloakroom and walked further down the corridor. She remembered a sunny morning room Deirdre had shown her the first time she had visited the house. As she got closer, she could hear the murmur of voices coming from the room. She flattened herself against the wall and listened.

'I told you we can't delay. If she discovers what we're doing…'

'Why do you always worry so much, Jaspar? We know why she's at Westminster and we know she's clever, particularly with the Holmes man, but we're way ahead of her. The documents are gone. They'll be in Berlin by tomorrow.' Ottilie knew the female voice was Tabitha Shaw's. 'William is already in Tebbit's office so he's in a good position. They see everything meant for the Foreign Office and the War Office.'

'And Evelyn?'

'She'll do what must be done.'

'You've trained her well.'

'Of course. She's my daughter. Like mother like daughter.' Ottilie's mouth dropped open. So Evelyn Green was not Tabitha Shaw's sister, but her daughter.

'What about Greta Deitz?'

'Gone. It got too hot for her here, particularly after she was spotted by Ottilie Divine and Sherlock Holmes at Waterloo Station. She's gone back to Berlin. Moriarty sent her. He said she could be a risk.'

Ottilie heard a slight chuckle from Jaspar Fairchild. 'You-know-who won't be pleased when he discovers she isn't in Britain. It was part of the agreement. Even Moriarty has a soft spot for her.'

Ottilie heard Tabitha sniff her disapproval. 'Everyone has a soft spot for her.'

'Even William?'

'He wouldn't dare. I have him where I want him.'

Ottilie bit her lip. She wasn't sure what to do. She knew she could confront them; she had her pistol with her, but there were two of them and she didn't know how they would react. Did they have firearms she wondered. She needed Holmes and Watson with her.

She slipped away from the morning room, heading down the corridor until she heard the click of a gun which stopped her in her tracks. Someone was behind her. Someone knew she had heard damning evidence.

Someone was prepared to kill her.

Chapter 40

Ottilie turned slowly, her stomach roiling. She gasped when she met the eyes of…Charles Wentworth.

'Miss Divine,' he said, the rather throaty voice of an injured and suffering man no longer there, but replaced by a much smoother, more confident one. 'Something tells me it wasn't the cloakroom you were looking for, but rather…information. Am I right?'

'Mr Wentworth. Charles.' Ottilie shook her head. 'What are you doing? This is a mistake, surely?'

'Not at all. I just wish you and your friends hadn't got involved. Everything was working out just fine until you turned up.'

'But how? You were being beaten? By Moriarty.'

'I was beaten yes. It had to look good, didn't it? We knew you were on our tails, but you took us by surprise. It's why I was thrown into the cell. I had been beaten, yes, by the guards because they wanted information for Klaus Fogel in Germany. They would have killed me. They enjoy their work a little *too* much.

'Professor Moriarty saved me from the guards, and he has a good story to tell, one I've come to subscribe to. I have pledged my expertise to them. He and Klaus Fogel are brilliant masterminds.'

'And what price are you paying for Moriarty's help…and his friendship? Surely, it's not just information. They have someone placed in the Palace of Westminster. We found your clues.'

Wentworth's face darkened. 'Not your business. And the clues were laid down before my epiphany.'

'But they led us to you.' Wentworth snorted with derision. 'Does Delia know?'

'Delia isn't involved in this.'

'Yet you put her…and your children in danger.'

He lifted his chin, and his hand trembled slightly. 'It wasn't meant to happen. Someone got their wires crossed.'

'I think *you* have if you think you're going to get away with being a double agent.' She narrowed her eyes. 'It's strange,' she said. 'For a fleeting moment during this investigation I thought you just might be involved…but then I thought about your children who clearly adore you and decided it could not be. How wrong I was…and how disappointed they're going to be when they discover their father is a traitor.'

Before she'd finished speaking, Jaspar Fairchild and Tabitha Shaw had joined Charles Wentworth in the corridor.

'Oh, it's her,' said Tabitha with obvious dislike in her voice. 'She's such a nuisance.' She looked at Charles and ran her hand down his arm which made Ottilie shudder. 'Well done, Charles. We might have missed her if not for your eagle eyes.'

Ottilie stiffened. They'd had the wool firmly pulled over *their* eyes as far as Charles Wentworth was concerned.

'Your family trusted you, Charles.' Ottilie frowned and shook her head. 'What happened to you? You were destined for great things. You had a marvellous job and look around you. Your family, those who trust you, and this amazing house. What more could you want?'

'A different life,' he said, angry he was being challenged. 'Don't forget I know exactly what goes on at Westminster and the kind of life I had in front of me if I stayed faithful to this country.' He laughed, but it was not with mirth, nor did it reach his eyes. 'I've been offered a different life, one with real power, and one with a woman who excites me, not this domestic suffocation.'

'Greta Deitz.'

Charles's eyebrows rose. 'You've been doing your homework.'

'We know about Greta Deitz. She was your contact until she went back to Berlin.'

For a moment Charles looked wrong-footed. Then he made a grim smile. 'It's all right, Ottilie. I know what you're doing. You're trying to unbalance me. Greta is in London. She's waiting for me.'

'She isn't. Ask your friends.' Ottilie lifted her chin to Fairchild and Tabitha Shaw. 'They know. She has gone back to Berlin. Go on, ask them.'

Wentworth side-eyed Fairchild. 'Where is she?'

'I'm sorry old chap,' said Jaspar Fairchild. 'She had to leave. Tabitha says it got a bit heated for her here. Moriarty made her go.'

'Don't worry, Charles,' said Tabitha in a cloying voice. 'You're needed here. Just get rid of this woman. We still have work to do, don't forget. Once you're given your elevated position in the government the sky's the limit.'

'I think you're getting ahead of yourselves,' said a female voice behind them. Instinctively they turned to the voice to find Sherlock Holmes, Dr Watson, and Deirdre Cheam, each holding a pistol. 'Miss Divine,' said Deirdre Cheam coolly to a shocked Ottilie. 'Adjust your position. Take the pistol from Wentworth. Do not pass them. There can be no trust here. Go out through the front door and come in through the conservatory. I trust you have your own pistol?'

'Yes,' said Ottilie, so shocked she couldn't say more.

Reaching forward and taking the pistol from Wentworth's hand, she watched as Dr Watson searched Tabitha Shaw and Jaspar Fairchild. As Deirdre Cheam suggested she followed the corridor to the drawing room, then into the conservatory where Delia Wentworth was holding a gun on William Shaw and Evelyn Green.'

'The police will be here soon, Ottilie.'

'Did you know, Delia?'

'Not for certain, no…but the more I thought about it the more I realised Charles wasn't the innocent party he claimed to be. It was only recently when he returned from hospital that my suspicions were confirmed. I heard him talking on the phone when he thought I was elsewhere in the house. It was obvious it was another woman. Then I heard the name. Greta. I knew I'd heard it before. You'd mentioned it. You asked me about her. I was so sure Charles would be faithful to me, but I was wrong, so very wrong.'

Ottilie went out of the house through the conservatory, and back inside by the garden room which was at the end of the corridor where Holmes, Watson, and Deirdre Cheam were holding Charles Wentworth and his cohorts.

'The police will be here soon,' said Holmes. 'I alerted Inspector Lestrade before we left Baker Street.'

'Delia is holding Shaw and Evelyn Green,' said Ottilie, proud of her friend who only wanted the best for her family.

She heard Tabitha Shaw sigh. 'Not just the prissy housewife then,' she said through gritted teeth. 'I thought she was minus a backbone, but it seems not.'

'Why, Mr Wentworth?' Sherlock Holmes asked. 'Why would you allow yourself to be abducted and treated so violently?'

Wentworth snorted a laugh. 'Come on, Mr Holmes. You know why. You've worked it out, I'm sure.'

'To be hailed a hero, to make it all look so very genuine. Something pulled you from the path of trust and loyalty to your country. Let me tell you what I think. I think you were having an affair with Greta Deitz. She made a mistake. I think they call it pillow-talk, do they not? She told you about Das Eisenhand, about Moriarty and Moran. You were shocked. You realised she wasn't a cultural attaché at all but a spy, a double agent if you will.

'Greta Deitz realised she'd said too much, which was why you were abducted, so you couldn't relay all she'd told you about Das Eisenhand's plans to your superiors, but she made you a promise. She promised to stay with you whatever happened. She confided her loose tongue to Moriarty but told him she wanted you. Whether in Britain or Germany she wanted you to be together. And so did you. He has punished her by sending her back to Berlin.

'The injuries were real. The violence was real. The intention was real. But Moriarty got to you. He promised you the earth if you would accept the position the government would give you after your heroic escape from Das Eisenhand so you could pass on information to The Reich. You knew Greta Deitz was part of it and always would be, an important part no doubt. A general perhaps. Moriarty's right-hand woman.'

Holmes lifted his chin and surveyed Wentworth under hooded eyelids.

'He promised her to you, didn't he?'

'And he will keep that promise.' Wentworth looked sick at heart; his pallor returned to one of a beaten man.

'He will not, Mr Wentworth. Moriarty is a monster...a criminal mastermind who cares not a jot for your emotional entanglements. You do not know him. I have heard the phrase "a swinging brick for a heart". It describes his anatomy perfectly. There is nothing he will not do to reach his goal.

'He has staged every part of this, and no matter what problem arises he will overcome it. He sees every occurrence as a mathematical equation, and he will find the solution no matter how difficult the problem is.'

At that moment, ten police officers rushed into the house through the conservatory and the garden room, followed by Inspector Lestrade. Charles Wentworth, Tabitha Shaw, and Jaspar Fairchild were handcuffed and taken out to a police van, as were Evelyn Green and William Shaw.

Ottilie went into the conservatory. Delia Wentworth was sitting on one of the conservatory chairs, her head in her hands. Ottilie sat next to her and put her arms around her.

'Delia? Delia, I'm so sorry. So very sorry. You have been treated appallingly.'

Delia lifted her face which was wet with tears. 'It's my fault, Ottilie.'

Ottilie was astonished. 'How can it be your fault? You trusted Charles completely.' She blinked. 'We all did.'

'But shouldn't I have known?'

'How could you know?'

'I'm his wife. Aren't wives meant to know everything about their husbands?'

'In my experience the wife is usually the last to know,' Ottilie said in a voice laced with irony. 'And, even if you noticed certain anomalies with Charles, you would have ignored them. You loved him...I'm guessing you still do. You probably didn't want to believe he was being unfaithful, not just to you, but to the country.'

'He's a traitor,' hissed Delia. 'How will I tell the children?' She glanced up at Ottilie with eyes pleading for understanding.

'Don't...don't tell them, not yet. They're too young to understand. When Dominic reaches the right age, early twenties perhaps, you can tell him about his father with complete honesty. Of course they must know at some point, but...no, not now. It's too soon.'

'We'll have to leave London. There are too many people in our circle who act as judge and jury without knowing the facts who will see it as their duty to tell the children before I have a chance to do it. They won't care about the damage they do. The children will need to leave their schools.'

'What about Dorset, Delia? You could begin a new life there.'

Delia nodded. 'Yes...yes, they know Dorset, so it won't be a completely new chapter for them.'

'Would your parents join you?'

'I rather think they would. It's a quiet place, a rural backwater. They have spoken about moving away from London with all its noise and dirt. Yes, I think they would.'

Chapter 41

Ottilie leant on her elbow and poured a cup of tea with her other hand, relishing the lie-in she'd had and thinking if she didn't take care, she just might get too fond of it.

She had spent the day before at the Daily Express Offices, typing up her story for Jonah Walsh, who was looking as proud as a peacock and walking around the reporters' room reminding everyone who would listen, *his* reporters always got the story first. In the beginning it was rather nice the conclusion of the investigation had put him in such a good mood, but after a while it became tedious, although rather amusing. His secretary, Maria, had rolled her eyes at Ottilie who had giggled, and had done her best to get Mr Walsh onto another subject so he would leave the reporters to get on with their work.

Ottilie had placed the article she had written on his desk. He had scanned it quickly, promising to give it a more in-depth read later on. Ottilie didn't care. She was so very tired she just wanted to fall into bed. Trying to spend the weekend in the laziest of ways hadn't done the trick. Scotland Yard wasn't about to let her off the hook so easily. Inspector Lestrade had wanted to question her, and she'd spent much of her time at Scotland Yard in a debriefing.

The debriefing had proved rather interesting. Ottilie had some questions of her own. The one uppermost in her mind was about Deirdre Cheam. It was clear "Deirdre Cheam" wasn't who she said she was. Ottilie had been shocked when she'd seen her in the corridor at the Wentworth house, holding a gun against Wentworth and his cohorts, and looking totally in charge, much to Sherlock Holmes chagrin. The thought of the expression on his face made her giggle.

'Deirdre Cheam is an intelligence operative,' said Inspector Lestrade. 'More than that I'm not at liberty to tell you.'

'But why was she there, in the Palace of Westminster?'

'There is a gentleman at Westminster called Mycroft Holmes. She's one of his. He put her there to keep an eye on Tebbit and Jaspar Fairchild. They'd had deep concerns about them for months.'

'Is Deirdre Cheam her real name?'

Inspector Lestrade raised an eyebrow. 'Even I don't know the answer to your question, Miss Divine.'

Jonah Walsh had acknowledged how tired Ottilie was after her "experience" and had given her the rest of the week off to recuperate…four whole days for her to sleep, to spend hours in a hot bath, and just relax.

The scandal of Charles Wentworth rippled through Westminster, gradually gaining momentum until the Palace of Westminster almost imploded. The moles, for there had been more than just the one they were expecting, had been revealed, incarcerated until they went to trial. Ottilie dreaded it. She didn't want to see any of them ever again.

She hadn't heard from Sherlock Holmes or Dr Watson. She assumed they were also enjoying some peaceful time before the war gathered pace. Christmas was just around the corner and Ottilie was looking forward to spending time with Camille, Richard, Cecily, Knolly and Aaron before taking on any other special assignments.

She should have known better. Dr Watson knocked on Ottilie's door on the third day of her "holiday".

'Sherlock would like to see you, Miss Divine. I rather think he has a story for you to investigate if you're interested. He has taken the liberty of speaking to Jonah Walsh who has given his agreement. A secretary for the Foreign Office has gone missing, a Miss June Butterfield. She hasn't been seen for weeks. And there have been new rumblings about Albertine Renault. She is not at all as innocent as she would like us to believe.' Ottilie smiled and nodded.

As she sipped her tea she sighed and thought about the day she moved into 221B Baker Street. Had she known what was in front of her would she have chosen to live there? She laughed to herself. Without a doubt. Life since had been exciting, dangerous, and eye-opening, the life she had always yearned for.

Ottilie was aware life would never be boring all the time she lived in the rooms above the consulting detective Sherlock Holmes, and his colleague, Dr John Watson. She thought about the war and what it would bring. Sighing, she took a breath and wondered about the weeks and months ahead.

She smiled, not just with her lips, but somewhere deep inside...221B Baker Street felt like her destiny, and she wasn't about to let it go. Something told her it wasn't just a place to live, but the beginning of everything...

Hello

First and foremost, thank you for choosing *Ottilie Divine's War – The Diplomat Who Vanished*. I hope you've enjoyed stepping into Ottilie's world, where danger, mystery, and wartime intrigue collide. Writing this novel has been an absolute joy, and I'm delighted to share Ottilie's first adventure with you.

The Second World War was a harrowing and horrendous time, affecting millions in unimaginable ways. My mother lived in London during those years, and she often shared stories of the challenges, the fear, and the small, fleeting moments of hope that kept people going. Her experiences have left a lasting impression on me, and I intend to weave them into Ottilie's future investigations, bringing even more authenticity to the series.

I'm thrilled to let you know Ottilie will return very soon! The next book in the series is already underway, and I can't wait for you to join her once again as she delves deeper into the shadows of war, uncovering secrets alongside her new partners—none other than Sherlock Holmes and Dr. Watson.

I truly hope you've fallen in love with Ottilie, as I have. She is brave, brilliant, and unyielding in her quest for justice, and with each story, I look forward to exploring the depths of her character even more.

Thank you for being part of this journey. Your support and enthusiasm mean the world to me. Until Ottilie's next adventure—stay curious, stay brave, and keep turning the pages.

With warmest wishes.
Andrea

OTTILIE DIVINE'S WAR

Thank you for choosing to read OTTILIE DIVINE'S WAR.

We wish you many happy reading hours.

Get the first book FREE from the popular series,

99 NIGHTINGALE LANE

by joining Nightingale Lane Publishing

info@andreahicks-writer.com

OTTILIE DIVINE'S WAR

The Locket Code

1940. London. The sky is ablaze—and so is the mystery.

A woman lies dead in the ruins, a locket in her hand…

Inside, a soldier's photo—and a code no one can break.

London burns. Secrets smoulder.

One locket. One soldier. One code that could change the war.

In the chaos of the Blitz, Ottilie Divine finds the truth buried beneath

the rubble.

Trust no one. Decode everything.

She chased the story. What she found could end it all…

Books in the Camille Divine Murder Mysteries Series
THE CHRISTMAS TREE MURDERS
MURDER ON THE DANCEFLOOR
THE BRIGHTON MURDERS
MURDER AT THE CHRISTMAS GROTTO
MURDER IN PARIS
MURDER AT THE CAFÉ BONBON
THE MANHATTAN MURDERS
THE WESTMINSTER MURDERS
THE SICILIAN MURDERS
THE EDINBURGH MURDERS
MURDER IN CAIRO
MURDER IN CAPRI

(The Honeymoon)
MURDER AT THE CHRISTMAS CASINO
MURDER ON THE 3.15 TO PICCADILLY CIRCUS

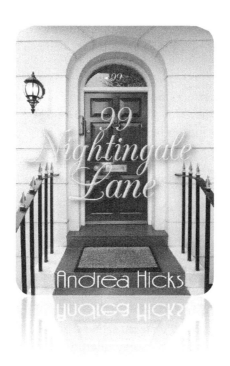

99 NIGHTINGALE LANE – THE COMPLETE SAGA
1295 pages on Kindle Unlimited
The complete series Books 1 - 8

London, Christmas 1914

Eighteen-year-old Carrie Dobbs harbours a secret that could unravel her world. When her parents uncover the truth, her mother, Florrie, intervenes with a drastic solution. To escape the whispers of Whitechapel, Carrie is hastily married to Arnold Bateman, a man she could never love. Arnold, a soldier bound for India, demands that Carrie accompany him, expecting her to play the dutiful wife to advance his military career.

India—a land she only knows from an atlas—fills Carrie with dread. Torn from her family and her beloved best friend, Pearl, Carrie embarks on a journey filled with uncertainty. Will she ever return to the place she calls home?

An Epic Tale of Love and Independence

As Carrie steps onto the unfamiliar soil of India, she is thrust into a world of vibrant colours, intense emotions, and profound changes. The country's mystery captivates her, offering unexpected solace and intrigue. When a kind stranger enters her life, Carrie dares to hope that love might find her again.

But choices have consequences. Carrie's decisions will shape not only her destiny but also the lives of those around her. Will she succumb to the pressures of her new life, or will she carve out her own path in this exotic land?

Why You Shouldn't Miss This Series

- **Free with Kindle Unlimited:** This expansive saga spans **1,300 pages** across eight captivating books, offering endless hours of engrossing reading.

- **Rich, Historical Setting:** Immerse yourself in the vivid landscapes of early 20th century London and colonial India.

- **Complex Characters:** Follow Carrie Dobbs, a young woman of courage and resilience, as she navigates through societal expectations and personal dilemmas.

- **Spellbinding Plot:** Experience a heart-wrenching and exhilarating journey filled with love, betrayal, and self-discovery.

-

What Readers Are Saying

"An epic series that kept me turning pages late into the night. Carrie's story is both heart-wrenching and inspiring."

"A masterfully written saga that brings the past to life with stunning detail and emotional depth. Highly recommended!"

"I really enjoyed how this story was written. Carrie is such a lovely character, such a sad life, and yet you know this probably has some truth back in time."

"Very well done, very hard to put this down."

"Excellent series. Very realistic. People feel real. Highly recommended."
READER REVIEW TOP 1000 REVIEWER

"One of the best fiction books I've read recently. Couldn't put it down.
Characters are very well described, and you "feel" them and what they are
going through. You either love them (Carrie, Ida, Pearl and so on) or you
hate them (Arnold, Carrie's husband). It is difficult to find books as easy
and enjoyable to read as this series."

Dive into the Series Today!

Join Carrie on her extraordinary journey from the cobbled streets of
Whitechapel to the exotic landscapes of India. **Discover the Complete
Series: Books 1 - 8** and experience a story that will stay with you long
after you turn the last page. Don't miss out on this exceptional value—
order now and embark on a literary adventure like no other!

"A wonderful portrayal of characters and the class system of Edwardian
England. I immediately liked Carrie and her best friend Pearl and felt
empathy for the suffering so many women went through during that time. I
read this book in one sitting as I couldn't put it down. Thank you Andrea for such a
great read." READER REVIEW

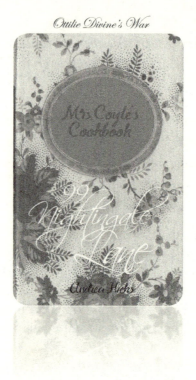

MRS COYLE'S COOKBOOK

INSPIRED BY STORIES FROM 99 NIGHTINGALE LANE and to accompany the popular series.

Stories and recipes from 99 Nightingale Lane from Ida Coyle

I do believe I was born thinking about food, which didn't do me much good seeing as we didn't have much of it. I know I'm lucky compared to many who had it harder than me…I've worked at 99 Nightingale Lane for most of my life, taken in by the family who lived there before the Sterns when my Ma was killed by The Ripper. They were an old London family, not that I would have taken any notice then. I was just a smidgen of a girl, one of many who worked here, nearly as many as the fleas on a dog's tail. And… this is one of the things I learned from Mrs Brimble, the cook who taught me everything I know.

'When I think about where I was born, where we lived over the tanners shop, and what my Ma had to do to put food on the table,' I shook my head, 'she wouldn't believe that I stood there in that grand room, amongst all those beautiful things. And now I'm here in this kitchen with you, cooking the Hamilton's luncheon. I so wish she could see me now.' Mrs

Brimble put a hand on my arm. 'She is watching, Ida, and I know she'd be proud of how well you've done and how hardworking you are, but not because of who you work for. She'd be proud of who you are, the type of person you've become. That's what's important, ducky, not money and things what can be bought. Not tables of silverware and fruits from the continents or gowns from the salons of Bond Street. You're just a little'un really, still young, but you will learn about what's important, and there will be more laughter and smiles and happiness below stairs around our simple table when we have our Christmas dinner than there will be in that beautiful room, you mark my words.' She lowered her voice. 'Y'see, Ida, they haven't learned how to count their blessings. This is just another day to them. They see rooms like that all the time, so they've forgotten how to be swept away by it. Do you think Lady Davinia will go into that room and widen her eyes in wonder like you did? Do you think Mr and Mrs Hamilton will take much notice of the table that the upstairs maids and the footman worked so hard to make look lovely? They'll give it a glance only to find an imperfection. It's how they are. They have plenty, they definitely do, but none of them appreciate it.' She stared at me. 'And that's for your ears only,' she whispered.

You see. I had the best teacher. This is my story, of when I was a girl starting work at the age of thirteen and how I fought my way through the ranks below stairs to become cook at 99 Nightingale Lane. And I've brought my favourite recipes with me, documented in MRS COYLE'S COOKBOOK for you to make yourself for you and your family to enjoy.

I hope you love my story and my recipes. It means so much to me that I've been given the opportunity to share them with you.

Warmest wishes from your friend, Ida Coyle, Cook at 99 Nightingale Lane

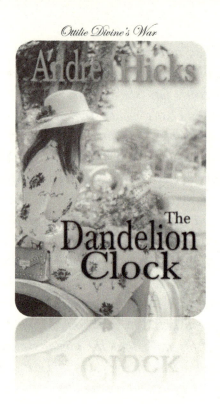

THE DANDELION CLOCK

Sixteen-year-old Kate McGuire has a secret. Her father, Joe, has disappeared, and Kate, her mother, Stella and sister, Emma are left to fend for themselves with little income and no one to turn to. For two years they are heartbroken, wondering why he left, or whether he is still alive. Kate decides she must take on a role she never wanted; as carer for her abusive alcoholic mother, and guardian of her sister who seems intent on finding the solace she needs her own way, a decision that leaves Kate almost unable to continue because of the hurt she causes. Kate is devastated because in her heart she is almost certain she will never see her father again and wishes for his return on the dandelion clock he gave her years before, the seed heads of a flower she wrapped in a piece of pink fabric and placed in her memory box as a lucky charm. Kate wonders if she will ever find the love and affection she craves and whether her dad loves her enough to return to them and the place they call home.

CHRISTMAS AT MISTLETOE ABBEY

A charming-to-read Christmas romance novella to snuggle up with under a tartan blanket, sipping a glass of spicy mulled wine. Enjoy! 'An enjoyable read that was entertaining from start to finish. It was simply delightful, and I highly recommend Christmas at Mistletoe Abbey.'

'From the first page to the last, this fun romance novel kept me hooked. A real page-turner I couldn't put down!'

THE CHOCOLATE SHOP ON CHRISTMAS STREET

The sweetest Christmas Romance to cuddle up with!

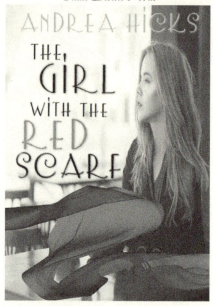

THE GIRL WITH THE RED SCARF

Tom Alexander has no memory of his life at House in the Hills orphanage on the outskirts of Sarajevo, or of his birth parents, the ones whose faces he wants to see, but doesn't remember. When he receives a letter from ChildAbroad, the agency that arranged his adoption in 1994, he is offered the opportunity to search for the boy he once was, Andreij Kurik—if he returns to Sarajevo. With Sulio Divjak, the driver and interpreter Tom befriends, he searches the derelict orphanage and discovers he has two siblings, one who was also at House in the Hills. Sulio uncovers a faded photograph in Andreij's file of a girl wearing a red scarf. She looks like Ellie; the girl Tom fell in love with at first sight in a café in Regent's Park. Devastated when he realises what it could mean, Tom goes back to the UK to get some answers. Accompanied by Ellie he returns to Sarajevo to find his birth parents, only to receive news that destroys everything he thought he knew about Tom Alexander—and Andreij Kurik.

A young love forged at the height of war, a chance meeting, and a collision of faded memories and half-truths, The Girl with the Red Scarf will appeal to fans of historical, women's and romantic fiction.

From the author of The Other Boy, shortlisted for the Richard & Judy Search for a Bestseller

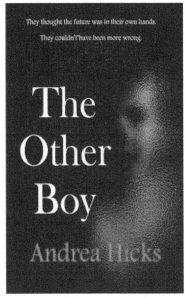

They thought the future was in their own hands.

They couldn't have been more wrong.

The Other Boy

Andrea Hicks

THE OTHER BOY
A Richard and Judy Search for a Bestseller Finalist

Their new home promises so much, an idyllic life in the countryside, a peaceful existence outside the busyness of London. She'd dreamt of it. A forever home. But something happened there, a heart-breaking tragedy infused in its walls. The history of the old house returns to haunt her, and when the memories she had buried return she isn't the only one who fears them.

Before you hide the truth, make sure the dead can't give up your secrets. If you love gripping, ghostly psychological thrillers that you can't forget, make a big pot of coffee - THE OTHER BOY won't let you go.

Find out why Amazon reviewers are saying, "Unputdownable and heart-breaking. Not just a psychological thriller, not just a ghost story, but so much more" …*Birdie Advanced Copy Reviewer*

"The Other Boy is beautifully written, as always. I expect nothing less from the author. This story is a revelation. By blending stunning writing with a heart-breaking ghost story and a psychological twist she had me captured from the very first moment." *MW Advanced Copy Reviewer*

'It's the other boy in the basement,' said Tobias. 'The other boy told me.'

Made in the USA
Middletown, DE
22 July 2025

11080150R00220